The Runes of Rahkfolk

First edition published in 2021

Editing by Mary Kern
Cover Design by Weird Wiring Studio

ISBN: 978-1-7360658-0-8 (Paperback)
ISBN: 978-1-7360658-1-5 (Kindle)
ISBN: 978-1-7360658-2-2 (Ebook)

LCCN: 2021904390

Published by Connor J. Hart

The Runes of Rahkfolk

Zardraken's Crypt

Connor J Hart

For my dad, who inspired me to imagine worlds beyond our own.

TABLE OF CONTENTS

PREFACE

ears ago when I sat down to play *Dungeons & Dragons* with my friends, the last thing on my mind was writing this many words to explain it. It was the summer of 2012 when I forged the beginnings of the world that became *The Runes of Rahkfolk* along with the help of some friends. I never imagined then how much that world would grow, and how much it would change my own life and career.

Growing up, I was always hands-on, drawing my own comics and making my own games. Words were never my forte but my friends and I would always tell stories. It was a fundamental part of how we had fun. I look back now and realize that we were essentially world building every time we played together. Even before the days when my dad showed us how to play *D&D,* we would run around outside pretending to be the characters we simply imagined into being. We would think of their backstories, draw up their costumes, and bring them to life with our play.

Once I got my hands on some dice, my dad's rulebooks and that old *AD&D 2.0* disc, that world building did indeed go to the next level. I remember spending countless hours on that old program making characters, creatures, items, and so on. Until the break of dawn, I would be telling stories with friends; contemplating how the next leg of their journey might unfold before my head even hit the pillow. Years had gone by just spit-balling adventures with my friends and growing a sixth sense for the right time to twist the plot.

By the time I was in high school, I was focused on making video games on *RPG Maker* and later working on video games with a small independent team for some time. But even then, no matter the medium, the end game was telling a great story. It wasn't until that day, now eight long years ago, when I tried my hand at turning a game into a book. Well, it turns out, there is a lot you can do with these little words, but there is even more they can do to you.

Of course, I would be crazy not to mention works such as *Star Wars*, *The Lord of The Rings*, *The Wheel of Time*, and *The Shannara Series* as deeply inspirational to creating TRR. Without the beautiful foundations of sci-fi and fantasy, my own thirst for building upon it would not exist.

With that being said, the story that lies before you now is as much about the journey bringing it to life as it is the subject matter of that very special *D&D* adventure I told years ago. It's a tale about the war between fate and destiny, the choice of revenge or justice, and power of miracle over illusion. It's a young man's journey through the wild world outside his home, yearning to find the truth many seem content on forgetting.

Connor Hart, 2020

1

THE MAPMAKER

875, Summer's 52nd Evening

he sounds of flipped pages echoed through the cold library of the Wisebeard home. Each solitary scrape of paper bounced from one wall to the next, sometimes accompanying the occasional scratching of a charcoal pencil. It was a sound its occupants had grown accustomed to; the sound of deep study.

Beyond cluttered aisles of countless books, tomes and scriptures, a young halfling fellow sat. Balamor Wisebeard was his name. His bare feet dangled from his chair, which was tucked under a small table in the center of the room.

As it was with all halflings, Balamor was a short man, standing no taller than three feet, yet the similarities to his kin were few and far between. Brown robes draped from his shoulders down to the tips of his furry feet; attire fit for a scholar, of which most halflings were not. His skills as a scribe and his passion to craft maps left him amongst books and stories rather than planks and mallets of his laboring kin.

Yet, he found no worry in his lack of woodworking skill. He was confident in his outcast passion. He believed his research would one day lead him to far more interesting places with far more interesting things to do. In fact, with the discovery of a very particular book, he was certain such a day would come sooner rather than later.

His short frame sat hunched over the table with his button nose deep within its shabby pages. From under curly locks of brown hair, his steel-blue eyes scanned the old book intensely. The line of his mouth was drawn between thick mutton chops outlining his square jaw, which he rubbed in thought.

Everything but the pages he turned stood motionless; the stale smell of paper and the smoky scent of incense filled the air, lingering along with the dust. He reached for a teacup to his right and sipped its warm contents carefully, not taking an eye off the text he read.

Contained within its leather bindings were the scribbled accounts of The Fourth Valorhorn, a ranger and one of seven men sharing his credo — *to protect the arcane and return the Valorhorn to the Island City of Delsis.*

The Valorhorn had traveled the lands of the south for decades, searching for the horn and the witch who had taken it. As the years had gone by, he documented his experiences in this book. Experiences which served as the young mapmaker's primary source of information — a witness to the strange land lying within the blank spot on his map.

The Valorhorn's journal had become worn from time and use, riddled with the scars of a traveler's journey. The leather was faded and ripped in spots, rings of coffee or tea stained its pages. The handwriting was ornate in style, but smudged in spots, sometimes causing Balamor to fill in the blanks. Frequently, he would turn to a thin notebook and write his findings down.

He paused and gazed off, rubbing his fuzzy chin in deep thought. Quickly snapping back, he began rummaging through various texts on the table, plucking out an old parchment scroll. He unrolled it carefully.

The light from the lantern beside him revealed a large map painted in painstaking detail. He removed his robes and hung them over the back of his chair before cracking his knuckles and then pinning the corners of his map with a few paperweights. Balamor quietly searched its contents. The warm light wavered across an artistic landscape of land masses and various waterways.

Unlike most maps, the details were not only articulated with geographical accuracy, but with the character of myth and legend. Dragons depicting rivers, kaleidoscopic gems and glorious castles of famed cities, and forests of fabled trees and creatures of folklore. Although most of its information came from the shelves of his very own library, the map felt more like a reality than his own small town. It was an ambitious work in progress but turning his project into a masterpiece was his mission. Large portions of the parchment were still empty or lightly sketched in pencil. He could only imagine the day when a famed traveler held a finished copy in his hands, guiding them on an epic journey. It reminded him of the work to be done filling those blank spaces. Work that now required a journey of his own.

Balamor scanned the lines of roads and rivers mentioned in the Valorhorn's travels. There was one in particular that interested Balamor the most,

841, Autumn's 32nd Night,

After all these years having abandoned my mission, it still failed to stay in the past. A man named Vildar, the gnomish bar hand at The Hogworm in Halden's Burrow, gave me a lead I couldn't resist.

He spoke of a place far within the Forest of Nim, where the truth about the old world was buried. 'Nature's Graveyard' was the name he gave it. He said it was once a forest tamed by men, but now it had been reduced to a cursed husk of its former self. A wasteland that would bury anything within its bounds, overstaying its welcome.

A fitting place to find the Valorhorn, indeed.

THE MAPMAKER

As Balamor traced the map, the details faded into a large blank spot. It had been weeks since the discovery of the strange blank spot. He had spent many long days piecing together the best maps he could find and using them to forge his own. He was comparing the recent surveys of Dario Lushwick to the older maps of Steel Islander, Sahn Mah Vi, when he realized both men had not charted the same area — an empty space surrounded by forest, deep in the southland.

Although the Valorhorn went into great detail of the events that took place during his travels, his documents of directions fell short once he entered the Forest of Nim — a woodland bordering the anomalous blank spot. The only clue the Valorhorn left was that within this forest there was an old tree which guided the wanderer to his destination — *the Mog Brush.*

841, Autumn's 42nd Dawn,

The Forest of Nim, it's been years since I passed through this place. I wonder if that kooky gnome is still around. I could really use a laugh these days. Nonetheless, I must find his tree and then I'll be on my way. The Mog Brush awaits this old man.

Only yesterday did he hear that mysterious name elsewhere. In an old folktale written by Hagron Soldo and passed down by his gnomish people; the story of *The Queen and The Guile.* The Mog Brush was described similarly as the forgotten land beyond the Thorned Ridge.

Within moments, his finger retraced a wide road cutting straight through the famed mountain ridge and thudded, pinning the map to the table. He pointed to the first place he would travel to — *the Greatstone Pass.* Many merchants of the southern kingdoms trek the ancient pass in search of business.

Others visited the pass for its age-old legend, but Balamor would travel there in search of the forest the Valorhorn spoke of.

It was famous for the gigantic path stones set into the earth. Some claimed giants had laid these enormous cobblestones in ancient times, constructing a glorious pathway through the ridge, while others insisted it was some kind of abandoned quarry.

Nowadays, the route was one of the busiest in the south, for it led to the Great Kingdom of Anstia. A great deal of valuables came through this pass from far and wide. The Anstian people lived lavishly after all, wearing the finest silks of the Crescent Coast, adorning themselves with Dahrisian gemstones, and fancying gnomish clockworks.

With goods coming from all the corners of the known world, coin was undoubtedly flowing through the ancient pass, lining the pockets of merchants and noblemen. Balamor knew all too well that anywhere coin traveled, highwaymen were one step ahead.

This of course meant trouble if he were by himself on such a road during the nighttime. He wouldn't stand a chance against more than one of them by himself, and they never traveled alone. The chances of finding another halfling who would travel beyond the Raehl were slim.

The halflings typically lived in solitude amongst the other races of man, and they had their own way of doing everything. Because of their small size and warm nature, most halflings avoided risking interaction with the grim nature of the wild. The other races of man, however, were more equipped for such dangerous eventualities. Dwarves were ruthless in battle, humans were great tradesmen, and gnomes were fond of tricks and schemes. Balamor felt he had no choice; the Mog Brush would remain uncharted if it were left up to the other races of man, too busy with war, commerce, and antics. If the land were to be charted, it would have to be a halfling, and he was the only halfling willing to do so. Balamor would do it alone and as carefully as possible. Travel at night was to be avoided at all costs.

With that, he shut the old leather book, *Sacred Lands,* By the Fourth Valorhorn and stacked it atop several other books. He looked at the map once more, nodding quickly and rolling it back to its original state. Turning to fetch his backpack from the cold floor, he stuffed the scroll into a narrow hard leather case within, beside it he placed his notebook. He removed his robes from the chair and put them on before tying off his backpack and throwing it over his shoulders. Gathering the remaining books into a stack, he carried them back to their places on the shelves as he found them.

As he filled the gaps in the bookcases, he came to the last book when its neighbor caught his attention. He plucked it from the shelf. It was a thick text upholstered in red fabric with a leather-bound spine that read *Runes and Runewords*. He paused and stared blankly at its cover. A wave rushed through his head and lurking below it was that creeping feeling. With an exhale, the thought was gone, now just another memory.

Or was it? Déjà vu?

Balamor shook his head and hurriedly flipped through the book's pages, when something strangely familiar caught his attention. A symbol on the page – three dots in the shape of a triangle. He'd seen it before on those charms from his grandfather.

Without further investigation, the book was put into his leather backpack and he started for the door.

875, Summer's 52nd Night

The heavy door stood ajar before crashing against the stone wall as Balamor walked into the warmth of the kitchen. His stepfather, Barris, was standing at a potbellied stove, cooking a meal for the two of them. His body was slightly taller and much sturdier than Balamor. A tan apron was tied over his red shirt, which was rolled up to his elbows. Below it were thick black pants which tapered off at his bare feet. His face was hardened, strict, and wrinkled with age. Beneath his thick brows were deep verdant green eyes. Most of his face was covered by a dark red beard which hung to his collar.

Balamor was only a baby when Barris Oakfoot took him and his mother in under his wing. He never met his real father, Ericho Wisebeard, who died before he was born. Growing up, Barris wasn't merely his stepfather, especially after the death of his mother Aliya when he was only five years old. Barris raised the boy as if he were his own child, and Balamor accepted him as a father. Although his demeanor appeared to be intimidating at times, his voice was calm and comforting as he spoke. "Done with your studies for the night, I see?"

Balamor nodded as he stretched his small frame.

"What is it that had you down there for so long?" his father added.

Balamor yawned and replied, "I was... looking through some old history books is all."

Barris chuckled. "You and those books about the past. The past isn't something you can change, you know? You should take a gander at those trade books down there and learn about a skill or two – something you can use in the present, to help the family."

"One day I might give them a read. It might be good to incorporate some other skills into my mapmaking," Balamor replied.

THE MAPMAKER

He and his father had talked a few days before about Balamor's trade as a mapmaker. They agreed he must travel to learn more about the lands if he wanted to craft accurate maps. Although Barris would rather have his only son following his own trade of carpentry, Balamor's grandfather, Farjadis, urged Barris to let the young man find his own trade. After all, the Wisebeard family was never a family of laboring professions. It was knowledge they were best with, and the secrets Barris knew of the family convinced him to let the boy do what he was meant to.

It was when he reached his adult years that his interest in cartography grew from a hobby to a passion. It was an odd trade to take up as a halfling, spawned from his time in the library as a child. Before his mother Aliya passed, she would take him down to the library, sometimes for hours, and teach him about the books and scriptures. He learned to read and write at the age of four, and began drawing maps of his village, the Raehl. By the time he was seven his interest in the trade eventually led him to making a map of the entire Southland.

His father wasn't pleased with the idea of a halfling traveling further than a few miles outside the Raehl, but he knew it would happen eventually whether he agreed to it or not. Farjadis would have changed his mind on the whole matter, anyway. As good of a father as Barris was to Balamor, the judgment of Balamor's only remaining kin far surpassed his own.

The tense eyes of Barris studied Balamor a moment, gazing upon him, trying to find anything beneath his vague response. He turned to the stove and continued cooking as Balamor left the kitchen silently, walking only a few feet before his father yelled out to him.

"Supper will be ready soon, Balamor, you should eat. An empty stomach won't do you any good."

Balamor replied from the hallway, "I'll join you shortly."

He proceeded down a wide tunnel-like hallway, the supports bowed to the traditional round structure of the halfling home. The doors he passed were of heavy oak cut into circles, each fastened to the wall by a large metal hinge. As he neared the end of the hallway, he drifted to the left and reached for the door to his room.

His hand came from beneath the long sleeves of his robes and wrenched the door open. He quickly stepped through and shoved the door closed. He stood within his small bedroom; its walls studded with wooden lathe which met a polished oak floor. Its surface was covered by a green throw rug, which laid pinned under various furniture. His small bed was up against the only flat wall in his room. The others were angled to fit the shape of the hillside the home dug into.

Adjacent to his bed, a hole cut for a window poked through the slats of wood, faintly revealing his village.

A crack of thunder jolted through the air, muffled by the glass and the sound of rain crashing against his window.

Balamor threw his pack onto his bed and searched its contents for the book he had taken from the library. Snatching it from the leather bag, the book was thick, its hard cover upholstered with red cloth which shimmered in the light.

This book.

He couldn't shake the feeling it gave him.

Runes and Runewords. He flipped through the pages until he found the symbol from before.

∴

He moved to his feet with the book nestled in his right arm and walked to the desk which stood by the window. Pulling back the drawer, he revealed a random assortment of charms made of different materials — some of wood, bone, and leather — while most of them were made of stone. Beside them was a silver flask, along with his various writing and drafting utensils. He started to browse through the stones; each had a symbol etched into its surface. His hands shifted through the stones, glancing back at the symbol in the book each time.

Ten of them nearly filled his drawer. Finally, he held the matching stone in his palm, referring to the book for more information. He quickly realized that the triangular symbol as well as many others were a mystery to the author as well. The only information he could draw from the text was that this symbol was a 'runeword.' It belonged to an ancient language the author referred to as the 'Runesong', a spoken tongue from the days before mankind, from the time of the 'First Folk.' These four ancient people forged the physical world with the power of the Runesong. The Rahkfolk of the mountains, the Merfolk of the seas, the Rootfolk of the woods, and the Wyndfolk of the skies.

The Runesong was not only expressed in the form of symbols but also in the way of mystical gestures, majestic tones, and even the solutions of otherworldly potions. The symbols were the most ancient of relics of the Runesong, created by the eldest of the First Folk, the Rahkfolk.

He learned that these runewords were found inscribed into different materials – objects the author called 'runes.'

Balamor was intrigued by the terminology, and so he read on.

These runes were said to be tools made to harness a powerful and potent force, each used to channel energy into different forms. It was unexplained how this was done, as the author was still searching for his own answers to the puzzle. The most he could conclude was the sequence of the runes reacted to the elements in nature. He flipped through the pages, passing by pictures of other runewords contained within different shapes and materials. The book stated that they each played a role in a rune's function.

He found himself reading over different stories of where some of the runes had been discovered. For the most part, these ancient items resided within the treacherous mountains of the north, somewhere he would not yet venture. As he learned more about the runes, he began to question the ten he had in front of him. In fact, he had more than the book itself.

His mind fell back to the journey he was preparing for. Weeks had been spent searching for obscure texts mentioning the forests surrounding the anomalous space, and of sneaking materials from his grandfather's house to sew himself a bedroll. All this so he could chart this mysterious land. Now, he realized those old marked trinkets were possibly ancient magical devices.

The day couldn't get more interesting.

He finished the thought when the voice of his father caught his ear. "Come eat before it gets cold!"

Balamor returned the rune to his drawer, shutting it softly. The book was closed and set atop the desk before he left to join his father.

His hairy feet thudded against the floorboards as he advanced down the hall. Barris was seated at a small table in the center of the dining room, consuming his food. Balamor gathered his robes and plopped himself on the chair across from him.

Drifting up to his nose was the smell of the meal his father had prepared. He looked down at his plate. Two pork chops sat amongst a baked potato, surrounded by an assortment of steamed vegetables. He reached for the cup of tea to his right and took a sip. Balamor quickly returned the cup to the table before grabbing his fork and knife. Within minutes, he finished the delicious meal and helped himself to a second plate.

Barris had become quite good at cooking over the years. It wasn't a very big interest of his, but a duty, nonetheless. Chances of Balamor cooking a palatable meal were frightening enough to force Barris to hone his own skill. The last time that Balamor attempted to cook, Barris spent the entire week wiping soot from every surface in the house and lighting candles to remove the acrid scent of Balamor's charred pot roast. Balamor had spent no longer than a walk through the kitchen ever since. He liked cooking though; there was a level of calculation to it that captivated him. His mother, Aliya, was said to cook the most delicious food in the Raehl, maybe even in the entire Southland. Barris kept her cookbooks after she passed. It was the one thing that kept her around even after a decade with her gone.

The two ate their food in silence for the most part. His father wasn't one to talk in any case, only saying what he did when the time demanded it. Balamor shared this trait with his father, but he was much more charismatic when he did choose to speak. He was a philosopher whose mind was focused on the task at hand — *a journey to the Mog Brush*.

It was something his father knew nothing about, and for his sake, Balamor wanted to keep it that way. If he were to find out where he was traveling to, his father would insist he not go alone, delaying his travel further, which wasn't an option. It was a risky decision to leave without telling his father beforehand, rather than telling him after, but he knew that risks needed to be taken, even as a halfling.

As his fork jabbed at the greens on his plate, he wondered when he would return home, and when he would eat another home-cooked meal. He would have to wait for answers to such questions. Right now, what mattered was how he would evade Barris.

He would have to leave at sunrise before his father awoke to work at the mill. If he could leave by then, he could be making his way down the River Faric during the early day; but he still needed to speak with his grandfather about the runes before he left. Balamor hoped he could provide the answers that the red book could not.

He finished his second helping quietly and began cleaning up when his father looked up at him. "Make sure you're up early, I need your help at the mill."

He stood up and handed Balamor his dishes before pushing in his chair and vanishing beyond the light of the lantern on the table. Balamor let out the usual sigh as he took the dishes and walked to the wash bin on the counter. There was no point in arguing with Barris when he asked for help. No matter how much Balamor was disinterested in woodworking, Barris would never fully give in to his son's passion. *Another day in this hole.* Balamor washed the dishes in silence, pondering his journey and his eventual departure from the Raehl. Quickly, he finished the chore and snuffed the flame of the lantern before making his way to his room. He pulled his backpack from his bed and fetched his notebook before taking a seat and opening his drawer slowly. Finding the ten runes he had, he gathered them and copied their symbols into his notebook one by one.

·⁰²₀ ÷· ⊕ ∴ ⊙ ⟨ठ⟩ ₮ ⠒ ·⫯·

After finishing his sketches, he shut the drawer and returned the notebook to his backpack, placing it on the desk. Knowing there wasn't a chance he could leave tonight; he shook his head in disappointment. Balamor stood his back straight and gave out a sigh. *Soon enough,* he thought to himself before he lunged into his bed.

Moonlight shined through the window, intensifying with tendrils of lightning as a vicious storm conquered the night. He watched the arcs of light dance across the sky, their steps resounding moments later in an echoing crescendo. His eyes soon become heavy, each blink longer than the last until finally his vision faded into the depths of his mind.

2

A MATTER OF TIME

875, Summer's 52nd Midnight

Rain drenched the Southland as a wicked midsummer storm rolled in from the east. The Watcher was looking over the secluded town where the Wisebeards lived, as he did every night.

The mighty storm was surging the river and howling like a beast. The Watcher hadn't seen such a storm in decades, perhaps since the fall of Delsis; the pitch-black clouds rumbling with thunder, the wailing wind groaning like a ghostly specter — the rain tasting like that of a murky brine.

A new age was upon the world, and storms like this would become commonplace for the folk of the Southland.

The magical bounds that the old king summoned would only continue to weaken as the storms grew stronger. One day, the monster living within would consume all it could reach.

Beyond the colossal cliffs of the Great Divide, the picturesque mix of wide-open plains and thick verdant forests would soon be trapped under dense black clouds.

An endless torrent of rain would bring floods and landslides. Trees would topple as their roots rotted from below. Darkness would slowly seep into the soil and morph the Southland into a series of dreadful bogs and dank wetlands.

That fateful day was to come much sooner than anyone had anticipated — aside from the necromancer responsible.

The signs that this prophecy would be fulfilled were becoming increasingly obvious as time ticked on. As days passed like a breeze upon the hills, seasons quickly turned to years, and those years were suddenly mounting in the hundreds.

The year is 875.

The Wisebeard's words started to trickle back into his mind.

The rain would not relent and nor would its vengeful source. This, the Watcher knew to be certain. He knew because it had all been foretold a long time ago, by Balamor Wisebeard himself.

Darkness lives here now...

Only days remained before he would finally meet the young halfling and obtain the answers he sought. Answers to an age-old mystery that has plagued him since the days of the old kingdom.

For now, the Watcher would wait, not risking interfering with the plan or revealing his identity. His small familiar would continue to be his eyes and ears, as it had been for so long. Under the cover of a leafy shrub edging the River Faric, he resided, observing the Raehl in the distance, watching its narrow bridge being battered by the storm. The last time he made a crossing, the young Wisebeard was merely a baby. He wondered where the halfling family would go next, where the old books and the ruby shard would end up.

It was only a matter of time before —

His thoughts were cut short as he felt a strange force drawing from his mana. Something otherworldly traveling in the distance, a being altering its form into raw power, twisting and warping the clouds with chaotic force as it zipped through the air. Its magical aura was one the Watcher knew all too well.

Glancing downstream, his beady eyes went wide, as an arc of lightning tore the sky open in a blinding flash of violet light.

3

WISE WORDS

875, Summer's 53rd Morning

Sunshine pierced Balamor's sleepy eyes as he fixed himself a cup of tea the next morning. He started for the front door, trying to keep his tea from spilling as he walked. The short circular door swung open as Balamor stepped out to breathe in the morning air. The scent of rain filled his nose along with the aromas of coffee and tea pervading from every halfling hole. A subtle breeze whistled along with the busy bodies of the townsfolk.

Balamor stood atop a wooden porch which rose a foot off the ground. It covered the front of the Wisebeard home; thick floorboards cut to make a semi-circle. A roof stood five feet high, posted on oak beams, each one carved by the hands of Barris Oakfoot. Barris took pride in his work, but his modesty kept him from boasting.

Standing quietly on the porch front beside his son, Barris crossed his arms and assessed the damage the storm had caused. His brow lowered in anger and his nostrils flared with heavy breaths. The scene wasn't pretty, especially compared to the picturesque state the town was usually in.

Trees uprooted, porch fronts dismantled, the farmer's barn required heavy patchwork, again. Yet what was ruined the most by the storm were Barris's plans to teach his son the woodworking trade. The sawmill was utterly demolished, as if the storm had a peculiar vengeance against Barris's beloved workplace.

His patience broke in a fit of rage. "It's always something! Now the town needs to be rebuilt and the sawmill is destroyed! Great, just great!"

He rambled on as Balamor sipped his tea, trying to grip the situation. "What a storm, huh? Surprised I slept through it."

Ignoring his comment, Barris turned to the door and stormed inside. Balamor observed the Raehl as he wiped the sleep from his eyes.

The village was a small but highly organized community. Halfling holes poked through the small hillsides dotting thin dirt roads. Each hole seemingly the same as the next. Some of them with porches and others with lush gardens. Although the storm had damaged the village structures, the halfling spirit and sense of community was strong.

It wasn't because of the destruction that they were a close-knit people, that trait was there even in the most mundane times. He gazed at his people fixing the village, always in large groups but performing as one. Just off to the left, he watched six men who were reconstructing the roof to a porch.

Three of them stacked atop their shoulders from the ground to the rooftop where a fourth was perched; each of them performing a separate task. The man on the bottom was the heftiest of the three; he held a bucket of nails in his left hand and a small hammer in his right. His job was to position the beam correctly and nail it to the foundation of the porch. The man above him was working a chisel into the beam, staying with it as it swayed to-and-fro. Little taps of his hammer carved out a design similar to the one on Balamor's own porch.

The third man was working with the fourth atop the roof. He too carried a hammer and nails, finishing off the work of the other two as he anchored the roof to its rafters. As the four men worked systematically from stud to stud, two others off to the left were sizing and cutting lumber.

Barris swung the front door open and quickly joined the two men, pointing out mistakes and taking new measurements.

He mumbled orders to the two men as he began checking the quality of the wood.

Balamor soon realized just about every halfling in the village spare himself had been helping. He felt the distance between him and his people grow, understanding now that he wasn't leaving solely to finish his map. He didn't fit in here. Not because he lacked the necessary skills, but because his purpose was meant for something bigger than his small town. His tea was almost gone when he walked off his porch and onto the dirt path. He had to see his grandfather, especially while his father was preoccupied.

He guided himself down the dirt road as the morning sun now greeted the entire town with its presence. The sky above was a clear blue with narrow streaks of white traveling further south. The feeling of freshness was in the air. Although the town suffered, the plant life was given its gift of rain, and now the light from the sun.

He turned on to a smaller trail which led to his grandfather's house. He approached the steps of the green porch front when he heard the voice of Farjadis Wisebeard.

"Balamor! Good to see you're still alive after all this. The men just finished fixing the porch a few moments ago." He was rocking in his chair on the porch with a book in his hand and a pipe in his mouth.

His face was old at its surface, showing the time he had spent on Earth. Although they were squinted with age, his eyes were just as Balamor's; steel blue and full of wonder — a strong trait that all Wisebeards shared. His long nose hung from his brow, dipping to the start of a long gray beard. He wore a brown vest above his shirt, and thin trousers flowed to his ankles. He was a jolly old man with more wisdom than anyone Balamor knew. Every time he spoke, it could be taken as well-intentioned advice.

"So, your father told me you want to travel outside the Raehl. He wasn't happy with the idea, but he wouldn't understand. A Wisebeard is no hermit. Even your true father traveled the land, and you must do the same!" He jerked his hand forward as the words escaped his mouth amongst a thick smoke.

Balamor was confused by his words. "But I thought my father was a bridge builder who lived here in the Raehl?" His small frame planted itself across from the old halfling. "Why would a bridge builder travel the lands anyway?" he added.

Farjadis puffed on his pipe, shutting the book in his lap softly. "You're right; he did live here in the Raehl, and he was a fine bridge builder indeed. But he traveled as well, taking his trade with him across the lands." His leg moved from his lap to the floorboards as he leaned forward. "Every Wisebeard must travel and learn as much as he can. Our lineage is special, Balamor, only you can prove that."

The old Wisebeard believed in the boy; he had to. It was his duty to keep his bloodline alive, and Balamor was the only chance he had. Farjadis's own son was gone for over two decades now. The old Wisebeard never did learn what fated him after being swept away by the Faric but dwelling on the thought further only saddened him. He was burdened with this responsibility after his time in Delsis, after his last words with the mystic Gantis.

The old mystic demanded Farjadis to retreat to the Raehl, for there was a chance he would've been sought out in his homeland. If he had failed at this, his bloodline would have been lost. Gantis told him more than his own fate depended on hiding the existence of the Wisebeards and saving the bloodline.

But he was done with hiding. He knew the purpose of being a Wisebeard, and not even he had the chance to live up to it. Balamor was the only option, even if he was far from being as great as his ancestors; time was wasting away at the opportunity.

The young cartographer sat quietly in his chair slightly rocking himself and his thoughts. Farjadis studied him, waiting for something from his grandson.

Balamor lifted his head as he felt himself being watched. Suddenly, he remembered what he had come for and reached for his backpack. Pulling it to his lap, he searched its contents until he found his rune and the red book. He pulled the items from the bag and began to speak.

"I came here to ask you something. Do you know anything about runes and runewords?" As he displayed the book and the stone to his grandfather, one brow rose in curiosity, and the old man replied.

"Ah, just what I was hoping you would ask next. Let me see here." He smiled and nodded as he put his glasses on. "So, I see you've been reading? What is it you would like to know?"

Balamor quickly summarized what he found in the book the day before, explaining how the symbols might be words from an ancient time, how he couldn't find any source which translated them, and how they might have even been used to do magic. The old man nodded along, silently listening to his grandson. Finally, the nervous halfling's question came forth.

"I was trying to figure out what this rune is for and if it might be useful to me on my travels." He searched his grandfather's eyes for any sign of an answer.

"Well, where is it you plan to travel to?" Farjadis asked with a half-smile on his face.

Balamor was reluctant to tell him, but the old man's eyes seemed to already know what he was about to say. He fumbled his words, trying to piece them together. "I was... You said a Wisebeard should travel and learn as much as he can." He fetched his map from its case and unrolled it slowly. "Well, I would like to go there."

His finger landed amongst the uncharted land; a blank spot on the map. Farjadis sat quietly, his wooden pipe hanging from his lips down to his bony fingers.

WISE WORDS

"An interesting place indeed." He paused for a moment, taking a drag of his herb. His brow curled as the young halfling peaked his curiosity.

"Going there by yourself is dangerous, but you understand risks must be taken, Balamor. I met a man who traveled there once; he called himself The Fourth Valorhorn. He said the Mog Brush is a very sacred land."

Balamor sat quietly; an unbroken stare growing wide and his mouth agape, shocked at the sound of the ambiguous name. If Farjadis met the man who wrote *The Sacred Lands,* By the Fourth Valorhorn, then surely that's how the book found its way amongst the shelves of the Wisebeard library. His eyes drifted to the floor as he began to ask himself where the other texts had come from.

Suddenly, he remembered there being very strange books which filled whole sections of the old library. Everything about them seemed out of place. Their spines were empty and some of their covers had symbols on them, which he now realized were runewords. But the pages had all been blank, not a word written on them. His thoughts escaped his mouth almost accidentally.

"There's... something else..." he hesitated. "In the library, I stumbled upon some... well, some very strange books. You always told me they were simply blank journals, but some of their covers are marked with these symbols—"

The jovial laugh of his grandfather interrupted him. The Wisebeard puffed his pipe once more as the silence hung over them. Their pale eyes met in a plume of smoke, blanketing their familiar features as the old halfling spoke, "Spellbooks."

He reached down to the basket beside him, retrieving a thin book. Flipping the six pages between the covers, he continued, "This was one of my own, ya know? A favorite, you could say. A mystic named Gantis Jacs gave this to me; you were only an infant at the time. I think it's time you held on to it." He handed the old book to his grandson as he smiled.

ZARDRAKEN'S CRYPT

The book was just as Balamor had described the others, but there was a detail he hadn't seen before. He studied the thin book; dark brown leather was stretched around a hardback. On it he found no trace of runewords, but instead, six words which resembled common tongue sat at the bottom of the front cover, each one separated by a dash.

Tyel - Aer - Hels - Theas - Maur - Firos.

Another piece to the puzzle, he thought to himself as he flipped through the empty pages, each uneven in size and shape. He didn't know how this could be used, but he didn't question the gift his grandfather gave him.

Rocking back in his chair, the old man felt a great weight leave his shoulders. It had finally been done; the book was held by the last heir of the Wisebeards. What concerned him now was what life had in store for the destined halfling. Balamor didn't yet know the truth about his surname, but his grandfather knew it was something only he could figure out.

Balamor shoved the book into his backpack, thinking deeply about its purpose. He knew it was far more incredible than its size made it out to be. Hopefully his journey would provide him with the answers to unlock the secrets of the runes.

Balamor realized he never got what he came for in the first place as he glanced at his grandfather. Looking down at his hand, he grasped the square stone rune, a triangle of three dots carved into its surface.

∴

WISE WORDS

Hoping Farjadis might know more about it, he lifted his head quickly. "But what of this rune? How will it help me on my journey to the Mog Brush?"

The old man leaned over to him; his gray beard shrouding the smirk on his face.

"It will guide the way when you need protection."

The sun towered high above the Raehl now, and the work on the village seemed nearly complete. Balamor and his grandfather sat in silence for a moment before a deep voice yelled out, "Balamor! Hiding over here with your grandfather I see!"

The stout figure of Barris Oakfoot was strolling down the dirt path toward the porch. Farjadis glanced over at him before returning to the young halfling who was studying the rune.

Before the opportunity was gone, Farjadis grabbed his grandson's attention. "For truth."

It was a look more serious than any Farjadis had ever given him. Balamor replied only with a quizzical look. No more words were spoken as he stuffed the map and the rune into his backpack. Standing to his feet, he marched down the porch stairs, saying goodbye to his grandfather. He walked the path until he met Barris, who waved at Farjadis before turning around and walking with Balamor toward their home.

The summer sun beat down on their backs as their furry feet thudded the earth below. His father observed without a word said. He watched young Balamor walking in short strides beside him. His lithe figure partially revealed as wind gusted against his robes. He wasn't as sturdy as Barris had hoped, especially if his son were to take up woodworking.

But Balamor was still very young; he turned over twenty years next fall, which was nearly half the age of Barris. With time, he could become just as good as his father, but it was time that concerned Barris.

How much longer would his son be here in the Raehl? How much longer until the day came that Farjadis told him of?

Shaking the thought away, he walked up the stairs to his home, exhausted from the work on the town. Balamor followed behind, quickly moving to the basement door and escaping down to his study.

875, Summer's 53rd Night

Hours had passed as the young Wisebeard turned the pages of the strange blank books lining the shelves. The smoky scent of incense pervaded the library as Balamor flipped page after page, each as blank and boring as the last. He sighed and shut the final book, dust billowing from the desk.

His curiosity about the strange books brought him back to his own six-page book his grandfather had given him. He flipped its shabby pages between his fingers. "Spellbooks," he whispered to himself.

The moon slid past the horizon by the time Balamor was standing at the wooden countertop, preparing rations for his journey. He decided he would take what he could without leaving his father with an empty pantry. There wasn't much to begin with, but he crammed his bag with a loaf of bread, cold cuts and various raw vegetables. It wouldn't be Barris's cooking, but it would have to suffice.

He closed his backpack — now plump with supplies — and looked outside the kitchen window. Heavy fog clung to the town, only silhouettes of neat hills could be seen in the distance. A clap of thunder left his hairs standing; a strange feeling in his body made him uneasy. He gathered his belongings and entered his room, closing the door quietly. Retrieving his square stone rune from his backpack, he jumped into bed.

Balamor ran over what his grandfather had told him about the rune that day as he was lying in his bed. He realized it wasn't an answer at all, but a riddle to which he had no obvious solution. The thought lingered within his mind until his eyes became heavy, and he was fast asleep.

4

NO TURNING BACK

854, Spring's 14th Dawn

he *thrashing waters of the Faric yanked at the halfling as he straddled the twisted ropes of a broken bridge. The river sucked him back and suddenly, he vanished. Seconds passed before the sturdy arm of the bridge builder reached out of the waves, latching onto a broken post, bobbing along the current. Just as he secured himself, the shout of a man rushed by him. "Ericho!"*

The sturdy halfling threw his arm out to the small figure being swept away. "Tarot! Grab my hand!"

Their stubby fingers were distanced by inches before he watched his comrade disappear downstream. He started up the tangled ropes slowly, exhausted with battling the river. The strained halfling climbed halfway up the ropes when the snapping of oak came from the only post holding the rope in place. Closing his steel-blue eyes, he whispered something strange to himself. The ruby pendant of his necklace shined with intense red light. He knew his fate now and took a deep breath as he grabbed the glowing pendant with his right hand. The last post splintered before the young Ericho Wisebeard was devoured by the raging waters of the Faric.

875, Summer's 54th Dawn

Balamor's eyes exploded open as he threw himself awake. He clutched the stone rune in his hand.

His recent memories littered his mind, a foggy remembrance of some nightmare. Sweat dripped from his brow as he gasped for air. He looked down at the rune in his hand, its carvings glowed a ghostly green.

∴

"Whoa!" he shouted.

In one quick motion, Balamor dropped the rune on the bed and jumped to his feet. The glow diminished as it hit the covers.

"Ericho?" he whispered to himself in contemplation.

Shaking the slumber from his eyes, Balamor turned toward the window. The sky was a gray blue and the frigid air of dawn cloaked the halfling village. The exact time eluded him but it was early enough. The sound of birds had not yet been triggered by the warmth of sunrise. His timing had put his mind at ease, but what had just taken place startled him. He couldn't ponder on the matter; he had to make sure he didn't wake his father who was sleeping in the room next door.

He crept to the wall and pressed his ear against the wooden lathe. He heard the rumbling snore of Barris, sometimes abruptly stopping and stuttering. He was in the clear. Moving to his desk, he slowly pulled his drawer open, revealing writing implements, the metal flask, and the ten engraved stone runes. He could only take two more runes with him; his bag was already over packed.

The first rune he grabbed was a stone in the shape of a disk. Cut into its surface was a cross extended past the edges of a circle. His second choice was a triangular cut stone. The word inscribed was four dots in the shape of a square.

Undecided, he glanced at the others. He needed to know what they all meant after he returned from the Mog Brush; it was an oath taken silently as he finished packing his belongings.

Balamor put the runes into a separate pocket in his backpack along with his flask and threw it over his shoulders. He snatched a piece of paper from the drawer before closing it lightly. Grabbing the ink pen in his right, he began writing a note to Barris, briefly mentioning he was going south to Anstia.

Father,

You might be wondering where it is I've gone, but do not worry too much. I will return home within a week's time. As you know, it is important I gather more research for my map, and there is no better place to go than the Anstian Grand Record. It is a long trip, so I hope you don't mind the food I have taken from the pantry. I know you aren't happy about this, but it is for the best that I seek out as much knowledge as I can. I hope you understand, and I hope the Raehl isn't too lonely without me there! Take care, Father, and please don't forget to keep Grandfather company every now and then.

Sincerely,

Balamor

He finished quickly, leaving the note on the desk before he walked to the end of his bed and opened a short wooden trunk. Snatching out a small hunting knife and sheath, Balamor quickly attached it to his belt before removing a bedroll and strapping it to his backpack. The trunk was shut softly as Balamor rose to his feet and started for the door.

Each step was taken softly as he moved to the door and turned the handle with both of his hands. He guided the door open; its hinges creaking with each slight nudge. The cold of the hallway crept up his legs, standing his hairs straight. He left the door ajar, not risking waking Barris in the room across the hall. His strides were slow and as long as his legs permitted. It was minutes before he reached the kitchen.

The cold tiles numbed his feet as he advanced toward the large oak door. His frigid hands grasped the brass handle and turned it slowly. The pins clinking free as he progressed, each of them amplified by his shaken nerves. The door released from the frame as Balamor snuck behind it, shutting it as lightly as he could.

He walked onto his porch, damp from a light fog, which cloaked the Raehl. He flipped his hood over his brow before leaving down the stairs. Although his muscles were tense from the cold air, he walked quickly through the small village without turning back. The sun would be up in a matter of minutes along with his father. Thankfully, most of the village was still sound asleep, leaving few to witness his departure.

The farmers were tending to their small fields of wheat as Balamor strolled by, only briefly glancing at his hooded figure before returning to their crops.

He traveled through the town silently, his feet pressing against the moist dirt and grass below. He reached the edge of the wide dirt path where a wooden archway stood over him, ivy wrapping itself through the intricate design consuming it slowly. Balamor paused to look back at his humble village, unsure if he should return, unsure if he would even have a choice.

A sigh broke the silence as he traveled to the bridge crossing the river.

His feet pushed against the wooden planks of the rope bridge, each one worn with age. Some of them were cracked, broken or missing completely. Halfway across, Balamor felt the frigid waters splashing up at his legs. Frequently, his hands gripped the ropes of the bridge as it began to shake from heavy gusts of wind.

ZARDRAKEN'S CRYPT

The Faric was roaring below him, white with foam, like a rabid beast hungry for unlucky travelers. He was almost to the other side when suddenly, he plunged into a large gap. He realized that the remaining planks had been removed as he reached for the ropes at his sides. His right hand missed but his left hand landed true and just barely gripped the braided rope. He struggled to climb back up as his feet dipped into the cold waters of the Faric.

A vivid flash of his dream struck him as he held on. He knew his real father wasn't as lucky as himself.

He shimmied across the unfinished bridge cautiously keeping as much balance as he could. As his feet touched the ground, he heard the sound of men shouting. His hand was at his sheath as he walked through what looked like a makeshift workshop. Wooden planks and iron nails riddled the path. Saws and spools of rope were scattered and knocked over. It was a bridge-builder camp, but the workers were nowhere to be seen.

A sharp yelp came from the road to the west before he pieced the situation together. He drew his knife and crouched as he glided across the path next to the short shrubbery. Peeking down the road, he saw two short halfling men fighting with a hooded figure. The halflings were sturdy and dressed in tan worker's garb. Large utility belts wrapped themselves around their waists and leather caps held down their curly hair.

Each equipped with hatchets, they swung furiously at their elusive enemy. The hooded figure was wearing dark leather armor which encapsulated his thin figure from head to toe. His hood was a black piece of cloth wrapped around his noggin, trailing in the wind behind him. A thin slit was left open for his eyes; the rest of his face was concealed.

He danced around with the two stout halflings, brushing off their attempts, but the halflings had much more stamina than a nimble thief. Balamor wanted to avoid confrontation with any of them at all costs. His best bet was to sneak by them through the trees. He looked past the combatants and saw a

31

caravan parked off into the brush. Their short-distanced blows now crashed against the bandit as Balamor crawled through the trees bordering their match.

He moved quickly through the thick brush, carefully making his way in and out of cover, only moving when the men were preoccupied. The darkness of the dawn was seeping into the green hills of the horizon as Balamor paused at the side of a damaged caravan. He saw a halfling man sprawled out in the grass beside him, two arrows stuck in his back. He glared at the horrible sight of one of his own, slain before he could return home. He shook the idea from his mind, looking back over to the fight on the road.

A cry pierced the air with pain as one of the small halflings thudded to the ground. Balamor quickly climbed into the caravan before he could be spotted by the hooded man. His eyes adjusted to the darkness as he pulled himself inside. Standing in the back was another highwayman searching through boxes and trunks. Before he could observe the items himself, the man turned around at the sound of his comrade outside, his voice muffled by the wooden walls of the caravan.

"What are you gonna do now, huh? Your other half is all gone, you furry-footed wank! Marik! What do you say we finish off this little scrap before we search the plunder, eh?"

Balamor stood frozen in his tracks, his hand slowly dropping to his small hunting knife.

The taller hooded man drew his sword from its sheath as he spoke to the frightened halfling. "Well what do we have here? Huh? Another halfling, eh?"

His grunt of a laugh continued, muffled under his cloth head wrap.

Balamor drew his blade in apprehension. He wasn't sure how to use it against someone twice his size but it was his only chance.

"Oh! We have another brave one, do we?" the bandit added.

His lanky arms thrust his sword downward to split the halfling in two, but Balamor was too quick, sidestepping the tall man and jumping behind him. The hooded attacker crashed into the trunks and crates, knocking them over and spilling their contents. Balamor ran to the back end of the caravan and undid the wooden latch holding the doors closed.

The man came to his feet and turned around to locate the nimble halfling, frustrated at his failed attempt to butcher him. He quickly saw the short silhouette of Balamor and reached to yank him from the ground. As his hand thrust through the darkness, Balamor ducked and sliced into his forearm. The bandit growled in pain and held his wound shut.

Balamor dove through his legs before the injured man could impale him. His broadsword broke one of the floorboards and planted itself into the earth below. Balamor quickly pursued the trapped thief and kicked him into the back doors. They crashed open as the tall man flung out onto the road.

Beside him was the last bridge builder who was hunched over the dead body of his partner. In the distance lay the body of the highwayman from earlier, defeated. The remaining halfling's face and torso were riddled with cuts and bruises, his clothes torn and stained from blood and earth. He glared at the final bandit before he stood up and swung at him with his hatchet.

Balamor quickly pulled the doors shut and secured them with the wooden latch. He looked around and saw most of the things in this caravan were useless to him — various building materials and a few large spools of cloth. He started to exit the side door, before a trunk which was knocked over caught his attention.

He stood it upright and saw its contents were of various knives and daggers. Most of them were basic iron blades fastened with wooden hilts — some rusty and dull, fair in quality. As he was searching the trunk, he made out the silver tip of a blade poking through the lattice of rusty knives. He removed the crude items one by one, revealing more of his discovery. Within moments, he held a beautifully crafted dagger. Its blade was a sharp silver, held into place by a porcelain hilt trimmed in gold. The dagger seemed almost too beautiful to be amongst the other shabby crafts. Balamor never laid his hands on anything like it — *he knew it was coming with him.* He wanted to know more about the history of the dagger and how he could contribute to it. His mind was set on the blade until the sounds of fighting rejoined his focus. He had forgotten about the bandit from moments ago, the blade somehow diverting his attention completely.

The racket of weapons crashing and feet shifting outside the caravan suddenly stopped. Only the sound of the bridge builder's whimpering struggle remained. He was almost done when the wooden doors of the caravan crashed open, showcasing the small-robed figure of Balamor. In his right hand he held his new dagger, its silver blade shined as he pointed it at the bandit sharply.

"Put him down!" the armed mapmaker commanded; his confidence amplified by his newfound weapon.

The bandit clutched the small bridge builder's shirt at the chest as he looked over at Balamor. "Oh! So, you didn't scurry away, huh? I'll take care of you first then."

His words were raspy and somewhat hard to understand, but Balamor knew what was in store as the bandit threw the squirming halfling to the ground. Lanky strides pushed the bandit closer as he cursed the robed halfling. His courage was only a facade which shattered like a mirror as the bandit approached him, revealing a terrified boy underneath. The bandit was in mid-swing when the sound of a large thud came from behind him. A deathly gasp for air was followed by the sudden drop of the hooded attacker, in his back dug the head of a small hatchet.

Balamor opened his eyes to see the bandit dead on the ground, and the short-kneeled body of the injured bridge builder, breathing heavily as he spoke.

"You... you saved my life you know? I figured... I would repay the favor." He drew a winded laugh as he picked himself up. "We have to... stick together, us halflings. You're the carpenter's boy, right? Oakfoot?" he asked, as he dusted himself off.

Balamor responded with the truth as it were. "Stepson. I'm a Wisebeard. Balamor Wisebeard."

"Oh my. I see. I'm very sorry for the trouble Mr. Wisebeard. You shouldn't have gotten caught up in all this," the bridge builder replied.

Balamor tried finding words to reply as he looked at the dead halfling only feet between them. "Is he...?"

"Dead? I'm afraid so. His bravery got the best of him." He paused. "We were fixing the bridge before we heard a raid down the road. I told him we shouldn't bother, but he insisted..." The man shook his head quickly. "I'm sorry, but I... I must inform his family of his death. Again, thank you."

Balamor studied the man's face, almost reminding him of his own. He had two thick sideburns and a wide jawline, but he knew there was no relation. The young mapmaker remembered his dream as he watched the bridge builder hoist his comrade from the ground to up over his shoulder before starting for the Raehl.

"Wait! I didn't catch your name!" Balamor yelled out, walking out of the caravan as he continued, "I must know the name of the man who saved my life if I were to tell his tale."

"The name's Finn!" the man replied as he walked down the dirt road.

Balamor studied his surroundings, two bodies of slain bandits sprawled out along the road. *What drove such men to rob and steal from simple halflings?* His thoughts contained questions he couldn't imagine answers for. The nature of halflings was incomparable with the nature of these men; although their agility would prove superior in thievery, violence was never the answer.

875, Summer's 54th Morning

Balamor waited a few moments, letting the aftermath of the encounter sink in. He didn't bother searching the caravan further. He was sure more bandits would stumble upon the remains, and he would join the rest of the corpses if he were to stick around. He started for the next river crossing further west, running over what had taken place this morning.

He was only a mile or so into his journey and already went against his plan to stay away from combat. He wasn't sure if it was something he could plan for on his travels at all. He realized his only knowledge of the land outside the Raehl was from the map he was working on. His mission seemed overly ambitious now, but his determination didn't allow him to stray away from reaching such a goal.

He had too much on his plate to put to waste, plus if he were to turn back and go home, his grandfather would be disappointed in him, to say the least. Failing Farjadis seemed like failing himself and more importantly their bloodline. He knew the old man's words were a bit outlandish, but there was sincerity behind them that served as proof to their validity. He opened his backpack and removed the mysterious six-page spellbook Farjadis had given him. It was now officially an heirloom, having been passed down from one Wisebeard to the next.

5

THE GREEN-ROBED WOMAN

875, Summer's 54th Afternoon

Balamor strolled down the edge of the Faric for hours, absorbed by his thoughts. He wondered why the Wisebeard name was so special in the first place, and if it dealt with the secrets of the runes. *Who was the mystic Gantis? Why did he give the book to Farjadis? What about the strange books in the library? How did they get there?*

He had so many more questions than he had answers. The only thing he knew for sure was that he'd barely scratched the surface of an even bigger question.

The sun glided across the blue sky peacefully as the mapmaker walked on. Occasionally, its light would dip behind a large cloud and return again with its blazing heat. Balamor felt the sweat drip from his brow down to the tip of his stubby nose. He was panting heavily before he settled next to the river to refill on water.

His backpack swung to his side, hanging from one strap around his shoulder. He rooted through its contents until he found his metal flask. He placed the leather bag down as he walked to the river. As Balamor drew closer to the edge, the sound of the rapids grew louder. Leaning over the edge, water splashed up in short waves, wetting his robes in spots and shivering his skin.

He dipped his empty hand into the rapids and wiped his face clean. The tired halfling let out a breath after he shoveled a gulp of water up to his mouth. He paused and studied the river. He was lucky to be traveling along the Faric. As nasty as it could be, it refreshed his dehydrated body. In fact, it was the first time he had a drink all day. He forgot to fill up on water before he left, but he wasn't willing to make the same mistake twice. He looked down at the flask while undoing its hard leather capping when something interesting caught his eye. As he rotated the flask, he saw small indentations etched out in the sunlight.

He held the flask closer to his eyes to make out what these engravings were. A large gasp was followed by a question.

"Are these Runewords? How did I miss this?"

He analyzed the flask further and saw there were six symbols which he had never seen there.

$$\overline{\underline{\mp}} \approx \ominus \approx \vdots \; \cdot ? \cdot \; \oplus$$

Balamor wasn't sure why they were on this flask, but he didn't have any way of further investigating their meaning. His sole interest was getting enough water to tide him over for the rest of the day. He skimmed the surface of the water with the flask, the heavy rapids poured into its mouth. He wondered why the waters of the Faric were so ravenous. It was something that even eluded his grandfather, along with many other Southlanders.

875, Summer's 54th Evening

Balamor watched the river flowing by for hours as he let his feet get some much-needed rest. As he soaked in the picturesque view of the Southland, he removed his flask and took a swig. Flipping the leather capping back over the mouth of the metal container, he studied the slight impressions of runewords, wondering what they meant.

His fingers rubbed up against the indentations in the cold metal as he pondered on the idea. He had a feeling he would get to the bottom of all this soon enough. The runewords disappeared as the parting sun fell behind a large cloud. At that, he removed his journal and made a note of his new findings — the first marker of his journey.

875, Summer's 54th Evening,

I've discovered my flask is, too, inscribed with runewords! Only a day into my journey and I have come to face bandits, obtained a brilliant dagger, and now this fascinating discovery. The Runesong is becoming just as mysterious as my destination. I shall find the Greatstone Pass tomorrow, hopefully. For now, I must rest.

He jotted down the remaining notes with his pencil before returning his journal to his pack.

The sun fell as he began his trek again, now running over the day's events. He couldn't have imagined the first day's entry to be full of such happenings. His journey had only just begun, yet each step brought him closer to the Mog Brush.

He wondered what made such a place so mysterious, forgotten by most of the Southlanders. It seemed almost wrong to lose such memories. Whether they were unpleasant or not, a lesson was to be learned from their remains.

Did something stand in its place before it was a tormented land? Or has the Mog Brush been a part of these lands since their conception?

The curious mapmaker had no answers to these questions yet asking them reassured him that his journey was not without reason. It was something which all men could benefit from. As much doubt as he had in himself, he knew someone must step up and do it if any benefit were to be made.

Balamor felt a sense of purpose now. He knew his mission wouldn't go unnoticed as the Mog Brush had for centuries.

Deep in thought, the halfling guided himself down a forested dirt path until suddenly he realized a strange silence hung over him. The sounds of life were absent, only the hushed footsteps of Balamor broke the stillness before he came to a sudden halt. Instinctively, he reached for his silver dagger, its polished steel resonating softly as Balamor guided it from its sheath.

Crouching beside a tree a few feet from the road, Balamor scanned his surroundings cautiously. Turning around, he saw nothing but the narrow trail he left behind thus far, forested on either side. The Faric was concealed beyond thickets and trees; its roaring waters muffled only slightly by the plant life.

Just as Balamor began to resume his trek, a thunderous crack down the trail whipped through the air along with a flash, filling the dim red sky with blinding white light.

Balamor was startled by the mighty sound, quickly scurrying off the road into the brush quicker than the flash which blinded him. His breathing ceased at the sound of footsteps to his left. His eyes followed a thin figure as they strolled past him. Satin green robes flowed to the earth, draping over an elegant frame, but their face was hidden beyond a deep cowl.

Stopping in the middle of the trail, the figure reached beneath its robes, retrieving a small leather bag and fetched three small stones from within. Throwing them on the ground in the shape of a triangle, the robed figure began to speak in hushed tones while grasping the pendant of their necklace.

Balamor watched in awe as the earth within the triangle began to gather at its center. Whipping past the hidden halfling, gusts of wind directed themselves toward the spectacle.

Within moments, the earth piled up to nearly match the height of Balamor.

The heavy winds stripped the mound of dirt in chunks that were only pulled back in, unable to escape an unseen force within the stones. Gradually, the pile of earth was etched out by the whirlwind, short stout legs protruding from the mound of dirt at its base. Running upward, the earth twisted itself into a torso which sprouted arms at its sides. Lastly, a short head formed amongst sturdy shoulders, eyes sunken below a thick brow line making up its only facial features. The winds calmed almost immediately as the stranger reached into the leather pouch and removed a glass vial.

Holding the vial in their hand, they spoke a mystifying tongue he had never heard before. *"Rhul theas manas firos. Guul ehn gehn mohr, ehn vis firos."*

The ancient words sent chills down the young mapmaker's spine. They rattled the leaves of the surrounding forest and easily intimidated any lurking predators. The lot of them could be heard scurrying through the trees, not willing to leave an encounter with the green-robed figure to chance. All had fled at the sound of the magical words, all but Balamor Wisebeard who peeked over the tree with a gaping jaw. The power this figure had was far greater than anything he could fathom.

The halfling had never before witnessed such magic, nor did he want to believe it. Yet whatever this earthen being was, it was real, and it was standing there on the road.

The stranger kneeled to the earthen being and began to speak, her feminine voice making it apparent she was a woman, "Now, little one, drink up before your quest begins."

A line in the face of the creature tore open into a gaping mouth as she poured the contents of the vial within.

Seconds later, a thin layer of light enveloped the being before it dissipated slowly, revealing a fully clothed figure of a halfling man.

Then the strange woman continued, her voice soft, almost nurturing, "There we are my child, now what was your name? Ah! Jabit, yes?"

Nodding in agreement, the small man started. "Oh, Mother, how I have missed you. What is it I can do for you?" His whimsical voice trailed into silence as the mystic woman removed another vial before tucking the leather pouch away beneath her green robes.

"You shall head east along the Faric until you find the Raehl, a small halfling village across the river. There you will find an old man who goes by the name Farjadis Wisebeard. Give this to him." Handing the potion to the short man she went on, "If anyone asks your business in the Raehl, tell them you are to deliver a message from Gantis Jacs to the old Wisebeard. Tell the old man that Gantis will be arriving within a few days, but he must take this potion to hide his presence in the Raehl 'til then. If he does not do this, then the library will be lost." She turned away, her green robes trailing against the dirt. "If he questions this order..." Her voice trailed into silence as the sun shined its final rays through the trees and down her green-robed figure. "Tell him the mystic Farah Lenook is here in the south, seeking his death." Her tone was strict, and Jabit's expression was that of shock.

Before he could muster up a reply, she disappeared in a flash of light trailed by a sharp boom which shook the ground beneath his feet.

Balamor stared at the short man as he walked away toward his home, the Raehl. His eyes were wide in astonishment from what had just taken place. He wanted to join him on the trip back to the Raehl and tell his grandfather he is being sought out, but he didn't want to risk being killed by Jabit or even worse the mystic woman who created him - or whatever he was. He would have to deliver the news alone.

Balamor crawled from the bushes, rubbing the numbness from his legs and brushing leaves from his robes before continuing west.

He searched the ground for anything which may have been left behind from the woman, but all was gone, even the three stones she placed on the ground. With nothing to scavenge, Balamor began his trek once more. He kept repeating the woman's words in his head. *Who was Farah Lenook and why would she want to kill Farjadis? And what about the library? What's in the library that would be lost to them?*

Suddenly, he remembered the strange blank books which filled most of the shelves in the old library.

"Spellbooks," he muttered to himself with wide eyes.

6

A GLIMPSE

875, Summer's 54th Night

 breeze brushed between Balamor's robes freezing the sweat on his skin. His body shivered as he tucked his flask away in his backpack. The cold night would only grow colder without a fire.

He couldn't locate the next crossing down the river without daylight; his travel seemed much longer than it appeared on his map. As much as he was against the idea, he needed to settle down for the night and try to sleep in this wilderness. It seemed impossible because of his encounter earlier. He would be completely vulnerable if he were to be found by more highwaymen, or some other dangerous beasts.

He made sure to study the flora and fauna of the Southland before he left the Raehl — packs of wolves, deadly snakes, and wild boar, just to name a few. There were toxic wildflowers and the various creeping bugs that would pester him, with a damning bite or a fatal pinch of poison. He wished he could stay on the move and avoid any of these possibilities. However, his body was exhausted from the journey thus far, and further travel would have to wait until sunrise.

He drifted away from the Faric, knowing it would draw predators as it did himself. His thin frame treaded the root-torn ground of the brush. Each step drained the energy from his body but he was determined to get away from the road.

He marched on mindlessly, dodging trees and searching for whatever timber was available. Grabbing only a handful of wood, he gathered the rest of his strength to start the fire before he laid out his bedroll and dropped himself beside a tree. The thud of his weary body echoed through the stillness of the air. He took a deep breath that turned into a yawn. One last look at the forest before his eyes closed, and he was fast asleep.

875, Summer's 55th Morning

Balamor awoke at the sound of footsteps. He rubbed the sleep from his eyes before lifting himself up and turning toward the noise. He was only a short distance from the road he departed last night. As he stood beside a tree, the footsteps faded. He crept toward the trail silently, hoping whatever was walking by had continued on its way.

As he kneeled beside the road, Balamor could see a figure of a short man wandering off into the distance. The mist of dawn shrouded the figure and dampened the dirt road the man traveled, but he knew this was surely no halfling for his silhouette was much too wide and bulky. Whoever it was, the halfling was cautious as he walked back to his makeshift camp.

Within a few minutes, he gathered his belongings. His bedroll was atop his backpack and the remnants of his fire were scattered. He turned to the road and silently followed the figure along the road's edge. He was hesitant to walk in the same direction, but his destination warranted it. Balamor slowed his pace as the fog was thinned with the sunrise approaching.

Miles had passed as he trailed the stranger, their distance increasing as the sun awoke the landscape. The birdsongs resonated from the vegetation which now nearly enveloped the road. As the morning dew began to dissipate in the sunlight, Balamor could see the figure was clearly a man. His features seemed to be Dwarven; a race Balamor only read about in history books.

From what he read, the dwarves are only slightly taller than halflings, but their strength and constitution go unmatched. The dwarves are the best miners the mountains have tested, and they're known to craft the most precious gemstones in the lands. However, stories said that the dwarves were some of the most fearsome warriors during the time of the Blood Wars, a reason Balamor knew he should remain hidden.

Historians, such as the famous Hagron Soldo, wrote of the wars only in retrospect. Hagron wrote very colorful tales recounting the happenings of the ancient wars — stories including giants, dragons, and the otherworldly consequences of dark magic. Many of his words were preposterous to put it lightly, yet the vivid nature of his stories always kept people telling them every year.

The Witch and the Guile was one of them. In that tale, the Dwarven people were said to be the strongest and most destructive race of mankind, known for killing a powerful being Hagron referred to as the 'Rahkfolk.'

But this dwarf Balamor trailed did not look harmful at all. In fact, he held no weapon amongst his back, waist, or even his boots. For a dwarf, he seemed underwhelming, considering Balamor's expectations.

Suddenly, the sturdy dwarf stopped in the middle of the road and fetched his pack.

Balamor quickly pinned himself to the base of a tree, hoping he remained undetected. The nervous halfling's curiosity couldn't be tamed so easily. Slowly, his head peeked around the trunk of a tree, its bark overgrown with moss.

The figure reached for his bag, and Balamor saw the man's entire right arm was wrapped in a white cloth.

A tremendous weight lifted from Balamor's shoulders. This dwarf was in no condition to start any trouble, at least not with such an injury. The curious halfling watched the stout figure crouch for a moment, feeling the earth beneath him. Balamor thought to himself, *What if he's tracking something or someone?*

The curious halfling crept forward for a better view, each step muffled by his hairy feet. Balamor stopped beside another tree and grabbed his leather backpack from his shoulders before he heard a crashing sound of earth ahead. He snapped his head up, but the sound ceased and the dwarf was gone, only a cloud of dirt settling in his place.

Gazing down at his bag, he caught a glimpse of a green glow. His hand thrust into the bag before plucking out the small book from his grandfather. He threw the book open and searched its contents, but the glow was gone; the pages were still blank. He dropped the strange book into his backpack. Returning to the road, Balamor checked for the mysterious figure as he crept out of cover, but the stranger was nowhere to be seen.

In the middle of the road, Balamor spotted the white cloth wraps which the stranger used to cover his right arm. But these wraps had no trace of blood on them at all, only stains from the earth below. Whatever this man was covering didn't seem to be a wound after all. Where he disappeared to was another question that brought new concern.

875, Summer's 55th Evening

Balamor trekked the road all afternoon and into the evening, keeping a close eye for any sign of the dwarf he was trailing. He would only stop to refill on water and rest his legs. He hoped he would reach the Greatstone Pass before sundown, but he wasn't sure how much further ahead it was.

The river was concealed with thick shrubbery and huge river rocks, and the mesh of plants made it impossible to locate the river crossing.

The journey was exhausting his body, but his mind tried to evade the matter and focus on the task at hand. There had to be some way to travel this river faster. He pondered the idea of building a raft to navigate the waters, but knew his strength was not nearly enough to steer in the rough rapids, not to mention his craftsmanship wasn't anything to brag about.

The remaining heat of the sun beat down on Balamor as he marched onward. The sound of crickets started to fill the air and nighttime began to take the Southlands under its wing. Owls occasionally would holler in the distance, breaking the eerily still atmosphere.

Balamor's steel-blue eyes were fixed on the trail ahead, waiting for a break in the thick bushes and trees choking the earth upon which he traveled. Winding along the edge of the river, the constricted trail was teeming with the life of the nocturnal. The young mapmaker trekked onward, taking a swig from his flask before stuffing it back in his bag. He looked at his square stone rune, its triangle of inscribed dots confounding him. He wondered what kind of magical powers the strange stone contained and if it was anything like the event he witnessed the previous night. The peculiar tongue in which the green-robed woman spoke lingered in the fringes of Balamor's mind. He searched for the particular words but only the last few came to him.

"Ehn vis firos."

The square stone rune flashed in a ghostly green light before he gripped it tightly. His eyes were filled with the same light and he dropped to his knees on the road. Starting from the tips of his fingers and rushing through his body was a mysterious energy that stood the hairs up on his skin. His muscles stiffened and his knuckles whitened as he squeezed the rune in his hand. Its symbol of three dots shined with an intense light as it shook wildly, fracturing with light, piercing through the cracks. An aura surrounded the young Wisebeard, illuminating the road and the dense wilderness surrounding him. As much of a spectacle as it was from an outsider's perspective, Balamor's own perspective was something else entirely.

A GLIMPSE

The moment that final word left his tongue, he felt like he was in another place altogether. His surroundings suddenly changed into a desert of billowing ash. Standing in the midst of powerful winds whipping against his body, he hadn't a clue where he was, but it sounded like a war was taking place behind him. Fires lit up the darkened sky as metal clashed against metal. Cries of pain and bellows of combat meshed together into a chorus of chaos.

Looking down at himself, he saw the landscape wasn't the only thing to have changed. His robes were those of long black satin and in his hands were three peculiar scrolls which he held with urgency. He studied them closely as ash surged around him.

Made of a coarse papyrus and fitted with ornate brass knobs, each of the scrolls were wrapped with a different color ribbon: red, yellow, and blue respectively.

Returning his gaze back to the ashen desert he started to wander through the wasteland. His mind was a scrambled mess of thoughts, some which he couldn't explain. Strange names entered his mind – those of people and places he had never even come across. Memories of past events that he never witnessed arose. Deep and vivid emotions of mourning, betrayal, and terror gripped him like a phantom and shook him to his core. His head began to ache, and his legs weakened with each pulsing throb of pain.

"Balamor!" a deep voice called out. One he had somehow remembered.

A tremor rumbled the ground below him as stone cracked with incredible force. He turned around to see a tall man standing several yards away. He too wore pitch-black robes and his pale, shaded face was otherwise concealed by his long black beard. A groaning roar erupted from the earth, thrusting ash and stone through the air and knocking Balamor to the ground.

ZARDRAKEN'S CRYPT

In a snap, the mystical vision ended with Balamor falling to the ground on the side of the road. He held his square stone rune in hand, the pale green glow emitting from its inscription faded. His sense of touch was numb, his muscles fatigued from whatever energy still coursed through his body.

He slowly gathered himself before searching his surroundings for any signs of others. The dirt road was heavily forested with no one forward or back. The Faric was raging beyond along with the buzzing drone of nocturnal critters. He returned his rune to his backpack before continuing toward the next river crossing.

Awhile had passed before Balamor regained his strength. The toll that the vision had taken on his body was an obvious cause for concern. He would make sure to leave a note of it in his journal once he found a place to camp for the night.

The sun was well beyond the horizon when Balamor finally saw a break ahead in the dense flora surrounding him. He moved with haste at the relieving sight, his furry feet thudding against the dirt before he felt the cold surface of stone beneath him. He scanned the ground and saw the dirt trail he was on became freckled with polished stone, each one greater in size as he moved on. After a few yards, he was out of the surrounding vegetation, amongst the open air which had brushed by his robes. The road turned toward the River Faric. The tired halfling turned his sight toward a humongous arch of Blackstone that spanned across the roaring water. He let out a sigh of relief as the first part of his journey had finally been met; Balamor made it to the Greatstone Pass.

7

THE MESSENGER

875, Summer's 55th Evening

Calloused heels thudded against the earth as Jabit Treadfoot trekked the forests of Gwendilae. He walked for what felt like weeks until finally breaking through the thick vegetation suffocating the road, along with himself. He strolled to the edge of the Faric cautiously, frightened by its turgid waters splashing up and soaking his hairy feet and legs.

Looking upstream, he saw huge cliffs towering above the horizon, cradling the life of the village below in a crescent shape. Dim lantern lights pierced through the dense evening fog, outlining a road which led to the edge of the Faric. There, a narrow rope bridge draped between large wooden posts, nearly skimming the river's surface.

Dropping his left hand to his tan vest, he slipped a glass vial from his inside pocket to his calloused palm. Jabit studied the vial closely. Its shape was that of a teardrop and pressed into its clear surface were four dots in the shape of a square.

: :

Within was a ghostly pale green liquid, streaks of bright white slithering like eels, mindlessly. Whatever this potion was, Jabit knew it was to be taken across that bridge before the sun fell behind the hills as his mother insisted.

He returned the vial to his vest and proceeded down the path to the Raehl, whistling to himself as he walked the dirt trail. There was comfort in the melodies, reminding him of his childhood when his mother would sing to him before he slept. The songs helped him ignore the awkward silences and the sounds of nature he found mundane.

Jabit had walked the south plenty of times, traveling between the small halfling villages and the kingdom of Anstia, making deliveries from his mother's farm on the outskirts of the small fishing town of Paetok. He wasn't living the dream, but with time taking its toll on his mother, she depended on him to travel and tend to the animals from time to time. If he didn't have such a burden, he would be out adventuring the lands in search of precious treasures, a tale to tell, and the fame of a hero. He waited for the day he could take on such a way of life.

For now, he would continue his travels to a familiar halfling village, the Raehl. He had to make a few trips there last season to deliver his mother's famous jams, but this time was different. Removing the tear-shaped vial from his pocket, he began to study it once more. Its ghostly contents twisted and occasionally glowed fluorescent green. Whatever it was, it certainly was no jam.

He thought it was rather strange that he didn't have his caravan with him, but this was the only item he carried, and the man who needed it, needed it urgently. His thoughts kept returning to the name of the man who must receive this strange tonic.

"Farjadis Wisebeard... Hmmm... Farjadis Wisebeard," he mumbled to himself quietly. "Ooh, hoo, hoo, I'll find you Mister Wisebeard. If not, I would be failing Mother, and I won't fail Mother, no, no, no." His ramblings became enraged until suddenly his attention was yanked from him.

Off to the edge of the road, Jabit saw the remnants of what looked like a raid. To his left was a wooden rundown caravan with its back doors busted open, and small boxes and spools of various fabric littered the surrounding area.

He gazed upon the caravan before he began twiddling his thumbs and looking around in anticipation.

The air was still, and the fog gripped the Southland as the messenger glided across the dirt road toward the caravan.

Looking inside, he saw many of the boxes and crates were ransacked, one of the floorboards shattered, and most of what could be scavenged was already taken. He stayed close to the wall of the caravan as he shifted himself to the back doors.

Jabit peeked around the corner when he found himself face-to-face with a man who was slumped over next to the caravan. Jabit jumped in shock before losing his balance and stumbling to the ground. He looked at the dark-clothed man, his milky blue eyes staring back at the halfling, his face concealed beyond a black cloth wrap.

Moments went by but the man remained motionless. A foul stench drifted up to Jabit's nose turning his stomach and gagging him.

This man was dead and could have been for days. He turned away and picked himself up before nearly puking from the disgusting smell. The interest in scavenging was short-lived and without thinking twice, Jabit returned to the road.

The mist gradually grew heavier as the warmth of the sun dissipated and the sky turned black. He approached the next crossing with haste, hoping it wasn't too late for a delivery. A mix of hoots and buzzing echoed through the landscape, joining with the constant flow of the Faric.

He paused for a moment to study the rickety bridge he was about to cross.

Two thick pairs of braided rope stretched across the entire width of the river, both secured by large engraved oak posts driven deep into the earth.

He remembered crossing this bridge before with his caravan. The bridge gave little to no clearance on its sides. At first glance it seemed impractical, but its defensive capability was impressive for a halfling village.

Thankfully for him, he was alone this time, and his only possession was no bigger than his palm.

Rough winds whipped the rope bridge to-and-fro as he slid his left hand over his vest pocket securing the precious potion within. A nervous breath escaped his lungs as he took the first step across the raging Faric. Gripping the rope railing tight, he guided himself from plank to plank. Travel was slow across the narrow bridge as he made sure he wouldn't become another victim claimed by the angry rapids below.

The water leaped up at his feet, causing him to jump and nearly knocking himself over.

The nervous halfling watched the thick oak planks pass beneath his feet, each one creaking as they pulled him closer to the heavy current of the Faric. His hands clenched the rope handrail as he neared the middle of the bridge.

His heart pounded against his chest, nearly breaking free from his trembling body. A deep inhale ended abruptly as Jabit watched a monstrous wave slam against the frail bridge, causing him to slip and lose his balance. His hand slipped free from the railing before he fell face first toward the thick planks below.

Slipping from his vest, the glass vial chimed as it skipped across the bridge in front of him.

Crawling frantically, Jabit chased the precious potion across the bridge. In one leap forward, the desperate halfling reached out and snatched the vial from the air with both hands. But his slippery palms lost their grip, leading him to juggle it wildly as he shifted himself to his feet. Each step drove him toward the end of the bridge, but no closer to securing the small vial which danced in and out of his clumsy fingers.

In one final attempt to save the potion, he dove forward and yanked it from the air, pulling it to his chest before his short frame slammed into the grass below. Too frightened to move from the stable ground, Jabit held his breath as he glanced down at the object in his hands. A metal latch still clamped the mouth of the tear-shaped container shut, the eerie substance still lurking inside.

Jabit's face relaxed as he let out a sigh of relief, hoping the worst part of the journey was over.

It was a long trip across the river, and one which made the messenger question the purpose of the entire situation.

He rubbed his noggin and looked into the night sky as he returned the vial to his vest. *Why would Mother be worried about protecting some old man in the Raehl?*

He knew this certainly wasn't a typical business transaction for his mother to be a part of, but he wasn't in the position to question such things, although he had a bad feeling about it.

His thinking ended abruptly when the sound of a man's voice called out for him, "Hello there, Mr. Treadfoot! I saw you almost took a dip into the Faric there!"

Jabit snapped his head up at the man relaxing by the bridge. He wore a dirty green tunic and loose brown trousers, but his weaved sun hat gave away his farming occupation. His face was soft for the depth of his voice. If they weren't alone, Jabit would have thought he was hearing someone else's voice.

An awkward silence fell between the two halflings as Jabit slid his hand over his vest pocket, shielding the precious contents within.

Jabit didn't respond, and so the farmer changed the topic. "I see you're without a caravan. None of your mother's jams yet? How is she doing this time of year by the way? If you don't mind indulging a halfling's curiosity."

The messenger looked down to the ground and tried to remember the stranger as he spoke, "She is well... Thank you for asking, Mister... Puddlebottom! Isn't it?"

The man nodded.

Jabit continued, "As for the jams... unfortunately not this time. She has me making a smaller, much more peculiar delivery to the Raehl. It's more urgent than her jams, I assure you!"

Puddlebottom rose one brow in curiosity before his question came forth amongst a laugh, "What could be more important than your mother's jams?"

Jabit leaned in slowly. "A message for a Farjadis Wisebeard from Gantis Jacs."

The light chuckle of the man broke at the sound of the name. His plush face tensed as if he could see the strange potion within his vest. "The mystic... I see, well then, you must be on your way. Don't let me hinder the delivery of such news. Though I would approach the subject lightly. The old man doesn't like to bring up his past with the mystic and the majority of the Raehl isn't very fond of magic in the first place."

"Yes, yes, thank you! And I am sure those jams will be here by the end of the month!" Jabit replied assuredly as a soft smile settled across his face.

Jabit proceeded through the wooden archway of the Raehl, a setting that felt strangely foreign this time around. His eyes were fixed on the crescent of giant cliffs which protected the halfling town. Their sheer size was intimidating, yet he felt secure in their bounds.

The messenger looked down at his destination to see a series of grassy halfling holes scattered around dirt trails like rolling hills in the distance. If it weren't for their wooden doors and porch fronts, the halflings who occupied them would have seemed like giants.

It was an interesting sight to Jabit. His experience in a town full of his own kind only came from his deliveries. His mother preferred to be isolated from towns, even if they were full of peaceful halflings. Jabit always thought about moving to such a town one day, perhaps when he was finally free from the farm.

His memory of the Raehl was slowly returning to him. It felt like ages had gone by since his last arrival.

He walked down the road for a moment before he spotted a familiar sign, *"The Watering Hole."*

Without a second glance, he yanked the two large semi-circle doors open, and entered the dimly lit lounge within.

875, Summer's 55th Night

The sound of chatter filled the entire room as the messenger guided the oak doors shut.

Lantern light danced across the surface of the small wooden tables, etching out the variety of halflings which occupied them. The mood was melancholy in the small pub, except for the bickering coming from some boisterous individuals in the corner to the left.

Jabit strolled to the bar, dodging patrons spilling their pints of mead onto the hardwood floor. He slowed as he approached the bar, scratching his head as he looked for an open stool. He paced back and forth as seats were claimed right before him, until he spotted the only remaining stool at the far left of the bar, sandwiched between two heavyset halflings clashing their pints ferociously.

He dashed to the seat and quickly came to a halt before clearing his throat. "... Excuse me gentlemen, I am—"

"Jabit!" the two men shouted in unison as they turned to face him.

Jabit studied them a moment trying to remember who they were, and why he had a feeling he knew them.

They looked nearly identical, both with thick sideburns and broad jawlines. The man to his left wore a bridge builder's uniform, his utility belt resting over his left shoulder. The man to his right wore a red tunic and black leather pants, dirt staining his hairy face and hands.

THE MESSENGER

The halfling on the right continued, "Well, of course you can join us. It's certainly been awhile since we had the likes of Jabit Treadfoot in town, hasn't it, Finn?"

The bridge builder chugged his pint before he replied, "Indeed it has, Lippin... Where did you go off to for the past two years, Jabit? I sure hope everything is okay at the farm."

The two men helped the messenger to his stool as he spoke, "Has it really been two years? I thought it was a while since I've been to the Raehl. Everything seems so new to me! Mother must have forgotten your village on my route this whole time! But I assure you that everything is certainly so back at the farm. However, I'm not here on the matters of my normal deliveries. I need to speak to Farjadis Wisebeard."

The two men looked at one another for a moment before they returned their gaze back to Jabit.

An awkward silence fell between them.

Lippin leaned closer to Jabit and hushed his tone. "Is he in danger? We've been hearing rumors of mysterious things going on along the Faric, and the word is that the young Wisebeard left the village just before the rumors surfaced. Finn says Balamor saved his life along the road after his clash with bandits a couple of nights back."

Finn nodded as he chugged his mead, allowing Jabit to interject, "The young Wisebeard? I wasn't aware there was more than one."

"The only two left, my friend. It's knowledge they wish not to share, for it might fall into the wrong hands. Whatever business you have with the old man, keep it between you and him. The safety of the Wisebeards means the safety of us halflings."

The bridge builder rested his right hand on Jabit's shoulder as he looked him in the eye. "It's the hole with the green porch. Oh, and do bring us some of them jams soon."

ZARDRAKEN'S CRYPT

Jabit jumped from his stool before the bartender could make it down to him. Within moments, he was making his way through the bar doors and back outside.

A slight breeze sent a shiver down his spine as he peered through the foggy halfling village. He strolled down the busy trail in search of the hole with the green porch front, recognizing only a few of the faces that greeted him.

It wasn't long until he felt like he was walking in circles.

The layout of the town confused him, leading him to walk for nearly half an hour before he spotted what he was looking for.

He must have passed it a dozen times.

Letting out a sigh of relief, he hurried across the dirt road toward the old Wisebeard's hole. It seemed like his steps became shorter as he approached the wooden steps of the porch.

The creaking of a rocking chair broke the strange silence, causing Jabit to seek it out immediately.

Before he could speak, the old halfling sitting in the chair across from the stairs started. "Ah, greetings! It has been a long time, Mr. Treadfoot. It's a bit late for you to be here making deliveries after sundown, though, I'm sure you have your reasons. I was beginning to think I would never taste your mother's jams again! How much are they now?" Taking a puff from his long pipe, he raised one eyebrow.

The messenger was startled for some reason — like he was caught committing a crime.

He was unable to answer the question before the old man paused and studied him. "Is everything okay, Jabit? You look like you've seen a ghost!" A cloud of smoke dissipated before the old man let out a jovial laugh.

"Yes, yes everything is very well... It has certainly been a long while since we last encountered, and sorry for the late arrival, but unfortunately I am not here concerning my usual business, Mr. Wisebeard."

THE MESSENGER

The air grew heavy around Jabit as he finished his sentence. He felt the joyful mood of the old man collapse.

It was as if time were still until the Wisebeard took a drag from his pipe.

Jabit felt the blue eyes of the halfling study him. Suddenly, he realized his hand was gripping his vest pocket.

"I see. Please, take a seat," Farjadis added.

Beside Jabit was another rocking chair. He sat down before he continued, "I'm unsure why I am here exactly, but I believe that it's beyond my purpose. My mother gave me this potion. She told me it was very important that I bring it to you."

Reaching into his vest, he revealed the glass vial to the old Wisebeard. Its contents still glowed an iridescent ghostly green.

Farjadis didn't flinch at the sight of the strange potion. He only rocked in his chair, waiting for the messenger to go on.

"She mentioned that a man named Gantis Jacs will be here in a few days, and that you must consume this to hide yourself from—"

"Farah Lenook." The old man seethed as he removed the pipe from his mouth, interrupting the nervous halfling before him. "She is here. Did you speak to Gantis yourself?" The old man's tone was strict, his eyes growing wide in concern as he waited for Jabit to respond.

"I'm afraid not. My mother must have gotten this from him while I was away on a delivery. I'm not sure why she would be dealing with this... Maybe this mystic is trying to keep it a secret? The reason is beyond me. I am merely the messenger." Reaching out to the old man, Jabit passed the potion to him.

Farjadis studied the tear-shaped vial closely, his bony fingers rubbing across the square of four dots pressed into its surface.

$$\therefore \because$$

He recognized this runeword, but he was not familiar with what was inside. He felt the urgency of the situation looming over him. Glancing over at the traveler beside him, he looked for answers he could only receive from Gantis Jacs himself.

He remembered when the old mystic last spoke to him nearly half a century ago, when he first moved to the Raehl. He was thirty-six. He knew Farah would eventually find him, but he hoped she wouldn't find Balamor.

Looking back at the strange potion, he studied the symbol once more. "Do you know what this symbol here represents, Mr. Treadfoot?"

The nervous halfling shook his head.

Farjadis went on, "It is an ancient word that stands for time, a runeword. This is a very powerful word; I've never seen it inscribed on a potion in my time. The old mystic must have something planned." The old Wisebeard placed the vial on a small table between them.

Jabit looked down at the table, and beneath it he saw a basket full of various books. "A library! My mother, she mentioned something about your library... becoming lost to you."

Farjadis let out a plume of smoke before reaching beyond his shirt revealing a silver necklace fixed with a small ruby pendant. He knew it needed to be protected. Balamor needed more time. But the effects of the strange potion he had just received were completely unknown to him. Caressing the pendant in his palm, Farjadis observed the gem closely. Moonlight shined against its surface and gleamed down its sharp contours. It was just a piece of a puzzle to him. He knew there were more, and Farah Lenook was undoubtedly after them.

"Gantis gave me this necklace. He said it was merely a fragment of the true stone it once was. I was to keep this away from Farah Lenook at all costs along with the books in the library. All these years I have held on to it, and I would rather have cast it down the Faric, but I knew my duty, my role in this world." The old man's steel-blue eyes became lost in the ruby before he quickly tucked it beneath his white shirt. He retrieved the vial from the small table before he continued, "I'm sorry you were brought into this. It is strange that Gantis would choose you and your mother to carry out such a task. Perhaps he wanted to ensure the safety of this potion. Well, no matter his purpose, I believe you have done your duty, Mr. Treadfoot. Now, I will do mine."

Jabit watched as Farjadis reached out his bony hand to meet his own. He felt the importance of the old man as their palms met. He wasn't sure what fate would bring the old Wisebeard now, but he knew his journey home would begin once their handshake ended. The two looked one another in the eye once more, each having a feeling it would be the last time they would have the chance.

8

A STRANGER'S WORD

875, Summer's 55th Night

he Southland was consumed by the darkness of the night. Its stars were jailed behind a thick shroud of gray clouds. Only the moon remained lit in the night sky, slightly dimming as clouds passed it by.

Balamor's short strides pushed him across the slight arc of a massive stone bridge. It was beautifully crafted with humongous boulders polished by heavy winds for what seemed like millennia, and assorted-like pieces of a puzzle climbing their way across the Faric. Not one visible speck of mortar was used to sustain this massive structure. Its design was godlike to Balamor. Even if he wasn't a bridge builder by trade, knowledge of the subject was instinctive for any halfling.

The bridge carried the young cartographer across the river within minutes. There he paused, looking at his map intensely. Tracing its surface with his finger and stopping at a familiar blank spot, he sensed his destination was in reach. The Greatstone Pass was found at last and discovering what lay beyond was now his duty. The map found its way back into his backpack before he started on the next leg of his journey.

The large stones blotted the wide dirt path he was traveling. The frequent touch of their cold surface became familiar to him, but the craftsmanship of the ancient pass was piquing his curiosity as well as his discomfort.

He felt confined within the towering walls which hugged the pass; a mosaic of giant stone bricks hawked the lone halfling down as he scanned his surroundings cautiously.

A STRANGER'S WORD

It was an odd mix of feelings Balamor was juggling. His thoughts dashed in all directions, a time-lapse of his past few days. What he's been through so far was known to other men, but few knew what danger the Mog Brush would bring, and an age-old fear kept most away. He would not let that fear corrupt his decision to uncover what was considered 'harmful knowledge', for all knowledge was neutral to him.

Balamor's mind slipped back to the spellbooks — how their pages related to the strange runes he held in his backpack, and the result of their power in the hands of the unknown mystic woman.

It wasn't her mysterious identity but her knowledge of his grandfather, and more importantly her knowledge of the Wisebeard name that left him pondering.

Farjadis never mentioned a woman in his travels, only Gantis Jacs; a man who must be just as powerful if not more so than the green-robed woman. He remembered she mentioned a name unfamiliar to him, Farah Lenook. She was seeking to end Farjadis, perhaps an attempt to vanquish the Wisebeard name once and for all.

Balamor gripped the hilt of his dagger tight at the thought of losing his grandfather.

The cool porcelain chilled his hand, but his anger ignored the cold until it was no more. Drawing the blade from its sheath as he walked, Balamor studied it thoroughly. It was in pristine condition, seemingly unused by its previous owner. Whoever that was didn't require its protection, but Balamor knew he depended on it.

He held the dagger firmly in his right hand, when he heard the sound of a man shouting in the distance. His voice accompanied by the snarling of horses and creaking of wooden wheels. Balamor couldn't make out the man's words, but assumed he was rambling on about the horses angrily.

Balamor searched the road for any escape, hoping he could avoid the man and his caravan until he passed by, but the large cobblestone road was barren. Minutes passed by before the man and his caravan approached the robed halfling. He held a lit torch in one hand and the reins of his horse in the other.

The man was short for a human. He wore a brown tunic and green pants. His face was narrow and bony but his eyes were wide with excitement. A thin goatee outlined a wide grin as the man spoke. "Hello there! Rather late to be on the pass alone, don't you think? Ha! But have no worries friend, I am not one of those filthy bandits! You would think they'd be out at night, but no! They wait for the earliest hours of the morning, ha! But not me, and certainly not yourself!"

Balamor began to reply, still holding his dagger in his right hand.

Before the words escaped his mouth, the short man cut in as he climbed to the ground, "Oh! I see you carry a very worthy blade! I could tell you quite a few things about that blade."

The curious halfling dropped his initial question and waited for the merchant to continue as he looked down at the blade.

"That fine blade there belonged to a king. The king of Hanson to be exact! How you found such a valuable weapon beats me!" The short man brushed himself off before he peered back at the young halfling. "But I know of a dagger even more worthy than a king's dagger!" He laughed to himself as he strolled to the back of his caravan, motioning Balamor to follow.

Balamor's eyebrows lifted in sudden disbelief as he followed behind.

"What kind of dagger is more worthy than that of a king?" Balamor asked.

The merchant quickly replied, "The kind which has a history. A dagger wielded by a fearsome warrior. A dagger which saved the life of the king, when the king's men could not. A dagger whose blade has seen more men than its hilt. That is the kind of dagger more worthy than that of a king." The man reached for the caravan doors as he looked back at Balamor intensely. "And I just so happen to own one such dagger!"

Balamor watched the doors as they swung open. His excitement was soon overwhelmed with panic when two hooded men sprung from the back of the caravan. The elusive halfling turned to break for the road when the merchant wrapped his arms around him, lifting his feet from the ground. He struggled as the two men walked toward him.

"Ha! You halflings are all so gullible! You should have stayed in your hole!" the merchant added, laughing as he wrestled with the halfling.

Balamor couldn't believe he fell for such a con. He knew he should have avoided the man altogether. He needed to escape but the merchant's grip was too strong. Glancing down, he saw he still had his dagger, its hilt numbing his hand as he struggled. The desperate halfling thrust the blade into the torso of his captor.

The short man bent over as he let out a sharp yelp, his grip broken by the halfling's daring attempt to break free.

Balamor fell to the ground as the first hooded man attacked. The blade of his broadsword pierced through the air, ready to pin his target to the ground. But the young halfling was too fast, rolling out of the way and landing behind the merchant who was now limping toward the caravan.

The highwayman dug his blade deep into the earth when Balamor shoved the merchant toward him. The two bodies toppled over one another before they slammed against the caravan spilling the contents of various baskets and small chests. The remaining bandit hurdled over them as he came running in Balamor's direction, his scimitar blade hissing as it departed its sheath.

The frightened mapmaker's feet pounded against the road in short strides as he fought to gain ground on his hooded predator. Suddenly, the earth beneath his feet shook rapidly before Balamor watched small waves of dirt rush toward him, raising the huge polished stones and dropping them back into place. Before he could leap to safety, the ripple of the earth knocked him off his feet, scattering the contents of his bag.

The merchant and the downed highwayman lifted themselves to their feet when they saw their comrade disappear under a thick blanket of dust. The wounded conman carried himself to the caravan and struggled to get into his seat. He took the reins in his hands and with a quick snap, the wooden caravan darted down the pass toward the stone bridge.

The other bandit chased down the caravan, dodging various stolen goods as they spilled out the back, the earth beneath his feet shaking heavily once more, slightly knocking the bandit off balance.

The young cartographer watched as a pillar of dirt rose from the flat ground, trailing the bandit as he tried to escape. Dirt and stone flung into the air wildly as a large man-like figure ripped through the pillar in mid-sprint.

Balamor glanced at this new towering figure as he frantically returned the fallen items to his bag. As he gathered his things to make an escape, a familiar green glow caught his attention. His eyes snapped to see his small spellbook flipped open to its fourth page. Every item, spare one rune, made it into his backpack as he hurried toward the glowing piece of parchment. Snatching the book from the ground, he studied it closely.

The page was no longer blank, but instead its surface was filled with lines of runewords, many he hadn't seen before. Four rows of the strange symbols glowed a warm shade of green which waved like light from a torch fire.

Flashing before him was the event he witnessed before crossing the bridge, when a similar creature was conjured on the side of the road. "The robed woman," he whispered to himself as he watched the earthen summoned chase down the hooded bandit.

The clay beast closed the distance between him and the final highwayman within seconds. Its dirt arms morphed together as they clasped the shaken bandit, squeezing the air from his lungs. As the last bit of air escaped the bandit, the dirt golem twisted downward, carrying the limp body with it.

Moments went by before a cloud of dirt settled and the golem was no more. In its place was the now unconscious bandit. His chin rested on the freshly turned soil, the rest of his body buried below the ground.

Balamor was on one knee, scanning the aftermath of the disastrous event as the madness settled into an eerie stillness. His face and hands were covered in scrapes and bruises, and his robes ripped and matted with dirt. He glanced down at his silver dagger uneasily, its blade streaked with the blood of the con artist who nearly kidnapped him. He felt a surge of pain rush through his left arm. Clutching his shoulder, Balamor saw his blood seeping into his palm. He snatched the remaining rune from the ground when the sound of a cough broke the lingering silence.

Balamor crept over to the remnants of the dirt wave which saved his life. There was the crippled body of the highwayman who struggled to breathe.

The man lifted his right hand to the air as Balamor slowly approached, spreading his fingers wide. *"R... ra... raji..."* His words were faint and distant as he spoke.

Balamor felt a strange sensation in his right hand before fixing his eyes on the disk-shaped rune in his palm. A cross cut into a circle glowed a bright yellow, illuminating the road around them.

The bandit let out raspy laughs, each one becoming more and more clear as Balamor watched the yellow light gather at the tips of his fingers before the cuts and bruises left the crippled man's face and body. He jumped to his feet and took off down the road, stumbling over the spilled goods from the caravan.

Balamor was in shock as the man made his escape, looking down at the rune, its glow beginning to fade just before Balamor whispered to himself, *"Raji?"*

The glow intensified at the sound of the strange word before the sensation in his hand began to course through his entire body. He felt his skin tighten around his wounds before their pain disappeared completely. He almost didn't believe what he had just done, questioning himself and studying the rune as its glow had completely faded. He yanked his small notebook and a wooden pencil from his backpack, swapping it with the rune.

The tip of his pencil panned to the top of the most recent page before halting at the symbol of the rune he just held in his hand. He marked down the first piece to the puzzle that was the Runesong — *Raji.*

As he scribbled down the last words of his report, he heard the sound of branches snapping overhead. He glared up at the verdant tree line which rooted itself to the brim of the cliffs surrounding the ancient pass.

9

A DYING OLD MAN

875, Summer's 55th Night

top its icy summit, the Peak of Rayguth was the epitome of isolation — a spire of rock ending far above the clouds. Sprouting from the Dahris Mountains, it towered over the north and could be seen from anywhere on Earth.

The races of man believed the Peak of Rayguth was taller than the sky itself. A place where the coldest air dwelled and the legendary falls gave birth to the River Faric.

Piercing through the clouds with awesome force, the waterfall that left the fabled mountain was immense. Its waters were unbelievably powerful, carving through the base of the mountain like a sword through flesh.

Since the beginning of time, when the Rahkfolk gave birth to the elements, this was the root of lakes and oceans — filled like a sink from a faucet.

The Faric was the arterial vein of the world. It was essential to life in all the lands, traveling east through the gnomish woods and cutting south into the vast lowlands. It twisted and turned with ease, defining the surrounding landscape.

It spawned countless streams and creeks along its turbulent journey. Filling up the Sarl Basin in the far southeast and sprawling west to carve out the Wynspur Sea of the Crescent Coast; the Faric was truly the lifeblood of the known world.

Its waters spanned the entire world in a single day and night. However, what was unknown to many was that it owed its life to magic.

Without the runes, the world would have no rivers, seas and lakes; no source of water to nourish its flora and fauna. Yet with that glorious life comes an inevitable death. The legendary Faric can only last as long as nature permits. For now, its current would travel far and wide fulfilling its purpose.

The same could be said about Jabit Treadfoot, the messenger who now crossed the treacherous rope bridge from the Raehl, the River Faric growling beneath him.

Fear was instinctive, but the common ground he and the legendary waters shared was uncanny.

He stood quietly on the new oak wood planks. His eyes were fixed on the river, but his vision was swimming in his thoughts. He couldn't get Farjadis Wisebeard to leave his memory. Glancing over his shoulder, his hand turned into a fist. The sun was retiring, and he had to do the same.

Looking to the northern sky, Jabit watched dark clouds rolling south cloaking the moonlight which signaled nighttime.

Paetok was only a couple hours away by foot. He needed to go now or he would be caught up in the approaching storm.

Moments passed before he left the bridge. Slipping his hand into his vest, he started to whistle softly as he began his journey home.

875, Summer's 55th Night

Farjadis studied the glass vial in his right hand after the messenger had disappeared from his sight. It was uncertain what would happen when he took the strange tonic. He could only have faith in Gantis — he trusted him implicitly.

ZARDRAKEN'S CRYPT

Just as the night fell over the halfling village, the old Wisebeard lifted himself from his rocking chair and started for the Wisebeard library.

The air was still as he walked the dirt path. The moon was full and shining bright in the sky with owls hollering in the distance. The trek across the foggy town seemed to take ages as Farjadis became absorbed in his thoughts.

He thought back on his journey to the Island City of Delsis with the mystic Gantis. He knew that Farah Lenook would never stop her search for the books, but more importantly, the pendant which Farjadis held dear. A pendant which he hoped he could pass on to his grandson when the time came. He asked himself how many times the mystic could keep good away from the grips of such evil.

How much could a dying old man do to escape such evil?

His final question brought him to the porch front of his old home.

He studied the beautiful halfling hole for a moment before he knocked on the oak door. Almost immediately, the sturdy figure of Barris Oakfoot swung the door open, still chewing a mouthful of his second supper.

Barris glared at the old man for a moment, raising one eyebrow in confusion before motioning him inside.

Returning to his seat, Barris grabbed his fork and knife, clearing his throat before he spoke. "Sorry, I wasn't expecting you. If you're looking for your grandson, I'm afraid he took your advice and half my pantry with him to Anstia."

The old man took a seat across from him, pouring himself hot tea as he replied, "Unfortunately, Balamor is not the reason why I'm here, Barris, though his safety is certainly part of it. I was visited by a courier today. He came with a message from Gantis Jacs... The *day* has finally come, Barris."

Barris quickly interjected before the old man could go on. "Balamor! This is why you told him to leave! So he could avoid the fate his father tried avoiding? Because he is helpless out there if she—"

"She won't," Farjadis cut in. His eyes were intense as he spoke. "She doesn't know about him, Barris, and neither did his father. As far as she is concerned, I am the last Wisebeard, and that is how it must stay! Do not underestimate my grandson, Mr. Oakfoot, he is our only hope."

Barris looked down at his half-finished plate, his appetite gone at the news he had received. He knew the worst was still to come as he looked back at the old halfling. The Wisebeard's steel-blue eyes stared at him with mixed emotions of fear, anger, and confusion.

"So, what now? She knows where the library is? How did she find this out? Where is Gantis?" Barris blurted out.

Farjadis removed his necklace from beneath his robes and handed it to Barris. "Your questions will be answered soon enough. What matters most is that you take this, along with those old blank books in the library and leave the Raehl tonight. I'm not sure where it is you will choose to go, but it's best that I don't know."

Barris felt his stomach knot at the seriousness of the situation. "Of course, but what about you? Where will you go? You can't stay in the Raehl and wait for a certain death!"

Farjadis answered him swiftly, his stare growing more intense by the second. "I must stay here, Barris. Gantis will reach the Raehl in the next few days, hopefully before the green-robed woman. If that is not the case, she will have to seek you out to find the books and the necklace. If you leave now, you'll have enough time to escape her."

"What about the safety of this necklace and the safety of these precious books? What about my own safety?" Barris shouted in frustration.

"The ruby will keep you safe." The old Wisebeard stood as his final words still lingered through the air.

Both of them had discussed this plan in the past when Balamor was only a small child, but back then the chance of it actually happening seemed almost impossible.

Without any more discussion, the two of them made their way into the cold, dank Wisebeard library.

The stillness of the dusty air was broken by the shuffling of their feet.

They split up, each taking an aisle and filling their arms with as many of the untitled books as they could.

Barris held one of the strange books in his hand, flipping through its blank pages. He didn't take the time to read the books from the library besides a few on cooking. He knew they were there, but he felt that they weren't meant for halflings. Holding something so powerful nearly overwhelmed him with fear. He convinced himself that power as great as magic was simply myth. Magic was nonexistent to him, but he made it that way.

Book by book his anticipation grew. He wanted to just up and leave but something inside fought against him. His arms grew heavy before he made his way upstairs and outside to his small caravan which was parked beside the porch. He slid the books up into the back through a thin tan cloth, making sure they were secure.

Quickly, he walked to the stables across the town which was nearly asleep. The stables were filled, mostly of ponies still awake. He began to pet them on their heads, hoping to not rustle them and wake the keepers sleeping in the hole next door. He made his decision with haste — a white and brown pony who seemed to be experienced as far as Barris could tell. He guided it from the stables quietly as he searched around cautiously.

Within minutes, the brown-spotted pony was fitted with the caravan and the sturdy carpenter was back to the library to gather the remaining luggage.

Nearly three hours passed before the last of the books found their way into the small caravan, along with a week's worth of food and supplies. Barris decided that he would travel north to the small halfling village of Mesmir. There, he would seek refuge with his sister Gilly and wait until news arrived from the mystic Gantis.

The two halflings exchanged their goodbyes mostly in silence. The situation had them both in a quiet mood. Nonetheless, they were both determined — focused on the task at hand.

Farjadis stood at the front of his old house watching his son-in-law depart the place he called home for all these years.

The rain began to spot the ground when the old Wisebeard slipped the glass vial from his vest pocket.

• •
• •

His fingers pressed against the symbol etched into its surface as he whispered to himself, "... *Payr*..."

The strange liquid inside suddenly became cold, slightly numbing his palm. He watched as the green glow intensified at the sound of the ancient word before calming back to its original state.

Farjadis slowly unlatched the metal capping, its cool breath escaping like an eerie spirit. Time stood still as he thought about his grandson. His memory gripped the old man as he drank the potion down to the very last drop.

10

A BLESSING

875, Summer's 55th Night

Small leaves fluttered in the moonlight as Balamor hawked the canopy above. His focus was broken as more branches fell to the ground behind him. He turned around to see something falling through the air and hurried to dash aside before being crushed.

A heavy thud was accompanied by a plume of dirt and dust. Through the cloud, Balamor spotted a short figure, stumbling into the base of a tree and striking its head. Raspy mumbling followed as it lifted itself from the ground, rubbing its head while swearing to itself angrily.

As the dirt dissipated, Balamor could clearly see this was no robed woman. This was a dwarf, and he was almost certain this was the same dwarf he was following before. His face was rigid and wrinkled with age, though the majority of it was covered by a thick brown beard. A green tunic stretched around the dwarf's heavy body and tucked itself into thick brown leggings.

Balamor glanced down at his book before blurting out his first words to the stranger, "You!? How did—"

Interrupting him sharply, the dwarf raised his right arm into his left hand. Balamor noticed immediately that there was something very strange about this man's arm.

"I call it a curse, but for you it's a blessing. Either way, you're lucky to have lived just now, little traveler. These lands are not meant to be traveled alone. The name's Awkid, Awkid Anvorbeard."

A BLESSING

He reached to shake the hand of Balamor, but the young mapmaker was awestruck by the strange limb. It was oddly larger than the rest of his body, but what startled him the most was that it was not of flesh and bone, but of Earth itself. Before waiting another moment, Balamor slowly slid his entire hand into Awkid's earthen palm before both of them gripped firmly.

Surprisingly, the frail hand of the mapmaker stayed intact.

A strange silence loomed over them before the dwarf gave him a curious stare.

"Oh! Right, sorry, my name is Balamor — Balamor Wisebeard. I—Uh... I don't know how to thank you..." Retrieving the silver dagger from its sheath, Balamor presented it to Awkid. "Here, take this. I'm sure it's worth something."

"There will be no need, Wisebeard. You need that blade more than I. And from the looks of it, that blade isn't the only thing you need. I have a camp a few miles west atop the Thorned Ridge. We can discuss the reason I had to save your life back there."

Pulling his map from his backpack, Balamor scanned the area they were in. "A few miles? Well I accept your offer, dwarf, but how do you expect we reach the top of these cliffs?"

"The same way I always do," Awkid replied with a short chuckle.

"Which would be?" the halfling asked as he packed away his belongings.

The dwarf's clay arm rested heavily on Balamor's shoulder as he kneeled to the earth below. "Through the ground, my friend. Now hold your breath!"

Balamor barely held a full breath by the time the powerful arm of Awkid Anvorbeard yanked him to the ground.

In one quick motion, it released the robed halfling and crashed to the ground. The mapmaker watched the amazing arm as it melded with the surrounding soil before tearing open a hole beneath their feet.

Within seconds, they were sucked in by the earthly whirlpool and consumed completely.

Balamor could feel the dirt rush through his robes as his body was twisted through the ground. Small rocks and thick clumps of dirt pounded his thin frame, making him nearly lose his breath.

The dwarf held Balamor over his left shoulder as he carelessly burrowed through roots, some wrapping themselves around their bodies before ripping loose.

In what seemed like only a moment, they busted through the topsoil to meet the frigid air of the night. A cloud of dirt cloaked them as Awkid fell to one knee before placing the mapmaker on the freshly turned soil.

Silence draped over the robed halfling as his eyes were fixed on the ground beneath him; his thoughts not yet clear. He stood up and began brushing dirt from his hair and robes as he turned his gaze to the stout dwarf beside him.

Pulling his clay limb halfway out of the ground slowly, Awkid reformed the bulky forearm and golem-like hand from before. He stood to his feet, and the dirt poured from his clothes as he motioned Balamor to follow him.

They walked a few yards before coming to a large tree. At its base, large wooden stairs were cut from logs. The two of them climbed the stairs as they spiraled up the tree until reaching a log cabin with a small porch front that sat beneath the tree canopy.

They walked across the porch to a large wooden door. Its hinges screeched as Awkid's mighty arm yanked it open.

Balamor coughed as a cloud of dust billowed out at them.

They entered the nearly pitch-black room. Its slight warmth greeted them as Awkid guided the door shut.

Balamor stood at the entryway, studying the craft of the small tree home as the dwarf strolled to a small wooden table and lit a candle with a piece of flint and steel. The small flame flickered silently, waves of dim light slightly etching out the rest of the room's features.

It was no bigger than his dining room back in the Raehl. The trunk of the massive tree pierced through the home at its center. Attached to it was a cloth hammock that stretched its way to a hook on the wall to their left. Various knickknacks and furs littered the surface of a large countertop that spanned the entire back wall. Though cozy like a halfling hole, it was scarce in features much like its Dwarven owner.

After lighting the candle, Awkid walked to the entryway and opened a wooden barrel which had a fine cheesecloth stretched over its mouth. "I know your backpack is full of dirt. You can empty it here."

Without a comment, Balamor walked to the barrel to his left and removed his backpack. Turning it over, he watched the dirt sift through the screen, revealing his things. His books, rations, map, and the three stone runes. He started returning them to their places when Awkid walked to the counter and prepared food and drink.

"I hope you don't mind the red-spotted hare. I finished the last stag yesterday."

"I'm sure it's better than the raw vegetables I've been eating. Thank you again, dwarf, but I must ask, did you build this home on your own? And why so far from the High East?" Balamor inquired as he seated himself at the table.

"I did indeed. It's no halfling hole, but it does the job. I've been living here in the Thorned Ridge ever since I left the High East, when I was thirty-six — over forty years ago." The dwarf continued as he lit a stone fireplace and placed the two small hares on a rotisserie, "My people were strongly against the use of magic ever since the time of the Blood Wars. They exiled me because of my arm, saying that it was the work of a necromancer. I still have no clue who the woman was that did this to me. Unfortunately, I owe my life to her and the curse she left me with."

He slowly poured the both of them a cup of mead before returning to the fire.

Quickly, Balamor took a large gulp, cringing at the bitter taste. "Wait, did this necromancer take you hostage? Or did you willingly accept her magic?"

Awkid spun their meal over the fire, almost ignoring the question for a moment. "Both. She found me on a road heading toward my hometown, Bhraeir, far northeast in the Dahris Mountains. I was nearly dead when she carried me to her home. I was in no condition to refuse."

"What happened to your arm before it was... like that?" Balamor added.

"I lost it. I was returning home from the Foot villages to the southwest when I was struck by a hijacked caravan crossing the Pass of Jemm. Just about lost my entire arm after, clipped off clean by the damn wheels. Not long thereafter, a Dwarven woman stumbled upon my body."

"The necromancer?" Balamor inquired, but Awkid's only reply was a stiff gulp of his mead. He wiped the foam from his beard before he continued, "I remember my blood staining the back of her white horse. I'm surprised she could even fix me... If that's what you want to call it."

Balamor took another dissatisfied gulp of repulsive mead as he replied, "Well, you might be surprised at the kinds of magic I've witnessed these past few days."

The dwarf raised one eyebrow in question as he rested their plates on the table.

The halfling went on, "Not even one day on this journey and I'm fighting off highwaymen, saving bridge builders! — who saved me of course. The next thing I know, I almost come face-to-face with this robed mystic figure. She conjures up a golem and turns it into a flesh and bone halfling!" The mapmaker took another gulp, now numb to its bitterness.

Awkid scarfed down his meal as Balamor continued, "The next morning, I'm trailing you along the Faric and you just disappear! I was surprised it was you summoning those golems in the pass, I was sure it was that woman. I mean, sure, now it makes complete sense with that arm of yours. Honestly, I'm wondering if I'm just dreaming because no halfling would believe such things were real, not even with their own two eyes."

The dwarf drew a heavy laugh and took a large gulp of his mead before he spoke.

"This journey you're on doesn't seem fit for a halfling, don't ya think? What kind of mission would force a halfling to leave his village except for fixing bridges?"

Balamor finished chewing his food before he replied, "I'm a cartographer. Well, I'm trying to be one at least, and that would require me to travel all the lands, eventually. For now, my destination is an uncharted land known as the Mog Brush."

The dwarf broke out laughing as he spoke, "A halfling on a journey to chart the Mog Brush? Ha! Are you out of your mind, boy?"

"No... I don't believe so, no," Balamor answered with a perplexed look.

Awkid's demeanor changed as he leaned forward with a grim stare. "There's a reason that land stays uncharted. It's not the wild, not the monsters, not the darkness, no. It's not the journey in between. It's the 'Bounds' that keep most men out."

"The 'Bounds?'" Balamor inquired.

"No simple mapmaker — let alone a halfling — can cross the Bounds of Akinn. Not without being reduced to ashes, that is. Even if you do cross, the land beyond is a ruin cursed far beyond the likes of this arm."

Balamor interjected quickly, "Wait, you know of the Mog Brush?"

The stout Anvorbeard finished his pint before he went on. "You may think I haven't seen magic past my own fist but I've traveled to that land. Only those who understand the magic of that barrier can make their crossing." He shoveled the final bite of his meal into his mouth, not waiting to finish chewing before he added, "However, I've seen your books, Mr. Wisebeard, and those stones you carry. You aren't just a simple mapmaker, are you? How much do you know of magic?"

"Not nearly as much as I would like to know. But I will tell you this, dwarf, I will not turn back now. Whether I understand that barrier or not, I will find my way in!"

"Ha! You're as stubborn as a dwarf, little mapmaker! But traveling to the Mog Brush is not something any mere *halfling* can do, especially alone."

"Well, you've been there, right? You can escort me there!" The excited halfling jumped to his feet before bracing his chair to keep balance. "I know it's a lot to ask, but you don't have to go in. Just get me to the border and I will make the crossing alone."

"To be honest, little traveler, I would rather just live in peace," Awkid responded with a stretch.

"And I would rather know the truth than drink mead and eat game," Balamor shot back, undeterred.

The dwarf smiled as his only normal hand brushed his beard. His expression again turned serious as he was considering the idea. Moments seemed to grow longer as Balamor waited for the stern remark from across the table.

Both of them were finished with their meals and their mead when the Anvorbeard finally broke the silence. "So, I take you to the Mog Brush, through the thick twisted forests and into the festering swamps? Past the ravenous packs of Tarwolves, or the even more deadly Parins? All the way up to the Bridge of Kaltas, so you can find a way in? What's in it for me?"

The robed halfling's excitement ceased as he tried to come up with some incentive, when suddenly it hit him. "If I return, I will bring you the name of the woman who gave you that curse."

The brown eyes of the dwarf grew wide before a chuckle caused them to close. "Ha! And how do you expect to find that in the Mog Brush?"

A BLESSING

Balamor immediately jumped on the question. "If this woman has any interest in magic, she would have no bigger interest than going to the Mog Brush. And considering what she has done to your arm, sounds like the Mog Brush would be right up her alley. If she isn't there herself, her name is." He paused for a moment as he realized he offered nothing tangible for Awkid's service. "Look, I know I'm paying you in knowledge, but that is all I have to offer."

The two of them waited in silence, both with their eyes fixed on the table — their thoughts scattered across its surface like battle plans.

Awkid leaned back in his chair as dormant memories filled his mind. He thought back to the time when his arm was lost to him. Even to this day his earthen limb seemed detached from his body. He opened his right palm, and small clumps of dirt fell between his fingers. A feeling of anger loomed over him as he tried to picture the Dwarven woman who cursed him.

Awkid rose to his feet and extended his right hand over the table. "You have yourself a deal, halfling, but I'm in charge of this expedition."

Balamor clasped the dirt hand tightly and nodded his head in agreement.

Awkid placed their dishes in a basin cut into the countertop before walking to a chest and removing a second hammock. He quietly tied off both ends and gestured to Balamor to rest.

The young mapmaker realized his body was exhausted and quickly scurried up to the hammock and jumped in.

Awkid blew out the candle before kicking off his thick leather boots and climbing into bed.

It seemed like only minutes went by before the hefty dwarf was knocked out. The sound of rain began to intensify along with the obnoxious snore of Awkid Anvorbeard.

But Balamor's mind was stuck on the Mog Brush no matter the background noise. He couldn't believe he had made it this far by himself. Awkid was right, traveling any further alone would not be wise.

Reaching to the floor, he lifted his backpack into his hammock and rooted through its contents until he came across the cross cut stone rune. The moonlight pierced through the window and etched out the symbol of what Balamor now called *Raji*.

He knew his knowledge of the Runesong was only starting to grow, but he felt a sense of familiarity when he spoke the strange word. He grabbed out his pencil and notebook to make his final entry for the night.

875, Summer's 55th Night,

Magic! First the woman on the road and now a dwarf with an arm made of earth! His name is Awkid Anvorbeard. He saved me from bandits — who I can't seem to avoid, mind you! Anyhow, thanks to his magical limb, those bandits didn't have a fighting chance. Not only this, Mr. Anvorbeard has agreed to escort me to the Mog Brush! My journey won't be so lonely after all, lucky me.

Speaking of magic, it seems that the strange three dot rune keeps giving me visions... First of my real father, Ericho, falling into the Faric. I thought it might have been because I was dreaming. Now, I triggered it by speaking the words the green-robed woman spoke.

Like a wave, the vision hit me, and this time I saw something I knew nothing about, yet something now I remember so clearly. Almost like a memory that has been repressed. There was a tall man wearing black robes. He seemed to know who I was. Strangely, I felt the same about him. I must tread carefully with this runeword.

He placed the items into his leather bag before returning it to the floor, repeating the word in his head once more. His eyes grew heavy within seconds as he pondered what it meant to be a mystic.

11

THE ROAD HOME

875, Summer's 55th Night

Dark clouds billowed northward consuming the milky starlit sky, the wind howling as another vicious storm rolled through the Southlands, pushing its way toward the Raehl. Thick fog clinging to the landscape warped with the fast approaching winds of the storm.

It seemed that the weather worsened as the fate of the world grew closer, and the Watcher was sure of it.

Along the River Faric in a small shrub, he arrived. He knew the mysterious crack of lightning from nights ago was not the same as those brewing this night. Farah Lenook was here, and she must have found what the Watcher worked so hard to keep safe.

Hiding was not familiar to him, but over the years he spent observing the Raehl, he became quite good at it.

A long time had passed since the Watcher came face-to-face with his green-robed nemesis. The power Farah possessed was undoubtedly greater than his, as it always had been. She exceeded him the most in performing spells of destruction and enchantment, yet he was a master of illusion and divination.

To succeed, he had to be discreet, let her go mad searching for him and any possible leads to his plans. He learned to craft peculiar recipes for concoctions that gave him the power to embody other beings — one of the many types of potions the ancient Merfolk invented.

These spirits were merely fragments of his own soul. 'Familiars' whose perceptions are felt in the depths of his own mind and body. These beings proved as useful vessels, giving him the ability to hide in plain sight and survey many locations at once.

It seemed for a while his majestic familiars had gone unnoticed by her — just as the Raehl had — until now that is.

It was always a matter of time. Unfortunately, that time passed by faster than the Watcher had imagined. At all costs, he would need to protect the library, the Bloodstone, and most of all, Balamor Wisebeard. The Watcher had prepared Farjadis for this day and could only trust things would go according to that plan.

Glancing at the narrow bridge that led to the halfling village, he waited to see whoever would be escaping its confines this night.

875, Summer's 55th Night

Jabit walked east down the riverside path until reaching a crossroads. The sign pointing northeast led to the village close to his home, *Paetok*. A second sign which read *Mesmir*, pointed north. A brief sigh left him as he turned north onto the narrow path which led him into a dense forest.

Leaving the Raehl behind him was a difficult task. The old Wisebeard's words seemed so comforting yet the symbol pressed into that glass vial worried Jabit. The halflings in the tavern also seemed worried about the fated family.

What about the young Wisebeard? His mother hadn't mentioned a second halfling. Was he too in danger?

The sound of the river faded in minutes and crickets began their symphony as nighttime was underway. The messenger's jovial whistling ceased when he gazed at the half-moon above. He realized he wasn't even tired this night, or even the night before.

ZARDRAKEN'S CRYPT

He had been traveling the south for two days, but it wasn't until now that he even questioned his lack of sleep. Perhaps his mission kept him alert. Even now, after the vial had been delivered, he felt an uneasiness deep within. He would have to ignore the lack of rest for now.

It was to his benefit if he wanted to reach his home before the storm laid waste to the land.

He stuck to the path for a while before moving several yards into the forest to keep away from highwaymen, yet they weren't his only concern. The beasts which roamed the forests at night were just as dangerous if not more so — wolves, bears, poisonous snakes, just to name a few. Then there were dangers spoken of in tales to scare children — magical creatures made to haunt men. He hoped he could avoid them all because otherwise he wouldn't know how to fight any of them.

He had no weapons to protect himself; his small size was all he could depend on. Nearly an hour had passed and the crackling of thunder in the distance was not a good sign.

The road to the left of him was familiar. Judging by warped trees every now and then, he could tell Paetok was close. If he could stay on course, he could be in the warmth of his home in another hour or so.

He wanted this journey to be over. One thing he knew for certain, this would be the last time he traveled without his caravan. His feet weren't aching yet, but his mind was strangely drained.

It felt like forever since he'd been home.

The memories of his home were faint, which struck him as odd. For a moment, he questioned how long he had been traveling the Southlands. Days and nights each seemed to pass like ages. He hoped this next leg of his journey would be easier than the first, but that hope was tested when the sounds of metal clashing echoed through the forest.

The smell of food and what sounded like swords clanging gave him no idea as to what was unfolding ahead.

THE ROAD HOME

He lowered his figure to the ground and crept from tree to tree. As he moved north through bushes and trees, the sounds of battle and the scent of cooked meat grew heavy. His stubby fingers grasped the rigid bark of a tall oak tree as he slowly peeked his head out.

In a brief clearing, waves of fire danced within a circle of stones, a rotisserie propped above it. Three tents stood several yards from the fire. It was a camp for sure.

On the rotisserie, a skinned boar was still cooking and next to it were two men fighting. Each of them wore fur pelts over their shoulders, and piecemeal armor of leather and iron.

As their swords collided, Jabit realized another man was behind the fire sitting on a broken log. He too had a pelt upon his shoulders, but his armor was lacking and beside him was a longbow. The contents of his wineskin soaked the ground below as he laughed at the combatants.

The halfling watched them, now realizing the trio was undoubtedly drunk.

The two men fighting were taunting one another to make fatal blows by dropping their defenses and showing their necks, but they were not foolish fighters. What seemed like vulnerability was actually advantageous to their technique.

Their burly beards and scarred faces showed that they were battle-hardened warriors who sparred even when being overly intoxicated. Although they looked like savage men, it was easy to tell they were master swordsmen, even when drunk.

One of them looked to be decades older, judging by the long gray hair. The other could have been in his twenties. His head was shaven except for a blond braid fitted with iron rings. Both of them were falling over their own steps as they swung their blades and continued to insult each other.

"You handle that sword like a wench!" the older man shouted as he stabbed at his younger opponent.

The young man quickly parried the strike and in one swift motion, the tip of his sword stopped at the older man's neck.

"You wish I had the hand of a concubine, old man. Even so, I'm afraid you wouldn't fill it!"

There was a pause which settled into awkward silence. The two fighters looked each other in the eye.

Jabit was absorbed by the situation, the suspense nearly frightened him. The ranger was also struck by the stillness, laughter fading into a slow and awkward giggle — his jaw agape in anticipation.

Then, the young man lowered his blade and the two warriors burst into raucous laughter. Snatching the wineskin from the ranger, they both drank until it was nearly gone.

Jabit was both relieved and confused by the outcome. He scanned their camp as the men sat by the fire, scarfing down hog meat and occasionally cracking jokes about each other's looks.

Moments went by before he spotted the contours of something in the moonlight. It was next to the road just yards from the camp. Adjusting his eyes, he couldn't believe what he saw or what he thought he saw.

A horse-drawn caravan still in one piece.

He didn't want to take the risk but entertained the thought of stealing it, when they finally slept, crossed his mind. He knew the idea was crazy, but he needed to do something or he would never make it through the storm.

As soon as he finished his thought, a crack of thunder broke the clouds. In seconds, the rain started and gusts of wind were howling through the tops of the trees.

The three men were finishing their meal when the storm began. Cursing at the skies with drunken slurs, they each stumbled to their small tents.

The messenger was without a bed and only halfway through his journey home. These human warriors were comfortable in the wilderness. Sleeping in the elements didn't faze them like it did Jabit Treadfoot.

The moon was obscured by thick dark clouds as he waited for the men to fall asleep. The fire in the middle of their camp was extinguished by the downpour and the remaining smoke mixed with the dense fog.

Minutes had gone by before Jabit wandered out from the brush he concealed himself in. The storm hit sooner than he expected, and it was much worse than he had imagined.

As he crept across the warrior camp, his clothes became soaked. He paused at the fire pit. Only charcoal remained but the smell of pork still lingered in the air. He didn't find it appetizing which was strange to him.

The caravan seemed more important at the moment.

He could clearly see it now, but he noticed something wrong. There was no horse.

The caravan was only a few feet away when he heard the snapping of branches above him. In an instant, something yanked at his ankle and pulled him into the air.

In a panic, Jabit shouted, "No!" The sound of the rain drowned out his cries.

Blood rushed to his head as he dangled upside down from a tree. He looked up at his ankle where a rope tied into a slipknot securing itself. The rain poured down into his eyes and mouth causing him to keep them shut. Heavy gusts of wind whipped against his small body as he struggled to get free. There was no chance he would get out of the trap. The men who set it, knew what they were doing and Jabit was ill-prepared.

875, Summer's 55th Midnight

Hours went by before a small caravan appeared, crossing the bridge slowly. The halfling guiding its horse was not who the Watcher expected — at least not alone — and so he trailed the caravan, hoping to find the precious gem and those sacred tomes.

Scurrying along the dirt trail beside the River Faric, the Watcher caught up with the man in a matter of seconds.

Being spotted was not an issue this night, for the halfling rider would not worry about the form the Watcher possessed.

There sat piles of books stacked to the ceiling, filling the entire caravan. Yet it was the Bloodstone shard that mattered most to the small pair of eyes glinting within the shadows.

Sprinting ahead of the caravan some distance away, the Watcher stopped and hawked the man down with its beady eyes.

Wearing a brown cloak over his red tunic and dark cloth pants, the man was familiar to the Watcher; he was an Oakfoot. Although a grizzly beard made him out to be intimidating, the halfling beneath looked uneasy and spoke to himself quietly. The Watcher's hearing was keen and so he listened.

"Damn it! I can't believe this is... Why when Balamor has gone to Anstia? And why am I the one with this thing?"

His pudgy halfling fingers reached beyond his red collar, revealing a small ruby pendant on a necklace which gave off a dim red light. "Damn it! If only—"

The bearded halfling jumped in his seat at the sound of bushes rustling. Searching around him, he held the red stone like a fierce weapon, but the Watcher knew he did not realize its power.

Hopping from behind a small bush, the Watcher revealed himself to the startled rider. Its body was tiny, even when compared to a halfling. Covered in white fur with red spots, its whiskers twitched as he sniffed the wet ground. Standing on all fours, it was obvious the Watcher was no threat to the halfling.

"Ah, it's just a hare... I thought I'd have to use this on you."

There was an awkward pause as the two studied one another.

The halfling felt strange looking at the small creature, but the hare looked normal to him. He pulled the reins of his horse and his caravan left at once, disappearing into the heavy fog.

The small hare remained silent. Across the River Faric, the Raehl did the same.

THE ROAD HOME

Farjadis must have improvised a plan in Balamor's absence. The Watcher wanted answers from him but finding Balamor mattered most. Reaching him before Farah Lenook or one of her accomplices would be a difficult task.

A bolt of lightning struck the ground, and the Watcher was gone.

12

A FAMILIAR HOLE

875, Summer's 55th Midnight

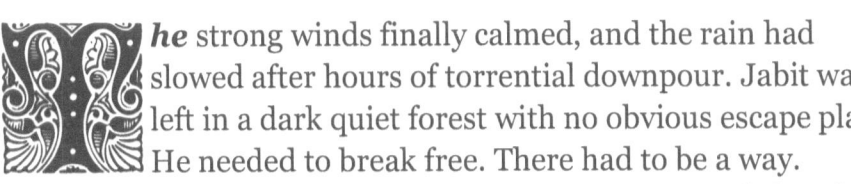*he* strong winds finally calmed, and the rain had slowed after hours of torrential downpour. Jabit was left in a dark quiet forest with no obvious escape plan. He needed to break free. There had to be a way.

The men were still asleep, but Jabit was worried that they would be more dangerous if he had awoken them. His only chance would be to do it alone. Suspended nearly six feet in the air, he looked around for anything to help him.

The stones from the fire were out of reach, but the caravan was only feet away. He wiped his eyes clear and looked closer. The wood was rotted and probably infested with termites. The surrounding vegetation consumed its wheels over time. After studying it for a while, Jabit could see arrows littered its left wall, most likely from the drunken ranger.

"That's it," Jabit whispered sharply, trying not to let his excitement wake the men in their tents.

He wiggled his body back and forth in an effort to swing himself to the caravan. It took a while for the small halfling to gain enough momentum, but he was getting closer with each sway.

The winds grew heavy once more and thunder joined them, but Jabit was determined to grab one of the arrows no matter the weather. The tree branches above creaked as he swung to-and-fro, the rain beginning to pick up as his efforts drove him closer to the caravan.

Grunting with every push, Jabit soon became frustrated. He cursed his small size. Being a halfling had no advantage in such a situation. He stretched his arms to their furthest extent, but they were still not long enough. The storm was greater than before. Lightning lit up the sky and the intense rain made it hard to keep his eyes open, but he didn't give in to the onslaught of the elements. He needed to reach one of the arrows. If he didn't, he would never get home and he would end up becoming bait for these warriors to catch another wild hog.

If he didn't break free, he would never see his mother again.

"C'mon!" he shouted as he drew closer to the caravan's wall. The rain forced his eyes shut as he stretched his small arms once more. He closed his hands and felt the wooden shaft of an arrow in his grip. His momentum caused it to be plucked from the caravan. He opened his eyes and saw he was lucky the broadhead tip was still attached. Wasting no time and summoning all of his strength, he lifted himself up and grabbed the rope tied to his feet. The arrowhead sawed through the rope slowly.

Jabit laughed as his plan unfolded.

With one final strike, the rope was cut and Jabit crashed to the muddy soil below. He picked himself up and looked at the camp in front of him.

To his surprise, one of the warriors was up and leaving his tent. He must have heard Jabit after all, but the halfling was quick, and by the time the man reached the rope trap he was too late. Jabit hid himself in the caravan away from the man and the vicious storm outside.

"Where are you?" the old warrior yelled as he drew his blade from its sheath.

Jabit looked in his hand where the arrow remained. He hoped he didn't have to use it. He had a strange feeling of nostalgia while studying the inside of the caravan. The shelves were filled with jars and beside him were barrels fitted with spigots just like those he held his mother's jams in. As he crept toward them, the floorboards creaked.

The man approached the caravan slowly as the rain streamed down the fuller of his blade and dripped to the ground, splashing in the mud below. In one quick motion, he wrenched the door open. Jabit jumped at the sight of the man, causing one of the floorboards to snap.

"There you are. A halfling, huh? You think you can steal from me and my men?" His breath reeked of alcohol.

He stabbed at the halfling but Jabit rolled out of the way, knocking over jars and shattering them. The tall man stumbled inside and slowly moved toward Jabit. His gray hair was plastered to his face by the rain, and his eyes were filled with rage.

Jabit held up his empty hand and pleaded, "No, mister, I wasn't stealing! I swear it. You see, I was coming through your camp by accident, and I fell into your trap, see?" He pointed at his leg with the cut rope still attached before he continued, "I am no burglar, mister. I am simply a messenger caught in a storm without his caravan."

The old man replied, "So you found mine and decided to steal it! Don't lie halfling, I'll cut you down!"

"No, I'm no thief, sir. I merely wish to go home. That's it, I promise you," Jabit added with concern in his frail voice.

The old warrior moved closer, putting the end of his blade to Jabit's small neck. "You halflings are helpless." He laughed, swaying slightly with his drunken buzz. His blade came closer to Jabit's throat.

Jabit glanced at the man's leather boots as he gripped the arrow in his right hand.

"You're wrong." Jabit jumped aside and stabbed the arrow into the man's foot with all of his strength. The old warrior screamed out at the top of his lungs as the arrowhead pierced his boot and dug into his foot.

A FAMILIAR HOLE

The floorboards shattered as the old warrior yanked his leg from them. Jabit fell through the hole it made and to the ground below. He started to crawl out from under the rundown caravan with all the speed he could muster.

The old warrior growled in pain as he ripped the arrow from his foot. Stumbling out of the caravan and into the rain, he saw the halfling being chased by his comrades.

Jabit ran for his life, moving in and out of the trees as he heard arrows zip by and thud into the bark. His feet kicked up mud and leaves as he maneuvered the forest in the rain. The storm made it impossible to tell which way he was going.

Forward was his only option.

He slipped into a puddle and scraped his hands and knees. An arrow struck into the tree in front of him as he ran, making his eyes go wide.

The ranger was skilled, but thankfully for Jabit, he was still too drunk to hit his target.

Jabit's breaths quickly became heavy and his body was weak from the chase.

The warriors were right behind him shouting out threats. "You're dead, halfling! When we catch you, we'll cook you alive! You hear me? We'll cook you alive!"

Maniacal laughter followed as Jabit broke away from the forest and quickly found himself crossing a dirt road. He heard the sound of hooves skidding through the mud and wooden wheels creaking along. He looked up to his right to see a bearded halfling pulling the reins of a small pony.

His caravan slid and crooked as it stopped just before crashing into Jabit Treadfoot.

The halfling was wearing a brown cloak above his red tunic. His green eyes were wide and full of worry as he looked at Jabit intensely.

He sensed something was wrong with the messenger, but before he could speak, the three hunters appeared from out of the forest.

They were startled at the arrival of the halfling rider and his caravan.

Looking at Jabit and then at the bearded halfling, the old warrior shouted over the sound of the storm, "Oh well, well! Looks like there are two of them! Is this your getaway? You rotten little thieves, we'll kill you both!"

The ranger had his long bow drawn and his aim was for the halfling rider.

The rider responded with a stern voice, "You would be mistaken, human. I do not know this halfling, but I am afraid you will not have your way with him. Would a thief travel with no bag to hold his loot? Lower your weapons."

"Who do you think you're commanding here? Me and my men?" The old warrior scoffed with laughter and rage.

"I'm a halfling, and I have more important matters to attend to than fighting with wild men!" the halfling rider shouted.

The old warrior walked closer to the caravan, ready to slay the rider. As he drew closer, the ruby pendant on the rider's necklace started to glow red.

"I will not repeat myself again. Stay your blade, human. This halfling has done nothing wrong and neither have I!" the bearded rider added with a strict yell.

With each step the old warrior took, the ruby shard glowed brighter and the man's rage seemed to diminish. Now standing only feet away from the caravan, the old man looked as if he were in a trance. He was fixated on the glowing ruby shard, its tender red glow reflected in his deep mesmerized stare.

Slowly, he returned his sword to its sheath.

The rider motioned his head toward the other men before the old warrior signaled them to stand down with a gesture.

"Are you serious? That little bastard is going to get away with this?" the young warrior argued, wielding his two-handed sword with checked rage.

He wasn't alone in his objection as the ranger pulled further back on his bowstring. "What is this, Sim? Some sort of spell you're under? Damn it! I could kill both of them right now. How could you let them belittle you like this?"

The old man snapped his head back to both of his men and shouted sharply, "Enough! Stand down, and put your weapons away. The rider is right."

"But—" the young warrior started.

"Now!" the old man shouted.

They didn't understand what was going on, and neither did Jabit.

He watched in awe as the others lowered their weapons. He looked at the halfling rider, his necklace gleaming in bright red light. He thought he'd seen him before, yet the rainy night made him second guess.

"Who are you, rider?" the old warrior asked, his eyes still fixated on the gemstone.

"My name is Barris Oakfoot," the halfling replied, his tone powerful.

The old man looked at him, confusion settling over his face, but he didn't ask any more questions. Instead, he looked to Jabit with empathy in his voice as he talked to him. "I am sorry, messenger, forgive me and my men. We had a bit to drink and I believe the mead drove us mad. We hope you find your way home." He turned to Barris and continued, "Mr. Oakfoot, my apologies as well. You are right. I have never met such a halfling as yourself, but I will tell the story of this encounter. My name is Simas Heldeir, and these are my men, Gerro Lakes, a great ranger, and Zeth, a master of the sword and also my son. We are with the Beshmere Arm."

With a bow, he let the two halflings continue on their way. His men contested with him, but he turned to them and pushed his hands against their faces to shut them up.

Barris looked at Jabit, and the glow faded as the men walked into the forest toward their camp. With a wave, Barris told the messenger to join him.

Jabit climbed up into the seat next to Barris Oakfoot and with a snap of the reins the caravan was off.

875, Summer's 56th Dawn

The storm was nearly over as they traveled, only a slight drizzle remained with the morning only a couple hours away.

For a while, the two halflings did not speak, the both of them only stared forward, lost in what had taken place behind them.

Jabit kept glancing at Barris and his necklace but nothing happened.

The awkward silence was broken as Barris caught the messenger staring. "They said you are a thief, Mr. Treadfoot. But from what I can recall, you are merely a merchant of jams. Now tell me you have some of those. I think it would be a fair repayment for my service this night."

Jabit stared ahead as he thought about the last time he sold his mother's jams. It was to a town called Trath in the east. It had to have been a few weeks ago when he made his delivery there.

The smell of wild strawberry and sweet kern-root jam lingered in his memory. His caravan was filled with all sorts of jams. Folks could smell it from trails away it seemed. His mind thought back to the broken-down caravan in the forest. The jars and barrels were strikingly familiar to him, as if he was standing in the back of his own caravan in a bad future.

"You okay, Mr. Treadfoot?" Barris asked, interrupting his thoughts.

Jabit shook his mind clear and replied, "I am sorry, I do not have any jams with me. When was the last time you had one from me?"

Barris thought to himself for a moment before he replied, "Ah, it's been years, but I still remember the taste of that sweet pomegranate filling in the pastries I baked back then." A soft smile settled across his face at the memory. "How come you haven't been around?"

Barris studied the halfling, noticing the perplexed look on his face.

Jabit responded, his eyes looking down at his lap, but it seemed he was staring deep into his memories. "I don't know, actually."

Barris didn't want to ask any more questions for he would arrive at the next fork soon. He needed to know where Jabit was going. He had a feeling something bad was going on in Jabit's mind but getting to the bottom of it was up to Jabit himself.

As they approached the fork in the road, he called for his pony to stop and asked his final question. "Where is it you are going, Mr. Treadfoot? I have to travel to Mesmir, north of here."

Jabit looked up at the signs which labeled each road. The one on the right read *Paetok*. "The farm is just outside of Paetok. I should be fine from here. Thank you, Mr. Oakfoot. You saved my life."

Barris nodded before handing the messenger a small hunting knife and a sheath from his belt. "Take this. You don't want to be defenseless if you come across anymore danger. Be safe my friend."

Jabit fastened the knife to his belt before returning a nod and starting down the road to Paetok. He listened to the caravan roll away as he walked on. He thought about what happened with that necklace Barris wore. It was like it had the power to change anyone's mind. It was magical for sure. In fact, it was just like the one around Farjadis Wisebeard's neck.

That realization had him turning back, and he started running to catch up with Barris.

He met the crossroads when he saw he was too late — the caravan was gone. He couldn't believe he didn't catch it sooner.

Who was Barris Oakfoot? Why did he have the necklace?

Looking down the road where the encounter had taken place sent a chill racing up his spine. He couldn't remember the last time he had such a view. As he turned away, he felt lost. The way home was clear but everything else wasn't.

Everyone had said years had gone by since his last visit to the Raehl, but that made no sense to him.

Why would his mother skip another halfling village on his route? Was it an accident?

He needed to ask her when he returned to the farm.

There were so many things that seemed out of place. He remembered traveling east along the Faric but not where he was coming from. Paetok was northwest not east of the Raehl.

Why was it so hard for him to remember?

He became frustrated with his bad memory. His mother would have the answers to such questions. Perhaps the lack of food and sleep were starting to affect his ability to think.

He finally made it out of the forest and into the vast plains where his mother's farm was visible in the distance. The sky started to turn a light blue, and after nearly an hour of walking, the morning sun blazed to life.

He finally made it home, and his mother would kill him at the sight of his clothes. Streaks of mud and torn stitches in his vest would drive her mad, but his journey was not easy and she would have to understand, eventually.

His furry feet were tired when he walked up to the wooden fence of the farm.

The animals were absent, but that was no surprise. The storm was one of the worst he had seen.

He gently pushed the wooden gate open, and a series of metal bells rung a familiar tune as he proceeded to his small halfling hole. Neatly trimmed rose bushes bordered its front, and a small path of stones led to its circular door. As he walked to the hole, he saw his mother beside their home. It was odd for her to be up this early.

As he drew closer to her, he could see she was placing flowers in front of a stone in the ground. He started to get a bad feeling in the pit of his stomach.

Only yards away, he spoke, his voice sounding confused. "Mom?"

She slowly turned around at the sound of Jabit's voice. She couldn't comprehend what she was seeing. Her eyes were wide in astonishment, the flowers in her hand dropping to the ground at once, their petals whisked away in the wind.

"I'm sorry I took so long to return home. I didn't mean to take this long, but I'm safe! Don't worry, I made it back alive," Jabit added, opening his arms as he walked toward her.

She backed away with each step he took, tears beginning to run down her face when she spoke, "No! Who are you?"

"Mom, it's me, Jabit. What do you mean?" He moved closer.

She shouted once more, "You're not my son! Who are you?"

Jabit looked at her and begged, "What is going on? It is me, Jabit! Have you lost your mind? How do you not remember your own son?"

Anger and confusion filled his mind. He couldn't figure out anything she was saying. It scared him.

Her eyes were filled with tears, and her wrinkled face became red in distress. "You are not my son! This is my son; this is what's left!" She stepped aside and pointed behind her where a stone stood — its surface was engraved with a name and date. "Why do you curse me?" His mother fell to her knees and held her face in her hands. Her words were shaky and cut off between breaths. "Why... Why are you here?"

Jabit became nauseous as he read the stone inscription. His hands began to shake as tears started building up in his eyes.

Jabit Treadfoot 844 – 873

"How? I'm alive! I made it back. How could you say I'm dead? What is going on?" he fumed, standing above the gravestone.

His mind was racing. Everything that happened on his journey seemed lost. But he knew it was true, he made it home.

How could this be his grave?

He looked at his mother as he started to cry.

She looked up at him before she answered, "She brought you here. Two years ago, she brought you to me. She carried your body right here!" Her crying was intense and her speech choppy. "She told me she found your caravan crashed... You didn't make it, but you told her to bring you here."

Jabit was without words. He searched his memories for answers. He remembered the road he traveled in his caravan. It was dark when someone appeared in front of him.

"A woman? I remember a woman. There was thunder and then a flash of light, and there was a woman. I couldn't control the caravan. I tried, but I couldn't! I can't remember, it's so hard to remember who she was. But I remember her voice!" Jabit stopped.

His mind flashed back to the strange potion which he now realized was not from his mother. His trip to the Raehl, to Farjadis Wisebeard, was a setup. Some twisted plan to have the old Wisebeard killed, and the rundown caravan on the road to Paetok, it was his. That green-robed woman did this, and he was sure of it.

Stuck in his mind was a voice – a single line she said to him as she carried his crippled body home. *Worry not, my little one. You've made it home.* It wouldn't leave his head.

"That woman used me!"

His mother stared at him.

He looked down at the grave. "This can't be me! I'm right here, who is this?" he objected as he fell to his knees.

His mother didn't respond, she couldn't. She was lost at the sight of him. She knew it wasn't real, but he started to convince her otherwise. The sound of his voice, his face and the clothes he wore were the same. Everything about it was right.

Jabit glanced at her and then back at the grave.

In a split second, he started to dig through the grass and down into the soil.

His mother tried stopping him, but her crying became hysterical as he dug up her son's grave.

His hands began pulling up mounds of dirt from the earth and throwing them behind him. "She did this to me! That woman did this!" he yelled as his hands became stained with dirt.

Minutes went by as he tore through the soil until he hit something sharp. He kept digging, revealing more and more of what looked like bones. His eyes became full of tears as he shoveled the soil from the shallow pit.

His hands were bruised and yet he felt no pain. He began to question if his mother was right. The remains of a halfling man were finally clear, still wearing the exact clothing Jabit had on himself. *Everything about it was right.*

His crying became uncontrollable as he lifted the corpse from its grave. He stared into the holes of the small skull, now fully convinced this was him.

The corpse broke apart as he turned to his mother.

The sun pierced the clouds shining its bright light onto his grave as he spoke, "I'm sorry. I don't know who I am, but I remember being your son." He paused. "I remember your love. I'm sorry, I don't remember my own death."

She held her hand out and rubbed it across his face. Looking into his eyes, she knew his soul was there.

He smiled at her soothing touch before he spoke, "I—"

In an instant everything that was living about him crumbled into a mound of earth as the dark spell that created him finally broke, filling the pit that was his grave.

His mother watched as her son was buried for a second time. Her cries echoed through the lonely farmland of the Treadfoot home, drifting into silence — or if you were close enough, a mournful sob. She glanced at the upturned grave when the light of morning sun revealed more than soil and bones.

Three distinct red gems drew Mrs. Treadfoot closer. She reached into the loose mound of dirt and retrieved three small ruby crystals, each fitting together to make a bigger shard nearly the size of her palm. The sun pierced the fragments sending scarlet glimmers of light cascading across her eyes.

13

FAMILIAR COMPANY

875, Summer's 56th Dawn

Silence gripped the woods as the remaining dark still loomed over the Southland. Only the sounds of insects and early birds echoed through the thick canopy of the Thorned Ridge. The smell of rain and wet ansi root drifted through the air as gusts of wind rustled the vegetation.

The storm from the night before drenched the entire landscape, small puddles gathering atop the waterlogged soil. Only a slight drizzle remained, but it was enough to worry the clay-armed Awkid as he stood atop the deck of his treehouse. Revealing a rolled-up cloth bandage from his green tunic, the dwarf began wrapping his strange limb from its fingers all the way up to his shoulder.

Though it brought great power to the lone dwarf, it was a burden, especially in the rain. He finished quickly, double-checking to see if everything was covered before he walked back into his home.

The room was dark aside from the dim light of a candle brushing against the walls of the small cabin. The dwarf closed the door softly, trying not to disturb his halfling guest who rested in the hammock across the room — exhausted from the beginning of an ambitious journey.

Awkid was still trying to figure out how the halfling managed to reach the pass alone, but more importantly, why he would want to go to the Mog Brush. He saw his books and the strange stones he carried. It was certainly magic; he had seen it before. Awkid had a feeling he was dealing with someone who could be of use to him. His eyes shifted to his now cloaked clay arm. It was a curse he didn't ask for, but perhaps a gift he deserved.

In the past, he told himself there was no reason to seek out the mystic who did this to him. Time simply passed by too quickly for him to question who she was. Yet, lurking in the back of his mind was the desire to understand the truth.

Grabbing the candle from the table, he walked to a short bookcase next to the door and lowered himself to one knee. The dwarf guided the candle across the shelves revealing an odd mix of books, some on hunting and foraging and others on cooking. There were even a few novels and stories he read on a rainy day. To Balamor it would have been a mess, but Awkid had his own way of organizing things.

Two books were carried to the vacant dining table along with a third under the gaze of Awkid Anvorbeard. His eyes were glued to the text within the shabby cloth book he made his journal. It was nearly falling apart as he flipped through its pages.

Years of travel were documented in this book.

He was almost a quarter through its contents when his bulky finger underlined the entry he was looking for. It was from his trip to the Mog Brush, or at least to its borders — the Bounds of Akinn.

849, Winter's 42nd night

I met the three Anstian men from the tavern on the Greatstone Pass. They arrived with a strange robed man. He hasn't talked much since we've been in the forest. He has been studying the trees very closely, like he was looking for something. Whatever it was, he was not willing to give up. I am glad I only signed on to get these men through the brush. I hope to make it there before tomorrow's moon, but for now

I'll sleep with one eye open. I'm unsure if I should be worried about this strange man, or the chance of Parins or wolves preying on us.

The memories of the time began to resurface as he read through his notes. He remembered something seemed different about the black-robed individual, and he felt the same about his halfling guest.

849, Winter's 43rd noon,

When I woke up this morning, the stranger with our party had disappeared. We searched for him all morning. Finally, we found him by himself in the forest. The fool only had a few books and a small hunting knife. When we found him, he was at the base of a tree reading one of his books. Now, more time has been wasted! We have to spend another night in this damned forest.

The Forest of Nim to be exact, a place he would undoubtedly have to visit once more, and his guest was eerily similar to that strange robed man. The robes, the strange stones, the books — especially the books.

849, Winter's 43rd night

I listened to the three humans as they discussed the robed man today. They've been calling him The Black Robe; he seems to be the chaperone of the little trio. But I know he is more than a simple bookworm, any dwarf would. The books he reads are far from ordinary, they're empty! Thankfully, he doesn't know about my arm.

Back then, Awkid concealed his arm from others and took to using an axe instead. After all, he didn't want to risk losing a job on a curse. He worked in Anstia, selling his axe for coin and escorting travelers around the Southland. But eventually hiding his curse became more of a burden than the actual limb itself.

849, Winter's 44th day

The robed man instructed the group to stay alert since we are close to "The Bounds", the border of the Mog Brush; that is where I begin my trek back. Finally, I can remove this armor.

He peeked up and stared at the back corner of the room, where dim candlelight drew contours of the clunky plate mail. He resented those scraps of metal more than that monstrous arm of his. Ever since his return from the Bounds of Akinn, the darkest corner of the room became the armor's final resting place.

849, Winter's 45th evening

We finally found the place The Black Robe spoke of after we nearly died the night before last. A group of Parins attacked our camp almost having me reveal my arm. I'm seriously getting tired of this axe.
We had finally found the edge of the forest when we saw, beyond a chasm, the ruins of an ancient fortress nearly swallowed up by the brush. That's when I saw the Bounds of Akinn, as The Black Robe calls it. It was an unbelievable sight, like a dome of white smoke spread thin over the old fortress.

I watched the robed man cross the narrow stone bridge with his three companions behind him. They stopped in the middle, bordering the strange barrier before the man cut a hole in its surface with his fingers.

Awkid placed the open journal on the table and rose to his feet, turning to the hammock behind him. He studied the brown-robed halfling who was still asleep within. The dwarf wondered if he was anything like The Black Robe.

875, Summer's 56th Sunrise

"Get up halfling!" Awkid's deep voice rang out, shaking the halfling awake.

The young mapmaker searched the dark room with probing eyes for the dwarf before he felt the heat of the candle beside his face. Its light quickly came into focus along with the bearded face of Awkid Anvorbeard.

"Your map," Awkid added with a demanding gesture.

Wiping his eyes clear, Balamor responded tiredly, "My map?"

The dwarf quirked an eyebrow before he continued, "Yes, give it here." His wrapped fingers fanned toward Balamor.

"Er... uhhh, yeah, of course," Balamor replied as he slid to the floor and rooted through his small leather backpack. With haste, he grabbed his map and handed it off to Awkid.

The dwarf quickly unrolled it on the table, pinning its corners with small paperweights.

The two of them seated themselves.

Balamor waited for the dwarf to start.

"This is where we are." Awkid's finger landed in the middle of the forest that bordered the pass. It would be a long trip to the Mog Brush. Awkid continued, "We need to make our way east until we reach the road to Anstia. If we don't run into any problems by then, we could be there around noon."

Balamor realized Awkid's camp was much further west than he thought. It had to be nearly a mile from the Greatstone Pass. The fact that the dwarf burrowed through the soil such a distance impressed him.

"What about that arm? You carried us nearly a mile from the pass last night. Why not do that again?"

The dwarf looked up at the ceiling in disgust. "This damn rain. It will destroy my arm if it gets wet. I learned that many years ago. An experience I regret having." He paused a moment with a clenched fist before he went on, "But that's beside the point — magic isn't always the solution and you need the experience, anyway."

Balamor nodded in agreement as he remembered his experience with the stone *Raji* rune. He wondered if Awkid witnessed the encounter with the bandit last night. A bandit he now realized understood the runewords far more than himself. His daydreaming was interrupted by the sound of a heavy thud against the table.

A thin cloud of dust sprung into the air making Balamor cough.

As it cleared, he noticed a thick hardback book in front of him — *Of Nefarious Nature*.

"Read up. If you want to survive the Mog Brush, then you better know what's gonna try to kill you." Awkid finished his instruction with a chuckle before he stood up and walked to the counter.

875, Summer's 56th Sunrise

The sun was just above the horizon and the storm from the night before left a bone-chilling cold in the air. The rain turned to drizzle, and the wind calmed as Mayn and Bear walked through the forests of the Thorned Ridge.

They were an interesting duo. Bear was the brawn with a head as thick as stone, while Mayn was quite the opposite. He was intelligent and had a strong enough will to possess magic in his blood; not to mention his skill with the sword was more than fair.

Their appearance is where they differed greatly. Standing nearly eight-feet tall, Bear was a giant in comparison to Mayn. His arms hung lower than most, and his hands could hold small boulders with ease. The oversized club he carried seemed unnecessary at times, considering how intimidating his size was, but a gargantuan man carrying a tree-sized stick was beyond intimidating.

Mayn, on the other hand, was cut from a very different kind of cloth. His slim figure only stood about five-and-a-half feet tall and was far from gargantuan. At average size, he was far from average. He looked unlike anyone in this part of the world. Perhaps that's why he covered his face with that long black cloth. When he revealed himself, it was hard not to notice his sharp features. From his narrow chin and nose to the tips of his pointed ears, he was far from ordinary, and he wanted that to remain secret.

On their travels, the two of them joked from time to time, but this particular mission was of most importance to their master. Mayn knew he was close to finding what she called the arm of the Avennoth.

He was almost positive his encounter last night was the work of such a powerful wraith. Those massive summons and waves of earth were controlled by something nearby. His mind flashed back to the young halfling they tried to rob. Mayn wasn't planning on actually helping those fools with the theft until he saw that silver dagger in that halfling's hand. After all, it was a dagger his master had been seeking for centuries. He never had a chance at obtaining it once the torrents of earth began. In fact, he would have nearly died if it wasn't for that halfling.

It would be the last time he traveled with such dimwitted bandits.

As he wrapped his head in a black scarf, he thought about what happened with the robed halfling before he met up with Bear.

Even if the halfling was holding that *Raji* rune, it wasn't what created those monstrous earth summons. But still he wondered who that halfling was, and where he received that *Raji* rune and the lost dagger of the Elf Queen.

What mattered more was who cast those spells. Mayn was positive it was the work of the Avennoth.

He didn't know much about it, since it has only existed twice. His master told him when an Avennoth is complete they can do almost anything, but this one was far from it. Only possessing the arm, the rest was unaltered — the rest being a dwarf.

"The dwarf has to be around here somewhere. I'm sure he was in these forests." Mayn's lithe figure stood in a clearing, looking around for any signs of a camp, but there was nothing to be found.

Bear broke the silence. "Don't worry, Mayn. We'll find that dwarf. And when we do, I'll crush him!"

"No, you will not 'crush' anything! Not everything needs to be 'crushed' by your damn hands," Mayn replied while making quotes with his fingers.

"What about the guards? You told me 'Crush 'em Bear!'... So, I crushed 'em," Bear added, also making air quotes.

"Okay, well when they are puny men you can do all the crushing. But the arm of Avennoth is not puny," Mayn cautioned as he began motioning his hands strangely.

Bear concluded, "You're a puny man."

Stopping his gestures, he looked over his shoulder at the big oaf. "I am not a man. I'm an Elf. There is a stark difference my friend."

Turning his concentration back to the forest, he continued motioning his hands with mystifying rhythm, a sign language which was majestic in its display. It was only moments before, his hands closed to form the shape of a monocular.

His gestures seemed to manipulate an unseen energy within his palms. Through his pale hands, Mayn manifested a lens giving him the vision of an eagle.

He scanned the forest for any signs of encampment. He looked southwest, past a huge fallen tree and just behind a forested incline. Short split trunks formed spiral stairs climbing up the bark of a tree.

"There." Dropping his hands to the hilt of his scimitar blade he gazed ahead. "Let's go. We need to check the camp ahead. Could be that our dwarf lives in the trees."

Bear nodded, and the two continued through the Thorned Ridge as dawn was nearly over.

14

NEFARIOUS NATURE

875, Summer's 56th Morning

**alamor** blew the remaining layer of dust from the cover, revealing a rare purple dyed cloth upholstery. He flipped it open. Its pages were trimmed with gold leaf, each paragraph initialed with a fancy drop cap.

~ Preface ~

To travel the lands of the Kingdom is no easy task, for even the highest hands of the Anstian Monarchy do not point fingers at such places on the map. Ever since the Necromancer was banished and the Anstian Kingdom was formed, these lands reek of foul creatures, lining its forests and rivers and the deepest of valleys to the highest of peaks.

The lands of the ancients were cursed by the hands of the Necromancer. These wicked creatures — spawns of ill-spoken word — they remain. A shameful reminder that man should hold his tongue. No matter the case, I write this text to shed light on such a dark and decrepit reality, hopefully to give the adventurous traveler foresight on their travels.

—Dansil Murko, of the Beshmere Arm, 652

Balamor went through the fine cloth-like pages, taking notes as his eyes scoured the contents. He copied the names and descriptions of the dark creatures, focused on learning as much as he could about them. Fine oil-painted illustrations of each subject gave him chills but his concentration was unshaken.

He transferred the contents to his notebook rather quickly, making sure to pluck out the important bits he would need for the journey. However, he couldn't help himself and read up on a few subjects which piqued his curiosity.

Nearly an hour went by before he was complete with his research.

The first of the demented beasts Balamor noted was a wolf which stood even taller than Awkid, its brown fur seemed slick with a pitch-black muck. Bright yellow eyes and a smoke-filled mouth seemed to leap off the page from behind the painting of a tree.

Tarwolves:

These rabid tar-covered beasts roam the darkest of the southern forests. I've come across quite a few in my time and it wasn't long before I learned they don't do well with fire. If you know this, then you know they are much less of a fight than they are intimidating. To take one down isn't a matter of strength, but dexterity. You must be able to outmaneuver them. Look for their bright yellow eyes; rarely are they hard to find.

Balamor scribbled down the author's accounts with the Tarwolves, even making his own sketches of the paintings in the book. He was conscious of the danger in the world around him even more now than during his time in the Raehl.

He never imagined such monstrous beings shared the Southland with him, lurking in uncharted lands.

After he finished his notes on the wolves, he moved on.

Various nasty beasts such as the fiery Searing Yemmings, and the brush tearing Paak Swarms made their way into his notebook, each subject taking nearly a third of a page.

After a while he found a very interesting creature Murko described as a brume of frost lurking through the brush.

Misks:

> *Many times have I felt the cold wind of the southern night, but there is a bone-chilling cold I've felt on my trips to the Lowlands of Leylancarr. Such a cold in those forests that you can see the air freeze around these clouds of tiny bugs as they swim in and out of the trees. Anything in their wake has no chance against the swarm. If you aren't as lucky as myself in escaping, then the Misks will devour you whole — I've seen it.*

These Misk swarms intrigued Balamor. He wondered if they lurked further north than the Lowlands of Leylancarr as Murko described. The traveler and his band of brothers trekked all across the Southland, yet he only placed these Misks in those lowlands — and the Tarwolves in the Forest of Nim. It was as if these creatures were bound to the lands more than ordinary beasts in this world.

The young cartographer studied his map on the table.

He had spent years filling in the names of locations he had never even seen. His finger traced a fancy calligraphy label; *Lowlands of Leylancarr.*

Balamor paused a moment before turning to Awkid who was packing luncheons for the two of them. "These... Misks. Are they a possibility on our trip?"

The dwarf didn't respond at first, almost ignoring the question as he prepared sandwiches of sweet maple ham and goat cheese — his finest ingredients he thought he would save for himself before Balamor showed up.

His bearded face peeked over his shoulder. "The Misks of the lowlands are no possibility. Those lowlands are their home and they made it that way. They are not the concern for this trip my friend, the Parins are the real possibility."

Balamor gazed down at the fine book, flipping its elegant page to reveal the next subject. At first glance, the shadowy creature seemed almost human in shape and stature.

Parins:

They are the fastest things I've ever seen. I swear it. The trees shuffled around us, but those black wraiths were gone. They are more intelligent than the other creatures in the south, but they have a weakness, as do all mortal beings. The light is their enemy. How they manage to avoid it during the daytime defeats me. You must use the light. It was my only chance when I became lost in the forest, thanks to the damned gnome. But I've seen the Parins up close — they are as sickening as they are horrifying.

The mapmaker looked up at the dwarf who was studying him as he read the purple cloth book. He knew all too well that Balamor was startled by the account on the twenty-sixth page.

Awkid started, "I've dealt with them, and you will too. We are trespassing in their territory. We are the intruders, Mr. Wisebeard. There is no doubt the Parins will protect what they consider their home."

Balamor quickly replied, "That's quite a perspective you have, dwarf, though I will have you know halflings do not defend before they welcome." He waved his finger in absolute certainty.

The peaceful halflings didn't believe such wickedness could be spawned by nature. Something or someone made it that way, and for reasons halflings couldn't comprehend.

He hopped to his feet and strolled to the wooden counter dipping his hand in the crate of various fruits Awkid was packing.

Grabbing a red plum from the assortment, he took an obnoxious chomp, still chewing as he spoke. "If you ask me, something has these strange creatures enraged. At least that's my perspective on things. Who was this 'Necromancer' anyway?"

The crate of fruits made its way to the thick floating shelf above them before Awkid poured himself a cup of mead. "A long time ago, centuries before you and I stepped foot on Earth, a time when the world was not what it is today, magic was prosperous. It was everywhere, and the Anstian Monarchy was nonexistent." Awkid took a gulp and sat at the table with Balamor to finish his story.

The young mapmaker was barely familiar with the tale, and so he sat quietly as the dwarf went on.

"The Old Kingdom was in power then. It was led by the hand of the Mystic Red King. It was said that he single-handedly reunited the races of man after the devastation brought by the End War — perhaps by using his magic. He chose one man from each race to join his rule. The humans, the dwarves, the gnomes, and of course you halflings lived under one sigil so to speak, and each of them ruled the Kingdom alongside the Red King. It was a peaceful age for mankind, and those five bloodlines led the Kingdom for centuries."

Balamor finally cut in, his curiosity besting him once again. "So, if these four families along with this 'Red King' were in power, then how did the Necromancer come about?"

Awkid swirled his mead in his wooden cup, amused by the halfling's impatience. "The trees sang their blissful songs with the wind, the birds with the beasts, and man played their instruments in concert. But after so much harmony, a string had to break under such great power. And so the tale says the sixth Mystic Red King became absorbed by his magic, slaughtering his entire council spare his queen. He cursed himself to prolong his life and sacrificed others to perform his blood ritual. The wife of the sixth Red King turned against his plans and started a rebellion against him."

Balamor wondered who this Mystic Red King was and if these monstrous creatures were cursed by him. He didn't want to become cursed by magic like this famed Necromancer. His fear on the subject seemed to grow as Awkid told him the story.

The tense green eyes of the wise Anvorbeard studied the young halfling a moment as he took his last chug and placed his empty cup on the wooden table. "That rebellion came to be known as the Anstian Monarchy. And ever since it defeated the Necromancer, the Kingdom has silenced magic."

The dwarf's last words lingered awkwardly in silence. Awkid realized what this meant to him as he finished telling the tale. His entire way of life centered around concealing his cursed limb and dismissing its attachment to him. He wished for a world that accepted those who possessed magic. As much as he felt cursed, his arm could save lives when a normal arm could not.

Balamor couldn't help but stare at the dwarf's concealed clay limb after he finished his speech. It was wrapped in white cloth bandages, shielded from the rain and from the eyes of the Kingdom. His steel-blue eyes scanned the single room of the log cabin. He knew this tree home was also hidden. He realized this man lived a very isolated life.

Balamor closed the thick violet colored book and studied its cover once more, *Of Nefarious Nature*. "So, Mr. Anvorbeard, when do we begin?"

Awkid grabbed a coil of rope from a hook on the wall and stuffed it into his backpack. Latching it shut, Awkid threw it to his back and looked up at the wooden ceiling of his home. He let out a breath before his eyes turned to Balamor. "Grab your map."

Balamor removed the small trinkets which pinned his map down and returned the large piece of parchment to his bag.

The dwarf snatched the small lantern from his shelf and tied it to his backpack with a loose leather belt. He swung the wooden door open and the smell of rain rushed in.

The rain outside wasn't as dangerous as Awkid imagined. At this rate, the bandages would suffice until they reached the road to Anstia.

"So with this rain, what happens when it gets to your arm?" Balamor asked as the two of them descended the spiral staircase of the tree home.

Awkid didn't bother making eye contact when he spoke, "You see that puddle there?" He pointed with his normal hand to the ground as they reached its muddy surface. "That is what happens."

A long pause ensued as they trekked through the forest.

The rain pattered softly against the canopy above.

Balamor held his hand out as a thick drop of water landed in the center of his palm. He tried to imagine what the dwarf had gone through.

875, Summer's 56th Morning

The Watcher was sprinting across the leaf-strewn ground of the forest, hopping over large roots which protruded the soil. His small body was exhausted, running the entire night to catch up with the young Wisebeard.

He didn't know where Balamor was exactly, but he knew where he was going — *the Mog Brush*.

Traveling there alone was not possible, but neither was traveling with another halfling from the Raehl. The Wisebeard had to be with someone, but not just anyone.

NEFARIOUS NATURE

The Mog Brush was not somewhere humans would travel to, especially since most of them would dismiss the land as myth. It had to be someone who had been there before – someone who possessed the strength and knowledge to survive the wilderness.

The clouded sky and slight drizzle made for an exhausting journey as the furry figure of the Watcher maneuvered the Thorned Ridge, but the urgency of the situation was a reminder that time was nearly out.

Darting past the humongous trees and thick patches of weeds, he searched for the mapmaker, knowing he had to make camp away from the road. But on which side of the Greatstone Pass is what eluded the Watcher.

He could only guess, and west was his first choice.

Dodging fallen branches and splintered logs, he started to lose his fast pace. His legs ached, and his lungs seemed like they were ready to burst. Miles of running took its toll on the hare and there was no way he could continue without resting. A mad sprint turned into a slow trot before finally, he parked beside a log.

The sounds of birds and insects were now eerily clear, and a strange stillness gripped the hare.

He crawled into the hollow body of the log — fungus and small bugs inhabited its interior. As the Watcher rested, his thoughts raced. He wondered where the halfling was, but more importantly, how close he was.

How long did the Wisebeard have until he was discovered by someone else?

The forest was quiet as the Watcher searched the brush. Glancing left, the dead trunk of a gigantic oak leaned against the remaining trees. To the right, a small clearing surrounded by bushes was littered with broken branches.

The occasional movement of birds kept the Watcher on edge. Minutes went by before he realized that he wasn't alone.

In the distance, he finally heard voices, two of them, and they were drawing closer. The sound of leaves crunching and twigs snapping grew louder as they approached.

Within moments, two figures stopped in the small clearing, the Watcher only yards away from them.

"Try to keep up, Bear. That camp was about a mile past this tree. I'd like to catch our dwarf while he's still sleeping," one of them said.

The Watcher studied the pair as they conversed with each other.

One of them was short, covered in dark crimson leather and a black scarf which concealed his face. The Watcher didn't know who this was, but his slender frame suggested he was no typical man, yet, the other figure startled the Watcher. Towering and built like a giant, this was no man — this was the work of magic.

Crawling out from the log and behind a tree, the Watcher knew they were not simple travelers. He could sense a peculiar magic emanating from the slim figure — elven magic. An elf meant one thing only, they were Farah Lenook's henchmen, and they were searching for the dwarf known as Awkid Anvorbeard.

15

BY A HARE

875, Summer's 56th Morning

owling past the thick trees, the wind was intense. The air was thick and cold, moistening their clothes, as well as the bandages covering Awkid's arm.

The clay surface of his limb became aware of the rain. A slight ache ran through the dwarf. He wondered how much of his real arm remained. How could he feel pain in this earthen curse of his? A question maybe Balamor would help answer in this journey.

The sun of the early morning made no difference in the gray sky above them. The weather was dreadful, and any passage of time went unnoticed, making their trip seem to go nowhere.

It felt like hours went by before they reached a clearing in the forest.

The thick grass they treaded was waterlogged from the night before.

Each step Awkid took was strategically placed. Even after all the years of traveling in the rain, his next trip never became easier than the last.

Looking up at the gray sky, the young Balamor searched for a break in the clouds, but it came to no avail. His hairy feet were soaked, and the cold wind made walking a chore. He watched Awkid in front of him. His strides were strong, yet they were taken with caution. Not once did he look back at his home.

Balamor couldn't help but think this journey was important to Awkid, even if it was unexpected. Whatever the strange woman did to his arm drove him to join Balamor's quest. He knew Awkid wanted to learn more about his own past.

They crossed the clearing and were beneath the trees yet again. The ground was riddled with broken branches and gnarled roots, making it hard to traverse for the halfling. Awkid, on the other hand, was a veteran of the forest, unlike most of his kind.

It took time for a mountain-born dwarf to get used to the Southlands. The climbing experience came in handy, but the lack of mountain game made past hunting experiences nearly pointless. Fruit and berries took over most of his carnivorous diet, something he dreaded at first. He had no choice. He needed to adapt to the Southlands if he couldn't return home.

The two travelers crossed the wet forest grounds for nearly an hour.

Balamor was tripped up by the exposed roots from time to time, and more often than he would rather admit, he required guidance from the Anvorbeard. His brown robes were drenched and riddled with grass and vines before he finally got a feel for the woodland.

All of a sudden, Awkid Anvorbeard paused, flashing his hand back for Balamor to halt. Something alarmed him.

Balamor didn't bother questioning it. He slowly kneeled at the foot of a large oak tree and waited for Awkid's command.

The dwarf studied the trees intensely. "Keep quiet. I hear someone ahead," Awkid whispered, joining Balamor on one knee.

"What do you hear?" Balamor inquired curiously.

Awkid didn't make eye contact when he spoke; his focus was trained on the forest ahead. "I think I heard men talking over there, but I'm not entirely sure." Awkid pointed toward a fallen tree.

Balamor peeked out beyond the cover of the tree trunk. Ahead, he saw the splintered remains of a tall oak, but only the sound of rain drizzling remained.

"Let me check it out." Balamor began to move before Awkid yanked him back.

"You are courageous, Balamor, but don't get yourself killed. Let's both move. Quietly now."

The dwarf removed his grip and nudged the halfling forward.

Balamor was at a crawl by the time they reached the broken tree.

Its size was immense in comparison to the mapmaker, and the sky had summoned an even greater power to strike it down. Twisted bark and fresh cut splinters tugged at his robes, ripping and tearing them slightly as he crept forth.

On all fours, he guided himself across the diagonal trunk which leaned against the surrounding trees.

His hands gripped the slippery bark before his curly head slowly peeked out. What he saw terrified him.

The young halfling was overwhelmed when his furry feet lost their grip on the oaken trunk.

Awkid's reaction was too late. He watched Balamor as his frail body landed in a thick patch of bushes.

"What was that?" a strange man's voice yelled out.

Balamor laid motionless within the shrubbery. His harsh breathing ceased but the pounding of his heartbeat did not.

Through the lattice of leaves and branches, he made out a tall dark figure framed in dark leather armor approaching. A black cloth wrap concealed his face.

Balamor's eyes grew wide as he slowly receded back into the bushes. His stubby fingers dug into the moist soil as the figure began to draw his scimitar blade from its sheath.

"Probably is nonsense... A hare or something," a deep hulking voice shouted.

Balamor couldn't figure out who it was, but it sounded like a giant.

Responding in arrogant fashion, the black-suited bandit held the blade firm. "Bear, I don't need your advice. Something is here, I can feel it."

The sun finally pierced the clouds, and the rain was gone. Bright light was gleaming on the edge of the cloaked man's blade. Its metallic hiss seemed to shake the entire forest.

Within a flash, the man thrust his sword into the bushes.

A yelp came from the bush, breaking the quiet atmosphere.

Awkid witnessed the event from atop the fallen tree.

The dwarf's eyes grew wide, a fiery blaze inside him almost charred the bark beneath his fingers. He was about to pounce on the unsuspecting bandit when the narrow blade was yanked from the shrubs. On its end lay a dead carcass of a red-spotted hare.

Balamor's hands released their tight grip on the wet soil as he opened his eyes. He looked around in confusion, wondering what had just taken place. He looked through the brush once more as the masked bandit tossed the body of the hare to his counterpart.

"Sometimes you're right, but only sometimes. Don't get full of yourself now." The man sheathed his blade in a swift and effortless fashion.

"Silly, Mayn, I'm too big for that. The only thing Bear is gonna get full of is this rabbit," his partner added with a deep chuckle.

Balamor could finally see the oaf of a man named Bear. A name that suited him well. His frame was much taller and wider than Mayn. He wore a loose brown tunic cut off at the shoulders. Thick red leggings were tucked into his leather boots. In one hand, he held a wooden club ringed with studded metal braces, in the other, hung the limp body of a hare.

Its death made Balamor uneasy.

"Anyway, we need to move on. We can argue all day about how you did or did not tear down this tree, but we can't forget why we came to this damn forest. If we don't find the one who wields the arm of Avennoth, then Farah will have the two of us blind and limbless!"

Mayn shoved Bear forward and the two of them walked away.

Balamor and Awkid watched the two men as they walked through the forest. It was hard for either of them to figure out the context, but Balamor knew Farah Lenook was also searching for his grandfather.

875, Summer's 56th Morning

The sound of an exhausted breath broke the air. Collapsing to one knee, the Watcher gripped the ash surface of the Rhethis Barrens, writhing in pain from the demise of his red-spotted familiar.

Surrounding him were huge beings made of stone. Their bodies were engraved with runewords from head to toe. They looked on as the Watcher began to stand up slowly.

"Is the Wisebeard safe?" one of the rock beings spoke. Its voice was that of churning gravel.

Dusting off his pitch-black robes, his frame was tall. His face was hidden behind the shadow of his cowl as he answered, "We can only hope. I had to sacrifice one of my familiars to save him." Looking up at them he continued, "There are two of Farah's scouts on the Thorned Ridge. They're searching for the Anvorbeard."

Another rock figure stepped forward. Its face was barren, only the blackness of eyes and a line for its mouth. "The dwarf who Farah has chosen to make the Avennoth?"

"Yes. The Avennoth is premature in him, but the threat for you Rahkfolk grows," the Watcher confirmed.

The Rahkfolk stood quiet as the reality set in.

BY A HARE

The tallest of the beings put its arm on the black-robed Watcher's shoulder as it spoke, "Thank you Gantis... It is time. We must gather the bloodlines..."

16

A STRANGER'S KEY

875, Summer's 56th Morning

For awhile, Balamor didn't move out of the small bush that concealed him. His hands were still and his eyes were fixed on the clearing that Mayn and Bear once occupied.

After the two men left, he felt lost. What they said about the Avennoth had his mind in knots.

The birds were singing and the forest around them was awake after a gloomy start.

"You know what they said, right?" Balamor asked from inside the bush.

A loud thump on the muddy earth and grass in front of him was accompanied by a grunt.

After a moment of silence went by, Balamor broke out of the bushes with his second question. "I mean, you know who? Right?"

Awkid Anvorbeard stood in front of him, glancing down at his earthly limb. His eyes were intense.

Balamor's patience grew thin. "They were talking abou—"

"About me? I'm quite aware of the possibility, halfling," Awkid interjected.

"The possibility? Well how many other people possess some special arm? And this close to your camp?" Balamor continued as he picked thorns and leaves from his brown robes.

Awkid didn't answer the young Wisebeard. It wasn't because he was being immature with his conclusions, but because Balamor was on to something.

The dwarf's large hand closed into a fist when he looked ahead. "Let's just keep moving. We don't know how many more hares will save your life in this forest."

Balamor finished with his robes and without waiting, took point.

His hairy feet flattened the moist dirt as he walked. He didn't talk for a while. Instead he thought about the duo he and Awkid just encountered.

It wasn't the fact that he nearly died in that shrub, or how a hare managed to save his life. To him the thing that mattered most about what happened was the name the two men mentioned — *Farah Lenook*.

She was the same woman in search of his grandfather, and now she was searching for Awkid. At least that's the only assumption Balamor could make. There was a mysterious connection between Farah Lenook, Awkid Anvorbeard, and the Wisebeards. Balamor was somehow in the middle of all of it, and his journey to the Mog Brush seemed to be fated.

The mapmaker looked over his shoulder at the dwarf with a smirk across his face. "You know, Mr. Anvorbeard... We're even now."

Awkid raised one eyebrow in disbelief. He found Balamor's statement amusing and quite credulous, in fact. "Is that so, Mr. Wisebeard?"

Balamor looked ahead. The wind brushed against his robes and the sun made him squint as he talked. "Sure it is. If I didn't convince you to leave with me to the Mog Brush, those men would have found you."

Awkid shook his head at Balamor's words. "You think those men would have killed me? I doubt they even thought the same thing! That's if they were even looking for me, little mapmaker."

Balamor giggled at Awkid.

He knew his clay arm would certainly put up a fight with his pursuers, but he also knew he would not be able to defeat

Farah Lenook once she arrived. Not if she was as powerful as he thought.

He wondered how powerful she really was, especially if she commanded men like Mayn and Bear around the Thorned Ridge. *And what about this Avennoth?* Mayn and Bear were just looking for the one who has its arm.

Balamor turned around to face Awkid Anvorbeard. He walked backwards as he asked, "So, if you have the arm of this 'Avennoth'—"

Awkid cut in, "If... This is all just your theory, Wisebeard."

The halfling continued, ignoring Awkid's interjection. "That must mean there are more, right? An entire body perhaps! Could you imagine your entire body being like that arm?"

Balamor realized he shouldn't have asked his question. He tried to take it back, but an exposed root tripped him before he could speak.

Awkid kept walking, not bothering to help him up. His mood didn't seem to change, but Balamor knew he wasn't happy with such imaginations.

Jumping to his feet, Balamor quickly caught up with the dwarf before giving his apology. "Ah, I didn't mean that. I am just saying what they are after is incredibly powerful, and we need to stop it. Sorry for mentioning it, I am just—"

"A halfling? Just keep your curiosities to yourself for now," Awkid commanded him. "This forest ends just ahead. Once we cross the road to Anstia, we will be in the next set of woods."

Balamor didn't respond. He knew he struck a bad chord with the dwarf; however, his idea was still a serious thing to consider. Balamor's suspicions seemed naïve, but Awkid was starting to think the halfling and his hunches were strangely accurate.

The two adventurers walked through the forest. The decline they traveled was steep which meant Awkid was right.

The Thorned Ridge was falling behind them as the sun rose into the sky.

The Anvorbeard was in front now; his cautious steps were a guide to Balamor.

As they walked, Awkid pointed out various plant life, telling Balamor which ones were safe and which ones were not. Being in the Southlands gave him a plethora of knowledge a typical dwarf would go without.

The mountains where the Dwarven people lived posed them with other dangers.

This knowledge made him appreciate the capability of the Southlanders, a people the dwarves mistook as unseasoned and well-off.

But the truth was that everywhere in the world had its dangers, and the races of man were equal in their ability to endure the Earth. It was the difference in their culture and their distance apart that made them look at one another with distaste.

One thing that Awkid was learning on this adventure was that one race in particular could see past the differences — the halflings.

Even though they were the most isolated of races, meeting a stranger presented them with an opportunity to befriend them.

There was an innocence in halflings that was undeniably special, but it was a trait that made them easily taken advantage of.

Awkid needed to be Balamor's guide, even if it was dangerous to himself. It was worth protecting the innocence halflings possessed.

875, Summer's 56th Noon

After they departed the Thorned Ridge, they found themselves on a cobblestone road.

To their right was the beginning of the Greatstone Pass. Its sight reminded Balamor of the past few days – his close calls with bandits and when he watched the mystic woman cast her spell on the earth.

He started to question what happened with Jabit and his grandfather.

It was all very strange to him. The fact that the woman had him save Farjadis from Farah Lenook. What was going on had started to frighten him.

He turned his head at the signs of an unknown fear. He needed to move on and finish his journey.

Looking to his left was the kingdom of Anstia; its beautiful architecture was visible from miles away. Polished white stone bricks shined in the sun. The towers of its keep rose high above its walls, each with a conical roof made of a scarlet flagstone. The glorious kingdom mirrored itself in the moat that surrounded it. The sight was amazing to Balamor.

"Don't let it fool you. What lies behind those walls is a prison for people like you and me," Awkid said as he watched the young Wisebeard stare westward.

Balamor kept his gaze fixed on the kingdom as he replied, "Do you know what was there before the kingdom of Anstia?"

Awkid was taken aback by the question. Not once did he ask it himself. But it didn't matter to him. Whatever was there before had been ruined by the Anstian Monarchy. "All I know is what stands there now, and it's hideous."

His own statement lingered in his mind. He had an awkward feeling after he said it, as if it was never even said or was not said enough.

He looked at the kingdom and then back at his arm. It wasn't his fault he was cursed. The cloth wraps were slightly stained with dirt as he began to fix them. He knew it was the only way to hide it from the power-hungry monarchs.

Even though they did well for their own people, it was their hatred for magic that drove them mad. They would do everything in their power to keep magic suppressed in the south if they could find it.

"Traveling to the Kingdom, I see?"

Balamor and Awkid snapped their heads up to see a guard atop a horse.

He was covered in iron plating and ring mail; leather strapping held a white cloth around him. On the cloth was a sigil, the same sigil Balamor saw on the flags of the Anstian Kingdom.

The head of a black dragon with a golden sword down its mouth — it signified the death of the Old Kingdom and the birth of the New Kingdom, The Anstian Kingdom.

The two travelers looked startled as the guard approached from the west.

Awkid quickly finished bandaging his arm.

Balamor attempted to answer the man's question. "Actually... We uhh... We are traveling south to—"

Awkid Anvorbeard quickly finished his sentence, his tone was serious as he looked the Anstian guard in the eye. "To the Kingdom of Elkhart. Don't mind my halfling friend here, he doesn't know the five kingdoms like you and I."

The man studied them. His hand was already holding the hilt of his sword. "I see your arm is injured dwarf. What business do you have in the lowland kingdom of Elkhart?"

Awkid looked to the forest as he spoke, "Simik venom. Only the healers in Elkhart know how to treat it."

"And the halfling?" the guard asked.

Balamor was unsure what to say. He glanced at Awkid who started to show he was lying with the arch of his eyebrows.

"Well? Do you have no answer for him?" The guard proceeded to draw his sword, and Balamor stepped back.

The suspense held everyone still.

Awkid Anvorbeard stared at the armored man. His focus quickly changed to the white stone keep of the Anstian Kingdom behind him.

"Get him! Stop that damn thief!" a voice called out. It was coming from the west and along with it were the sounds of hooves clacking against the cobbles of the road.

Whistles from riders and the occasional cry from their horses came closer.

Awkid and Balamor looked up to see who was coming but the Anstian man who held them up was too slow to make the same move.

Before the guard could turn around, the men on horseback about to trample them; two more guards were chasing down a blue-hooded man.

Balamor froze in the middle of the road, his legs wouldn't work for him this time.

They were only feet away when Awkid pushed Balamor out of the road and reached for the blue-hooded rider with his bandaged arm. As he gripped the blue robes, he lost his footing and pulled the rider from his saddle.

The other guards quickly pulled their horses to a stop when Awkid Anvorbeard and the hooded rider crashed to the ground. The sounds of metal clanged against the cobblestone.

Balamor was still getting back on his feet when he saw various metal trinkets littering the road. He looked closer as one guard gathered them into a bag, while the other two detained the hooded thief. The metal pieces shined in the light; some were polished while others lackluster. While he walked toward them, their details became clear.

They weren't just trinkets, they were keys.

"A thief stealing keys? He must have broken all of his lock picks to get these. How ironic!" one of the guards exclaimed while handling the blue-hooded rider.

Awkid remained on the ground as the three Anstian guards hogtied their prisoner and threw him over the back of his horse.

The horse was stolen too. It was easy to tell since its saddle matched that of the pursuers.

The guards turned to Balamor and Awkid before continuing to Anstia.

They all looked the same, which made noticing the original guard from before impossible until he spoke, "I hope you get that Simik bite taken care of. Thank you for aiding in this arrest. The Kingdom is grateful. Good day."

Awkid nodded as he was lying on the cobblestone road.

Balamor followed suit with a nod and waved to the men as they left. He turned to Awkid and tried to help him to his feet.

Awkid laughed at his attempt and managed to get himself up after a moment. He dusted off his clothes and looked at Balamor with a smirk before opening his wrapped palm.

He revealed three keys to Balamor whose jaw dropped at the sight.

One was a typical cast-iron key with a loop handle and two squared teeth at its end; nothing special Balamor thought. The second key however was magnificent — it looked to be made of sterling silver — its handle was in the shape of a clover and studded with precious gems.

He wondered who owned such a key, and what valuables it gave access to. The many intricate teeth showed it was certainly a key to a complex lock.

He looked up at the dwarf who motioned for Balamor to have them. "Go ahead, take them."

The curious halfling grabbed them from Awkid in excitement before he realized he hadn't looked at the third key.

He moved the others into his bag before he examined the final key. It was polished like the silver key was but darker than any metal he had ever seen. He noticed it was also smaller than the rest and had no teeth on its cylinder shaft — as if it was never finished.

It felt strangely cold in his hands as he rubbed his thumb against its flat disk handle.

"Wait," Balamor whispered when he turned the key over to see its other side.

"What is it?" Awkid asked.

"It's a rune."

Balamor looked on the handle to see another runeword had found its way into his journey and it was one he hadn't seen before.

Balamor quickly retrieved his journal and jotted down notes about the discovery, including a sketch of the key and the shape of the runeword. A line drew downward into a box made of five points, like a key into a lock.

"This came from the Kingdom of Anstia?" Balamor asked as he nestled the key in his palm.

"It seems so. What do you think it is for?" Awkid inquired.

"I don't know just yet, but what matters more to me is why a kingdom who forbids magic owns a key like this?" Balamor shut the book and put both items in his leather backpack before returning it to his shoulders.

Awkid put his hand on Balamor's back and nudged him forward. "Let's keep moving. We don't want those guards coming back for us after they realize what they're missing."

The young Wisebeard didn't have any objections; on his mind was the old tale Awkid gave him the night before.

He had a feeling this key was from the time of the old kingdom, from a time when magic was accepted.

They walked south off of the road and into the next forest.

17

THE TREE OF NIM

875, Summer's 56th Afternoon

he sun was still up, and the sounds of life surrounded them. Minutes went by before the road behind them was no longer visible.

The trees were unlike those on the Thorned Ridge. Their bark was twisted, and the leaves gave off an unfamiliar scent. But the travelers were not surprised, especially the Anvorbeard for he had been here before.

Looking around at the trees and shrubs, Awkid was reminded of the notes in his old journal.

Years have passed since he stepped foot in this place. The last time was no simple journey. The old man they traveled with was the reason for that. Always disappearing and making it impossible to stay on track.

He knew this time would be different, but how different?

The young halfling was very similar to the Black-robed Man.

The trees shuffled and Awkid stopped. He started to remove the wraps from his arm as he waited for something to pounce on them. He was ready this time, and his arm wasn't going to be a problem either. His mind shifted to his encounters with the Parins. He hoped they wouldn't encounter such creatures this early on.

Crawling down the trunk of a tree came a squirrel. It stopped and stared at the two adventurers before scampering away into a small bush.

Balamor sighed in relief but Awkid was still on alert.

It was a squirrel this time, but it could be something much worse next.

"So this is the Forest of Nim, huh?" Balamor asked as they continued to walk.

"Yes." Awkid scowled.

"I read about this place. The man who came through these woods said there was a tree that guided him." Balamor looked around and scratched his noggin after he made his statement.

Awkid chuckled. "Is that so? A tree in the woods? Well, I have been in these woods, Mr. Wisebeard. Besides myself, the only guide I had was some crazy old man. A lot like yourself."

"Yeah? What was his name?" Balamor reached into his backpack and grabbed a red plum. He began eating it as they walked.

"Never found out, and neither did his party."

"Strange," Balamor replied as he chewed his fruit.

"Indeed, but I never asked. No one did. But the men who traveled with him seemed to be his students."

"Students of what?" Balamor asked.

"Didn't matter to me. They spoke of him plenty. That's all I remember."

Balamor chucked the pit of his plum on the ground as they walked on.

His hunger wasn't satisfied, but he would have to wait until they made camp. He looked up at the sky as he took a swig from his flask.

The trees obscured any bit of the sun. It could have been late afternoon by now, which meant they might be out of the forest before dark.

Reaching into his backpack, he pulled out his map and unrolled it carefully.

The blank spot was close now, judging by the size of the forest which surrounded it; his assumptions could be correct.

Possibly another five miles stood between them and the Mog Brush. The number felt small, but he knew the forest was harder to trek than the blank spot on his map made it seem.

He closed it and packed it away.

Awkid was walking slightly ahead of him observing the forest for any signs of trouble. He was smart compared to the dwarves Balamor read about. Perhaps his life here in the south made him different, or the stories he read were misconceptions of the Dwarven people.

Balamor started to wonder how much the dwarf had been through. He traveled further than Balamor could imagine, all the way from the Dahris Mountains, from the Peak of Rayguth to the forests of the Thorned Ridge.

Whatever he had experienced in his travels to the south made him adept for a world such as this. Danger lurking around every corner whether it be nefarious creatures or the other races of man. Awkid has seen his fair share of both and dealt with it enough to live on his own in the wild.

Balamor respected him even when his own people didn't.

Just because he was cursed didn't mean he was evil. In fact, the curse he was stuck with was what made him admirable. Otherwise, he would never have the drive to help a halfling or a crazy old man and his students.

"I see something ahead," Awkid claimed as he pointed south.

Balamor snapped back to reality at the dwarf's words. He pulled his journal out and began looking through his notes. "It could be the tree I have in my notes. It has a marking on it so we should know for sure when we find it."

Awkid continued south and Balamor followed him. His journal was still in his hands as he walked.

"Whatever it is, it is far away. I barely caught a glimpse through the trees," Awkid said thoughtfully.

The foliage of the trees started to rustle again. First, it was in front of them, then behind them.

THE TREE OF NIM

Awkid held his hand up to signal Balamor to halt, but when he stopped so did the movement in the trees.

It was so quiet that fear began to fester in Balamor's mind.

He thought back to the words of Dansil Murko. His accounts of evil creatures in the Forest of Nim were enough to stop the life from moving or even making a noise. The eerie stillness found its way under the young halfling's skin.

"Parins?" Balamor asked with a shaky voice.

"Not now, it's too early." Awkid was scanning the trees, his eyes showing concern but the rest of his expression was confident.

He couldn't find out what was there. Before he could think any further, something plopped on the ground behind them.

They turned around and scanned the forest.

Awkid thrust his arm into the ground, a few feet in front of them sprouting a hand to crush whatever made the noise. His arm burrowed back through the soil and he pulled it back from the earth.

Balamor flinched as Awkid opened his palm. Within was the crushed remains of an acorn.

Balamor began to laugh slightly, but Awkid's death stare caused him to stop immediately.

"Damn vermin!" Awkid shouted as he threw the broken acorn to the ground. "Let's go before I tear these trees down and cook every one of these rodents," he added as he turned around and started walking away.

Balamor followed. He looked down to see his hand gripping the hilt of his silver dagger, still within its leather sheath. He didn't even notice he held it; it seemed it was now pure instinct.

It took him a few seconds to catch up with the speedy dwarf who was in a hurry. This forest had him frustrated, and they'd only been walking for an hour.

They passed the twisted trees which obscured what was ahead.

The ground was relatively flat now, making it easier to navigate than the Thorned Ridge.

Balamor was still on edge from minutes ago. The relief he had gotten still wasn't enough to settle his mind. He looked up at the trees, the feeling of being watched made him uneasy.

After several minutes, they both could finally see what Awkid spotted moments ago.

It was a tree, but unlike its neighbors, its bark was a light shade of brown and the grooves were lined with a strange golden residue. Its leaves were gold and shined in an unseen ray of light.

For a moment they were both quiet.

Balamor glanced between his journal and the golden tree.

"This is it! See this symbol?" Balamor ran ahead and pointed at the tree as he looked back at Awkid.

The symbol was the shape of a circle with a diagonal dash at its center. The contours of it melded with the bark and were filled with the golden substance. It wasn't carved, that was obvious to both of them; but it wasn't normal either and that meant one thing.

"Another runeword," both of them said in unison.

They looked at each other and then back at the tree. Awkid had never seen the tree before, but the Wisebeard was right. Balamor knew now that they were close to the Mog Brush.

18

WHISPERS FROM THE TREES

875, Summer's 56th Evening

Pages fluttered as Balamor scrambled through his notes, trying to find out more about the mysterious runeword on the tree. It meant something, and it was here for a reason. Whoever or whatever put it here was giving others a message.

What that message could be was unknown to Balamor, but the symbol was not. When he found it, his stubby finger nearly punched a hole right through the page. "Here, I knew I had seen this before. Except the one in my notes has the line drawn horizontally." He rotated the journal to match the symbol on the tree.

"Where did you see this?" Anvorbeard asked.

"In my other book, on the fourth page." Balamor grabbed his spellbook from his backpack.

Its red cover and disproportionate pages flapped.

He stopped and the both of them investigated the fourth page intensely before Awkid rose an eyebrow

Balamor sighed. "It looks blank, I know, but the symbol was there when I was in the Greatstone Pass."

Awkid shrugged and looked back at the tree before gripping it with his earthen hand. With all of his might he tried to turn the symbol, but his strength was not enough. Twisting the bark of a tree was obviously unlikely, but Awkid was not one to leave brawn untested. He growled in frustration when he heard the sound of laughter behind him. His head snapped back to Balamor.

"You find this amusing? Would you like to try?"

"What? That wasn't me," Balamor replied as he looked around.

Awkid stared at him with an arched brow before he started to walk away.

Balamor was close behind. "Wait, where are you going? We need to figure this out."

"What is there to figure out? We just need to keep moving," Awkid said as he pushed past the young Wisebeard.

Balamor looked back at the tree before turning to catch up to Awkid.

They walked for a few minutes before Balamor requested to stop. Awkid growled as the young Wisebeard searched through his notes. There was nothing else The Fourth Valorhorn mentioned on his travels.

He had found a strange type of tree which was his key to finding the Mog Brush but that was all he wrote.

"Perhaps it's a marker of some sort," Balamor guessed.

"Perhaps, let's keep moving," Awkid agreed.

No more conversation took place as they walked.

The only sound was the crunching of twigs and feet stomping the dirt ground. Another hour had passed, and the surroundings were becoming mind numbing.

Awkid was concentrated on his task — he had been here before — and he hadn't fared well then. The thought of Tarwolves hissing as they approached in the night lingered in the back of his mind.

Balamor on the other hand was lost in his notes as he walked, a skill he gained in the past few days. His journal rested in his right hand, he read about The Fourth Valorhorn's accounts over and over for more insight, but there were none. His gut told him there were details missing, but the forest gave him no clues. There was the strange tree, but he knew too little about the magic of runewords. He glanced up to see where Awkid was when he spotted something.

"There! Another tree. See it? I was right." Balamor was excited.

He nearly danced to the tree with his book in his hand.

Awkid was behind him with a disappointed look on his face.

The Wisebeard had a knack for being right.

They looked at the tree; the symbol pressed into its gold-lined bark was the same as before.

Awkid felt the symbol with his normal hand, tracing the diagonal dash with his fingers, his eyes following it into the forest.

"Maybe this line points in the direction we need to travel?" Awkid looked out into the forest to see where the symbol guided them.

Balamor pulled out his map and unrolled it, holding it in front of him with both hands while glancing between it and the sun's direction. "Good observation, Mr. Anvorbeard, but the lines have no defined direction. Do they point us northeast or southwest?"

Awkid didn't look at the Wisebeard. His tense eyes were fixed on the forest in front of him. "They point forward."

He stepped around the tree and left Balamor's sight.

The halfling looked up as he let out a sigh. He rolled up his map but kept it in his hands as he walked toward Awkid.

875, Summer's 56th Sundown

The two adventurers walked for hours, passing by the golden trees and following the marks to the Mog Brush. The surrounding vegetation was becoming annoyingly familiar. Tree after tree they walked on, hoping for something to appear but there was nothing.

Balamor removed a plum from his bag. Soft spots showed it would be rotten soon. He didn't bother worrying about it, his boredom was giving him an appetite. A juicy bite of the fruit distracted him from the dread of the forest.

He thought about his small village as he consumed his snack. He didn't miss the Raehl, but he did miss his family. Days had passed since the last time he had seen a halfling. His time outside the Raehl offered him nothing but dangerous encounters with bandits and the company of a rather strange dwarf.

In fact, strange wasn't even scratching at the surface. Awkid Anvorbeard was far from the dwarves Balamor read about. He carried no weapons. He wore only basic clothes and boots and of course he had his curse.

Balamor knew Mayn and Bear were looking for it — the arm of the Avennoth.

He dropped the pit of the red plum on the ground as he finished his thoughts. He looked up to see another golden tree only yards away.

Awkid looked back and motioned to Balamor. "Check your map."

Balamor unrolled the map and ran his finger into the blank spot. "According to our travel by these trees, we should have made it close to the Mog Brush by now."

"We never even came across the swamp! Something's off, Mr. Wisebeard, and it's probably your directions! I'll take point. Let's go while we still have what's left of the daylight," Awkid fumed before he began walking off.

He made only a few steps when something cracked against his head.

A small chuckle let out behind him.

He rubbed the sting with his palm and turned around with fire in his eyes. Balamor was looking at his map still trying to figure out where they were.

"You do that one more time, halfling, and you won't make it out of this forest."

"Do what?" Balamor looked up in confusion.

Awkid pointed down at the broken acorn that struck him. "That."

Balamor contested, "That wasn't me! Something is going on here, Mr. Anvorbeard. We're being watched."

Awkid shook his head in disbelief and turned around.

Balamor scanned the trees.

The air was still and the sounds of life were quiet.

The young halfling couldn't spot anything out of the ordinary so he followed Awkid and stared at his map. He walked silently. Sometimes, he would glance up at Awkid to keep track of him.

Looking over their travel, he knew something wasn't right about this forest. The way the inscribed trees were laid out seemed so random. Any intelligent being would know how to make an obvious trail, but this wasn't even slightly obvious. It was as if the point was to confuse someone rather than guide them.

All of these symbols pointed either northeast or southwest, but when Awkid and Balamor spotted the next tree, it was either directly east or west of the last tree. Nothing was adding up, and Balamor felt like he was traveling in circles.

As he took another step, something tripped him.

His map crinkled up when he fell to the ground.

"Yeah, yeah, laugh it up, Mr. Anvorbeard." He cursed as he rubbed his noggin but what he saw lying on the ground paused him.

Chewed and left behind was the pit to the red plum he discarded earlier.

Laughter from above made him jump to his feet and look around.

Awkid peered over his shoulder when Balamor gathered himself.

"You know, sitting there isn't gonna get us to the Mog Brush. Get up, there's another tree up ahead," Awkid commanded with a strict voice.

There was an awkward silence before Balamor's eyes snapped back at the remains of the plum and then right back at Awkid. "Something's going on in this forest, Mr. Anvorbeard." Balamor felt like he was on to something.

Awkid didn't say anything, but he saw the look on Balamor's face — it was serious. Something gave the young mapmaker a sign.

Awkid watched as Balamor walked off.

"Follow me."

"Like you know where you're going!" Awkid complained, his cursed hand balled into a fist.

Awkid went along anyway, staying behind Balamor as he walked onward through the forest.

19

THE RIDDLING BARK

875, Summer's 56th Sundown

As the sun was going down, the cold southern night was creeping in, and Awkid was finally starting to question what was going on in this forest. He tried to just get through it but there was no sign that he was traveling in the right direction.

"Have you ever read *The Tales of The Vanishing Woods*?" Awkid asked while he trailed Balamor.

"I have indeed. Do you think these trees will eat us, Mr. Anvorbeard?" Balamor chuckled.

"I believe in the Old-World fables of legendary men who were devoured whole on a simple trek through the forest. Whole armies would disappear through the brush and never be seen again," Awkid stated firmly, his eyes squinting with tension.

"Well, they must have lacked practice in basic experimentation." Balamor pulled out his silver dagger and went to mark a random tree.

After slicing into its thick bark, Balamor realized there were other marks above it, and they were much older.

After a few minutes, Awkid realized they were moving away from the gold tree.

"What's your plan, halfling?"

"For hours, we have followed these strange trees and they've brought us nowhere. I want to know where we end up when we avoid them," Balamor explained.

Awkid looked at him blankly before his hand opened and he motioned forward. "Lead the way."

875, Summer's 56th Sundown

The Forest of Nim was silent while they walked away from the gilded tree.

Every so often, they could hear birds leave the trees.

Awkid watched as the mystifying glow disappeared behind the lattice of scarred trunks.

Balamor batted away a thick shrub with his dagger as they walked through the forest.

The sun tinted the vegetation in red, casting long shadows as it fell behind the horizon. The wind was still when they approached another tree — a lot sooner than they expected.

Balamor held his dagger in his right hand, its blade reflecting in the sunlight. He stared at the canopy above them, but the brush remained undisturbed.

The strange tree in front of them gave off a fresh scent; flakes of gold dust slowly floated their way to the root-torn ground.

Balamor turned to face the tree, its beautiful bark seemed oddly perfect, no scars or fungus of any kind.

Awkid watched him as he glanced at his dagger for a moment before slicing into the tree.

The two adventurers watched as the deep slash made by Balamor's dagger sealed immediately.

Balamor held his breath in shock while Awkid looked to him for answers.

Balamor turned away from the next golden tree.

He knew magic ran through its bark, but how far did its roots spread? It seemed every sighting came sooner than the last.

Their patience was growing thin and ache was settling in the soles of their feet. They walked the entire day, and the majority of their travel was in these woods.

The rune-marked tree appeared time and again, but still the Mog Brush remained undiscovered.

Balamor and Awkid felt lost, and it seemed both of their plans would amount to nothing.

The dim skies of dusk were only growing dimmer with each step they took.

Balamor scanned the trees. He knew what he was looking for, and it wasn't the strange runeword. He marked the trees for a reason, to see if they really were walking in circles. He spotted a few marks ahead. He knew they were his, he could tell since he made each mark a tally. This trunk had four vertical slashes, meaning ahead should be the last mark he made before finding the tree.

The final tally was nowhere to be found; not at thirty, forty, or fifty paces.

Balamor could not grasp the elusive system behind the Forest of Nim.

The folktales of lost woods rung true. This place was a thief — of your time and peace of mind.

There had to be a way out. There had to be a system.

Awkid stomped his foot with fury and aggravation.

Balamor instantly turned around. The enraged dwarf shouted, "That's it, Mr. Wisebeard! I'm done with this! We're trapped in the woods by some damned magic, and I am no fool to what magic can do to the mind. I'll go no further!"

Balamor stared in shock when Awkid spoke, but he would not reply.

Awkid stared back, but the look on Balamor's face was placid.

After a moment, Balamor pointed and Awkid slowly looked back.

Facing him was the gold-lined trunk of the infamous tree they had been trying to avoid. Gold dust floated through the air, sticking to his clothes and into his long brown beard.

THE RIDDLING BARK

Awkid stepped back while glancing between Balamor and the tree. His clay arm gripped its trunk with impressive strength. Bark splintered as he fought to wrestle it from the earth, but the tree would not relent. The wounds Awkid inflicted were sealed by its magic. Its deep roots were fettered within soil. Awkid's brawn would not suffice, so he gave up and backed away from the tree.

He saw Balamor was nose deep in his books — similar to his experience in this forest. He never saw the golden tree then, which seemed impossible to miss this time around.

The day's light was spent here, camp needed to be made — another night sleeping in the Forest of Nim for Awkid Anvorbeard and the halfling.

"Can you get me into this tree?" Balamor asked as he stood to his feet. "I'd like to test something."

Awkid gave him a curious look. "What for?"

"To get a better look at these woods," Balamor said while motioning his hand toward himself.

Awkid thrust his arm into the earth. It melded with the soil and formed a mound of dirt beneath Balamor into a large hand. Roots and insects deep underground were clinging onto the large limb as its five fingers closed to shape a cup.

Balamor lifted himself into the tree and quickly found his way to the top. Gold residue glittered on his robes and the locks of his hair. He broke through the dense foliage with a cloud of gold dust.

"What do you see?" Awkid asked.

"Strange..." Balamor replied.

He looked around slowly to find a way out, but there was nothing but trees in all directions.

The Forest of Nim was endless — no distant mountains, no Peak of Rayguth, no Mog Brush.

"It's just... trees. Forever!" Balamor shouted as he looked down through the foliage. He paused when he saw some leaves were stuck to his robes. He quickly yanked a handful of leaves from the tree. He wanted to save them.

Maybe in the future they could be of use, but for now they would be concealed in his backpack. After a final look, he climbed down the tree.

"Illusions. We're being toyed with, Balamor," Awkid claimed as he looked around in suspicion.

"I have an idea, but we need to test something." Balamor paused.

Awkid was silent.

"Okay, we need firewood, right? Well while you gather wood, I want you to walk straight. Don't turn around, just keep walking," Balamor ordered, confidence lurked behind his words.

"You better hope you're right, or else I'll be fine to keep on walking," Awkid replied.

"Just trust me, Mr. Anvorbeard," Balamor said as he turned around.

At that, Awkid walked away leaving Balamor up in the rune-marked tree.

Minutes had gone by as Awkid gathered the driest branches and leaves he could find. He was angered with this journey but it was something he agreed to take part in. He knew what could happen on the way to the Mog Brush.

The trees shook behind him and then quickly to his left.

Awkid didn't fret, his eyes were peeled — something was around and it was very fast. Whatever it was, Awkid knew he needed to track it. He walked in a creeping stance, his arms full of branches and leaves.

Above him the canopy shook, leaves feathered their way down onto him. Again, yards in front of him the trees rustled. Awkid ran forward chasing the sounds of branches snapping. He tried not to veer off course, but the sounds were luring him.

Tree after tree, he trailed behind. After a moment, he began to see the tally marks Balamor made; each in chronological order. He made it to the fifth. From around its trunk, the mysterious glow of the rune tree greeted him along with the young Wisebeard.

Awkid froze and for a short moment he forgot why he was even running until a small laugh came from the trees behind him. He knew it couldn't have been Balamor, which meant one thing...

"You were right," Awkid mumbled

Balamor wrote down his notes while he spoke. "The ends of this forest meet. You walk south and you end up north or possibly any other direction, Illusions? Possibly," Balamor concluded as he nodded and shrugged.

"That and the trees are laughing at us. We're damned in this place," Awkid said quietly as he scanned the forest.

"Wait, you've been here before. How come you didn't find this tree then?" Balamor asked.

Awkid walked over to him and began placing sticks and leaves in the shape of a circle. "The Black-robed Man. He must have figured out this labyrinth. He would leave without notice and then return in the middle of the night."

Awkid paused and removed a piece of flint and steel from his boot.

Sparks leaped onto the wood and quickly caught fire.

Awkid cupped his hands and gave the fire breath before he continued, "Your books, he too carried strange books. Perhaps he performed some spell on this symbol here?"

Balamor rubbed his chin a moment before he dug into his bag and retrieved his six-page spellbook. He looked at the cover for a moment like he was missing something.

The sun was kissing the horizon and the urgency of the situation pressured his thinking. "I have no way of figuring out how to speak this language. I've read about the Runesong, but there's no recorded pronunciations of the symbols."

Awkid looked over his shoulder. On the dark leather cover, he saw six words spanned the bottom edge. "Hm, how many pages are in your book?"

"Six," Balamor stated after flipping through them.

Tyel - Aer - Hels - Theas - Maur - Firos.

"Well, it looks to me like these words on the cover are labels," Awkid suggested as he pointed to the six words.

A moment of silence went by as Balamor absorbed the theory. "Ah! Genius!"

Awkid's idea was so basic that Balamor overlooked it this entire time.

The fact that the book was magical made him assume it was too complex. He held the book with both of his hands as he thought back to the encounter in the Greatstone Pass.

His focus was the fourth word stamped onto the bottom of the cover. "... *Theas.*"

The book jolted open to its fourth page.

The feeling of pins and needles overwhelmed his body when the blank page illuminated with warm green runewords.

Balamor studied them as the sensation diminished. Quickly, he picked out the runeword he saw on the golden tree.

"There, that is the same symbol. And see how it repeats along the page?" Balamor pointed to the symbol on each line before he went on. "It must be some sort of activation word. Which explains why it is written in common tongue on the cover. If that's true, then..."

Balamor placed his palm against the diagonal runeword on the golden tree. Once he touched the strange bark, he knew that he was being watched — being tested.

"*Theas.*"

20

KNOW WHERE

875, Summer's 56th Night

B*eneath* his palm the gold-lined bark of the strange tree started to glow; within the bounds of the symbol a warm green light gathered and intensified. A powerful energy emanated from the bark and through Balamor's entire body. Slowly, the strange force twisted and warped the bark, turning the runeword to its correct position.

$$\Theta$$

Balamor slowly removed his hand from the sparkling bark and looked around. His skin still coursed with a numbing sensation.

The forest was quiet and the darkness of nighttime only made the situation nerve-racking.

"So... I suppose that's it?" Balamor asked, looking at his notes and then back to Awkid.

"Well that was step one, Mr. Wisebeard and Mr... Anvorbeard? Ah, yes."

The two adventurers snapped their heads back to the pitchy voice behind them.

There stood a very small figure, even smaller than that of Balamor. He wore black boots and light brown knickers with a tattered blue vest over a dingy yellow shirt. His complexion was old, and judging by the condition of his clothes, he had been here for a long time. What was left of his gray hair was spiked out to the sides and his bushy eyebrows made his emerald eyes hard to see. A long tuft of gray hair on his chin was braided and tied. His large round nose bobbed as he paced back and forth with a large scroll in his right hand.

"Yes, yes, you were hard to put a finger on. Anywho, there's just a few questions to answer, some papers to sign, and Voila! You'll be on your way!"

Balamor and Awkid were both caught off guard by the small man's appearance.

Without making a noise, he managed to get so close to them. His presence was strangely non-threatening, and his character was whimsical in both voice and gesture.

"How do you know who we are?" Balamor asked.

"I know all who pass through the threshold. Trust me, the list is rather long, and showing its entirety would revolve the hands of time," the small man replied.

Awkid balled his hands into fists and stepped toward the small man. "It was you! You're the one driving us mad! Damned gnome!"

"Madness, madness, madness… Well there's a thing about madness that we all seem to forget. It starts with a simple pick — pluck — strum of each individual fiber of our very own emotions. If you play the right notes, it can make a show that sends the audience into madness! We, Mr. Anvorbeard, drive ourselves mad. I am merely here to add to the variety of it," the colorful man jibed and winked.

"Don't test me with your words!" Awkid shouted as he quickly stomped his cursed hand on the soil.

The gnome didn't budge. He stared into the emerald eyes of Awkid Anvorbeard intensely. "Don't forget that cursed limb feeds on anger. Would a dwarf's wisdom allow such idiotic acts? No. It. Would. Not. Now, let's not be hostile, Mr. Anvorbeard."

Awkid replied with a drawn growl while he removed his earthen hand from the ground. He turned to Balamor who was staring at the gnome with a deep look in his eyes.

Balamor flipped through his journal and stopped at his notes from Dansil Murko. "You're the gnome I've read about. What's your name?"

The old gnome nodded and winked once more. "That is the question, is it not? For I am a gnome, but I am simply not... any gnome... am I? I will tell you where my name is, but it is you, who will tell me what my name is."

"Damn riddles. I am in no mood for riddles," Awkid responded as he removed mushrooms and greens from his bag and pierced them with a sharp stick.

"I'll answer your riddles," Balamor said as he removed a charcoal pencil from his bag.

"Good, good. Now listen to the words as I speak them. Write them down forward and backward if you must. I will not repeat myself and I certainly will not wait. Time is part of your answer," the gnome continued, pacing as he spoke.

His movements were animated and his character was beginning to drive Awkid up a tree.

The colorful gnome cracked his fingers before he began.

Balamor held his pencil tightly and flipped to a new page in his notebook.

Awkid patiently twirled his veggie kabob over the fire as the gnome spoke; each sudden pitch making him flinch.

"My name is nimble in the beginning and always at the center of this inanimate forest. You can see my name within unimaginable places, like an eye in between the ending of dawn and the beginning of midnight. You can find my name through the trees and under the bushes, in the midst of the animals. Now that you have heard my name, tell me, Mr. Wisebeard — who am I?"

Balamor scribbled down the strange gnome's words into his notebook. He studied them in silence, making sure he didn't overlook the small details. If he should have heard his name then it must be hidden within the riddle.

Quickly he underlined specific words; inanimate, animal, unimaginable, nimble... There was something they all had in common.

The small gnome stared at Balamor. His eyes squinted and his smirk drew up his left cheek.

Who was this man? How did he come to be in such a place?

All Balamor knew was that the eyes he felt lurking in the trees belonged to this man and his riddles suggested he was protecting something — something that was his.

"Nim!" Balamor yelled out as he poked the page with the back of his pencil. "Like an eye between the ending of dawn and the beginning of midnight, N-I-M," he concluded. "Each found in the beginning of the word nimble. The center of the word inanimate. Amidst the word animal and within the word unimaginable. You are Nim, and this is your forest!" His pencil popped against his notebook in conclusion.

The gnome stopped and pointed upward. "Congratulations! You are certainly correct, Mr. Wisebeard. However, I have more questions for you — may they guide you to your destination."

Nim began to pace slowly once more, exaggerating his small steps as he continued, "It does not breathe. It does not leave. It does not eat or even sleep. It sees through darkness above the trees. Above you, above our eyes, above all mortals and even I. It changes space in due time and in its place a pearl shines. One round the clock it goes away — one round more to show its face."

Balamor's handwriting was sloppy as he jotted down the second riddle with haste.

Awkid scratched his chin while he planted himself on the ground.

The two adventurers seemed stumped for a moment and time was of the essence.

Balamor's mind kept him from resting his legs. Over and over, he read the ambiguous text but nothing came to his mind.

Time grew thin as Nim tapped his foot on the ground.

Awkid handed a roasted kabob to the young Wisebeard who quickly accepted it.

"It's the sun," Awkid answered.

Balamor threw his hand in the air, baffled that he didn't think of such a thing.

Nim slowly clapped as he walked back toward Awkid. He leaned in to speak to him, "True... But you are not Balamor Wisebeard." Nim winked.

Balamor shook his head as he looked at Awkid.

The dwarf responded by letting out a sigh and slumping his shoulders.

The moon was rising and the cold fog was beginning to grip the southland once again.

Nim quickly looked back to Balamor and snapped his fingers. "Question number two! Its time is not now and never was before. It has no place, but it held today in store. The closer it gets the less it exists, yet some hope to live it while others wish they didn't. Death steals it, patience reveals it, but time is all that conceals it. No one knows what it will be, but every day it's next to see."

Balamor finished his notes and read them slowly, searching them for any patterns or references to spelling. Nothing stuck out of the seemingly illogical text. He finished his kabob while he quietly read.

Nim began looking up at the trees, impatiently tapping the tips of his fingers together.

The young mapmaker couldn't realize any obvious solutions. He began thinking out loud. "Judging by the first three lines it is definitely something abstract. Hmm... Death steals it, and 'it' is something that is not now... and never was before. So, it's not in the present and not in the past... '*But every day it's next to see.*' Hmm." He looked up toward the sky, through the lattice of leaves he saw the moonlit sky — it hit him. "Tomorrow... It's tomorrow," he said while scribbling down his answer.

Nim stretched and let out a long yawn, making Balamor second guess himself.

The young halfling's eyes widened and quickly he began reading back over the riddle.

Awkid stood up and looked at Balamor's notes for the answer, even if he couldn't help, it simply bugged him.

Nim finished his stretch and slowly strolled up to Balamor. The atmosphere became intense with each step. "I was beginning to think tomorrow would greet us before you figured it out. Ah! Speaking of tomorrow..."

Balamor and Awkid both let out a sigh while Nim looked around once more before removing a pocket watch from his vest.

It was made of brass and hung from a thin chain hooked to one of his buttons.

They could hear it ticking as Nim studied it for a moment. He turned around in a circle slowly, referring to the device in his hand as he spoke in hushed tones.

Awkid paid no mind to the gnome as he rubbed his fingers together above the fire; small cursed specks fell into the flames and burned up instantly.

Also sitting by the fire was Balamor whose full attention was on Nim.

As the small gnome checked his watch, the young Wisebeard tried to listen to him but he only made out the last few words — they were runewords. "... *Ehn vis payr*"

The words were eerily similar to those he heard the green-robed woman speak — words he once spoke himself.

The brass watch shook before its backside illuminated the palm of his hand in a familiar pale green hue. The same pale green glow Balamor saw the morning he left for the Mog Brush.

He realized there was a connection between the runewords and the colors he had seen before.

The glow slowly faded when Nim stopped and became strangely quiet.

"Last question." He winked again. "Where to go? Know where to be. Of course a place only few have seen. We all will go. We all may see. Who wins the race is a matter of speed. What I ask is simple, I swear, if two trek south to somewhere, who is someone going to know where?"

Balamor finished writing what he heard the gnome say. He studied the words quietly. He quickly gathered that they referenced Nim, Awkid and himself, but the rest was too ambiguous.

He looked up to speak to Nim when he realized he was walking away.

"Hey! Wait! Where are you going? I was about to answer! And what about the papers?" Balamor yelled out.

"A race is a race, Mr. Wisebeard," Nim replied.

"But where does this race end? How do I get there?" Balamor stood up and stepped a few feet forward as Nim walked further away.

"Know where!" Nim shouted as he disappeared beyond a lattice of trees.

"Nowhere? How—"

"You'll figure it out tomorrow. We need to rest," Balamor was cut off by Awkid.

"I'll take first watch," Balamor declared as he let out his bedroll and sat down to study his notes. "If I hear anything, I'll wake you."

"Very well," Awkid responded. He didn't think it was the best idea, but he could sense Balamor was too uneasy to sleep.

KNOW WHERE

The dwarf took his backpack off and laid it on the ground as a pillow. He carried no bedroll or hammock, waking up with nothing to pack meant less to forget in a hurry. He rested his eyes but his mind was not at ease in this wilderness.

Balamor looked over the riddle in silence.

Occasionally, he would add sticks and leaves to the fire to keep it burning.

The frigid air made him pull his robes close to him.

He scanned the page with his finger. "Nowhere..."

21

A FESTERING EVIL

875, Summer's 56th Midnight

he night sky was left unclouded after two vicious storms ripped through the southland.

It wasn't common in the summer to see such nasty weather, yet that picture was soon to change. This wouldn't mark the end to the roaring thunder and sheets of rain, no. The hand of a dark magic presented itself once again. A time long awaited by Nim and the few remaining bloodlines that stood against such evil.

They spent decades running and hiding from the east coast to the west, and with each passing year, Nim's paranoia worsened. Each dark spell would course through the mana that was his blood — making taps in the depths of his mind. Ever since the fall of Delsis, even the smallest of forces he felt were noted in his list, but rarely would he feel those of great power. Those that would send ripples through his veins and stand his hairs straight. Although rarity was no reason for them to go unmentioned. It was obvious there was an unchecked magic deep within the forests to the west.

Nim sat on a thick tree branch with a pipe in his mouth. Small clouds of smoke would billow from the canopy as he thought to himself.

The wind was calm this night, leaving his forest awkwardly silent. The creatures awoke when the night was at its peak, creeping, crawling, some even flying — though all lurked for their prey. Even Nim was no exception to their diet, having to fight them off plenty in his time.

Yet, the creatures were utterly silent this night, no scratches of bark or the slight flap of wings — *where were they?*

He paused and widened his eyes, dropping the pipe from his mouth as he felt it. Traces of magic belonging to more than his green-robed nemesis.

She wasn't alone.

Quickly he caught his pipe on the top of his foot and kicked it back up to his right hand. Reaching beneath his robes, he revealed a small scroll buckled with a leather strap. He left the pipe to his lips before he spread the scroll with his hands and held it tight. As he took a deep breath, two symbols etched into the wooden shaft of his pipe shined with a sky-blue light.

"Ahn Lim Dran." His words escaped with a cloud of smoke that rolled toward the scroll in his hands. Brushing up against its parchment surface, the smoke held it still in the air — unmoved by the wind like a weightless slab stone. He reached above himself with his left hand and yanked a handful of leaves from the branches. Quickly balling them in his fist, he spoke quietly once more, *"Onos yus, manas theas aer."*

His closed hand flashed with a green light before he opened it.

A small ink puddle remained at the center of his palm.

He lightly whistled twice before an opaline owl fluttered down to his shoulder. Grabbing a loose feather from the air, he dipped it into his palm.

"Awa jar," he said before writing his letter with haste. The ink upon the page glowed a ghostly green hue with each finished stroke he made. The message nearly filled the small scroll.

Friend,

I write you with urgency. The skies grow sick in the south with each passing day; sick with a darkness that hides in the brightest of sunlight. The forest is silent and I fear the storm we await is being conjured with the help of other hands. I know you, too, have felt what dwells in the west, but there is something we overlooked, or perhaps there is someone else against us. No names shall be mentioned in this letter should it fall into the wrong hands. We must see eye to eye on these matters as soon as the southern moon finds the ashes of the north.

I'm on my way,

- A friend

Seconds after he finished, the text flashed and quickly faded from the page. He rolled up the small scroll and tied it with the leather strap. Attached to the strap was a small cuff which Nim fastened to the owl's leg. Lifting his hand up to the sky the owl took off.

Nim climbed down from the tree and began his trek.

The owl flapped its wings against the air as it ascended into the night sky.

875, Summer's 56th Midnight

The lands were dark and the torchlight of scattered cities could be seen for miles. Small villages and magnificent kingdoms all surrounded by wilderness. The fog of the lowlands crawled up from the deep south and clung to the vegetation.

Heavy northern winds rattled the message on the owl's foot as it crossed the Faric.

A FESTERING EVIL

Twisting through the southland, the famous waters cascaded over the rocky cliffs of the Dragon's Head, down into Rayguth's Scar — a massive canyon whose walls bent the Faric back north. Starlight glistened off the rapids and pierced the dense foliage of southern woodlands.

Even in times of growing anticipation, the world looked strangely innocent from above. The usual acts of murder and larceny were almost forgettable at the sight of the gorgeous terrain.

Any other owl would think that the lands were simple, but this owl was a familiar. An extension of Nim that allowed him to travel beyond the bounds of his forest. This particular owl's spirit was gifted with ages of foresight and wisdom. Thanks to Nim, it was aware of the evils lurking the lands and the history it left behind.

The owl was also aware of this point in time. A time that would mark the beginning of a new age — a time when tales were written.

Of course, whoever strikes first is who determines how that tale begins.

In these times the only tale that remained was one spoken with distaste and horror — the Blood Wars. But few knew of the tale that was only decades old. A time when a great fortress was besieged and the Knights of Valorhorn were reduced to seven swords.

Passing over the Midlands, the owl glided toward the Great Divide, a colossal cliff made of jagged Blackstone. It stretched from the furthest east to the furthest west and stood hundreds of feet high. At its base was the grave of a large lakebed; plant life consumed it over the decades, slowly encroaching the island at the center.

It was there where the owl saw the ending of that forgotten tale — the ruins of Delsis.

Great walls made of Blackstone laid broken by the same darkness that threatened the present. Massive bastions were knocked from their foundations and scattered like toy blocks. The keep was a magnificent structure of ingenious defense, now left abandoned by its men — left to become a dark and wild place.

Over the years, the earth reclaimed the old fortress remains, erasing a great history along with it. Every stone and splinter of the famous island city was left in the desolate bed of Mystfalls Lake.

Nim's memory was stuck in the lustrous owl's mind, and so were the deep emotions attached — the downside of its magical nature. Those emotions belonged to another part of Nim, another soul he was slowly forgetting about. Memories from a man who lived in high spirits and worked with ornate scripture. Distant memories whose time was fleeting. The scent of books, the sound of that old clock ticking, and the numerous faces of those that passed through that majestic threshold. The blissful feeling of having a place amongst the most knowledgeable individuals of mankind.

However soothing the memories felt, Nim's owl had a mission and this man's past emotions would only hinder its focus. Only once did the familiar let the past conquer its mind.

Back then, those feelings led to a trap set by evil hands, by the mastermind that was Farah Lenook. She tried many times to lure Nim's owl off course, but she gave up on brash means of gaining information years ago.

Farah Lenook's game was now silent, divertive, and patient.

Unfortunately for the owl and its master Nim — it was working — and she knew that determination can leave someone blind to what's staring right at them.

Atop the crooked high tower of Delsis, the velvet green cloth of Farah's robes churned in the wind. From behind a broken parapet, she walked to the edge of the cylindrical mass of Blackstone bricks. Off in the distance, she gazed at the letter rattling in the wind.

A FESTERING EVIL

The owl's feathery wings fought the height of the Great Divide.

She opened her robes, revealing her pale lithe figure beneath. Runewords were drawn on her soft skin, signed in blood now dried and smeared. Her face was sharp and menacing, yet strikingly attractive — as it was with most elves. Arched eyebrows edged her aquamarine eyes and thin nose. Her black tapered lips were an accent to the straight jet-black hair that draped down her body.

A perfect emerald rested at the center of her chest. Thin twisted vines attached to it and wrapped around her neck. The flapping of wings came from within her robes before three small bats took off with haste.

They kept a far distance behind the owl, each of them waiting for it to deliver its message.

The ash covered ground of the Rhethis Barrens wisped through the air. Sheets of ash broke apart as they crashed against the spires of rock scattered across the ancient plains. The heavy winds did not let up in the north, making it nearly impossible to see, yet sight wasn't essential to Farah Lenook's winged scouts.

They listened to the prismatic owl as it disappeared through the dense cloud of ash below.

Minutes went by before a dim pulse of light pierced the storm and they could hear a faint ring from below.

In a flash, the winds ceased and the ashes slowly feathered to the ground.

Three figures stood in the middle of the barrens – two of them armored and wearing the red and black stag of the Kingdom Elkhart. One carried an ornate lantern as they accompanied a very tall man dressed in black robes.

The pearly owl perched atop his shoulder while he held the small scroll in his hands, a dim light emitting from its surface.

The bats listened to the man as he whispered to himself, *"Ahn Jar."*

The parchment flashed a white light, and he quickly strapped it to the owl and sent it off.

22

BEYOND VANISHING WOODS

875, Summer's 56th Midnight

hree figures headed south, the Black-robed Man taking point and moving quickly. His long strides were unmatched by his Elkhart counterparts, though they did their best to keep up. The bats followed them for a moment, still waiting overhead for the next move.

The men walked across the dead plains for a long while, treading over the barren wasteland leaving a trail of prints in the ashy dunes.

The sky was a blanket of milky stars cascading by. The two Elkhart soldiers had no clue where they were, or how long these plains stretched. The man they were with told them travel would be short and the pay well worth the trip. However, they didn't imagine finding themselves in a place like this.

The air was as dry as the ash they walked on; slight wisps of wind brushed against the trio as they traveled. The seemingly boundless terrain started to ache their legs. Perhaps hours went by but there was no way to tell.

One of the men would periodically wipe dust from the glass of his lantern as he walked beside his comrade.

Their eyes would lock every so often, but no words were spoken.

The man they traveled with had a reputation for knowing things before they unfolded. Where they were going would be left a mystery, for now all they could do was follow the tall stranger.

His personality was enigmatic to them, his age, complexion, even his intention were all presumed by the stories they heard. He was the man who spent his days in secret; a scholar of magic and ways of the old world. Some travelers said they met the Black-robed Man, witnessing the awesome power embodied in him.

Lightning would leap from his hands and devour the likes of demons and devilish beasts of only myth and legend. His voice would echo through stone and shatter it to dust. Some would say he single-handedly defeated the legendary Necromancer in the days of the Blood Wars.

Yet these two Elkhart men were skeptical of those tales until the robed one stopped and stared at them beneath his deep dark cowl. His right hand revealed a wand made of polished redwood while his left halted them.

There was a long silence as the Elkhart men waited nervously behind the Black-robed Man. They looked up at the dark sky, anticipating it might fall this night.

The Black-Robed Man was a sign of bad times ahead.

Stories of his legend filled the halls of the Elkhart garrison. He arrived when the world needed him, when an evil unbeknownst to them would strike. The fear of death crippled their minds and left their hands shaking.

The man holding the lantern wanted to speak but his words were lost.

In front of them, they watched as the air began to change and the ashy ground slowly morphed into earth. A blurry wall of green and brown shades filled an area several yards across before quickly snapping into focus. Plants and trees could be seen scattered across leaf-strewn soil.

The soldiers were in awe as the small patch of forest appeared from nothing.

The bushes quickly shuffled sending leaves into the air before a very colorful gnome rushed toward them. He stopped at the edge of the portal-like apparition.

"You know we forbid this! It's too dangerous to leave your forest unwatched. We can't risk the remaining scrolls!" The Black-robed Man contested.

"She's not alone Gantis, you know this!" Nim shouted as he stomped his foot. A fierce wind erupted from his sole.

The soldiers winced but Gantis stared Nim down.

A sense of apprehension held both of them still.

"We mustn't lose our heads! Don't surrender your patience at a time when it is needed most. You'll know when it's your time to act, but for now you must go," Gantis said as he looked the gnome in the eye, his words trailing off into an eerie silence.

Nim stared at him in silence. He knew Gantis was right, but he couldn't wait as their plan fell apart. His mind began to race, but he remained solemn as he turned away and walked. His ears twitched at the sound of slight taps from above the trees. The quiet amplified the smallest sounds. He cocked his head and closed his eyes to listen.

The Forest of Nim was beginning to fade from the Rhethis Barrens when the air became deathly still.

"No!" Nim cried out as he turned around.

A tremendous crack of thunder ripped through the air. Nim's vision was flooded with a bright white flash and a gust of wind knocked him off his feet. A high pitch rang his ears as he staggered to his feet and removed a gnarled root wand from his vest. At the edge of the forest was Gantis Jacs, his black robes slowly undulating as he stood behind a wall of violet light.

A stream of blue flames nearly blasted its way through the magical ward he conjured. Arcs of electricity snapped and sparked as the fire began to spill over its edges.

From behind Nim, the two soldiers gathered themselves and ran forward fumbling their weapons. They shuddered as they gripped with the incredible reality. They looked at each other with regret in their eyes,

"We need to go!" one of them yelled over the sound of spark and flame clashing as he scanned the area for a way out.

"We need to fight, nothing else!" the other responded, his hand gripping the leather-bound hilt of his blade. He grabbed the tunic of his comrade and looked him in the eye. A sense of determination fell over him and he turned his gaze to Nim, who was staring down at his wand, lost in the situation. "How does this end?"

The gnome raised his head and glared at the Elkhart man.

Gantis fell to one knee, and the barrier began to weaken.

Nim glanced back and forth between the men and Gantis as the flames engulfed the shield of light.

Stepping forward, he pointed his wand at the collapsing ward and shouted, *"Tyel Siras Lim!"*

The runewords that covered Nim's wand shined in white as the bright violet ward exploded outward. Electricity swallowed the now broken stream of blue fire.

Unshaken by the blast was the thin figure of Farah Lenook, and her long bone wand — smoke rising from its singed tip — aiming into the forest at the bane of her twisted ideals. Her green robes trailed in the ashy barrens, the cold grin beneath her dark cowl was hidden but Nim and Gantis knew it was all too certain. She lowered her wand and waited. The emerald Rootstone rested upon her chest, shining brightly against the darkness of the night.

Suddenly, one of the soldiers charged from behind Gantis, his long sword and steel kite shield gleaming in the moonlight as he sprinted forward.

Gantis held his comrade back as he screamed, "Kleo! No!"

The Elkhart swordsman was roaring with each step but Farah Lenook was unmoved by his battle cry. He held his sword high as he closed in on the green-robed woman. From above him, a small bat screeched as it dove through the air, black smoke churned from its body. In a split-second, the bat burst into a cloud of darkness and morphed into a thin gray-robed figure that crashed into the unsuspecting soldier.

The figure slammed him to the ground and stabbed the swordsman in the throat with a small dagger. The blood pooled around the hilt before the fatal wound glowed a pale green and his entire body was reduced to ash.

The remaining soldier broke from Gantis's grip with tears in his eyes and darted toward the gray-robed mystic. Holding his long sword low and his shield square in front of him he was fearless.

The gray-robed mystic turned around and blasted a bolt of blue fire at the enraged soldier but it glanced off of his kite shield and whizzed past Nim and Gantis.

In one quick motion, the soldier's gleaming blade lopped off the gray mystic's head. Blood erupted from his body as it collapsed to the ground.

The soldier's deadly strike left him breathless, but he was determined to finish what he started. He lifted his sword from the ground and charged his second blow with an angry holler.

Farah Lenook reached into her green robes and cast out three stones at the soldier. They lit up as they landed on the ashy surface and surrounded him. With a snap of her fingers, the Elkhart soldier stopped in mid-swing. Unable to move or even speak — he was paused — Farah Lenook held her pale wand to him. "So this is what good is, yes? You bring along some meager foot soldiers — one who is mediocre — to just watch them die for the 'greater good?' All thanks to what you wear around your neck!"

Gantis threw down three stones of his own and gripped his redwood wand.

They crossed into the Rhethis Barrens and shined.

Two more bats descended, becoming two other figures who landed next to their green-robed master.

One of them wore purple robes and held a short wooden staff. He pulled down his hood and pushed up his spectacles. The other wore crimson leather from chest to foot, a long black cloth covering the bottom half of his face. Both of them had sharp narrow features and long pointed ears. A green glare glossed over their eyes.

"The Rootstone... How?" Nim whispered.

"Nim, you must go," Gantis replied, not taking his focus off of Farah Lenook and her apprentices.

"You'll be perfect for Bear, now hold still," the leather-armored elf said as he revealed a silver dagger and stabbed it into the chest of the suspended soldier.

The soldier murmured as its clear glass hilt filled with his blood.

The elf ripped it from his body and waved his hand over him rhythmically as he bled out.

The soldier's groans began to escalate into screams as his body contorted into a new shape. His muscles grew in size and his bones shifted and stretched. The nightmarish scene continued to unfold as the two parties stared one another down.

Nim balled his fists and looked down to where his forest met the Rhethis Barrens. He knew he couldn't cross — he couldn't save the Elkhart soldier from his fate.

His screams began to grow deep along with the features of his face. Seconds later the transformation finished with the loud roar of the newly formed man. The stones shattered as the massive figure dropped the now short steel sword in its hand and flexed the armor from its body.

"Nim go now!" Gantis demanded as the giant blood familiar charged at him, the two dark mages at his side.

"No! You won't win this!" Nim shouted at him.

Gantis reached beneath his collar and yanked a small gold chain from his neck. Attached to it was the shard of a ruby, its red glow diminished as he turned and threw it back to Nim. "Go! Shield the Wisebeard!"

ZARDRAKEN'S CRYPT

The ruby necklace chimed through the forest border and landed in Nim's palms. Gantis turned around and swept his wand across the stones. A shock wave rushed forward and stumbled the charging figures.

Rising into the air from behind them, Farah Lenook pointed her wand toward Gantis.

"Gantis! No!" Nim yelled out as he watched the black-robed man cross into the Rhethis Barrens and everything faded into a quiet empty forest.

23

RIPPLES IN THE POND

875, Summer's 56th Midnight

Balamor's eyes jolted open at the sound of thunder, his bare feet shuffling the pile of ash and warm coals that was his fire.

His journal fell from his chest as he panicked. The trees shook with a forceful wind. He quickly scuttled to a tree and pinned himself to it, peeking his head out toward the wind.

The moonlit contours of dense flora swayed as the heavy gust passed. Leaves slowly flickered against the ground as the still darkness ensued.

Balamor looked around nervously. He rubbed the sleep from his eyes before he remembered his resting companion, Awkid Anvorbeard. He found the cursed dwarf lying at the foot of a tree, unmoved by the wind. If it wasn't for his occasional snore, Balamor would have mistaken him for a rock. The halfling looked around and reached for his dagger. He drew it as quietly as he could, but the quiet of the forest was unnervingly so.

His ears strained to make out something around him, but there was nothing, not leaves crunching or insects creaking. The air was thick with a dewy fog, so much so, he could taste it. He held his dagger tight and waited for something to appear or for his nerves to calm, whichever came first.

Minutes seemed to pass by the second before he heard distant shouts muffled by the fog.

He glanced between Awkid and the noises ahead but a scream in the distance made his decision. He crept forward without a sound, the moist soil dirtying his feet with each slow stride.

Through the thick fog he saw violet blue flashes and stopped behind the wet trunk of a tree. Unsure what was ahead, the young Wisebeard held a cold breath and continued to the next tree.

Minutes went by as he crept closer and closer toward the strange lights. Voices could be heard but their words were too muffled to make out clearly. He tried to focus when something heavy landed upon his shoulder and yanked him back. He tried to yell but a large hand covered his mouth and another held him tight.

"Easy, little mapmaker," Awkid whispered as he released his hands and held a finger to his lips.

Balamor tried to catch his breath as the dwarf looked around.

"Stay close," he whispered. With a wave of his hand, he crouched low and moved back to their camp.

Balamor followed behind him and quickly gathered his belongings. Voices could be heard yelling as he tried to keep up with Awkid who moved ahead.

Bushes whipped against the two adventurers as they started to jog, not knowing where they were going next.

"Kleo! No!" another distant voice cried out from behind them.

Balamor kept looking back, afraid of not knowing what was taking place behind them.

The fog illuminated once more in blue and faded into the dark.

The Wisebeard went forward through trees and thick bushes, now running behind his companion, but the dwarf was nearly impossible to keep up with in the forest. Awkid moved with ease and veteran swiftness, each step thoughtfully placed between exposed roots and crowded trunks. Balamor was losing his breath as he held his hand in front of him and batted the vegetation from his sight.

Ahead, the sturdy figure of Awkid quickly stopped and raised his right hand.

Balamor forced himself to a stop and slid through the dirt to the edge of a rocky cliff.

Awkid quickly reached for the robed halfling and yanked him back. Stones tumbled into the ghostly white haze that swallowed the land below.

The two adventurers posted themselves behind the trees, hugging the cliff side, their legs aching and burning in the intense cold. Their heavy breathing was the only sound they could hear. The peaks of warped dead trees were all that could be seen in the foggy land ahead.

"Wait, is it safer down there?" Balamor asked in an anxious whisper.

Awkid fished through his bag and retrieved a rope coil. He unraveled it as he spoke in plainly, "Are you willing to wait to find out?"

Balamor's eyes went wide.

Awkid secured the rope to the tree and tied it off with all of his strength. After looking back, he tossed the rest of the rope over the cliff edge.

"Wait! What about what's up here?" Balamor whispered sharply with his body stiff against the tree trunk. Faint echoes of men screaming slowly waved through the fog.

"What about it? Now, let's go before we end up like them." Awkid replied. He grabbed the rope with both of his hands and began his descent. The surface of his earthen palm grinded to dust as he slid down.

A gust of wind blew past Balamor as he hesitated. When he looked down, Awkid was gone. In that short moment, Balamor felt the weight of his journey. He glanced back again at the forest gloom before sheathing his weapon. He took a deep breath as he grabbed the rope and carefully lowered himself off the rocky cliff side. His hairy feet walked against the cold stony surface while his hands guided him down the rope.

He wanted to look down for Awkid but his fear of heights had his eyes fixed on the cliff wall.

The air was becoming numbingly frigid as he got closer to the ground. Thick green moss and twisted vines clung to the jagged stone face.

The wind churned heavily once more, making Balamor grip the rope harder and squeeze his eyes shut. His feet slipped, and he swung from side to side. Spinning around, he slammed into the wall and shrieked in pain.

His eyes opened to see the rope quivering below and the stout figure of Awkid still putting hand under hand, impervious to the cold wind.

Balamor closed his eyes for a moment before he continued the climb downward, his face and hands now riddled with scrapes and bruises.

The night sky was still infant as they resumed their long trek, and Balamor could feel the lack of sleep in his eyes. He reached the end of the rope and let down his feet.

A shock shot up his spine as he entered a cold body of water.

He removed his backpack and held it above the surface of the murky waters.

Awkid grabbed a roll of bandage from his bag and wrapped his clay limb starting from the fingers. He finished quickly and unbuckled the lantern from his backpack. Flipping open the brass capping, he removed his flint and steel. With two quick strikes, the wick ignited and illuminated the surrounding bog in a warm yellow shade. He locked the brass cap with a small latch and turned to Balamor who was nearly chest deep in water.

"We move slowly now," Awkid said quietly.

Balamor nodded in agreement and unsheathed his silver dagger once again.

His teeth began to chatter as they walked through the disgusting waters.

Awkid held the lantern in front of him and searched the dreary swampland for any signs of danger.

Crows cawed as oversized insects winged through the air and bore holes through the plant life. Balamor occasionally swatted them from his view as he gazed at the strange place.

The trees were twisted and abated with disease, their leafless gray bark overgrown with moss and the strangest mushrooms Balamor had ever seen. The gills beneath their large wart caps glowed a dim blue light, casting an eerie mood over the daunting bog.

Balamor drew close to the peculiar fungus, his hands reaching out for it when a large insect landed on its surface. Balamor pulled his hand back and observed the bug.

Its four translucent wings buzzed before it pierced the mushroom with its long mandible. The mushroom lost its glow and quickly deflated before the mosquito-like bug took off, its clear abdomen filled with a bright blue liquid as it flew into the fog — small blurry flickers of blue surrounded the marsh.

Balamor kept moving forward behind Awkid who kept his eyes peeled and his ears alert. He'd been here before, but the Black-robed Man was with him then. The mystic told Awkid something dreadful lived here, something that was someone a long time ago. It lived off dank carcasses and the insects they bred.

It was a long time ago — twenty-six years to be exact — when Awkid first trekked these parts of the world and when the Black-Robed Man saved his life.

He didn't know back then, but now, he knew — that musky smell that turns sour in your throat, the baritone croak that never seems to fade, the ripples in the water. He knew what the signs were when looking for the one they called Du'gahr, and none of them were present, yet.

The sun wouldn't show for hours.

RIPPLES IN THE POND

Balamor could feel the particles of dirt, limp grass, and mortal remains brush up against his legs. Dirty bones and skulls of men littered the placid water, once belonging to souls and now left as a clear and daunting sign. Balamor's heart began to beat against his chest as his curiosity suddenly melted into fear.

Awkid found a small patch of land rooted with three trees and motioned Balamor to follow.

They slowly made it through a dense pad of cattail grass and walked out of the murky water.

Awkid kneeled at the foot of a twisted tree, covering a large blotch of its bark was a thick iridescent slime. Awkid rubbed the cold substance between his thumb and forefinger. "It's saliva," he said as he looked at Balamor.

"From what?" Balamor asked.

Awkid wiped his hand onto his tunic before he answered, "From Du'gahr, The Blind Prince."

"The Blind Prince of the Steel Isle? Didn't he die in the Blood Wars?" Balamor whispered. His only knowledge of the time was from old journals, textbooks, and poetic tribute to the name.

"Enough questions. Stay quiet, we're not far now," Awkid commanded along with a gesture forward.

Balamor followed without a word, but in the back of his mind he tried to find his own answer. He only knew what was said about Du'gahr in writing, from first-person accounts of his triumphs to the old land claims made by the Swords of the Steel Isle.

They nearly conquered the entire southwest up until the start of the Blood Wars. It was then when the Kingdom of the Steel Isle fell from a war on both sides.

Balamor read poetry and was told nursery rhymes exemplifying Du'gahr's rise and fall but he knew anything he was told had loose ends and blanks to fill.

He wondered how a man could live for centuries here, drowned in a depressive land that seemed to feed off itself. Du'gahr especially.

The Steel Isle was a place of tropic scent and crystal-clear beaches in the middle of the Shining Sea.

Balamor knew the southern swamps were no place to live for a man of the Steel Isle, let alone a famed prince. But he was here, he didn't doubt that, and what kept him here for so long had to be against his will.

The muddy ground was unpleasant to cross as the two adventurers walked with clothes dripping wet.

Awkid held his right arm high to avoid the water, a weakness that worried Balamor a great deal. Until now, Awkid seemed unstoppable. He was a thick-skinned veteran of the land with the ability to control an awesome power, but in this swamp, that power met deadly odds with the waterlogged soil.

The water to their left splashed making them both jump.

Balamor turned with his dagger in hand to see a large tadpole push through the muddy water.

Their soaked bodies slowly crept across the wetland. A large tree was knocked over toward another patch of land; they looked at each other and both nodded.

Awkid moved to the splinted trunk. He saw its surface was grown with more mushrooms and covered in the same iridescent spit. He strapped the lantern to his backpack before crawling on all fours across the downed tree, his bandaged arm carefully avoiding the slime that splattered over its bark.

The moment was tense as Balamor watched.

Steel-blue eyes scoured the foggy marsh while awaiting his turn.

Awkid finished his crawl after minutes of agonizing suspense, now waiting for the young mapmaker to join him.

The Wisebeard returned his bag to one shoulder and began to cross. He gripped onto the spongy moss with his hands and slowly moved forward. He glanced at Awkid ahead, who was hardly visible. The dwarf looked to his left and right as he fanned Balamor forward.

The halfling began to pick up his pace when his hands slipped in the gooey substance across the bark. He yelped as he grabbed onto a broken branch and yanked his leather backpack before it fell.

The chirping of bugs died down instantly and the mighty sound of a whip echoed through the mist.

The young halfling was frozen, now halfway across the fallen tree.

Awkid knew the sound and immediately huddled next to the closest trunk. He felt a deep vibration grow into a long guttural call.

Balamor quickly pulled himself atop the fallen tree and looked down at the water. Large ripples waved across its surface with the sound of a distant thud before fading to nothing.

Balamor looked for Awkid but the fog was too thick, his breaths becoming still when he looked back at the water below.

The large round snout of a frog poked through the littered surface, its two bulbous eyes — ghostly white with cataracts — stared at the robed halfling with nostrils flaring.

Balamor held his breath as the creature rose from the swamp on his legs to the height of the tree bridge. Its spiny skin was a dirty shade of green and spotted with gray and black patches. Balamor couldn't take his eyes off of the monster that stared him down. Some grotesque figure of a frog-like man fitted with the remnants of rusty scale mail and wearing the Twin Pillars of the Steel Isle. A light blue tongue crept from the monster's wide mouth and slowly brushed over the fallen tree trunk.

The smell of death made Balamor's stomach turn. He closed his eyes and fought to hold still when suddenly something splashed into the water.

The frogman whipped back his tongue before peeking over his shoulder. "Hm, hmmm... Well, well!" he said with a half-smile, his smoky voice trailing with a hiss. "Who dares disturb Du'gahr? Don't be shy... It has been... awhile since Du'gahr has had any visitors." He rolled his tongue and blinked his blind eyes.

24

A BAD TASTE

875, Summer's 56th Midnight

S*aliva* covered Balamor's feet as he continued to inch across the trunk. His eyes fixed on the blind prince as he crawled hand over hand.

Still Awkid was nowhere to be seen, but Balamor knew the distraction was his.

The sky was pitch black and everything but Balamor stood still. He felt like he was days away from the land only yards in front of him. Slight scrapes of his dagger against the dead bark shook his nerves. He paused as he watched the frogman turn his head back.

Balamor jumped from the log with blistering speed, adrenaline overwhelming him in a split second. He landed short of the island and splashed into the water, paddling his feet as fast as his legs allowed him.

The loud sound of a whip cracking shook the hideous bog as Du'gahr speared his blue tongue through the water and latched onto Balamor's foot. The halfling whizzed backward through the water before slamming into the fallen tree bridge. He stabbed into the bark with his silver dagger and struggled to hold on. His fingers began to slip when a loud roar came from across the water.

In a fiery flash, Awkid's brass lantern crashed into the blind frog prince, its flames exploding across his slimy face and singeing his wiry mustache.

Balamor felt his foot come loose and quickly yanked his dagger from the tree.

A BAD TASTE

Awkid ran toward him and rushed him ashore, water splashing in their mad escape from Du'gahr.

They both sprinted wildly across the wetland terrain, oblivious to what direction they were headed. Behind them they heard the enraged croak of Du'gahr followed by a loud splash and the snapping of trees. The wind whistled past their ears as they ran through the swamp.

"This way!" Awkid shouted.

The two adventurers cut left just before the cursed frog could pounce on them.

His powerful hind legs crushed the surrounding trees and stomped into the muddy soil.

The sky split open with a crack of thunder and rain started to wave across the misty swampland.

Balamor followed close behind Awkid as he glided over the root-torn soil. The bandages that protected Awkid's arm became damp from the rain but he didn't stop for a second.

Du'gahr tore through the wild bog with unmatched speed. In a few long strides, he nearly caught up with the adventurers.

They both ran across a shallow body of water in a panic.

Balamor fell at the edge of a dirty shore, broken bones and pieces of wood piercing his feet and hands. Lying beside him was the skeleton of a fallen warrior, hollow eye sockets staring at him. He jumped back from the remains just before they were crunched by the webbed feet of the blind prince.

Now overtop of Balamor, the frogman croaked once more and twiddled his knobby fingers. "Hmm, hm, hmm!" He took a mighty inhale and nearly stole the air from Balamor's lungs. "As you know... halflings have a rare scent, but do you ever wonder how it is they taste?" he asked before flicking his blue tongue upon his mouth. His body language was strangely calm; a slight imbalance in his stature made him unpredictable. Twisting the end of his narrow mustache he continued, "It's a thought that crosses your mind when you're like me. Imagine the sound bones make when they snap... it's fascinating, really."

Balamor wanted to speak, but his mouth was motionless. The hilt of his dagger numbed his hand.

Wielding a rusty battle-axe, Awkid delivered a stunning blow to the monstrous frog prince. Blackened blood spluttered through the air and stained the dwarf's green tunic. He wound up a heavy overhand swing as the creature stumbled back into the water. Awkid's loud roar echoed through the swamp after he struck once more. Du'gahr dropped into the water while Awkid growled. Broken boney hands and cobwebs still clung on to the old battle-axe, fresh blood now coating its surface.

Balamor quickly got up and ran as a loud thrash of water erupted from behind him.

Awkid Anvorbeard watched the slimy frogman jump out of the water with tar-like blood seeping from the gash across his face.

The dwarf charged at the blind prince and attacked him again. The heavy battle-axe sliced through the air and sparked against Du'gahr's rusted chest plate with a glancing strike.

With incredible strength and speed, the blind prince of the Steel Isle grabbed Awkid Anvorbeard by the throat and lifted him from the ground. Du'gahr's blue tongue slithered from his mouth and down across Awkid's face to the cursed limb that fought against the frogman's grip. His tongue returned in a whip of saliva before he began a snickering laugh.

"Ah, Yes... We meet again, Mr. Dwarf Dirt. Now tell me, have you come to finish me off? Necromancy is contagious isn't it!" he said with a devilish smirk. "It seems you're just a bit too, short." His grip began to tighten and Awkid started to panic.

He felt Du'gahr's large hand begin to crush his windpipe and a numbing sting flow down his legs. With little strength remaining, he swung the old battle-axe. Its rusty blade dug into the frogman's side making him shriek in pain.

He released the cursed dwarf and cupped his webbed hands over the wound.

A BAD TASTE

Awkid fell to the ground and rolled to his feet, his weapon splashing into the muddy water.

Du'gahr unsheathed two wide crescent blades from his lower back and switched his stance into a wide crouch. He licked his lips before a wide grin crept across his face. The gash on his cheek was now sealed with a thick black scab that stretched as he croaked.

Awkid started to move in a circle slowly, his green eyes focusing on the blind prince who joined in the standoff.

Balamor was without a plan as he watched his companion face off Du'gahr, who was nearly three times the size of the dwarf. There was no obvious way to help Awkid take down the blind prince. He looked around the gloomy swamp but every path was smothered by the cold fog.

Awkid was surrounded by water and muddy soil without a weapon.

Du'gahr was facing down his prey and fully in his element. The swamp was his lonesome lair and its nasty air corrupted his once human mind.

Awkid's steps were thoughtfully placed, but he had no obvious plan. His clay arm was useless to him and his opponent sensed his hesitation to strike first.

Du'gahr's cloudy eyes blinked twice before his gullet expanded with a gurgling croak.

The air was uncomfortably thick as Balamor took a chattering breath.

Du'gahr leaped forward and slashed at Awkid with his rusty curved blades, but Awkid's steps were clearly calculated and took the frog prince by surprise. A second and third attempt failed and the famed warrior's eyes twitched. His slimy mouth puckered in frustration with each sly maneuver Awkid made.

The dwarf glanced back as he moved closer to the edge of the murky pond.

The old battle-axe was only feet away with its cloth-bound hilt sticking out of the water.

ZARDRAKEN'S CRYPT

The gripping tension was suddenly broken when a distant yell resonated through the quiet swamp, but the words were smothered by the fog.

Du'gahr diverted his attention toward the noise when Awkid quickly made a dash for his weapon. The water thrashed as the dwarf clutched the war-torn hilt of the axe with his wrapped hand and lunged it toward Du'gahr.

Balamor heard the blade part the thick air before it ended in an abrupt pop. The old axe collided with the ground and broke apart. Dark blood spewed across the ground from Du'gahr's right arm; beneath him was his webbed hand — now departed clean from the wrist — twitching with the crescent blade in its grasp.

A split second of silence was followed by a tremendous roar.

Du'gahr slashed wildly at Awkid with his remaining blade but Awkid parried the heavy strikes with the broken handle of his axe. Wood fragments chipped away revealing a fresh red layer of oak beneath. The mad frogman battled back and forth with the cursed dwarf.

His exposed wrist gushed tar-like blood across the swamp as he hacked through dead brush with each failed attempt. The fight tired Awkid's legs and turned his clever footwork into a breathless stagger. He stumbled next to the blind prince and out of the littered water, his lungs feeding the fiery pit within his chest.

He fell to his knee and shrieked in pain as Du'gahr twisted his slimy figure to face the dwarf and walked toward him.

The black scab that formed over his wrist started to bulge and crack apart. A nascent hand slowly broke through, trembling and covered in a thick iridescent slime — its pale skin began to harden. After three earthshaking strides, Awkid's exhausted body stood up and held the whittled axe handle in front of him.

Du'gahr quickly slashed the weapon from the dwarf's weary grip and lifted him from the ground with his newly formed hand. His lips curled into a disgusting grin as he flipped his blade slyly in his left hand. Rage ran through his eyes and into his vile words. "It would leave a bad taste in my mouth."

He grinned before jabbing the crescent blade through Awkid's stomach.

Balamor couldn't speak. He wanted to scream but the fear in his gut pushed him deeper into the swamp. He took several shaken steps back before falling against the foot of a twisted tree, crushing a patch of the strange glowing mushrooms.

He watched Awkid's mouth gape with blood, each slight effort for breath a gurgling struggle. Even from afar, he could see disdain in Awkid's eyes.

Du'gahr snickered before tossing the limp body of his opponent into the shallow water.

A large splash consumed the dwarf and the strength that defined his character vanquished.

Balamor's eyes began to well up as he fought with himself over what he now felt were naïve aspirations. The closer he was to his destination, the worse the toll it took on his mind and now on the lives of others.

Halflings, they're not meant for this world, not for this type of burden.

He couldn't think of anything else. He should have known Awkid couldn't win, not without the help of that crazy old man, whoever he was. It didn't matter. There was no chance he would amount to someone like that man.

All he could muster was cowardice and far-fetched imaginations.

Du'gahr stared at the dwarf as he lay in the water, his clay arm dissolving with each passing second. For a moment, he looked around and took a few deep breaths, round nostrils flaring while his tongue flicked between his lips. He turned his dead gaze to his left where Balamor was hiding.

Warm breath slowly escaped Balamor's lungs and pushed against the fog.

The blind prince scanned the area with his nose sniffing heavily. His webbed feet stomped into the mud and shook ripples across the water.

Balamor waited for his last moments to come to an end but there was nothing. It seemed that Du'gahr was lost. The young Wisebeard reached for his dagger when he felt a bright blue muck covering its sheath along with his tattered brown robes. Spreading the blue substance between his fingers he cringed at its pungent scent. Balamor looked at the monstrous frog prince and back at the putrid slime.

Du'gahr stood still with his nose held high, searching for Balamor's scent. A sinister grin crept across his slimy face before he shouted, "You won't last long!"

Du'gahr started laughing before crawling into the water and swimming away silently.

Balamor blinked his eyes as if to shake off a dream.

Seconds passed before a groggy cough pulled him from shock. He grabbed his knife and slowly crawled across the swamp. Balamor arrived at the edge of the water where he saw his companion, Awkid, had washed ashore.

His blood filled the water around him with red, and his right arm was reduced to muddy bones. Short stuttered breaths meant he was alive, but for how long?

Balamor felt a surge of energy run through his body. He reached for the dwarf and pulled him from the water, then, he dragged him to a patch of the strange mushrooms and yanked four from the ground. He cut into one of them and squeezed out the blue muck onto himself and Awkid. Returning the others to his backpack, he continued through the swamp without thinking where to go. The dwarf was heavy, but Balamor was determined to drag him somewhere safe.

A BAD TASTE

Adrenaline sent a numbing sting to his feet and hands as he hurried Awkid through the fog, avoiding the water as best he could.

His eyes snapped to his left where he heard a distant scream and a loud whip crack. He didn't stop, not even at the thought of someone else in danger. Whoever it was might prove just as dangerous to him.

Balamor could trust no one else, and it was a feeling that scared him.

He looked at Awkid's arm, now reduced to darkened bones rattling against the rooted soil.

Everything went wrong. That was all he could think about as he pulled his friend to whatever safety he could find.

For a while there was nothing but the silent dreariness of the bog around him. Soggy footsteps through dead shrubs and bone-littered earth made his legs burn. Awkid was unconscious, blood stained his beard, and a slight wheezing came from his lungs.

Balamor's back slammed into an unexpected rocky surface and he winced in pain. Behind him was a sharp crag of rock protruding from the ground with a small mouth to a cave carved out. Long dead grass and weeds entangled the entrance.

With a few slices of his dagger, Balamor broke through and pulled Awkid inside.

25

SEALED BY MAGIC

875, Summer's 57th Twilight

arrow stone walls tugged at Balamor's robes as he dragged the limp body of Awkid Anvorbeard through the rocky passage.

Darkness consumed its confines; the sounds of hushed footsteps and breathing were all that could be heard.

Balamor reached for the wall to feel for an opening when his fingers brushed over a series of strange circular holes. He froze in his tracks.

His calves were burning as he crouched to the floor with caution. Swiping across the holes quickly with his open hand, he tried to trigger the possible trap. He yanked it back quickly, but there was nothing, not even a sound. He proceeded slowly, dragging Awkid down the narrow interior with sharp breaths in his lungs.

The adrenaline began to fade just as he could feel an opening in the wall to his left.

With the rest of his strength, he pulled the dwarf through the passage and collapsed. His lungs were churning with cold air when he sat up and reached his hands out in front of him.

The cold darkness left Balamor without sight as he searched for Awkid's body. Minutes passed before he could find the dwarf's boots. He reached beneath the laces of one of them and quickly removed the flint and steel that was tucked away.

Tearing a large strip of cloth from his robes, he hurriedly wrapped it around the blade of his dagger.

Several strikes against the fire-steel and the cloth ignited. A small flame illuminated the room in warm scarlet and revealed the sharp contours of the walls.

Blood rushed from the deep wound in Awkid's stomach as he laid on the jagged stone floor.

Balamor quickly put the flint and steel in his bag and cupped his small hands over the wound.

He pressed against it but the bleeding was too heavy. Blood seeped through the cracks between his fingers and stained his hands red.

Awkid's breaths became wheezy and scarce.

Time was running short as Balamor scrambled to save the life of his cursed friend.

The dwarf's right arm laid under sloppy wraps trailing in a streak of mud. Pale yellow bones were still connected from his shoulder to his fingers, lying on the floor motionless.

Balamor looked through his leather backpack frantically, and under a mess of spare veggies and papers he found his runes. Three stones whose surfaces were inscribed with a symbol of the otherworldly Runesong. There was only one of them Balamor needed, *Raji*. The flames nearly devoured the cloth around his dagger by the time he held the stone disk in his palm. His nerves sent his hands into an uncontrollable shiver, sweat gathering upon his bushy brow line.

Slowly he placed one of his hands over Awkid's wound and let out a long breath. *"Raji."*

The cavernous room flashed in yellow light before settling into a tender glow within the bounds of the ancient symbol. Cracks slowly stretched from within the deep grooves as the rune shook with some wild force raging to escape.

Starting from the tips of his fingers, Balamor felt his body begin to tighten. A mystical zephyr waved against his robes and the curly locks of his hair. His steel-blue eyes began to roll back to bloodshot white as Awkid's wounds sealed shut. Cuts and bruises diminished to normal flesh and the blood pouring from his gut ceased.

Balamor's short frame fell back against the cave wall and slumped with exhaustion.

Weakness plagued his arms and legs and the frigid air shuttered his breath. The fire was but a mere flame smoldering ash around his silver dagger.

Balamor began to cough as he leaned against the pale interior. A trace of energy surged through his blood and shook him to the cold stone floor. His foggy vision suddenly cleared and his hairs stood straight with a great gasp of air. Balamor's eyes darted around him, the slight red glow of embers shining off the silver blade of his dagger.

Quickly, he moved to the center of the room and grabbed its porcelain hilt. Ignoring the heat, he waved the remaining light across the dwarf.

Awkid's stocky figure laid on the ground, blood soaking his tunic but his breathing returned to normal.

He moved his hand to the left of the cavern and the small patch of light revealed the broken leg of a skeleton. Balamor jumped before slowly tracing it from the foot to the shattered end of the tibia. His hand moved the faint light toward the wall where the dry bones of a man were slouched against a broken pole-arm.

There was a torn white banner draped against the wall, on its surface an elaborate black crest of a cane and a sword crossed below a curved horn.

Who was this man?

Balamor contemplated the figure, thick rust consuming the metal plating of his heavy armor and flakes littering the long white tunic beneath.

Then, Balamor caught a glimpse of a satchel and the last bit of cloth around his dagger burned out. He sheathed his blade and slowly felt for the old leather backpack. Shifting the arms and torso of the rattling corpse, Balamor could finally slip the bag free.

The darkness made the cold bone chilling and the decayed leather felt coarse against his hands as he searched the contents with haste.

Long moments passed before Balamor emptied the flag bearer's backpack onto the cave floor. The sound of metal jingling and a heavy wooden thud echoed through the cave. Balamor reached into his bag and removed the flint and steel once more.

He struck against the fire-steel, spawning cherry red sparks and flashes of bright light.

Balamor examined the items with each strobe, hoping there was something of use.

The first was a small pouch made of fine ring mail, and inside was a strange black stone. Balamor rubbed its polished surface with his fingers, surprisingly, no symbols appeared. The black stone and ring mail bag made its way into his backpack before Balamor moved on to the second item, a small amber-shaded chest.

It was made of sturdy vespine oak and coated in a thick layer of lacquer. The flat metal latch holding it shut was locked. Balamor shook it next to his ear, a few small thuds verifying something was inside. He placed it into his bag before striking the fire-steel again, the flash of light revealing a bundle of dark metal rods.

Balamor leaned closer and struck again, the white light splashing against the cave interior and the surface of what he now gathered were torches of some sort. He grabbed them from the ground and placed two in his backpack. He felt its smooth surface and at the very end the wet bristles of a wick.

Placing it back on the ground, he grabbed the flint and steel and struck once more. Sparks ignited the wick end of the black steel rod and filled the area with a fierce blue light.

Balamor retrieved the strange torch from the ground and looked around the small cavern. There were two narrow exits, one to his left and another with a streak of blood and dirt trailing off to his right. He looked at Awkid and immediately noticed the pale bones of his right arm.

Kneeling next to the dwarf, he checked his stomach but the hole in Awkid's bloodied tunic showed no wound. He slumped back in confusion and placed his torch on the ground.

Staring at the ceiling, he remembered the first time he spoke the word *Raji*. He could still see his wounds diminish before his eyes, like nothing ever happened. But this time was different, and Awkid's curse was the reason for it. Balamor could only wonder the logic behind this power and why it would reject Awkid's limb.

It was beyond the young Wisebeard's knowledge.

Slowly his eyes shut and his mind clouded with sunken esteem.

The days that passed all seemed like a blur and Balamor felt stuck in a trance of inconsiderable burden.

875, Summer's 57th Dawn

His eyes slowly opened to study the fiery blue torch in his hand. Strange, yet common amongst the souvenirs he salvaged on his mission. The steady flame suggested its make was of high craft, but its age was mysterious.

Balamor's steel-blue eyes shifted to Awkid's arm, the dirt and bandage surrounding its bones was now dry from the fire. The consequences of such dark magic frightened him. He looked down at his bag, its contents were a mess — his map, his runes, his grandfather's spellbook.

They were all just vague questions with the same deep ties to the magic that cursed Awkid Anvorbeard. Questions with answers veiled in ancient history.

The torchlight remained undisturbed as he contemplated his journey and the meaning behind the runes. He opened his journal and flipped through its pages.

The coarse parchment leaves were smudged with dirt and furled at the edges. His sketches and encounters were defined in shaky lead print. There were notes of texts from the old world to the accounts of lost roads traveled by men of myth and legend. All of them from centuries steeped in mystery and magic.

These tales of blood and virtue ran parallel with the crusade against magic. Of course, they were written by the famed scholars of Anstia and he expected the truth in their words was lacking if not completely absent.

He flipped past a few more pages of his journal — sketches covered the parchment and this time they were the symbols he copied from the ambiguous text, *Runes and Runewords*. Ten inky signs he had since his last night in the Raehl.

The pages flipped between his fingers before the covers clapped shut in a plume of dust.

Balamor could only depend on himself to uncover the truth behind it all.

After a moment, he removed the leather upholstered book his grandfather gave him and laid it on the ground along with his journal; he then studied the mysterious six-page spellbook.

The circled dash of *Theas* was dug into its cover above its label, but five other words were missing symbols.

A snap of his fingers seemed to ignite the clockwork in his mind and he flipped his journal to the previous page. Placing his hand over the first symbol — two points divided by a vertical line — Balamor gazed at the spellbook, unsure what to choose.

"... *Aer?*" he whispered.

He stared at the page but there was nothing. Unconvinced, he spoke again, this time with command.

"*Aer.*"

A slight echo bounced through the small cave.

Nothing, not even tingling in his hands. He moved on to another word, this time the first in the series of six.

"*Tyel.*"

The sketched page of his notebook crumpled and disintegrated to ash as another echo carried away — but this time he felt it.

It was a different feeling than before. His entire body felt weightless and his mind was quickly overwhelmed. The six-page spellbook jolted open to its first page, and three rows of pure white runewords nearly blinded him.

The light shined against the cave in a great flash and diminished to a faint glow within the symbols.

The young Wisebeard grew a pounding headache and could barely catch himself on one knee. He staggered to his feet when the light from the fire became too bright for his eyes.

Shielding his vision, Balamor hurried toward the metallic torch on the floor and stomped out the flames with his calloused heels.

The pitch-black darkness brought dead silence to the cave.

Balamor was only inches away from Awkid's resting body when he heard something coming from down the tunnel to his right.

In a rush, Balamor grabbed everything from the ground — first was both of his books, then the torch, and most importantly his unconscious companion. Gripping behind the collar of his green tunic, Balamor dragged the heavy dwarf into a small dark crevasse within the stone cavity.

The skeletal remains of the flag bearer crashed to the cold floor. The shuffling of footsteps and wheezy breaths were quick to hush when a shrill voice crashed against the walls.

"Did you hear that? What was that?" There was a pause and the man started up again, his voice trailing with his movements. "Damn these eyes. Light a torch damn it! We'll be de—" A series of spastic coughs interrupted his words.

Balamor removed his brown robes and waved them over him and Awkid as the men drew closer. He took a quick glance toward the tunnel, warm torchlight illuminating the walls and the floor where the streaks of Awkid's blood were still fresh and easily noticed by the figures of two men.

Both of them wore robes, but one of them stood out. Sharp pointed ears were nearly a spectacle to Balamor's eyes if it weren't for the imminent danger.

He knew too well, and after a second take he was certain, this was an elf.

Balamor's steel eyes peeked through a slit in his robes, fixated on the duo only yards away.

The other figure was surely human. Within his right hand was a small vial and, in his left, a makeshift torch. He passed it to his counterpart and unsheathed a small dirk from his side. Perching himself over the trail, he skimmed Awkid's blood into the mouth of the glass vial with its sharp edge.

"This is fresh, follow it," the man claimed in a brash tone of voice as he stuffed the vial into a small leather satchel.

The two figures followed the trail for a few feet before the elven man broke course and began examining the strange walls of the cavern. Just as Balamor had felt earlier, a myriad of holes covered large swathes of these walls.

The elf peered into one of the deep pits, an unsettling darkness stared back, seemingly fit with never-ending depth.

The human figure grabbed the torch from his comrade and kept forward. "Do you wish for death? It really does amuse me," he said to the elf who was quick to respond as he followed behind.

"I never let my death stray too far from my will, but this is no set snare. This is something beyond that..." His pointed fingers brushed across the series of deep inky pockets.

The human figure held the torch in front of him. The upper half of his face was obscured by the hood of his gray robes.

Balamor held his breath as the light from the man's torch entered the rigid cavity where he was hidden.

What sounded like the squeaking of mice made the man turn his head. At first, it was subtle but his elven companion was already on the move. The torchlight waved wildly as the elf rushed past him.

Almost instantly, the subtle noises grew into a raucous shriek that echoed through the cavern from within the deep holes surrounding them.

The gray-robed stranger took off after his elven partner while the cave was roaring with high-pitched mayhem.

Balamor watched the torchlight fade off to his left.

The figures of small bat-like beings poured from the walls with tar dripping from their bodies. Their screaming escalated as they smashed into each other in a disorganized attempt to fuse together. Moving in hive-like patterns, their twisted frames winged into position and formed the silhouette of a man.

Balamor reached into his bag and felt for his runes, rummaging through all but one, a square stone with a triangle of three points sunken into its surface. He had no plan nor the time to make one.

He needed to wake Awkid.

They needed to do something.

He reached for the dwarf beside him and began to shake his left arm.

More of the creatures were screeching and running through the tunnels madly. Balamor started to panic. He pushed against Awkid's chest and clutched onto the rune in his left hand. The dwarf would not wake. Balamor looked down at the remains of the cursed arm and placed his hand over it. He knew that he didn't know magic, but it didn't faze him. He closed his eyes and focused, and everything seemed to disappear.

The magical words he spoke once before were the focus of his mind – words he still didn't understand. *"Ehn vis firos."*

. .
. .

Balamor's eyes exploded open, pale green light shined from them. Snapping into his focus was yet another strange vision.

As if he were seeing from someone else's perspective, a woman whose green cloak was billowing against heavy gusts of rain as she sprinted forward.

She was running from something. Balamor could sense that terrible fear beating in his own heart.

The terrain was mountainous, deep valleys disturbed by small rocks tumbling as they traveled a narrow road. Lightning flashed, momentarily blinding him.

His vision returned to see a tall man wearing long black robes reaching his hand toward him. His face was hidden but a deep voice commanded him. "Balamor, give me the scrolls! We have not time!"

Balamor found himself lying in the dunes of gray ash whipping in the winds of a ferocious storm. He started to back away from the tall man as he looked around him. Streaks of fire trailed humongous stones through the air accompanying the sounds of devastating battle. He glanced down to see the same three scrolls from his vision along the Faric. Each of them ornately designed with brass knobs and each tied with a different colored ribbon. One red, one blue and one yellow. However, this time he noticed something different; another ribbon, absent of any scroll. Its emerald green color was contrasted by a deep red stain across its surface.

"Balamor! The scrolls!" The black-robed man yelled. *Balamor glanced up at him and suddenly a name came to mind,* "Gantis?"

Before the strange man could respond, Balamor's vision faded to darkness.

26

SCRIVENKIN

875, Summer's 57th Dawn

Chains rattled from deep within the vestigial confines of the Whispering Tree. Down below the vast rainforests of Wynspur — where the ancient roots bore holes through bedrock — steel could be heard creaking along with a faint breeze.

Each dark metal link led from the abyss of the ceiling to the top of a narrow metal cage. Slouched against its dark steel bars was the black-robed figure of Gantis Jacs. Beaten, bloody and bruised, the old mystic's tall frame was curled up and defeated. His pale haggard face and grayish black hair were stained with ash and dried blood. Bags and dark circles formed under his gilded brown eyes.

Iron braces bound his hands entirely, not even allowing him the use of gesture magic. With the little strength Gantis could muster, he threw the iron bindings against the steel cage.

A metallic ring traveled through the cavern before bouncing off of distant walls.

He was far from the likes of mankind, trapped in the Blackstone lair of the Elf Queen. There was no easy way out for the old wizard this time. Even if he could perform a spell, the likelihood of it killing him was too much of a risk.

His essence had been all but drained in his battle against Farah and her elven apprentices. They and that lummox of a familiar were a sure challenge, but the Elf Queen was simply too powerful, even more so than in the days of the Blood Wars. He was lucky enough to get rid of his Bloodstone before it too had been captured.

His eyes slowly opened, and he looked around the cavernous den he was trapped within. Darkness was in all directions spare the cool dim lit catwalk below. Roots and vines entangled the narrow footway and wrapped around the Blackstone altar that stood at its abrupt cliff end.

The stench of stagnant blood fumed from below, invading his sense of smell with its foul odor. His stomach twisted and churned. He could taste the iron with every inhale, its source sending chills down his spine.

Madness.

Gantis sat up with his back against the cage, searching for a gate within its steel bars, yet the cylindrical cage was absent of any latches or locks. There was no escaping, not even from the floor or the pointed ceiling above. How it was he ended up in this prison was indeed a mystery.

The sound of his cell swaying was accompanied by an eerie stillness. He could feel a glaring set of eyes staring him down, peering through the darkness like a cat who has cornered its prey. Gantis awaited the Elf Queen's vile remarks, yet he only sensed her nefarious smile as it widened with the silence.

"The year is 875." Gantis's words traveled down the catwalk toward his green-robed nemesis, curdling her expression in an instant.

In the abyss beyond the catwalks end, she sat in her root-strewn throne of chiseled black bedrock. She lifted her long bone wand and gestured toward the caged wizard. "Is that so?"

Piercing through the darkness was a warm green glow that emanated from the Rootstone around her neck. The wizard watched as the light intensified along with the sound of roots slivering toward him. Stretching across the cavernous walls and up onto the jagged ceiling, they crawled like vipers on the hunt.

"And where is Balamor now? Will he open one of his magical doors and come save you?" Her grin slowly returned as Gantis stayed silent.

Blackstone stalactites crumbled and fell, some crashing into the catwalk and shattering into pieces. Gantis could sense the rage in her magic as it drew from his own mana.

"Prophecy," Farah said with the sarcasm of a laughing crow.

The chain holding his cell jerked and rattled before a metallic snap came from above. Gantis was tossed around in the steel cage as it was ripped from the ceiling. Pale roots traveled down the chain, spiraling through its metal links before entangling the dark metal bars of his cell. He stood up and tried to keep his balance as they crept across the floor and onto the ends of his tattered black robes.

Slowly, the narrow cell was carried through the air and down the stone catwalk. Torches of cool blue fire passed him by as he waited to meet his nemesis face-to-face. Her pale roots slithered around his ankles and locked him in place. He felt them continue to lurk across his skin, spreading up his chest and around his bearded neck. The emerald stone she wore illuminated her throne in an eerie green light.

"Balamor was certainly right about one thing..." The Elf Queen paused as the black steel cage drifted up close. The green glow of the Rootstone wavered across her smooth pale skin as she leaned close to Gantis and whispered, "Darkness lives here now."

Gantis wrestled to break free, but the roots were far too strong. "Balamor will bring your demise, Farah!" he shouted.

She sucked her teeth and shook her head. "I'm afraid that Balamor Wisebeard will be nothing but a false memory, my dear Gantis. Nothing but an imaginary friend to comfort you in these dark times." She stepped back from his root-entangled cell, turning away as she continued, "Did you really think I wouldn't find out where the old man and his son, Ericho, were hiding? I must admit, you did a good job hiding them in a shabby village such as the Raehl, not to mention all of those precious books. Oh, how long it has been since I've read the books of that old library! I do hope those dirty little moles have taken good care of them."

The green light of her emerald amulet followed the queen as she strolled toward the cage once again, this time brandishing an empty tear-shaped vial in her other hand. A runeword was pressed into its surface, four dots in the shape of a square. "It's a shame those poor people will suffer because of you; Farjadis most of all... though, I'll keep him entertained." She held the vial up as an eerie green liquid dripped from its capping, slowly filling its glass confines. The drops of the strange substance swirled and wavered with pale green light before an apparition coalesced within. Distorted and wailing with a ghostly howl, it was the figure of Farjadis Wisebeard, and he was trapped by the Elf Queen's magic.

Farah Lenook sneered at the fire growing in Gantis's eyes. "You didn't know? I really thought you had your eye on the old man. You went to such lengths to keep me from him. I thought my messenger would most assuredly be caught."

"Messenger?" Gantis muttered.

"The old Wisebeard was given a magical solution to all of his problems – a gift from you of course." She stirred the contents and the soul inside subdued before she returned the vial to the inside pocket of her green robes.

"You expect some stranger to be so easily trusted giving out potions? Farjadis is no fool," Gantis shot back.

"You really have always thought so little of me, Gantis. As if I would really use a stranger to win over the old man's trust. But you weren't aware of how long I've known about the Raehl, were you? How long I've studied those who cross that bridge — and those who have tried and failed." She smiled, showing the edge she had over him now. "Oh? You thought the Faric washed him away?"

"You monster!" Gantis shouted.

She laughed, "Now, he may not be a great bridge builder these days, but a Scrivenkin he will always be."

Gantis felt his soul sink as the Elf Queen turned and called out with a gesture of her bone wand. "Krassus, come greet our newest guest! I'm sure you will find him to be a rather useful specimen."

Emerging from the darkness was the silhouette of a short-hunched figure. His bare footsteps were accompanied by the taps of his pale staff — a scepter whittled from the finger bone of a giant and fastened with a bubbling black cauldron. His frail crippled figure was draped in ragged brown robes that trailed across the stone floor behind him. Tied to his waist was a small orange velvet bag and a ring of black metal keys. The disheveled bookmaster lowered his hood as he met his queen, revealing his sunken and grimaced face. Gantis's eyes went wide at the sight of the strange man.

Krassus wasn't merely another servant of the Elf Queen, his steel-blue eyes and long black and gray beard showed he was of particular halfling blood.

"Ericho! What has she done to you?" Gantis shouted before Farah's roots tightened around his neck.

Krassus looked at the old wizard imprisoned before him, his eyes glossing over with pale green light before he spoke, "Mother, I think this one has Krassus mistaken for someone else. Why does he do this?" His craggy voice trailed with demented ramblings.

"Delusions haunt him, I'm afraid," she responded.

"Delusions... yes, yes!" He leaned in to study the caged wizard prodding him with his bloody staff. "Easily frightened, highly suspicious, experiencing hallucinations... Yes indeed, all symptoms of psychosis, my queen. These are issues Krassus can fix! Yes, yes, he can fix them, my queen! But first, the blood of one's kin..."

SCRIVENKIN

Gantis tried to resist the strange halfling's prodding as best he could but the roots held him still. The spur of bone at the end of the staff slowly sliced open the wizard's cheek. Gantis growled as blood streamed down the sharp bone jag and dripped into Krassus's dark iron cauldron.

Farah let out a joyful laugh, as the wizard's blood sizzled and smoked upon touching the bubbling surface of its crimson contents. "He still bleeds! And here I thought I might have been too late. It looks like eight centuries of magic hasn't replaced you yet, my dear Gantis!"

Krassus stepped back from the cell and stood by Farah Lenook. "The ritual is ready, my queen."

"Splendid, Bookmaster. Now, please demonstrate to our guest how important his contribution is to our cause."

27

FROM THE BONES

875, Summer's 57th Dawn

Krassus laid his staff to the ground and snatched the black iron pot from its end. With a twirling gesture of his open hand, the bloody mixture began to churn and flash with intense scarlet light. Gantis struggled to break free from the roots as the maddened halfling performed his blood ritual. "Ericho, you must break... free..." The old wizard's words were muffled as roots spread over his mouth.

Krassus continued his spell, yet that name lingered in his mind. He heard it from somewhere else.

Ericho...

The thought was shaken from his mind as his cauldron began to tremble. Swirling smoke gathered at its center, whipping streams of hot blood into a powerful helix.

The bookmaster was consumed by his magical performance, waving his hands in patterns around the bloody twister fueling it with more and more power. Blue fire ignited at the center of the pot and the smoke grew darker. Before long, the bloody pool in the iron pot was completely consumed by the hellish vortex.

The intense heat upon Gantis's face made sweat drain from every pore as he helplessly observed from his cell. The stench of burning blood fumed toward him along with the billowing smoke. His eyes teared up and his vision blurred. Farah laughed maniacally as the spell churned around the cauldron, her aquamarine eyes filled with both fire and glee.

Krassus pulled his hands closer together and the mass of gore, smoke, and flames condensed at the center of the helix, forming into a charred bulbous mass bigger than the bookmaster himself.

The blue flames grew hotter as Krassus spun the amorphous blob into a tightly wound ball. The magical force of the bookmaster's spell twirled the fire into a blazing shroud that engulfed the strange ball of cooked gore. The ball started to shake and contort its shape before its charred skin cracked open. The hot blue shroud swimming around it was sucked in and spit back out in a massive explosion of fire, blasting off the blackened surface and revealing a cherry red organ beneath — the heart of a dragon.

Its meaty surface was covered in hot blood and glowing igneous rock. The mystical heart came to life with a powerful rhythmic throb. With each echoing thud, its veins shined in a fiery blue light. Gantis watched in awe as the estranged halfling completed his spell. The brown-robed bookmaster was unfazed by the powerful feat of magic. No sign of fatigue plagued his already crippled body. Ericho Wisebeard was indeed a powerful mage, but a spell of this size would surely have cost him a great deal of power.

What has she done to him?

As the heart lowered to the ground, Farah fanned her hand forward and roots sprawled across the stone from the darkness behind her, twisting and weaving as they spread. Softly caressing the massive organ, the queen pulled it closer to her. "Impressive, indeed! A beautiful spell performed by our beloved bookmaster, wouldn't you agree, Gantis?"

Gantis wrestled with the roots, his voice covered by their sturdy grip.

She strolled down the narrow catwalk with victorious stature. Her satin green robes shimmered in the passing of blue torchlight. Krassus hobbled behind her as he reattached the cauldron to his bony staff. The pale roots of the Whispering Tree held both the cage of her nemesis and the beating heart of a dragon.

After several minutes, they arrived at the catwalks end where a Blackstone altar stood. The roots carefully rested the heart on the altar before slithering away. Farah Lenook slowly slid out of her robes as she approached the altar. Bloody runewords covered her pale shapely figure from the nape of her neck to the base of her petite ankles.

The emerald Rootstone around her neck dimmed along with the blue torchlight as an aura of energy was drawn toward the altar. She held only her narrow bone wand, which she waved over the dragon's heart majestically.

The heart grew intensely hot and glowed like the bowels of a furnace. Krassus stood back, watching as his master conducted a spell that would surely change the course of history. It was something he studied for years; a feat of magic only performed once by the First Folk. Krassus had written thousands of runewords, read hundreds of ancient texts, and gathered countless ingredients so that this day would become a reality.

Bringing to life a creature that had been extinct for centuries was now in their reach. That creature would accomplish her age-old mission — destroying the remnants of the First Kingdom. Every artifact, every mystical scripture, the monuments, the traditions, each and every single mark left on the culture was to disappear. The Bloodstone, the spellbooks, the bloodlines that once ruled society were to be found and brought to justice. Magic was only to be trusted in the hands of the elves, and with it they would finally bring the races of man to heel.

Farah raised her wand high and started to speak the mystical words of the Runesong with a powerful tone, the bloody runewords drawn upon her bare skin shined crimson red as she called upon each of their symbols in sequence.

𝄆 ⌒ – ⦚ ⁒ ⏀ ÷ ⦚ ⁓ ≋ ∼ ⊖ ⊙

"Yev ris, onos firos ahn yus. Lim firos ehn dran, manas theas guul." The heart of the dragon levitated at her wand's rhythmic command, floating further out from the altar.

Below, the massive pool of blood began to ripple and churn as mana flowed through it. Slowly breaking the thick scab-like surface were a series of pale bones. The queen waved her wand, and the bones twirled and flipped into their correct positions, hundreds of them all forming into the skeleton of a massive creature. First its spinal column twisted into shape, formed by thick spiked vertebrae whose size tapered as it formed into a whip-like tail. Ribs were lifted into place two by two, forming a bony cage around the searing heart of the dragon. The bloody bones of its limbs and wings finally clicked into place before she continued her spell.

"Rhul ris ehn hels, manas theas guul. Awa jar, manas theas guul, ehn hels khin." Her godlike voice echoed with the power of a chorus as blue fire erupted from the dragon's heart. Black smoke billowed upward into the shape of two massive lungs, pulsing and stoking the heart of the fire. From the wisps of the dancing flames, runewords coalesced, each of them a small ember that raced toward the dragon's bones one by one. Upon their pale bloody surface, these fiery words were branded, flashing with jet blue light as they were bound by magic. The queen reached into her robe pocket and revealed three small ruby gems, their crystalline structure unmistakable by the imprisoned wizard who observed from afar — *bloodstones.*

⊙⊖⚬ ˹⸣˸˹ ⊡

"*Mohr theas guul, ehn firos siras.*" The stones shined with red light before Farah tossed them toward the spectacle unfolding before her. Each of them spiraled within the forming body of the dragon. Tendrils of blood shot toward them before consuming them completely. They spun and convulsed as the blood transformed them into the dragon's guts. Her words went on as the walls of her cavernous lair shook.

"⊖⚬⩊⍫⊕⩆⊕˷⌖

"*Dahn theas guul wyl yus. Eyon yus ehn raji.*"

The webs of blood leeched onto the dragon's bones, wrapping around their fiery markings and transforming into cartilage, veins, and muscle.

⸾⸣˸˹ ˷≋⸴⊙≋⸴˷≈⫫⸴⸰−⊕⚬

"*Vehs firos ehn dran, mohr dran ehn aer, yev hels onos yus guul.*" The black clouds of smoke were coated with red tissue, contracting and expanding as they pulled air toward them. Soon the entire skeleton was consumed by the tendrils of the growing nascent body. Blue fire pulsed through its lattice of veins as a watery fluid emerged, swimming and splashing around the dragon's body.

−⊕⚬˶⩙∼⊕⚬˸⋔⊖⩙

FROM THE BONES

"Onos yus guul ahn deun, manas yus guul ehn maur, theas deun." Layers of flesh spread over the fluid, one atop another forming the dragon's thick scaly skin. Spiraling from its lower body up to its massive head, dark red scales covered the dragon entirely.

The red runewords upon Farah Lenook's pale skin each turned to ash and fell from her body as she spoke the final words of her spell,

$$-\, \text{//} \, \therefore \sim \therefore \, \text{``} \cdot | \cdot \sim \oplus \sim \{ \text{:} \} \sim : \, : \sim ?$$

"Onos ahn vis, manas vis ehn tyel, manas raji, manas firos, manas payr, manas gehn."

Two horns protruded from either side of the dragon's menacing face, each of them curling into a ridged spiral. White orbs shuddered and twisted around the bridge of the dragon's snout. Within their pearly confines, magical projections of godly wisdom flashed and shined with power. Crimson blood and jet blue fire seeped into them, exploding with a raging spirit who roared at their unwary awakening.

A snarling set of teeth was dripping with saliva as the dragon's monstrous scream sent a mighty blast of putrid breath toward the Elf Queen. The beast flapped its massive wings as the magical force levitating it gave way. Another shrieking call came from the beast as it studied its darkened surroundings. Its glowing red and blue eyes stared down at the queen in silence. The gusts from its horned wings rocked Gantis's black metal cage.

The old wizard was stunned by the incredible power the Elf Queen possessed. To summon a dragon from bones and blood without even the slightest sign of weakness was unbelievable.

There had to be a price.

Every single spell — no matter its source — came at a cost. What that cost was remains to be seen, though it would be undoubtedly paid.

Farah Lenook smiled as her pointed fingers reached to meet her newly formed familiar. Even with the will of a god, the magical bond between the dragon and the queen held great sway over its mind. "Idhissat, my wonderful child, I have waited far too long for your return," she said with a mystifying gesture. A green light waved over its eyes before it lowered its snout to her. "My queen, what has happened to me?" Its words stretched with a rumbling hiss.

"You have been reborn," she answered as she placed her hand upon its red scales.

"For what purpose do you return me to this world?" Idhissat asked her.

"Vengeance, against those who put you to rest."

"*Men...*" The dragon's raspy tone trailed into a hungering growl.

28

FOLLOW THE SHADOWS

875, Summer's 57th Dawn

*he* slight glints of Awkid's eyes greeted him and the young Wisebeard dropped the square stone rune from his hand. He screamed but the large hand of the dwarf muffled the sound.

Moments passed with Balamor's heart beating intensely. He couldn't trust his eyes until Awkid spoke.

"Where have you brought me now, halfling?" His strict voice faltered with a grimace of pain.

Balamor was laying back against the cold stone floor as he looked to his left and right frantically. "I-I don't know... I... Are-are they gone? Those men and... And-and those things?"

Awkid responded with a raspy tone, "Parins? Sure... For now, but they'll be back. It doesn't take long for Parins to tear a man's flesh from his bones, trust me." He balled up Balamor's brown robes and shoved them into the halfling's chest.

"I couldn't..." Balamor said while lifting himself up from the ground. "I couldn't leave you behind, not like that."

"Oh no, of all places, the cozy den of Parins is surely best fit for my last days," Awkid said sarcastically as his now lifeless arm scraped against the stone floor.

Balamor looked toward Awkid. The darkness only allowed the low glints of his eyes and the slight contour of his stocky silhouette to be seen. He ignored the dwarf's attitude and fished through his bag for a torch. He felt for the metal haft and quickly removed one. He struck his fire-steel and blue flames leaped from the ground where it was placed. Awkid raised one brow, the color of the flames flickered in his wide eyes.

"Strange, I know… I found them in here, on the corpse," Balamor said as he looked between Awkid and the skeleton awkwardly.

He turned to his bag and retrieved two plump tomatoes and passed one to Awkid.

They ate silently.

Occasionally, Balamor would study his companion, unsure of what he was thinking.

Awkid stared at the remains of his arm for a while.

The two of them went through all six of Balamor's tomatoes before Awkid finally spoke. "What happened in that swamp? I have never been that close to death. That creature… that place… that is what we don't speak of to any man. There's a reason why no one should know of those things."

Balamor was quick to disagree. "You're wrong, Mr. Anvorbeard. What happened back there with that monster… That is fear that must be addressed. Stories are stories, but the ignorance of a festering evil like that? That is just the ignorance of a guilty conscience."

"Well said, halfling, if only you were that good with that dagger," Awkid said with a hushed laugh that quickly faded. His skeleton arm rattled along the stone as he took it into his left hand.

"Your… Your arm, I couldn't—"

"It's no fault but mine," Awkid interrupted as he held the lifeless bones of his right arm in his palm.

"Can you… still feel it?" Balamor asked curiously before palming his face at the afterthought.

"I can feel all of it. Everything that's missing. Only these bones are mine, these bones. That's it. Whoever she was, wherever she is — she too will feel this pain." Awkid turned his gaze to Balamor.

"Farah Lenook. That's who did this," Balamor said sternly, his eyes unmoving as he stared back at the dwarf. "She seeks your arm... and she seeks my grandfather's death," he added as he looked down toward the fire.

"So, you know those men who were lurking near my cabin? You never thought to tell me?" Awkid asked.

"I met one of them... Mayn, the one with the black wraps upon his face. He escaped the night you saved me. I thought you might have recognized him yourself. He knows magic, and he works for this Farah Lenook, that I'm sure of. It was three nights back when I learned of her name from another powerful woman, with robes of green satin draped long over her body. She summoned some creature of the Earth... Like something straight out of an old kingdom tale..." Balamor paused a moment while he gazed into the strange blue fire. "After she fed it a potion, a bright light gathered around the thing, as bright as a summer day sun. Within seconds it faded, and beneath was a fully grown and clothed halfling. I've never seen real magic before that, nothing like it..."

Awkid removed the capping from his water canteen and took a swig before passing it to Balamor. "Hard to believe, considering only days later you're sealing my wounds with the same magic."

Balamor leaned over and snagged the canteen, taking a long gulp and wiping his mouth. "Before I left my village, my grandfather told me that my blood was special. I thought nothing of it until things like this started happening. Whatever it means, I still know nothing compared to that woman."

Awkid removed two luncheons he packed with his good arm. Grabbing one, he passed it to Balamor who caught it and untied the leaf wrapping. "So, you believe this woman to be Farah Lenook?" Awkid asked before tearing into his own. A rather stuffed pocket of venison and veggies spilled out the side as he took a chomp. His stomach growled, awakening from a day without a proper meal.

Two bites in, he answered Awkid's question. "She gave the halfling man a small vial and a message to deliver to my grandfather — for him to drink the potion to hide his presence until Gantis Jacs arrived – a man I've only heard stories of. She told the halfling that Farah Lenook was here in the south." He took another two bites and swallowed before he finished, "At first, I was sure the green-robed woman was someone else entirely; another mystic my grandfather knew of. But if she was helping my grandfather then why didn't she just go to the Raehl herself and deliver the potion?"

"Sounds like a ploy to me. Of what blood was this woman? Human?" Awkid asked as he secured his skeletal limb to his chest with the dirty cloth wraps.

"Unsure... maybe a human. Her features were strikingly elegant, almost frail," Balamor replied.

"Well, the woman who did this to me was of the Dwarven kind, my own kind. A strong woman and most certainly not frail. I believe there's more than one woman with an ability to course magic."

"Perhaps," Balamor said with a sigh.

"Besides, what would any woman want with a cursed dwarf and some old halfling like your grandfather?" Awkid asked almost rhetorically.

"Not just some old halfling... He is a Wisebeard, as am I. I do not yet know the story behind our family, but I believe it has everything to do with your power... and mine." Balamor finished his answer while gazing into his palms.

He was uneasy about his ability — where his power had led him and how its influence could discern both good and evil. There was a reason for it nonetheless, as there was with anything in the world.

Silence seemed to hang heavily over Balamor before he felt Awkid staring at him.

The young halfling looked back.

"We should leave before the Parins return. If we're lucky, they've died from something worse." Awkid rose from the stone floor as he spoke.

"There were two men who passed through here before awaking the Parins. An elf and a human – robed men. I thought you should know." Balamor packed his belongings as he spoke nonchalantly.

Awkid looked confused at first but soon a small fit of rage caused him to shout. "What is it with you pestering worms and wearing robes?" He balled his fists and looked over at the young halfling who was fitting himself with his own brown robe.

"Everyone needs a good robe, Mr. Anvorbeard. Whether it be for concealing or not, a good set of robes can give a man purpose, or at least it seems to," Balamor said with a smile.

Awkid rolled his eyes and shrugged before quickly returning to the topic. "Were they lost? These robed men."

"As lost as you and I. Strange. What would someone else be doing here?" Balamor rubbed his chin at the question.

"Hmm... Let's go." Awkid ignored the question. He didn't like the idea of others being here. It could only mean a harder journey ahead, especially if they have another encounter like before.

Balamor reached for the metal torch and waved it across the room. The blue light flickered against the scattered skeleton of the flag bearer. Rusted plate mail tugged the white tunic that barely held his torso together. The long white banner lay pinned under the mess of bones.

The embroidered sigil upon its surface was peculiar. He wiped the fabric clean and stretched out the wrinkles. In deep black thread was the assortment of a cane and a sword crossed below a large curved horn. Oddly, he thought it might appear again on his travels, another piece to the ever-growing puzzle. Balamor crouched and dug it out from beneath. He removed his dagger and quickly cut the banner from its pole.

FOLLOW THE SHADOWS

The emptiness of the cave was eerie as they began their departure.

Awkid grabbed the flag bearer's pole and with a swift kick broke it down to size. At its end was a rusted pike which he studied for a moment.

As they moved down the hall, the swathes of holes covering the walls were dripping with an inky black substance.

Balamor held the grip of his dagger in his right hand and the torch in his left.

The jagged walls of the swampy grotto opened to show a thick fog, barely lit by the early morning sun. The sky snuck through the overcast in wide rays but the ground beneath was as lifeless as before.

Twisted trees and sick grass hugged the small path from the cave.

Awkid stopped and peered over what looked like two sets of footprints. His eyes followed them down the trail — one set was wider and deeper than the other — a sign that the other was light on their feet.

The tracks became harder to see as they crossed a narrow clearing of dark wet grass.

Beyond the clearing, Balamor made out the face of an ornate obelisk made of stone, like that of the Greatstone Pass. Moss and dirt were spread across its lower half, staining the stone with hues of green and brown.

As they neared its base, Balamor could recognize some of the various rune markings found in his books. The runes bordered the edges of the tall stone prism. A band of sunlight fell upon one face casting a long shadow to the ground.

Awkid studied the shadow and quickly looked to the sky. "Follow the shadows, Mr. Wisebeard. I've been here once before and I owe it to that advice alone."

Awkid moved forward with his eyes peeled. Whatever tracks he was trailing were too hard to trace. His body was still exhausted from the night before, catching the two men was a lost cause. His stomach would frequently ache and cause him to stop as Balamor stayed close behind.

The young halfling held the hilt of his dagger tight as he went along with caution. His torch evaporated the fog around its wick and mixed with the orange sunrays of dawn.

Both of them moved slowly and silently through the dead wasteland.

Small puddles of mud occasionally bubbled and popped and flakes of ash fell from the dying bark of trees.

It was a truly unimaginable part of nature to witness, but Balamor didn't think twice on removing his notebook. The torch was snuffed out and his journal nestled in his left arm as he jotted down descriptions and made rather chaotic sketches of the scenery.

Pages were filled by the young Wisebeard when he was finally granted a moment of research.

875, Summer's 57th Dawn,

—The Mog Brush is close

The silence broke as Awkid spotted the next stone marker ahead. "Another obelisk."

Balamor closed his book and snapped his head up to see it was only yards away.

In moments, he held his torch to it. The blue fire shined against the obelisk yet there was no shadow.

Balamor seemed stumped as he began to circle the base of the rock structure. He was more than halfway around when a shadow appeared.

Awkid was quick to recognize and took point toward what he hoped was their destination.

The air was calm, and the fog thinned considerably as they walked.

875, Summer's 57th Sunrise

The wetness of the swamp dissipated and the dreary forest surrounding them was swimming with a strange glowing dust.

Balamor watched as the small specks of light drifted to the root-festered soil and flickered away. Trees and plants were missing most of their foliage and what remained was drained of color. Twisted trunks stood tall over Balamor as he imagined them in their normalcy. Their bark was etched with deep grooves and coated in a copious layer of ash. The curious mapmaker held his hand out in front of him catching a few of the odd particles in his palm. At the touch of his skin, they broke into gray flakes.

He looked to Awkid who began to answer his unspoken question. "The spirit of the trees, that's what confounds you."

"Fascinating... Unlike any trees I've ever seen," Balamor replied quietly.

"That's because they're not just trees, they're folk," Awkid said with a glance over his shoulder.

"Folk? Like you and I?"

"Rootfolk... That's what the Black-robed Man called them, anyway. Some ancient spirits bound to the flora and its rotting soil."

"These folk, do they speak?" Balamor asked while running his fingers along the bark of a towering trunk.

"No more than the wind whispers at night. Their days have long since passed, only their essence remains. The man told me this place was once more alive than the rainforests of Wynspur," Awkid responded as he glanced around the forest.

ZARDRAKEN'S CRYPT

Balamor looked around the dismal place trying to imagine what it looked like once. "What happened?"

"War, blood, and death happened," Awkid said disgustedly as he strolled his weakened body forward with the help of his new pole-arm.

The two of them finally made it to the next stone spire.

Balamor's torchlight swept across its border of signs, filling each with a cool shade of blue. Again, the halfling searched for the shadow with its flame. The light waved against the surface as he approached the marker's leftmost side. A long shade grew from the opposite face and stretched across the ground beside them. Balamor was still amazed at the logic behind it when a long distant howl broke his attention and pierced his ears with a caustic and gurgling cry.

It passed through the dying forest and slowly faded.

Fear held Balamor in shock but Awkid quickly nabbed him and ducked them both behind a tree.

The silence resumed, but this time with heart-stopping suspense.

Balamor gripped the dirt below and held his breath. The bright particles patiently floated their way to the ground as a subtle rumbling escalated into a thundering stampede of beasts.

The creatures stopped only feet behind them and trotted the dusty ground, snarling at one another. Their hulking frames stomped the soil and could be heard sniffing the air for a scent.

A deafening bark shook the atmosphere and Awkid snapped his eyes to Balamor.

Paws shuffled heavily, and another yelp screeched through the forest.

The dwarf nodded toward the Wisebeard's dagger as the footsteps drew closer.

The creatures were yapping almost painfully as they neared the adventurers.

Awkid gripped the shortened pole-arm in his left hand while the young halfling peeked to his right. A thick black liquid dripped to the ground, sizzling as steam wandered up from its shiny surface.

Balamor slowly lifted his eyes to see the long gray snout of a grotesque beast moving around the tree. Fanged black teeth lined its jaw, razor sharp and coated in hot black tar. Balamor's chest was beating with fire. He wanted to run, but he knew there was no chance. He glanced at Awkid who readied his weapon to strike.

Another dripping monster approached from around the trunk to the left, sniffing out the dwarf with ease.

In a flash, Awkid jabbed the spear through the side of its mouth and Balamor immediately followed after the other.

29

THE BOUNDS OF AKINN

875, Summer's 57th Sunrise

A ghastly yelp rang his ears as he shoved the silver blade of his dagger through the beast's gullet and into its massive head.

Tar and blood gushed from within and spilled onto his hand, boiling the skin beneath.

Balamor screamed as the beast's head slumped to the ground and its bright yellow eyes faded to black.

The forest was now roaring with demon-like chatter as Balamor and Awkid jumped out of their cover. The dwarf wrestled the spear from the other creature's head when Balamor finally saw the terrors in full.

*Tar*wolves — he was certain of it. Almost twice the size of any wolf he had ever seen. Their gray fur was matted with hot black tar from head to toe, oozing to the ground with steam billowing from their bodies as they approached.

With eight in all, only six remained, snapping their jaws at Balamor and Awkid.

The dwarf finally ripped the broken spear from the lifeless beast beneath him and slowly moved back.

"The torch!" Awkid yelled to Balamor as the remaining wolves were closing in.

Lying in the ashen dirt only feet between them was the dark steel handle of the torch, the sunlight revealed the etching of a runeword Balamor must have missed in the cave.

·⁊·
o

Balamor scrambled to its position, kicking up a cloud of dust as he secured the torch in his hands but it was too late. One of the wolves leaped through the air with its jaws wide and pounced onto the halfling.

Awkid quickly stabbed into its back with the best of his strength.

Balamor screamed as he fought the beast on top of him. Shoving the handle of the torch into its mouth, he tried to wrestle it off.

Another dove for Awkid and barely missed as he jumped away and dug the rusted pike into its gut.

Balamor was losing his grip when the claws of the wolf began tearing through his robes and into his skin. Tar flung spastically from the beast when Balamor shouted in one last attempt to save his life, *"Aer!...Firos!...Hels!"*

At the sound of the last word blue fire exploded from the torch and engulfed the wolf in flames. Its face began to melt before his eyes as it shrieked and flailed in pain. The beast jumped off of Balamor and fell to the ground, twisting and thrashing wildly as the fire whipped around its body. Horrific screams faded and the remaining wolves backed away at the vicious sight, but Awkid was too quick.

He thrust his pole-arm into another before dragging it to the ground and finishing it with a final blow.

Balamor laid on his back with the torch still burning bright. A blistering cold wave flowed from his gut to the tips of his fingers before his lungs released a cloud of frigid air.

Awkid lifted the young Wisebeard to his feet and took the torch from his hand. He waved it at the few wolves that were left.

They barked madly while shying away from the blue flames.

Balamor watched as the fiery blaze devoured the wolf only inches away. His robes were now covered with a thick muck and burns blotted his arms and face.

"Run, Balamor! Run now!" Awkid yelled as he swung the torch with his left hand.

The halfling looked behind him and quickly grabbed his dagger.

They both moved backwards through the forest but the wolves would not relent; snapping their tar-filled jaws at the dwarf and yelping between foul coughs.

Balamor looked ahead but the next marker was nowhere to be seen. He reached into his bag and shuffled through his relics for his square stone rune, a triangle of three divots assured him of his choice. Removing it from his backpack, he began to sprint through the dying woods.

The Tarwolves jumped at Awkid but he batted one away with the torch, igniting it in a fiery blast of blue flames. Their cries racketed through the forest as he took off toward Balamor.

The young halfling held the square rune in his left hand, battling with the idea of using it again. The consequences of performing magic and the toll it took on his body, the uncertainty of it all only worsened when running from wolves. The ground ached his bones as he trampled through brittle brush and over fallen branches. He glanced back at Awkid and the two wolves charging behind them.

Risks must be taken, he thought as he clutched the rune in hand and began to speak the mysterious words he barely knew. *"Ehn vis payr!"*

∴

Surging through his body, a powerful vision overcame his mind in an instant and a great energy filled his eyes with pale green light. His vision turned foggy and out of sync with his steps as he struggled to run faster.

The woods were dark and strangely quiet and now the fresh smell of rain filled the air around him. Balamor tried to keep pace with the ground ahead as thick green trees whipped by faster with each stride. He knew this was someone else — someone else's eyes — as he tried to fight it, but his vision flashed before him as he felt himself tumble to the ground.

From behind him, he could hear Awkid yelling along with the barking of Tarwolves.

Reality returned in a snap as Balamor was crawling to his feet.

A mix of adrenaline and the magic running through his veins seemed to blur his surroundings. Up ahead through his tunneled vision he could see another stone marker. His bare feet pounded against the soil as it drew closer. Specks of light were falling like a brisk snow before his eyes flashed with pale green once again.

The dewy scent returned along with the sight of lush vegetation. In front of him, a woman's hand rose out of long satin green sleeves, thin and pale in comparison to his own. Hovering above the palm was a white ball of light that shined before jolting toward the rune-marked obelisk. He watched a shadow extend along the dirt floor to his right before the vision ceased in a split second.

As his sight returned, he could see a large tree lay fallen before him. His balance wavered with sloppy steps as he barely had time to traverse the dead wood.

Awkid was only feet behind, trailing the halfling to wherever it was he was going. He saw the marker pass him but the cloudy sky hid its shadow. The young mapmaker quickly cut right and Awkid followed after almost losing his footing.

One of the tar-covered beasts slid and slammed against the trunk of a tree but it was quick to recover. The other turned with ease and started to gain ground over the dwarf.

Balamor and Awkid could both hear the heavy panting behind them growing louder with each step.

The halfling tripped and crashed to the ground holding the rune to his chest.

Awkid ditched the torch behind him before yanking up the halfling by his ragged robes.

The woods were now jarring with the sound of hungry wolves.

The Wisebeard quickly surpassed the dwarf when they both could see something in the distance. Through the remaining trees, the gray surface of large ground stones became more and more frequent. Before the young halfling could behold the entire sight in front of him, his vision changed yet again.

Plants now whipped past him and the wind whistled in his ears. The stone beneath his feet was numbingly cold as he finally broke through the thick brush. Ahead, massive walls and structures of black stone were crumbled and eroding along the edge of a sheer cliff. Stretching from the edge was a narrow bridge hanging with moss and vines. Segmented with beautiful lancets, the ancient bridge spanned hundreds of feet far across a pitch-black chasm.

The halfling felt himself drawn closer when he could make out the flickering light of some glassy barrier. Halfway across was an enormous dome of some magic encompassing everything beyond.

The wind was whirling when the sound of Awkid's voice finally broke through. "Balamor, no! The Bounds of Akinn, you cannot cross!"

The Wisebeard's vision broke as he felt himself slip. Falling to the cold ground, he looked around in a daze. Staring down, he could see the pale face of an elven man; his eyes were wide and blood stained his face and blue clothes, but he didn't move. Balamor jumped in shock as he saw the long slit across his throat. There was no time to react, he needed to keep moving.

THE BOUNDS OF AKINN

Awkid pulled him from the ground once more and they both staggered onto the bridge. The wolves charged across the stone ground throwing sparks behind them with their sharp claws. Nearly halfway across the bridge, Awkid skidded to a stop and pulled Balamor back. The trails of his robes crossed the magical barrier and instantly turned to ash.

Balamor lost his breath just as another vision stole his mind.

The same stranger's hand rose just before the mysterious bounds and Balamor traced its path with his own. A circle cut into the glowing translucence as he followed. The Wisebeard finished the symbol with four dots at the center and pushed his palm forward as the magical vision diminished.

Awkid watched as Balamor's hand slowly passed through the barrier along with the rest of his body.

The young halfling turned back and reached for Awkid. "Trust me!"

Awkid gazed back at the Tarwolves only feet away before clutching Balamor's hand.

The mapmaker pulled the dwarf through the mystical enclosure with the rest of his strength and the two of them fell to the ground.

They watched in awe as the wolves leaped through the Bounds of Akinn and their monstrous figures disintegrated into a cloud of ash and smoke. The adventurers were still catching their breaths as the madness settled along the bridge.

Balamor stood up using the stone railing for support and brushed himself off. Scanning from left to right, he couldn't believe his eyes.

Blackstone ruins extended beyond a huge broken archway as far as he could see. He looked at Awkid with a grin. "Welcome, Mr. Anvorbeard. Welcome to the Mog Brush."

30

REFUGE

875, Summer's 57th Morning

iercing through the clouds in bright rays, the early sun shined its warm embrace down on the ancient Palvista Hillock.

Upon the grassy headland, the small halfling community of Mesmir resided, quiet and seemingly deserted if it wasn't for the few dim candles in windows.

Off in the distance, dark clouds rolled southward with cracks of lightning clattering miles away.

Leaning against the railing of a small circular porch front, Barris Oakfoot stared into the small town before him, scratching the railing impatiently. The cold metal of the ruby necklace in his hand reminded him that the passing storms were only the least of worries for him and his people.

A place such as Mesmir, isolated and almost antique when compared to the modern world would be gone if everything Farjadis had told him were true. Barris didn't want to admit it, but he was sure that every bit of it was.

He looked down at the ruby pendant in his palm and let out a long breath before returning his gaze to the large windmill at the center of town.

Standing high above Mesmir, the damaged wood vanes of the old mill slowly creaked as birdsongs emanated from the forest. The cylindrical wooden body of the windmill sprouted nearly three stories from a large halfling hole. Its polished wooden surface was ported with four circular windows, each with a sill adorned by hanging plants. Around it were four cisterns made of Blackstone and treated wood — the pre-war basins of Gwendilae.

Long ago, the reservoirs were the place of tribute to the forest spirit Gwendilae, an ancient being who once protected the people of the forest thousands of years ago. Now they were used by the people of Mesmir as water reservoirs. After the storm that passed, they were filled beyond their limit, drowning out the surrounding grass and shrubs.

Decorated halfling holes encircled the hilltop mill and between them was a maze-like ring of vibrant berry bushes and short fruit-bearing trees of all kinds. One could get lost in the meticulously crafted rows of flora and the mix of aromatic scents permeating through every inch of the village.

In the warm seasons, many would come to visit the famed fruit gardens of Mesmir, the one place to find any sweet nectar to sink your teeth into. Yet it wasn't why Barris arrived in the past stormy night. This time around was far from vacation just as it was six years ago on another dismal day.

"Few come to seek refuge in Mesmir, Uncle. So, what's really got you out of your hole these days?" the jovial voice of a young girl asked from behind him.

"Refuge, that's a big word. You know that one?" Barris slipped the necklace into his trouser pocket before he turned around to face his niece, who he hadn't seen in years.

"Yep! I learned it yesterday!" she replied gleefully.

He nicknamed her "Marie" though her full name, Marigold, was just as simple.

She gave him a curious stare with two shabby mugs in hand.

Wearing a red buttoned-up cardigan, a white blouse and gray skirt, she was a maturing young girl, which only made Barris feel older considering how long it had been. Last time he'd seen her, she was barely a year old.

Long strawberry blonde hair brushed against her freckled cheeks as she handed a small ceramic mug to her uncle. Black coffee steamed in the cold air of dawn.

"I do not seek any refuge in this repugnant hill of a town," Barris said in distaste.

"Well, what about your caravan? What's in there?" Marigold asked, being nosy.

"They're things. I'm taking them to someone."

"Oh, what kind of things, Uncle? Sweet things? Fun things?" she asked curiously.

Barris saw where the conversation was headed and was quick to end it. "Where's your mother?"

"She's right here," a woman's voice resounded through an open window.

Marigold sneered at him and pulled the door open by its centered knob.

Stepping through the circular doorway, wearing a pastel floral dress beneath a blue buttoned bodice, a petite halfling wrapped an apron around her waist and glared at Barris. Her red hair was covered by a blue headscarf and her green eyes peered into those of Barris'. She was younger than him by four summers, making her thirty-nine, but to Barris she looked no different from the last time he'd seen her.

"Marigold, dear, why don't you go inside while I speak to your uncle?" she said in a soft tone of voice.

Marigold glanced toward the caravan outside before fleeing behind the door and pushing it shut.

"So, after six years you finally missed the lovely gardens?"

"Hardly," he replied with a smile. A long pause ensued.

She approached the railing and looked out into the small hill town as the sun was rising. "You pull a caravan now?" she asked.

Barris nodded and sipped his coffee before palming the hot surface of his mug with his other hand. He stared into the swirling black brew and became lost in his thoughts turning the silence disturbing.

"Why are you here, Barris?" she quickly demanded.

Barris lifted his head to the sky, stars fading in the rise of the sun. "Look, Gilly, I can't explain... Not the caravan and not a single reason why I'm here. I just can't. Not right now."

She hawked him in silence as he took a long gulp of the bitter dark roast and winced.

"What is it?" she insisted, gripping the railing and jerking her head toward him.

"Balamor is in trouble, as am I," Barris replied in hesitation, gazing off in the distance. He didn't need to see her to know his sister's look when it flared up. "I am here because I need help, and I need you to trust me. I know it means nonsense right now, but it's just for a time. I need somewhere to stay until I figure it out, until—" Barris was cut off as he lifted his head and met the heated stare of his sister.

"Until the thickets grow legs? You footed off to the Raehl, Barris. You left me and Mum. Now you happen upon some daring burden and you wish to drag me into it? All before you considered sending an owl to say hello?"

"I... I couldn't," he said as he kept himself from yelling. "There were many days, Gilly, that I wanted to write to you and Marie but if you were to know even the slightest thing, the consequences—"

"Consequences? What is it you've gotten into, Barris?" Gilly asked as she looked between him and his caravan. He quickly dodged the question and put it plainly, "Will you help me or not?"

Gilly balled her hand into a fist and slowly unfurled it over the railing. She looked through the circle-cut window of her home, the small noggin of her daughter ducking out of sight. Then she looked back at Barris, their gaze locking before she drew a long sigh and rolled her eyes. "Fine." She began to walk across the wooden porch. "Whatever it is you have in that caravan; you best bring inside in case another storm passes. There's an extra room down the left hall, t'was for storage so you'll have to make do. Get settled in for now. You can explain all this over breakfast."

"Well, it's a rather long and confusing story," Barris said distastefully.

She arrived at the door and grabbed the handle, looking over her shoulder as she pulled it open. "Good, in that case I'll prepare for a second breakfast and set out cakes for elevenses."

The door shut and the creaking of the windmill was the only sound. Barris stretched out his stocky frame and yawned, placing his elbows atop the railing. He rubbed his eyes and thought about how he would explain the story, especially without being called a kook.

There was no right way of telling it – no obvious beginning or definite end. What Farjadis told him fell somewhere in between the two.

He looked down the twisted dirt paths connecting each home to the gardens. A few halflings could be seen sweeping their porch fronts and feeding birds stale bread. The gardens were slightly rustling in the wind. Leaves and fruits both gracefully waiting to be trimmed or picked.

The town was the same as it was six years ago — the same birdsongs, the same early morning dew, and the same lovely gardens.

It was as if this place would never change no matter the world around it, but Barris knew such thinking was merely ignorance.

Things would change, as they already have for Barris.

The weight of that knowledge seemed too heavy, but the fear gave him an odd sense of courage in the face of a dangerous mission. Everything Farjadis told him couldn't be taken lightly. The old halfling was too wise to talk delusions.

Whatever the change would be, Barris could only do what he must.

REFUGE

He took the last sip of coffee from his mug and looked down at his caravan. Tan cloth upholstered its rounded wooden frame, still wet from the storm. He strolled down the porch steps and made his way to the damp caravan and lifted the back cloth open.

The books inside were still dry, which was a surprise considering the storm he'd been through. Hundreds of them were piled halfway to the ceiling, some in wooden milk crates and others loosely stacked.

He shook his head at the massive hoard and the strong musty smell of paper wafting from within.

"Marie!" he called out playfully before taking a small stack into his arms.

In seconds, Marigold wrenched the door open and skipped down the stairs. "Yes, Uncle?"

"How old are you now? Six?" Barris asked as he squinted his eyes.

"Seven!" she answered gleefully.

"Ah well, has your mother taught you reading?"

Marigold quickly nodded and clasped her hands behind her.

"I will let you read one of my books before I return home." Barris smiled and waved one book from the top of the stack in his hands.

Marie rose to her tiptoes and became antsy.

"But you have to help me carry them to my room. Think you can do it?" he bargained.

"Easy as pie, Uncle Barris, but... Can I choose *any* book?" she inquired with wide blue eyes.

"I'm not so sure you would understand some of them," Barris assumed, scratching his chin.

"Uh, huh! I'm smarter than you think, Uncle," she said, stomping her foot to the ground.

"We'll see," Barris replied and handed the books to her. She grabbed them and hurried through the open door.

"Careful now. Those aren't just *any* books," he cautioned as he lifted a large crate into his hands and followed behind.

The two of them moved through the cozy tunnels of the halfling hole.

The wood floors were polished, and the walls were made of a smooth eggshell-painted plaster trimmed with cherry molding.

Ornate throw rugs stretched through the hallways and the ticking of a grandfather clock resonated softly.

He moved behind his small niece, her arms clenched tight to the books as she strolled past cabinets of porcelain knickknacks and colorful indoor plants.

She stopped at a wooden door, old blue paint flaking and chipping off of the oak beneath. An iron ring was fastened for a handle. Barris leaned his weight against it and shoved the door open. The room was nearly vacant aside from some spare household tools and a wooden trunk occupying the corner.

Barris walked to the opposite side of the room and placed his crate on the dusty floor. Marigold followed suit before snatching a book from the pile curiously.

"Oooh! Can I read this one?" she said as she moved her face closer to it.

"There's more than that, Marie. You can look at them when we're done," Barris replied.

Marigold jumped up from the floor and followed him outside.

They spent another hour moving the precious books from his caravan to the old storage room.

The sun was shining above the trees and the garden hill was fully awake. The savory smell of home fries and freshly seasoned eggs filled the halfling hole of Gilly Greeneburrow.

Barris placed the last of the books on the floor and moved to the only free corner of the room.

His niece was looking through the texts quietly when he spoke, "Did you find the one you wish to read?"

"Yep! Most of them are empty or boring, so it didn't take long. I wanna read this one," she replied while holding out an old ragged leather book.

Barris looked at the cover from across the room, in deep red ink it read: *Sacred Lands,* By the Fourth Valorhorn.

The old carpenter heard the name before — *Valorhorn* — and quickly gestured to see it.

Marigold saw the perplexed look upon her uncle's face, even through the thick brown beard he wore.

She handed it to him, and he flipped its cover open.

"You know this one, Uncle Barris? Looks like someone was reading it, so it must be good!" She laughed, but Barris was unnervingly serious.

He turned the pages until he reached where the red ribbon marker was placed.

The silence grew as he read on. Paragraphs of text finally led him to two revealing words: *uncharted lands.*

"Balamor..." Barris whispered.

The clock in the other room began to ring and Barris slowly handed the book back to his niece.

31

UNCHARTED LANDS

875, Summer's 57th Morning

Dead wood dotted the rough terrain of the Mog Brush, desaturated and buried deep in the dirt ground surrounding them. Hills of debris and vast mounds of earth covered entire structures and ruined colossal statues. Splinters of bark and lumber littered the soil along with the rubble of buildings completely overturned within.

A deep hum reverberated from the mystical dome enshrouding the ancient land and everything was dead still, even the air was unmoved.

Pillars of black smoke could be seen beyond the rolling hills of ruins and earth, their dark ashy substance remaining in place and fresh with heat.

The sun was overhead with its warm light phasing through the milky Bounds of Akinn, warping and splashing against the surface.

Stretching past large stone debris, two shadows slithered like snakes along the ground, cast from the withered bodies of Balamor Wisebeard and Awkid Anvorbeard.

They stuck to a narrow path made of toppled stones, scanning the area in silence. Silence that seemed amplified with death and shaken nerves.

Balamor's brown robes were stuck with dry tar and stained with dirt, blood, and the remnants of glowing mushrooms. Ripped and torn where they met the ground and where they covered his dirty hands; they were far from good condition.

UNCHARTED LANDS

Awkid walked beside the young mapmaker, looking even worse than his counterpart. His green tunic was cut and torn from his battles with Du'gahr and the bones of his arm now tied to his chest.

The two adventurers finally arrived in the Mog Brush, now in search of answers — answers they hoped would be worth the risking and saving of each other's lives.

Here, in a land cursed to be forgotten by all, they hoped to learn something about its history — something about the old world it was once a part of. Yet, what mattered most was finding answers about themselves, and Balamor had a strong feeling those answers were here somehow.

After all they had been through to find this place, he felt beholden to the deal he cut with Awkid. Thanks to the dwarf, the Mog Brush was now Balamor's to uncover and document.

He removed his bag and searched its confines for his map. Its frail edges flaking in spots as he unfurled it with both hands. Upon the aged parchment, black ink had been drawn by Balamor himself to mimic the biggest landmarks and main roads he knew in the Southlands.

Unlike most maps, he chose to depict parts of its content based on old world tales of myth and legend. For Balamor, a map wasn't just a tool for directions, but a story in which the world and its deep history could be shown to guide travelers like himself.

Looking at the map, the most vivid illustration was the long snake-like body of a fierce cerulean dragon, twisting and tearing its way from the cold northeast to the wildly unkempt southwest. Along its scale filled back in deep crimson ink was the calligraphic title, *The River Faric*.

Balamor remembered how it took months to finish the devilish beast, and twice as long to clean the dye from his hands.

His eyes moved to the very top of the parchment where the vast bed of Mystfalls Lake was drawn. A horseshoe shaped mass of a dehydrated land was shown with fissures and cracks spreading to its edges. An octagonal gem fell within its bounds, representing what Balamor only knew as the Abandoned Island City.

The vast forests of the south were illustrated with detailed trunks and canopies, outlining swathes of land still unnamed and unexplored.

Balamor's steel-blue eyes traced the thin roads he traveled thus far, each one decorated with the appropriate vegetation found in the area. Between the monstrous spine-like ranges of the *Thorned Ridge* was the recently labeled *Greatstone Pass*, the latest addition to his map.

His gaze slowly moved to the large blank spot in the deep southland. It was hard to believe he stood somewhere in its unknown confines. Filling such a void would be part of his mission to bring certainty to an uncertain world.

"You expect to chart this land?" Awkid said, seemingly amused by the idea.

"That's the plan, my friend, but first I must take notes and characterize the landscape. Then I shall try to determine the borders by counting paces and so on. Without the proper measuring tools, you must do with what you have, and I have my feet," Balamor explained confidently as he returned the map to his backpack and fetched his notebook and pencil.

"Have you ever done this before?" Awkid asked, testing the young mapmaker's confidence.

Balamor turned away and scratched his head. "No, but that shouldn't be surprising considering that cartography has existed for generations, and most lands have been discovered long before my time. Plus, halflngs are a laboring people. I'm probably the only halfling who studies such an outstanding field."

Awkid grinned and raised an eyebrow.

Balamor shot back undeterred by Awkid's picking. "How many times have you been saved by a halfling? Oh, this is not just a day of 'firsts' for me, Mr. Anvorbeard."

Awkid growled and looked away.

Balamor chuckled and went on, "However, I am no one to speak. You did bring me to the Mog Brush after all. My debt to you is far from repaid." His view shifted away from Awkid and searched the land around him. "I will find out who gave you that curse, and what this 'Avennoth' is. There must be a bottom to all this. I haven't stumbled upon you by some coincidence, Mr. Anvorbeard. Me, you, this place... We're all just smidgens, part of a bigger picture, and I want the whole picture."

Awkid relaxed his hand and looked at Balamor studying the land and jotting down his notes. He wanted to say something to the young Wisebeard but there was nothing more to say. He could only stare down at the soil and contemplate the reason he joined Balamor on this risky mission. It wasn't because he was certain Balamor would fulfill his end of the deal, even if there was a chance that he would. Before he met Balamor, there never seemed to be a chance, and now even against the odds he felt determined.

Years had gone by with him living day by day, catching game and keeping his home warm. The curse bound to him became a problem beyond his solutions and beyond his understanding. Acceptance was a simple way to describe it all, until of course, he stumbled upon Balamor Wisebeard and sensed a unique importance in his character. It was something he couldn't quite put his finger on but accompanying the young halfling on his journey seemed like the right thing to do.

Now, he was within the Bounds of Akinn, the barrier he watched the Black-Robed Man disappear through many years ago. Whatever brought that strange man and his company here was undoubtedly powerful.

Looking around the path, Awkid saw a blaze of a fire near the crushed ruins of massive walls. Inanimate flames and embers of blue fire trailed in sharp formations from a charred boulder dug in the soil.

Bodies of elven soldiers surrounded the area in gruesome display. Some only remained as hunks of flesh littering the ashen surface, while others were either buried by the earth or in the midst of retreat.

Awkid drifted from the stone trail to the devastating scene, motioning Balamor to follow him.

As they drew closer, the smell of rotting flesh and smoldering bone became nearly unbearable for the young halfling. He cupped his right hand over his nose and mouth and took Awkid's lead.

The air was hot and heavy to breathe as they stood only yards away from the paused flames engulfing the boulder.

Awkid crouched to the body of a fallen elf, an archer still gripping his longbow and covering the bloody wound in his stomach. His face was grimaced, paused in the midst of screaming.

"What in the world..." Awkid said, baffled by the sight.

"Everything is frozen still, but how?" Balamor was utterly confused by the scene.

"Magic. Powerful, dangerous magic," Awkid answered sternly.

Upon closer examination, he saw the archer wore very fine metal armor, something he never knew elves to wear. Yet, all the soldiers were dressed in the same silvery light scale male and equipped with high quality arms and supplies.

"These soldiers... They're elves, but I've never seen any elves like this," Awkid said, trying to wrap his head around the still flames and paused expressions of the soldiers.

"I was expecting skeletons, yet here are the seemingly alive bodies of elves in the middle of some obscure, demolished ruins. What happened here?" Balamor asked as he examined the still figures around him.

Awkid scanned the area and started to see more figures and flames scattered along with the debris. "Unsure really. Lots of elves, fire, plenty of destroyed structures. My guess, there was a war here. Before then? Perhaps it was a fortress, or —

"A kingdom?" Balamor asked, almost rhetorically.

Awkid reply with a shrug. "Perhaps." He pushed his hand through a frozen plume of smog. "I've never witnessed anything such as this... As if time is absent."

"Indeed. That barrier must be holding everything still, a stasis of some sort," Balamor gathered, but that wasn't the only thing that intrigued him about the Mog Brush thus far. "Whatever happened here didn't happen recently, or we would have heard something on the way here. So, I'll assume whatever it was, it must have happened a long time ago. Take a look at the placement of everything. Something about it doesn't sit right with me," the young Wisebeard said as he felt the grayish earth with his hand.

"Not surprising considering the context, but you're right about one thing, I'm getting a bad feeling about this place," Awkid said quietly.

As they passed through a thick black trail of smoke, dark ash, and soot stuck to their clothes, making them cough and brush it from their faces.

After a moment, they navigated their way back to the stone path and pushed on deeper into the strange land. The steep hills on either side of them covered ancient siege weapons fitted with silver hardware and made of vespine oak. Suits of dark steel armor littered the path, each of them absent of any bodies.

Far in the distance was a colossal Blackstone tower whose flagstone peak nearly pierced the apex of the magical bounds. Surrounding the tower was a spiral of mounds and hills, most of which were comprised of a thoroughly mixed mess of soil and ruins. The huge Blackstone spire was a glorious vestige of the monumental fortress it once was a part of.

Somehow, it was still standing amidst the maddened landscape while almost everything else had been reduced to piles of pulverized rubble. The remnants of any other standing buildings were few and far between the spoiled wastes.

Awkid walked behind Balamor, studying the Mog Brush with great suspicion. The presence of magical power could be felt in the air and heard in a deafening silence nature itself could not produce. Passing by another suit of dark steel armor he paused and studied it further. Half buried in the soil the black steel body was trapped. Its confines were hollow and devoid of any man, yet its orientation showed otherwise.

He placed his left hand upon the ground. A strange sensation numbed his skin as it dug into the grayish soil. Slowly the once lifeless earth started to grip his hand. A chorus roared through his mind, screams of countless men and women begging to be freed. Their ghostly voices clashing with the sound of gurgling earth.

Avennoth... Save us... Return us... We must find her...

He stumbled backward, ripping his hand from the ground startling Balamor who stood in front of him. A frigid breath of air filled his lungs in a gasp. "No! Stop!" he shouted, his voice echoing in the distance along with the voices in his head.

"Mr. Anvorbeard!" Balamor reacted as he scurried over to help him up. "What happened to you? Are you alright?"

For a moment, a look of terror was upon his face, but he quickly shook it away. He shrugged off Balamor once he finally regained his footing, shaking the encounter from his mind and dismissing it completely. "It's nothing," Awkid growled, his green eyes narrowed as he looked ahead.

"Didn't sound like nothing to me." Balamor replied as he brushed the dirt from his robes. He shot a glance at the dwarf who quickly glared back.

"I said it was nothing, Wisebeard. Leave it. We should keep moving anyhow."

Balamor didn't want to press him any further. Knowing the rage dwarves carry, it wouldn't be worth the reaction. He closed his notebook to get a better look around himself. He climbed to the top of a bulk of stone debris and gazed out with a hand fanned over his eyes.

In the distance was the buckled foundation of a massive building. A broken archway stood by its lonesome far above the scant remnants of thick walls dotting its contours. Shattered panels of ornate stained glass were scattered throughout the building, mixed with various papers and broken wooden shelves. Long throw rugs and splinted floorboards were signs of a once elegant interior. Even amongst the scattered debris of other structures he was almost certain of this building's purpose. "A library, up ahead."

Climbing down from the stone ruin he continued, "Perhaps there I can find some records about this place."

"Perhaps you'll find a map there instead, then we can leave this forbidden wasteland," Awkid concluded.

Balamor started to walk toward the distant ruin, looking at Awkid over his shoulder as he spoke. "'Forbidden,' now you're starting to sound like an Anstian mouthpiece."

"Never associate me with those pretentious humans, boy! I may only have one good arm, but it's all I need to shut that mouth of yours!" Awkid threatened, his bearded face growing red in an instant.

"Duly noted, Mr. Anvorbeard. No need to make threats over such jibes." Balamor flipped open his backpack and removed a carrot from inside. He snapped it in half and tossed one piece to Awkid who caught it with a growl. "Plus, you are free to leave here whenever, if that is what you truly desire. Our terms were that you'd escort me to the Bounds of Akinn, nothing more. Your end of the deal has been fulfilled."

Awkid took a bite of his carrot before he replied, "Leave you here in the Mog Brush? Sorry, but I like having a clean conscience, Balamor. Leaving you here is signing your death wish."

Balamor smirked before pointing at Awkid with the bitten end of his carrot. "I think it's deeper than that, Mister

Anvorbeard. It's deeper than keeping a clean conscience for you, and it's deeper than drawing the lines of a map for me. I believe you and I have come this far for the same reason... To find the truth. No matter what anyone says, or what anyone does, the truth cannot and must not be forbidden."

Awkid looked around the Mog Brush as the Wisebeard's words drifted into an eerie silence. The ruinous landscape was indeed a mystery that he could no longer ignore. For twenty-six years he never questioned what was within the Bounds of Akinn. After helping the Black-robed Man and his entourage reach the famed bounds, he put it all behind him. The armor he wore, the axe he wielded, the security he offered adventurers, it was put to rest after that journey.

"Perhaps we do uncover the truth about this place, what then? What good will come of it? How do we know the consequences?" he asked.

Balamor thought to himself for a moment. The right words were always so elusive when right questions were asked. He finished the final bite of his carrot before chucking the leafy end aside. "Honestly, I don't know, but are you willing to accept ignorance for the sake of peace?"

"Good question..." Awkid replied.

At that the two adventurers finally stood at the entrance of the fallen library. A lone archway stood nearly seven feet high. Its finely chiseled curves and sophisticated patterns were signs of the building's once glorious past. Its cherry red door was almost torn from the threshold separating Balamor and Awkid from its confines. Balamor gripped the tarnished gold knob and pushed the door open, its hinges creaking as it swayed. They began to cross the threshold when a deep bellow came from the distance. They froze and looked at one another as the strange noise rippled through the soil like a wave.

Moments passed as the noise died down and the Mog Brush returned to utter silence. Balamor shrugged his shoulders prompting Awkid to do the same. They started to walk slowly into the demolished library; their eyes peeled and scanning the open interior.

Danger was undoubtedly close. Awkid felt it as a pit formed in the depths of his gut. "We shouldn't be here..."

32

THE HANDS OF TIME

875, Summer's 57th Morning

 ***ithin*** the ruins of an ancient library the two adventurers stood, still suspicious of the strange noise they heard just moments ago. Balamor took point and crept forth passing piles of earth, hunks of Blackstone and the remnants of an interior once lavish in nature. Wooden shelves were tossed about the half-buried foundation where patches of buckled floorboards were left cracked and splintered. Shreds of paper and leather book bindings littered the soil. Balamor lifted an old book from the soil. Its pages were torn and charred black.

"So much for a souvenir," he said quietly.

"At this point our lives are the only souvenir we should be concerned with keeping," Awkid responded as he walked ahead.

Balamor tossed the book to the ground and continued toward the center of the demolished structure. Awkid led, looking around him frequently for something — anything.

Someone is watching us... he thought to himself as that shivering cold feeling crept up his spine. He couldn't shake it, especially with the lack of shelter getting in the way of prying eyes.

They passed broken columns and slabs of Blackstone suspended in mid-collapse. Inanimate flames clung to wooden rafters and shelves, turning them into black smoke.

Thousands of books and scriptures were completely torn apart or burned to crisp – a sight that bewildered the young Wisebeard.

THE HANDS OF TIME

Awkid slowed his steps as the leaning structure of an old grandfather clock came into view. "There's some kind of clock ahead," he said to Balamor, who quickly took notice.

"Indeed... A rather intricate clock, look at all the different measurements... A shame it is to be left here in these ruins," the young mapmaker said as he approached it.

The body of the clock was made of vespine oak carved with impeccable detail. Four balusters stood atop its wide base, each spiraling with filigree patterns that edged beautiful panels of wooden inlay. Its lower and upper doors were made of a peculiar crystalline glass whose hue seemed to change ever so slightly.

He had studied very little regarding gnomish clock making, but from what little he knew, this seemed to follow the same basic framework of most case clocks – an upper door displaying the time by minutes and hours and a lower door for housing the pendulum and its three drive weights tied to cable pulleys. However, there were some obvious differences that left him puzzled.

Within the lower chamber were nine cylindrical weights, triple the usual amount. Typically, the middle weight powered the pendulum, while the right was for the chimes and the left for striking upon the hour. The weights would fall for seven days before being reset to keep the clock ticking.

What could be the purpose of the other six?

The weights hung above a crooked blacksteel pendulum which was even more peculiar given its engravings. The disk-shaped metal bob was stamped with a ring of runewords, a sign of its connection to the magical Runesong. Balamor recognized a few and quickly began to record them into his notebook along with sketches of the clock.

The upper chamber was far more complex than a typical case clock, featuring a series of hands for measuring different patterns and cycles. The clock face itself was made of four concentric rings each with a unique purpose.

Around the edge of the outermost ring was a series of gilded letters arranged in alphabetical order, with the last letter 'Z' meeting the first letter 'A' at the twelve o'clock position. A black metal hand was paused between them. What these letters represented was not yet obvious to him, though their position around the clock face showed their importance.

Within that ring was another narrower ring. Half of it was labeled with a series of numbers while the other half remained blank. The numbers ranged from one to 849 where a small dial rested. "If I'm not mistaken, this indicates the year was 849 when this thing stopped ticking... Wait, that's—"

"Twenty-six years ago..." Awkid interrupted him, his eyes becoming intense as he stared down at the grayish soil.

"Wasn't that when you traveled here with that black-robed man and his students?"

Awkid only nodded in response.

"Well then, the clock was stopped in 849... twenty-six years ago. Simple enough."

"I'm afraid it's never that simple, Mr. Wisebeard," Awkid replied as he leaned in closer to study the clock himself.

The third ring was a painted depiction of the four seasons, from the breaking spring rains to the deep freeze of winter. It was a self-explanatory work of art. Balamor fawned over its aesthetics, trying to sketch its details with the best of his ability. Around its edge was a sequence of numbers ranging from one to ninety-two, one for each day of the season. A thin black metal hand was stopped at forty-six, while a shorter hand hovered over the middle of winter.

"I see... It was the forty-sixth day of winter. Fascinating!" Balamor exclaimed with wide eyes, inspecting it and glancing toward a steely faced Awkid with excitement.

Last was the innermost ring that consisted of the usual twelve-hour clock at its center and the dial of the sun and moon around its edge. Balamor was familiar with dials such as these. They were referred to as 'sky dials' and they were typically found above the clock face. However, having a sky dial around the clock face itself rather was strange yet beautifully clever.

"A sky dial! I think that's what this part is. Usually they aren't this... Cool. But yeah, I can read this one as well. With the dial showing the sun making its passing right here," Balamor pointed toward the sun hand of the dial, "means this was the sun's clock when it stopped working. Therefore, the hands of the sun were stopped six minutes into its fourth hour, in the afternoon!"

"Around the same time I was making my way back home from the Mog Brush," Awkid said.

"And the same time that the black-robed man was here," Balamor added as he rubbed his chin.

He searched through his notes for more information as a hunch formed in his mind. "The Bounds of Akinn, they were here when you arrived?"

"Indeed, and what land I could see within was as dead as a corpse," Awkid answered.

Balamor flipped the pages of his notebook back to his early research. "Nature's Graveyard... Hmmm."

He stopped at his notes from The Fourth Valorhorn, his index finger pointed at the date of his entries. "841... So, eight years before you arrived here this Valorhorn fellow made his own journey. He mentioned this place was 'where the truth about the old world was buried.' That suggests this place was around well before anyone we know stepped foot here." He looked up at the milky Bounds of Akinn as he continued, "So, if these bounds are keeping everything paused and they were here before the year 849 then the clock should have been stopped long before then..." Balamor paused and pointed out a small hole just below just below the clock face. "Perhaps someone changed it?"

Awkid had something else in mind. "Or the Bounds of Akinn aren't always this stable."

"Think you can get me up there?" Balamor asked as he rooted through his backpack for something.

Awkid growled in suspicion. "What's your plan, halfling?"

Balamor removed a small blacksteel key and revealed it to Awkid. It was only a day ago that Awkid first retrieved the key, along with others after their run in with the guards and the thief. This particular key was most curious, considering the rune it was marked with.

"Maybe this key can fix the clock?" Balamor contended, gesturing Awkid to lift him up.

The dwarf let out a sigh and cupped his hands together to hold Balamor's foot. The young Wisebeard climbed up to the height of the clock face and held the key steady. Awkid's face started turning red as Balamor squirmed to reach the strange hole.

The key clicked into place and he felt the hairs on his neck stand up. He whispered a phrase that led him into the Bounds of Akinn, *"Ehn vis payr."* Balamor watched the runeword upon the key's surface flash an orange hue. He turned it to left and held his breath.

"Well? I can't do this all day!" Awkid growled. He was growing angry at the idea of him being a stool.

Balamor exhaled and looked at the clock, everything remained unchanged.

"Never mind. Must not be what this key is for," Balamor said as he climbed down to the ground.

Balamor brushed himself off and looked around as he spoke, "Either way, this place is much older than that clock puts on. Judging by the rarer materials such as the Blackstone and the vespine oak, I would say it's from the days of the Blood Wars."

"Agreed. In order to quarry this much Blackstone, one would require countless tools made of dragon glass... I once knew Dwarven stone masons that would kill a man for some dragon glass." Awkid shook his head as he tried to imagine the fortune it would cost.

"Well, there's not much else here for us to find. Let's keep moving. A few more stops and I will have an idea of the scale of this place." Balamor started to walk forward counting his steps as he went on. "One, two, three, four..."

They walked off across the desolate wasteland, as the young mapmaker made his progress on charting its bounds. They were a distant pair of silhouettes when the sound of gears clicked into place and started ticking. Dust fell from the leaning wooden case of the ancient clock and its once paused pendulum began to swing off kilter.

Slowly the year began to run backwards and the outermost metal hand started to turn forward.

Tick Tock...

Tick Tock...

The hand rolled away from the last letter of the sequence and toward the first. The soil beneath started to churn and undulate slowly. Another distant bellow erupted from the Mog Brush.

Tick Tock...

Tick Tock...

33

THE PAPER TRAIL

875, Summer's 57th Morning

**re** you okay, Uncle?" Marigold said over the sound of the clock.

The seventh bell was struck and the ticking of the clock resumed.

"Breakfast!" Gilly's voice yelled out from the kitchen.

Barris turned to Marigold and motioned her to the kitchen. "I'm alright, let's go eat."

The delicious scent billowed from the kitchen as Barris and his niece made it to the dining table.

Gilly stepped through the doorway holding three plates, two in her hands and the third balanced on her forearm.

She placed the plates upon the table and sat in the remaining floral cushioned chair.

Barris looked at his plate and rubbed his hands together in anticipation. It was indeed a sight to behold, especially for a hefty halfling like Barris on an empty stomach.

The home fries were a gorgeous golden brown and mixed with sautéed garlic and onion. Beside them, a slice of rye toast and two large servings of scrambled eggs and maple-glazed bacon. The heavenly mix of fresh parsley and Dahrisian salts pervaded with the rising steam.

Barris looked up from his plate and shot a glance at his sister who smiled and poured him another coffee from the brass flagon at the center of the table.

"Thank you, it has been ages since I've had someone else's cooking," he said as he grabbed a quartered potato with his fork.

"Since you've had *Mother's* cooking, you mean?" Gilly replied, pushing the mug toward him.

He took a bite; the buttery seasonings charmed his taste buds causing him to pause and close his eyes. "Indeed... Do you have her recipes?"

"Luckily for you, I do," she said, pouring herself a coffee and placing the flagon back on the table.

Marigold ate in silence, only the scraping of her fork could be heard as she consumed the hot meal.

Barris was lost in his food. Nostalgia took him to his childhood.

The same grandfather clock would ring every morning and his mother, Rose, would have the table set. He and Gilly would try to guess what their mother cooked that morning, but some new recipe always fooled them.

"She was magical, Mum was, and her cooking was her potion," Gilly said.

Barris paused at the words, reminded of what brought him here, away from his own home.

"And now you're magical, Mom! And maybe one day, I'll be magical!" Marie cheered as she raised her fork with glee.

Barris pushed his food around with his fork before grabbing his mug and taking a long swig.

Gilly studied him between bites, his eyes wandering from time to time and the shaking of his leg against the floor.

"So, you say you're in trouble? You and Balamor?" Gilly asked after wiping her mouth with a cloth napkin.

Barris looked out the window into the sunlit town. "Balamor left the Raehl, four days back. A day later his grandfather, Farjadis, was visited by a courier. Someone is after him and Balamor, Gilly, and they could come after me."

"Come after you?" his sister asked.

"For those books and for this..." he said as he reached into his pocket and retrieved the ruby pendant, placing it on the table before him.

Gilly didn't respond, she and Marigold both looked at the fastened ruby shard and then back at Barris.

"Farjadis calls it the 'Bloodstone.' Look I know, it sounds like nonsense to say the least, but this necklace and those books are part of something that is beyond just us halflings." He paused and stared into Gilly's eyes. "There are very powerful people in this world, Gilly – some on the bad side of the hill and others willing to keep these holes safe." Barris picked up the pendant and glared into its crystalline structure. "The Wisebeards, they aren't spun from the same thread as most halflings. They come from the old world, when there was one kingdom for all the races. It was always fairy tales to me though. Halflings, dwarves, humans, and gnomes all living in harmony? But twenty years ago, when I took the Wisebeards into my home, I learned the truth about those fairy tales and about magic."

"Magic?" Gilly asked with a raised eyebrow.

"The old man told me who the Wisebeards really were; where they'd come from. Their name goes far back, possibly even millennia before there were any kingdoms of men ruling this world. The people of old knew the Wisebeards as 'Scrivenkin.' Scribes of powerful words given to them by beings Farjadis called the 'Rahkfolk.' I don't know all the details, but what I do know is that the Wisebeards were the curators of this powerful knowledge, this magic... And since the Blood Wars that knowledge has been threatened."

"Scrivenkin? Sounds a bit outlandish of a title to give halflings. If you're certain this to be true, then who are the people on the bad side of the hill?" Gilly asked while placing her fork down on the emptied plate.

"A woman. Some say she is a beautiful human being; others say she's Fey, but all know her by the green robes she wears. She was once the queen of that old kingdom, and also the destroyer of its rule."

"And she lives today? How?" Marigold contested, chiming in after being lost in the tale from Barris.

"I don't know, but she does live today and she mustn't learn I'm here," Barris said before taking the last bite of his home fries.

"Where is Balamor in the heat of all this? Did he run?" Gilly asked.

"No, unfortunately Balamor doesn't know any of this. He left the Raehl alone on some journey, foolish boy. Where he travels now is hard to tell, and not in the least bit safe. Cartography he calls it. His grandfather always did defend him tooth and nail when it came to his mapmaking," Barris said as he shook his head.

"There was always something special about that boy... I knew it the day I sat for Aliya. Balamor was the only young'un whose toys were books," Gilly said softly, her emerald eyes scanning the sunken state of Barris. "He'll come back, Barris," she added.

Barris nodded and put the pendant back in his pocket.

Gilly stood up and grabbed their dishes from the table and walked to the kitchen. She placed them into an oak water basin and began scrubbing them with a porous Wynspur sponge.

Marigold lifted herself from her seat. "Thanks, Mum! I'm going to read now. Uncle Barris has so many books!" she said joyfully and proceeded to the room where Barris was staying.

"You're welcome, sweetie. I'll call when second breakfast is ready," Gilly said as she scrubbed the ceramic plates rigorously.

For a short moment, it was quiet aside from the sound of water occasionally splashing.

Barris leaned back in his chair and closed his eyes.

So many people flooded his mind — Balamor, Farjadis, and now the green-robed woman who hunted them both. His memories of the day he was thrown into the mix began to surface.

It was only two months after he moved to the Raehl when he met Farjadis Wisebeard. That fateful night seemed far darker than most nights as the stars were lost beyond thick clouds.

Three figures came strolling into town – two halflings and a very tall black-robed man guiding them. They moved through the town quietly avoiding contact with passersby. Barris was sitting on his old porch front — which now belonged to the old Wisebeard — as they stopped at an old shanty halfling hole.

Back then, Barris believed some hermit lived there, but he learned that night that it was a home to no one. Yet, purposeful was its abandonment, for the tall figure had planned its future occupancy.

Barris was curious about the cloaked trio and so he approached them. The other two figures waited behind the black-robed man who was cycling through a ring of keys.

He asked who they were and the tall man was quick to speak his name, *Gantis Jacs*. He introduced the others as Farjadis Wisebeard and his son *Ericho*. But what seemed like a simple greeting quickly turned to a serious command.

The black-robed man told Barris that he was to not speak of the Wisebeards to anyone. He remembered his deep, distressed voice, and it would be decades until he spoke of their name to others.

Gantis insisted that the Wisebeards live peacefully, quietly, and undisturbed; for the fate of all halflings was at stake. He made sure Barris would understand.

"So, do you know this woman's name?" Gilly asked, pulling Barris away from his thoughts.

Barris stood up from his chair and turned to face his sister. "'Lenook', that's what the old man calls her, anyway. Perhaps a surname, or even a title. But he believed it was unwise to tell me anything about her. Knowledge only Wisebeards seem to burden themselves with."

"I see... So, what will you do now?" Gilly asked.

"Wait." The clock kept ticking as he contemplated how long that would be. "It's all I can do."

"Wait? For how long?" Gilly was perplexed by the idea.

"Until—"

Barris was cut short by a knock on the door.

They both froze at the unexpected sound, which came again, now with heavier beats.

Barris approached the door and wrenched it open by the brass knob.

Standing before him was a rather slender figure dressed in elegant purple robes and fixing the small spectacles upon his nose.

"Excuse me, didn't mean to disturb you, but I couldn't help but notice this book outside your hole." He revealed a dark leather hardback with no title or text on its covers. He flipped its empty pages and continued, "Rather fascinating really, as it is similar to books I've seen before... You see Mister...?"

"Oakfoot," Barris answered with an uneasy tone.

"Ah, Mr. Oakfoot, well you see I am traveling with milady, and she too finds the placement of such a text, well, odd to say the least. I assume someone must have dropped it. You perhaps?"

Barris looked out to the road and saw a carriage of pristine quality. Gold trimmed its wooden walls and two beautiful white horses were at the reins. Out of a side door, the woman this man spoke of appeared, hooded and draped in long satin green robes.

Barris quickly looked back to Gilly through the doorway, fear plastered across his face. He took a breath and gathered his nerves, almost unable to believe who he was seeing.

She scanned the small halfling village and glanced toward the man at the doorway. "Aerendyl, does this halfling own this text?" Her voice was strong yet sweet and mystifying.

Barris turned to face the thin man before him, the green-robed woman waited only yards away for a response. "I'm afraid I am just as lost as you, friend. Books are no interest of mine. However, I did see a man cross these grounds at dawn. His gear showed he was certainly the traveling type. He could have dropped it."

"Hm, odd indeed." The man turned back to the green-robed woman and answered her question. "He does not, milady. He thinks a traveling man may have dropped it."

"Take the book, if he is lying, he will regret it," she said as she stared at Barris, her face hidden beneath the cowl of her robes.

The thin man closed the book and left the porch front slowly. "Thank you for your time, Mr. Oakfoot," he said with a sly voice.

"Of course," Barris replied as he watched the man stroll to the carriage and climb onto the upholstered bench.

The woman kept her gaze on Barris after she returned to her own seat. Even though her face was hidden, her stare stood him still.

The slender man yanked the reins to signal the horses to move and in a matter of seconds, the two strangers were gone.

The wooden wheels could still be heard squeaking as they drove away.

Barris shut the door quietly and turned to lean his back against it.

"Who was it?" Gilly asked as she walked toward him.

"It was her... Farjadis was right... I can't stay here much longer, Gilly. She will be back, and next time, she'll find what she's looking for."

34

NATURE'S GRAVEYARD

875, Summer's 57th Afternoon

hey both slowed their pace after hours observing the Mog Brush and visiting the larger landmarks that could be defined. Balamor made a note of them and their location from one another, using the tower as a reference. He contemplated how this place was destroyed.

Was it an ancient flood? Landslides? Perhaps some kind of series of earthquakes? Or was it the war itself?

It was undoubtedly a fortress, a massive one with a mysterious origin.

Balamor's eyes became heavy and the strength in his legs started to diminish as he walked on. The thoughts were coming together, but his lack of sleep made it hard to focus.

Awkid too was losing strength. Not only was he tired, but he was still weak from the struggle with Du'gahr and then the run-in with the Tarwolves. His strength was laughable compared to his better days.

"We should make camp. We haven't had good rest in days," Awkid suggested as he stopped and raised his arm for Balamor to halt.

"Good rest? In the Mog Brush? You're kidding?" Balamor raised an eyebrow and laughed.

"We either rest or pass out from exhaustion on our way back through the swamp. Your choice," Awkid finally replied.

"True... Plus, I could use some time to make some sketches," Balamor said while he closed his notebook and fitted it into his backpack. "Where to then?"

NATURE'S GRAVEYARD

Awkid looked around for a place, yet every which way seemed no different of a choice. There was no truly suitable set of ruins for them to occupy. Toppled buildings that may have once been grandiose were no better a place than the remains of peasant shacks.

Mixed up altogether as if there was no real layout to anything, these ruins baffled the dwarf as well as his halfling companion.

Awkid gazed off into the distance, squinting his eyes to focus, and he spotted the rippled fabric of an emerald banner. Dirt nearly consumed the entire pole it was attached to. It stood near the crooked and broken structure of a large building. Beside it, wooden dummies and archery targets poked out of the earth in random fashion.

"There." Awkid pointed. "A barracks of some kind," Awkid said, as he walked toward it.

Balamor followed him back to the stone path they traveled before, glancing at the ruins around them.

The still bodies of elven soldiers and empty suits of black metal armor were scattered across the wasteland. His expectations of the Mog Brush were surpassed by its reality, and the story of what happened here was more mysterious than he previously imagined.

For a place called "Nature's Graveyard" it must have been a place occupied only by death. Yet around him were the seemingly alive bodies of an unknown elven army. Their weapons and armor weren't covered in a single speck of rust.

Flames from a fiery battle still lingered with heat as if they were fresh. Stone and wooden structures that once belonged to a more stable place were toppled and displaced without any apparent reason.

The path led them to the green banner and the remains of the old barracks it stood for. At the center of the banner in bold white contours was a gemstone encircled by a braid of thorns; the sigil of yet another unknown kingdom.

They both moved slowly through the arched stone threshold and stopped at its thick wooden doors.

Without hesitation, Awkid grasped one of the iron rungs and slowly dragged the tall door open. Digging through the hill of dirt that covered its lower half, a passage became clear and with it, a stream of earth pouring out from within.

Balamor quickly moved aside and watched as the dirt spilled out of the doorway.

The two adventurers looked at each other and then back at the doorway as the dirt finally settled.

Awkid raised an eyebrow as Balamor traversed the new mound of dirt into the old barracks. Awkid trailed him through the narrow opening, grunting as he struggled to fit inside.

They both pulled the heavy doors closed and the humming of the ancient barrier became nearly silent. The air smelled of musk and mildew as flecks of dust lingered in a stagnant haze. The stone floors were barely visible under a sea of earth and scattered weapons.

More elven bodies and dark steel armor suits were half buried by the dirt — paused along with plumes of earth.

They walked by a series of long wooden tables, each coated in a layer of dirt. Some were flipped while others were broken in pieces. The contents they were meant to hold were scattered around the room in random fashion; plates, bowls, cups, and utensils all made of steel were spotted in every direction.

The remains of meals and decorative fruits were also thrown about the place without one speck of mold upon them. They quickly gathered this area was a mess hall of sorts but eating any of the meals would have to be out of the question.

Balamor looked in his bag, reminded of the fact that he hadn't had a meal in days. To his surprise he still had a few carrots, tomatoes and even a couple baked potatoes left for him and Awkid to share.

His journey home would be a different story that made the idea of taking something from this hall tempting.

He shook his head before walking to the other side of the room where another emerald banner hung from the low ceiling. Balamor shoved an abandoned suit of armor out of the path and slowly snuck by.

Through the passage was a dark and narrow hallway with more earth spread unevenly throughout. Bodies could be seen eerily poking through the grayish-brown surface as Balamor and Awkid moved onward. Balamor lit one of his metallic torches and blue flames spawned from its wick, casting an aura of cool blue light around them. Halfway down the hall, they came to a heavy oak door. The Wisebeard lowered himself to the ground and shoveled the dirt in front of him when he felt a strange numbness spread through his left hand. He paused and lifted it up, letting the dirt pour through his fingers before staring intensely. After a moment the feeling subsided, and he placed his hand on the soil once more. He waited but there was nothing.

His curly head shook in disbelief as he rose to his feet.

Awkid looked at him but didn't question what was on Balamor's mind. His own mind was slipping with exhaustion and the only thing he could think of was rest. Although his wound had sealed, weakness plagued his body as he moved to the iron rung and pulled the door open.

The room inside was toppled with broken furniture and fabrics all mixed in a thin layer of soil. Looking around, it became obvious this was the living quarters of soldiers.

A few mattresses were still amongst the remains of bunks, covered in dirt and haphazardly placed. Wooden trunks were still filled with various supplies belonging to the men who once called this place home.

Balamor leaned over one with the torch in hand and observed its contents.

Papers and shabby journals were found along with a few valuable trinkets. He grabbed a small necklace and observed it quietly.

Hanging from a leather cord was a small wooden figurine of a bird, perhaps whittled by the man who once wore it. As his fingers rubbed the grains of the strange wooden bird, he looked around.

What was left of these living quarters didn't come close to telling its story. This all seemed like a dream in some kind of omniscient wasteland. Sleeping here would be a chore to say the least.

Awkid snooped around the dormitory for a moment, kicking over random litter to find a reasonable place to sleep. He pulled a single mattress from the soil and placed it on the ground flat.

Balamor finished observing the random belongings he could find before nabbing a dusty journal from the chest and plopping himself next to where Awkid was resting. After placing down the blue lit torch between them, he reached into his bag and grabbed two carrots. Tossing one to Awkid and chomping into his own, he brushed the dirt from the journal's cover and flipped the rest from between its pages. A cloud of dust billowed out in front of him before colliding with the stone wall across the room. He let out a breath before opening the fresh leather cover.

"Doryn Beldavale," Balamor said with an intrigued look upon his brow. He flipped to the marked page and widened his eyes when he saw the signed date.

> *"212, winter's 3rd day..."* he said with a glance to Awkid, who propped himself up on one elbow as Balamor continued to read the passage.
>
> *"Blasphemy! All this talk about 'The Great Red King' has my guts turning! This leader of ours is failing not only in this war against these Fey, but in his own fight for sanity! If it wasn't for this war, I would be long gone to The Steel Isles, a*

place where a sword can be put to good use. A shame it is that a blind prince can lead an army better than a famed ruler of the world's most powerful Kingdom..."

Balamor paused, taking another bite of his carrot and rubbing his chin in intrigue. "Well, this confirms our suspicions. Looks like this place is hundreds of years old, but what about the war he mentions?"

"Men against Fey? The Blood Wars, no doubt about that," Awkid answered.

"But this is from over six centuries ago... that can't be right... The Blood Wars ended almost three centuries ago... By 602, Anstia finally secured their power in the Southlands and the Steel Isle of Wynspur fell to a den of thieves sometime after Du'gahr's supposed death. If proven right, then this would mean Du'gahr has lived longer than the Anstian Monarchy."

Awkid responded swiftly, his mouth full as he spoke, "An ugly comparison, nonetheless. I think the real question is not when the Blood Wars ended, but when they really began... and for how long did they continue?"

Balamor agreed, as he studied Mr. Beldavale's entry. "Indeed. The exact date when the wars began is vague on most accounts. The great scholar Hagron Soldo did claim that that the history of the Southlands was laden with amnesia. Hmm, it was the year 212 that Doryn mentioned 'this war' in his writing. Perhaps, it was the only war at the time? The Blood Wars may well have started early in the second or third centuries," he added, seemingly perplexed with their deliberation.

"Four hundred years of war?" Awkid asked impatiently.

"There's more," Balamor claimed.

"But all is not yet lost. There is word that the Knights of Valorhorn are sending support; perhaps Abbott Valorhorn will try and seize the Breadth of Man himself... I don't believe

*he would usurp any throne, especially that of an ally... 'Ally'
what does that term mean when your life is at stake?*

*"Seems fitting that this place became depressed as the
sun became fallow... This Necromancer and the corruption
they breed will be all that remains in this place. I'll find a way
out of here on my own. Hopefully Nim can extend a branch in
my favor."*

Awkid looked at Balamor and watched him absorb the
context. The young mapmaker snapped his fingers and pointed
at the page as he spoke, "That name... *Valorhorn*... the man I
mentioned earlier, who traveled here in 846. He called himself
'The Fourth Valorhorn.'"

"Besides the old horn itself, I haven't learned much about
the Valorhorn name... though I have laid eyes on that famous
island city... over forty years ago," Awkid reminisced.

"Delsis? All I've learned about Delsis was that it was
home to the 'oldest horn in the world', and it was once my
grandfather's hometown. Before that old lake dried up, anyway,"
Balamor chimed in as he laid another mattress atop the grayish
soil.

Awkid paused and looked down at the floor. "832 was the
year, a long time ago... I was on my way south to settle in the
forests of Gwendilae. After being exiled and living off the
highlands for two years, I was finally able to cross the Great
Divide. I traveled the Mystvein for days before the river became
sick with something foul. The current slowed to a mere creek,
and all the fish died, bleeding from their eyes and gills. It only
took four days for that river to die and a week for that foggy
lakebed to run dry. By the time I descended the Great Divide
and came across the famous city, the entire fortress was in ruins
and the Mystfalls were mudflats. If it weren't for the small fires
remaining, I would have thought the place was abandoned for
centuries."

Balamor seemed stumped with Awkid's story compared to his grandfather's modest version. "A fortress? I always thought it was a simple town..."

"Far from simple. The walls alone made any Dwarven structure seem petty in comparison. It was a man-made mountain, really," Awkid replied with a gaze into the blue flames of the torch.

"Before I saw those ruins, I didn't know much about the island city... Only that the Blackstone it was made of was ancient; perhaps it's from the same time as this old place. Either way, whatever destroyed Delsis in those days possessed enough power to toss massive blackstones an acre's breadth from their foundations. Hard to fathom."

Balamor looked to the ceiling in thought. "My grandfather never spoke of this destruction you witnessed, but he never did go into detail when speaking of 'the old days', just that the lake eventually dried up and the people were forced to move elsewhere. I wonder if he was there when the fortress was destroyed, too..."

Awkid sat up to continue his story, the bones of his cursed arm rattled as he gathered himself.

"There was a human kid I met that day; I think his name was Sam. Found him fighting off wolves deep in the forest. A talented swordsman, but a poor hunter. After slaying the wolves, we became acquainted. Made camp, drank mead, split the meat, that sort of thing... After a while he told me he was from the Island City. He said that he survived an onslaught nights before. In the dead of night — when I was camped out along the dying Mystvein — he was with his brothers fighting to hold the southern gates of Delsis."

"Against what?" Balamor asked impatiently.

"Against a creature, and the sorcerer who controlled it. The kid said his commander called it the 'Windwraith' or something of the sort... Said it stood as high as the city walls, and its body was made of dust and storms."

Balamor wouldn't have believed it before, but he saw the green-robed woman conjure up a smaller yet similar creature only days ago – *Jabit Treadfoot.*

"A sorcerer? Was it a man or a woman?" Balamor inquired, curiously trying to piece it together.

"Didn't say... He said in one moment they suddenly appeared, standing atop the high tower of Delsis — where the ancient Valorhorn rested — and in a flash the sorcerer disappeared, taking the horn with them. By then the creature had torn the city walls down and ravaged the entire city."

"This human... Sam, he survived all of this?" Balamor asked.

"Indeed, he and six others trapped themselves in some old cellar. After days had gone by, they rose from the rubble, only to find their home was demolished. Sam said they gathered anything 'worthy of the Valorhorn credo'. Whatever that meant, I haven't a clue. After that, each of them split ways; taking an oath to seek out the horn and bring it back."

"A courageous mission... Seems odd there haven't been books written about this," Balamor added.

"That's because most of the world still doesn't know it happened, or how it happened. Anything truth tellers who dare speak of such things like 'Windwraiths' are labeled as 'Whispers' by the Higher Hand of Anstia. And, every commoner knows not to trust Whispers," Awkid finished in distaste, both for the Anstian Monarchy and for the conditions of this forsaken place. He looked around at the remnants of the living quarters. The ransacked area was flooded with dirt and debris, smelling of stale grain and moldy earth.

Balamor kept flipping through the old journal in his hands. His tense stare seemed to hawk the pages for something peculiar. Each page flip echoed through the room, one after the next; the scrapping of paper and crackling of strange blue flames was all that could be heard.

Awkid rested back his head and Balamor looked further into Doryn Beldavale's accounts.

The journal entries filled the pages of the shabby old book, all the way back to the beginning of the second century — when Mr. Beldavale's outlook was much less tragic.

200, Spring's 16th day

At last... The First Kingdom... Oh what a truly magnificent place! I would say the journey to its walls was the best any adventurer could imagine, but it seems the land beyond is of another world altogether! The people, the music, the food, and this wine... Oh the wine is just splendid in this place!

Never have I met so many folks who all share my world view and still fight with grit! Hard to imagine they all live under one rule, but even the Red King himself can walk the streets without dissent dragging behind him like some fleshy cape. His mere presence illuminated the heart of the city, as if his own enlightenment was contagious! Fantastic, I will write Maldyaer as soon as I am settled down. Wait 'til he learns of the First Kingdom and its people... They are far from being as ignorant as Beshmere suggested. These folks are rather motivated.

My sword will prove useful here after all.

Balamor gazed off into thought as a familiar name picked at his mind. He removed his notebook from his bag and searched its pages. He knew that name, Beshmere, and just as he remembered why, he turned the page to reveal his recent notes from Awkid's bestiary, *Of Nefarious Nature*.

"Dansil Murko, of the Beshmere Arm," Balamor said, speaking his mind aloud. "What is 'The Beshmere Arm' anyway?"

Awkid answered his question after a long pause, "A group of hunters."

"Hunters? Of wild game?"

"No, not your typical hunter. The Beshmere Arm hunt monsters and the dark magic that created them," Awkid replied as he closed his eyes.

Balamor became absorbed by the new snippet of information. *Yet another name to remember*, he thought to himself for a moment. For him, even the smallest, most unrelated information was still part of something bigger, something intangible yet essential to uncovering the truth.

Written here in this old journal were the words of a common man, yet his words pointed toward something beyond their mere context. Mr. Beldavale may one day be the key to understanding the Mog Brush and the days of old.

This realization struck Balamor as he tried to remember all the names he had heard in his own time.

He quickly turned to a new page in his notebook and removed his charcoal pencil. In scratchy print, he titled the new section, *Names of Legend,* and began listing all the important names he had heard throughout his journey.

Each one was given its own description – some short and vague like that of the summoned halfling *Jabit Treadfoot* and Mr. Beldavale's unknown acquaintance *Maldyaer*. While others such as *Awkid Anvorbeard*, and the mysterious *Gantis Jacs* went on and on with both clue and question. He added the names of famed kingdoms such as *Anstia*, and forgotten kingdoms like *Delsis*, and from the *Valorhorn* name to his very own name, *Wisebeard*, the list became more of an undertaking than he imagined. There was *Finn*, the bridge builder who saved him from the bandits. *Mayn*, the strange mystic highwayman who nearly killed him on two separate occasions, and he couldn't forget Mayn's oversized companion, *Bear*.

Each name added to the list was a reminiscent flash of Balamor's seemingly long and impossible quest, but one title that intrigued him the most was that mentioned on three different accounts.

The title appeared in Awkid's old kingdom tale and also in the dwarf's own story about when he received his curse. He read the same title in Dansil Murko's preface to his work, *Of Nefarious Nature*. Now, in Doryn Beldavale's personal journal, Balamor has come across it once more.

Who is the Necromancer?

The thought lingered on as he finished his description of Nim and his bewildering forest.

If Awkid's old tale was true, then it would be the sixth Mystic Red King who became the Necromancer. Perhaps being the 'Sixth' could have been a symbol of the current century.

Well of course! He said to himself, nodding slowly.

Then it would line up perfectly with the recorded birth of the Anstian Monarchy. The pieces fell into the place, and for a moment his exhaustion seemed to fade at the onset of a conclusion.

He finished the next entry and began to look over his list. As he panned down the page, he realized there was a problem with the connection between the old tale from Awkid and Balamor's hunch — The Necromancer who cursed Awkid was certainly no king, but instead a Dwarven woman.

Could there be more than one?

A possibility that only complicated the history even more.

All the names reminded him of how intertwined the world could be and how many faces quickly had become involved in his own tale. He knew the list would only grow, and he started wondering how many pages such names would fill.

As he finished his ambiguous entry on the alleged *Necromancer*, he caught the sound of a low stuttering snore from across the blue fire of the torch.

There Awkid Anvorbeard lay still, grasping the dark and dirty bones of his right arm like a steel dagger in the night. Only imagination could describe to Balamor what the strange dwarf felt or didn't feel for that matter.

The curiosity kept coming back to the young Wisebeard and returning each time with it was the promise he made to the dwarf — The name of the woman who cursed him.

He looked down at his list of names and wrote his final entry — *Farah Lenook.*

35

IN THE SOIL

875, Summer's 57th Midnight

nce again — after what felt like ages of absence — the Bounds of Akinn trembled and the Mog Brush had finally awoken. Arcs of fluctuating light splashed in and out of the dome-shaped barrier as a growling vibration echoed through the landscape. Like the sighing breath of an old, old man confined by the ancient bounds, not by virtue, but by a lonesome burden. Like the breath of a prisoner who wishes for death, but only finds another aging exhale instead.

As the deep hum of the magical bounds spread to the very edges of the Mog Brush, the grayish soil within started gradually to shift and churn. Deadwoods and Blackstone ruins tumbled in the sluggish current. The air had awoken after years of dormancy, pushing pillars of flame and smoke into motion and reigniting the sounds of a long-forgotten battle. Screams of rage and agony began to fill the entire landscape in a bizarre form of reality, both past and present.

At the center of the once sleeping land was the ancient high tower of the First Kingdom. Made entirely of megalithic Blackstone. The old tower was built with magnificent style and skill. Its form was that of a lathed baluster with protruding rings of Blackstone and intricate hexagonal patterns etched into its surface. Twisting upward into a conical roof of charred flagstone the great spire of rock stirred like a buoy in a sea of soil.

Far up the tower, a large section of the cylindrical wall was demolished. Courses of huge Blackstone lay broken and scattered by whatever ancient impact struck the tower long ago.

IN THE SOIL

From within the large cavity was a streak of blood that stretched to the base of the ancient tower's foundation. Slowly it began to flow once again, and its crimson color pulsated and glistened with amber light as it mixed with the earth. The soil swirled around the base of the tower, carrying entire buildings and the remnants of other Blackstone structures with ease. The bodies of elven warriors once paused in time were now alive and being tossed and turned by the earthly whirlpool.

Their screams echoed, and those that were still standing could be heard fighting as metal clashed against metal. Empty suits of armor that once lay scattered around the ancient land could be seen moving as if men wore them. The soil devoured the iron bodied warriors close to the tower, smashing many with large Blackstone ruins and drifting trees.

The Mog Brush was pulling everything in like quicksand.

It was a battlefield being twisted by a powerful spell, and its combatants were unaware of the madness around them. As corpses and ruins were drowned by the earth, the souls of lost warriors and cursed men began to manifest into beings made of soil and crushed bones. Like earthly apparitions whose bodies were dissolving like sand slipping through frail fingers. Their amorphous figures leached onto soldiers and ruins alike, consuming all in their earthly reach.

The once still air turned into a roaring crescendo, as the Mog Brush tumbled whole buildings and bastions like river rocks. Blackstone structures once completely buried ripped through the ocean of regolith crooked and lopsided, only to crash down and capsize like dying vessels. Closer toward the edge of the calamity, the remains of once forgotten barracks drifted and bobbed as it was pulled closer to the ancient high tower. An emerald banner that hung from the archway of the old barracks snapped under the pressure of the turbulent landscape.

Before long, the building began to keel over and the doors of the mess hall finally crashed open, flooding it rapidly and forcing a torrent of corrupted earth into the main hallway.

Earthly souls tore past large debris, melding into one another and viciously forming and deforming their tormented bodies within the soil. Their screams raced down the hallway closer to the doors of the sleeping chambers.

The sound of vespine oak creaking and cracking joined the deep snores of Awkid and Balamor. Sprawled across a dirty mattress with his six-page spellbook covering his face, the young Wisebeard slowly awoke as soil punched a hole through the hallway door to his room. He removed the book from his face and rubbed his eyes in confusion.

Suddenly, the room rolled over and the stone cracked as Balamor slid off of the bed into the wall. The contents of the room were flipped over and dirt swarmed in, breaking the rest of the door from its iron hinges.

Balamor looked around for Awkid but the room was flooding too quickly and the dwarf was nowhere to be seen. He grabbed his bag and spellbook and hurried toward the back of the room. As he rushed across scattered furniture, something yanked at his bag and pulled him to his knees. Glancing back, he saw earthen wraiths grabbing at his legs and ripped robes, dragging him further into the soil. He yanked at the bag and flew from the dirt-formed hands, rolling and slamming into a crooked stone wall.

Winded and dazed, he looked for a way to escape the carnage when the barracks started to tumble once more tossing him across the room into an open wooden trunk. The walls buckled and the wave of earth finally demolished the entire room when the trunk slammed shut, locking Balamor inside.

Careening across the crest of an earthly wave of barrack ruins and deadwoods, the trunk jostled along toward the tower.

Balamor flung to-and-fro within the dark contents of the chest. Earth scraped against the wooden confines in a violent thrash, his breaths began to chatter and the occasional thump from large debris left Balamor in a panic.

IN THE SOIL

The small wooden trunk surfed the rumbling terrain past earthly eidolons attempting to snatch the trunk from the soil. The sound of screeching metal and tormented men whipped past the trunk in a confusing blur of commotion.

Balamor fought to gather his stability and the rest of his belongings in the churning ride through the Mog Brush. His runes were scattered and each of them were glowing brightly against the darkened interior of the chest. Without a thought, he stuffed them into his bag and grabbed his spellbook. Many of its pages were filled with glowing runes. He tried studying the words, but the chest tumbled once more and thrashed him around inside.

Then, something massive slammed up against the wooden trunk and nearly broke it apart. Wooden planks came loose and cracks spread through others as the entire chest started to fill with grayish soil. The creaking wood barely held up against the earthly torrents clawing their way toward the young Wisebeard.

He peered through the cracks as the waves pushed him closer to the tower where fires and havoc consumed the land. Elves and their metal opponents were torn apart and mixed into the earthly concoction surrounding Balamor. A heavy thud below the trunk shook him from his daze and the wooden chest finally splintered open throwing him forward.

Swiftly rolling out of the debris was Balamor Wisebeard, clutching his six-page spellbook and gathering his footing atop a huge slab of Blackstone. Quickly stuffing his spellbook into his backpack, he glanced around for somewhere to go.

Only seconds passed when a monstrous wave of earth started to fold and crash down from behind him.

He sprinted toward another large jagged rock and made a daring leap through the air. His furry feet hit the Blackstone and his momentum began to build, jumping from stone to stone as the wave consumed everything in its path. As he advanced, another wave approached from his front, rolling and tumbling trees and stones alike. He jumped to another stone and searched for a path away from the destruction ahead, but the Mog Brush charged him from all sides.

The souls in the earth all raced from the edges of the waves like serpents looking to consume the young mapmaker.

There was no sure way out.

The two colossal waves raged toward one another like the hands of a titan crushing its prey.

Balamor was stuck on a slab of Blackstone with nothing to save him but himself. He closed his eyes and tried to imagine a way to stop the Mog Brush, a way to remove the corruption from the earth. He kept saying the words over and over while the waves began to merge their earthly crests into one collapsing tunnel.

The screams and echoes of battle were muffled and all Balamor could hear was the earth tearing into itself. Yet, the sounds of the runewords overpowered the roaring noise.

He reached his right hand into his bag and grabbed his *Theas* rune; its encircled dash symbol glowed a warm green.

He looked intensely at his left hand as he spread his fingers wide — a force between them felt strangely familiar.

The tunnel was seconds away from consuming the young mystic when he yelled the makeshift spell with a mighty call, *"Raji ehn theas!"*

It was a mix of words he only barely felt made sense, but it was a spell more powerful than he could imagine.

Around him the massive waves of soil exploded outward with amazing force before disintegrating into a warm green light that rapidly swirled into the tips of his fingers.

He felt the strange weakness deep in his bones but resisted the strong power overtaking him. The slab of stone he stood on rushed to-and-fro through the narrow tunnel of earth that now dissipated around him. As he sailed between the crashing waves, he saw ruins and trees being forced out of his way.

The sled of stone he was on drifted into another and threw Balamor off balance, breaking his concentration along with the spell he was casting.

Quickly, he gathered himself and ran as fast as he could from the tail ends of the crashing waves of soil. With each step more Blackstone slabs gathered in front of him, making a path through the dangerous landscape.

He didn't stop to question the strange forces at work in the Mog Brush. His only option was to follow the path away from the havoc unfolding behind him.

Ruins and debris were thrown wildly toward him, shattering stone and crushing the swirling brush with ease.

Balamor kept his feet under him as the Mog Brush hunted him down with all of its power.

From between the pathway of Blackstone tiles gathering before him, he saw arms and bodies of cursed earth climbing out of the ground looking to tear him from his feet. Pieces of the path were dragged beneath the soil by the earthly figures in an effort to sabotage Balamor's escape.

The pathway narrowed and, in the distance, the robed halfling could see something huge breaking through the soil.

Earth poured off of its Blackstone walls and darkened roof as it rose from the ground.

The halfling sprinted toward the unknown building with the Mog Brush swarming after him.

The thin path continued to extend all the way to the entrance of the building, seemingly unmoved by the raging landscape. Hurrying across them, Balamor's feet lost control, and he tumbled to his knees.

Still holding the *Theas* rune in his hand, he tried crawling back to his feet but something grabbed him from behind.

A series of earthen arms snatched at his legs and body in an effort to swallow him whole.

He struggled to break free but the swarm of hands latched onto his tattered robes and pulled him from the path. He jerked his small body forward in a twist and slipped out of his robes before they disappeared into the earth. Now, he was left wearing his white tunic. He glanced over at his leather bag as it too was being pulled into the soil.

Quickly, he rushed toward it and wrestled it from the tormented figures, throwing him onto his back. He felt a large hand grab his legs and begin to drag him away. He tried to break free once more but its grip was too strong.

His stubby fingers held onto the Blackstone slab with all of his might while the rest of his body was being consumed. He knew he could only hold on for so long before his soul joined the others trapped in the cursed earth.

With one last gasp of air, he closed his eyes as his hands were ripped from the Blackstone and the earthly limb finally pulled him down into the Mog Brush.

He could feel the soil racing around his body and tearing against his flesh like sandpaper. Roots and other litter crashed against him when he felt something grab his torso and drag him along.

He could feel his limbs growing numb and his consciousness slipping further away from him. Reality soon became a faint blur and his thoughts were all that he could sense, like a dark boundless room with only flickering sounds of familiar voices.

He didn't know where he was, who he was or where everything was before. All he knew was a tender voice that called out to him.

A warm and mellow voice that started to burn intensely the more he focused on the words. *"There we are my child, now what was your name?"*

IN THE SOIL

It was a woman's voice, a woman who had no face, but a woman with a name he thought he would never forget. The words trailed... *now what was your name?*

He didn't know any name, not the name belonging to this burning voice, not even his own name. The woman's voice dimmed out, but the burning became more profound.

Balamor focused with the last of his mind on the heat of this fire he felt within.

Soon, the darkness became divided by the embers of a white flame whose light grew into a blinding bellow of fire.

He lost his sense of reality but where he was now seemed to be all that there ever was. As he focused on the fire, the burning became a comfortable caress and the light started to pulse between various colors and elements.

All else seemed gone before the sound of silence broke and cold air filled his lungs.

His steel-blue eyes exploded open to see the stout figure of Awkid Anvorbeard carrying him under his left arm while charging through the ground with his magical limb.

Awkid tunneled out of the earth with incredible speed. Ripping through soil and ruins, the cursed limb he possessed had been reformed by the Mog Brush itself.

Before the mapmaker could begin to think, Awkid threw him over his shoulder and leaped onto the narrow stone path. After a few moments, Balamor felt the numbness subdue and, in its place, pure adrenalin rushed over him.

He looked around at the monstrous landscape churning and mixing everything into chaos. With his *Theas* rune and bag somehow still in his grasp, he squirmed out of Awkid's grip and landed on his feet, darting ahead down the Blackstone path.

Awkid glanced back and saw the path behind was being ripped into the rolling wasteland and quickly joined the fleeing halfling.

The both of them had no other path to take.

The fact that a path existed at all seemed stranger to Awkid. Yet after what this place has become overnight, nothing could surprise him even slightly.

They hurried down the rock-strewn road as the Mog Brush around them attacked from all sides.

Awkid rushed toward Balamor when a wave crashed onto the path and divided them. Awkid acted quickly as he saw the path breaking apart and ripped a tree from the wave to bridge the gap. As he dragged the dead oak into the path, the sound of a deep guttural roar shook the entire landscape around him.

Awkid ran across the grayish trunk and rushed toward the halfling who abruptly stopped before a second wave crashed against him.

By the time the dwarf made it to him, Balamor was beneath the crest as it folded over.

Awkid reached his arm in Balamor's direction when he saw a green light shine through the soil.

The wave exploded into a warm green stream of light that absorbed into Balamor's hand.

Awkid watched the dirt that formed his earthen arm begin to whisk away into that same green light. He reeled his cursed arm away from Balamor in shock and the young halfling stared back, bewildered.

"Run! Damn it! There's no time!" Awkid shouted as he pushed Balamor forward.

Balamor started to sprint with his hand spread out in front of him. The green glow continued to spiral into his fingers while the scrapes and cuts riddling his body sealed shut. The earth around him disintegrated from all sides as the roar that shook the land sounded once more, only this time it was right behind them.

He glanced over his shoulder and his eyes widened at the sight.

IN THE SOIL

Tearing its way onto the path was the colossal figure of a giant wearing armor plates upon his thick skin, charging for the two adventurers in magnificent strides.

"Giant!" Balamor yelled, as he dropped his spell and rushed toward the building at the end of the path.

Flying through the air, a flaming ball of stone soared toward the path ahead before smashing in an explosion of fire. The impact destroyed the slabs of stone making the path, leaving a vast swathe of dead earth in their place.

Just as Awkid prepared to take action, another buried structure punched through the gape of earth, filling its place and rocking like a ship against the sea.

The two of them kept running, traversing broken ruins that fell from the ancient building and hobbling past its crumbling threshold.

Inside, the litter of the Mog Brush rolled and snapped as soil breached the windows trying to consume it. As they moved forward, they could see another threshold leading outside, but the stones holding it up started to crack and break apart.

In seconds, the armored giant busted through the entrance and chased them down, sending ripples across the stone floor with each step.

The adventurers were losing ground to their massive predator as they ran for the tumbling doorway.

Another fiery boulder crashed into the pitched roof of the ancient hall, and the building started to collapse.

The giant shouldered through the ruins with ease, splitting the trembling hall in two.

Balamor and Awkid barely slipped past the exit before it crumbled, but the giant was still close behind, bursting through the back of the building down the remaining path.

Awkid was catching up to Balamor, who tumbled over debris raining down in front of them. In a swift motion, he yanked him by the back of his tunic with his left hand and leaped onto another slab making up the path.

Balamor gained his balance and continued to run as he looked ahead to see the strange Blackstone building was still there; sitting completely still while the Mog Brush raged around it.

Unbroken and in seemingly perfect condition, the building waited for them, holding off the wasteland around it.

Two large chiseled statues guarded a stone door that began to open as the adventurers drew closer.

The Mog Brush grew increasingly wild, the closer they made it to their destination, as if it was working to stop them. Debris flung toward them and waves of earth lifted up high before rolling toward the sides of the path.

Ducking under a dead tree, Balamor and Awkid moved like the wind. They were seconds away from the entrance but the giant finally closed in and reached to yank the two of them from the landscape.

Sliding and tumbling into a secluded hallway, Balamor and Awkid heard the deafening roar again, only this time it came to an abrupt and gurgling end.

As Awkid looked back toward the entrance, he saw the slouched figure of Balamor Wisebeard only inches away from the reaching hand of the giant.

Slowly the monstrous arm fell limp and Awkid saw the two stone guardians had come to life, thrusting their spears into the armored chest of the giant who quickly faded. Red blood drained out of his wounds and from his mouth before Mog Brush reclaimed him.

The two adventurers stood in awe, frozen in the moment as the heavy stone door slammed shut and left them in complete darkness.

36

EIGHT CENTURIES

875, Summer's 58th Sunrise

**eaves** glided through the air gracefully, flipping and turning as they fell toward the forest floor. Sunlight was beginning to break through the foliage in the thick trees.

The ground was covered with leaves upon leaves. Some were old and deep in the dregs of the earth, while others were still green and gilded in a powdery golden haze. Drops of rain started to patter against the canopy as the wind churned the leaf-strewn ground from dormancy. A faint trace of an echo bounced off the trees of the dense woodland, becoming louder as they replayed in Nim's mind.

"Go! Shield the Wisebeard!"

Nim was left stranded in the forest once again, remembering the last voice he heard.

This time it was the voice of an old friend, but more so the voice of a man he watched mature from an orphan boy into a timeworn magician. A great one indeed. A mage who's done more good for the races of man than any king, or other folk have.

Nim looked ahead, a memory of the Rhethis Barrens only being yards away. Two days had passed, yet the memory was as real now as it was then. He opened his palm. Within it was the red ruby shard necklace Gantis had given him, a fragment of so many things — of peace, of ignorance, of a time before the other end of this forest died.

EIGHT CENTURIES

This small ruby was a bigger risk than its size granted. Giving its beholder a power impossible to foretell; the prospect of mutual peace at the cost of mutual ignorance.

It didn't go so well the last time – he remembered those days so vividly now as he felt the ruby in his grasp.

Closing his eyes almost transported him there, centuries ago. The day he had become bound to the roots of this place — a life sentence. He tried to remember what it was like before then, but it was so far back now.

The strange sound those bells made when the door opened. The sight of each familiar face coming and going to his desk, returning books or unlocking new ones for study.

He remembered watching that humongous clock ticking forward not for the sake of time, but for the sound of peace. It was a clock that was said to never stop after all.

But he remembered the time that day, of that moment.

It was nine minutes past the sun's fourth hand when he blinked, and everything changed.

At first, he thought he'd merely awoke from a daydream. Yet the clock read six minutes past four. Days went by as he tried to convince himself it was his eyes that were mistaken, but his mind obsessed over it.

Every day after, he watched that clock ticking away. Never again did he watch it with the same peace of mind. It was that slight difference that consumed him entirely. Three minutes before the bells ring, he would stare, waiting for something to happen once again.

He opened his eyes; his fist was nearly senseless from squeezing the ruby so tight. Placing it into his vest pocket, he removed his brass pocket watch and inspected its exterior. Three dots in the shape of a triangle, neatly engraved into its surface.

$$\begin{matrix} \bullet \\ \bullet \quad \bullet \end{matrix}$$

ZARDRAKEN'S CRYPT

"Lohn khin onos ris. Ehn vis payr." The words came out in one mystifying breath as he flicked the timepiece open.

Behind the glass cover, two brass hands ticked onward, yet everything else about the clock was strange. Atop the hands was a third hand – a dial made of dark steel that spun around its circular rim where the four cardinal directions were engraved.

Suddenly the dial stopped. It pointed northeast — the same direction it always faced. Nim let out a brooding sigh and closed the watch and stuffed it away.

"Perhaps one day," he whispered to himself.

The windy drizzle was soon joined by a thick swirling fog, dirty with dust and the scent of death. It was a scent he knew all too well, the remnants of an age-old disaster he barely escaped.

Although the memories were vivid, it became difficult to discern those of the two souls he shared. Both of them filling in blanks for the other, slowly fusing into one.

He began to walk through the repugnant fog and rain, drawing closer to its deadly source. His clothes became moist and dirty as he trekked the familiar woodland. The trees wavered in the whistling wind, leaves twirling and splashing against his body.

After a while, the Forest of Nim was blanketed in the dirty mist, making it impossible to see at a distance.

The old gnome was not concerned. The distance was a mere illusion to any normal man traveling these woods. His focus was beyond the fog, on a place the young Wisebeard lurked; a place he had awoken with his presence. The sounds of trees creaking and snapping grew louder, but he paid it no mind.

The ground beneath his feet changed from that of his forest to the cold touch of stone. As his small strides pushed him closer to his destination, his fears of Balamor's fate consumed his thoughts.

After all these years, that prophetic day when they first met was never lost to him. He stopped at the base of a tree and motioned his hands to the foliage. Slowly its branches curled and lowered themselves to him, softly plucking him from the ground. With his hands still twirling, the tree carried him to its peak and created a nest for him to sit. He finished his mystical gesture by reaching for a branch and plucking a thick scroll from its grip.

There he watched — through the dense fog — as silhouettes of dark stone ruins churned beyond the weakening Bounds of Akinn. Looking down at the ancient scroll in his hands, he slowly opened it. On it was a list of names, many he remembered, but many more he had lost. Almost halfway through the list he found what he was looking for, the name faded by the passing of eight centuries.

Balamor Wisebeard.

37

A FORGOTTEN KING

875, Summer's 58th Morning

heir raspy breaths were accompanied only by silence. Gathering themselves and feeling for the cold stone walls, they moved down the hallway with racing thoughts. Still shaken and confused by their miraculous escape, they both started to wonder what brought them here.

Balamor knew it wasn't by chance that they ended up in these dark confines.

From the mysterious stone path appearing and escorting them through the Mog Brush, to the perfectly preserved building that seemingly invited them into its shelter, it was more than luck. It was something aiding their mission.

But why?

In a flash, a blue light leaped from the wall and they snapped their heads in its direction. A familiar metal torch was resting upon a dark metal sconce, emitting a mystical blue fire.

The two of them glanced at each other and then back at the torch before the halfling walked forward.

Standing beneath the flames, he realized it was well out of reach. "Give me a lift," he said with a wave of his hand.

Awkid approached, looking around in suspicion before cupping his hands and hoisting Balamor up. The young Wisebeard barely reached the mystical metal torch upon the wall while Awkid's sturdy frame held him high.

"I don't like this, one bit," Awkid said quietly, still glancing back and forth.

"It's better than the alternative," Balamor replied as he grabbed the torch and hopped to the stone floor. "I mean, you've seen it out there right?" he added while brushing off his dusty white tunic.

Awkid only shot him a look, one Balamor knew all too well. He motioned forward to the young halfling who eagerly took point.

The blue light illuminated the Blackstone surfaces of the long dormant hallway.

The two of them traveled quietly, scanning the floors and walls for traps. Balamor had no real experience like Awkid but reading of the myth and legend of treasure hunting has taught him a few things.

Pressure plates, hidden crossbows, poison gases... anything was possible in a place like this.

But treasure wasn't why he trekked through a presumably dangerous place. Unless knowledge could be considered a treasure. To Balamor it most certainly was and risking his life was worth knowing the truth. He still felt the same way as he did the day he shook Awkid's hand and promised to find such elusive answers. He felt closer to that goal, and each unexpected turn had only fueled his ambition.

They walked down the hallway cautiously before reaching an unexpected end.

Balamor stood in front of a dark stone wall, studying a large runeword etched in the blue lit surface. He recognized the symbol from one of the runes he left home, however, that didn't give a clue what it meant.

"Looks like a flame to me. Perhaps try your torch," Awkid suggested.

The symbol was a deep engraving of a small open circle with two dots above it, separated by a waving vertical line.

$$\cdot\overset{\cdot}{\underset{\circ}{\text{\reflectbox{?}}}}\cdot$$

He moved the dark metal torch close to the symbol, its blue flames danced and swirled around the wick.

"Hels," Balamor said.

As the words echoed through the cold air, the blue flames of the torch filled the deep engravings of the runeword. He removed the torch from the wall at the sound of grinding stone.

In seconds, the giant chiseled brick of Blackstone divided, revealing a stairway spiraling deep underground.

Without another choice, the two of them descended the cold stone steps.

Awkid trailed behind the young Wisebeard as he looked at his newly formed dirt arm. Under the blue light of the torch he could see, it wasn't the same as before. The earth that formed its disproportionate shape pulsated with each beat of his heart. Encasing more than just the thin bones of his arm, the strange limb seemed to have grown onto his chest and shoulder blade. He knew it wasn't a good sign, but without it, he and Balamor would have been buried by the Mog Brush.

Even though they walked in silence, Balamor too was thinking about the mystical limb Awkid possessed. He couldn't explain why it took the Mog Brush to bring it back. It was a detail that haunted him.

'The Avennoth' became a much more foreboding and threatening title.

What did those men know that Balamor didn't? What did those two men want with Awkid?

His imagination could run wild with the possibilities, none of which were good for Awkid and himself. The only thing that became clearer was who was behind Awkid's curse, Farah Lenook. If she used the Mog Brush to create the arm, then she must only want the cursed dwarf for one reason, to finish what she started.

Just as he ended his thought, the two of them stood at the bottom of the stairwell in the threshold of a darkened stone room.

A FORGOTTEN KING

Balamor slowly walked through the archway, illuminating the dusty surfaces of the silent room with his torch.

As the presence of the adventurers entered the room, torches on the walls to his sides began to ignite. After a moment, the depth of the chamber was revealed and standing before them was a tall statue of a man. The details were finely crafted to show a robed figure with a crown upon its head. His face was strong yet wrinkled with age. Outlining his thin lips was a long goatee. Garnet stones were in the place of his eyes, glowing with dim scarlet light.

"Is it like the others outside?" Awkid asked, referencing the stone warriors who saved them previously.

After a few moments, Balamor approached the statue and poked it with the metallic torch, but there was no response. "I don't think so..." Crouching down, the young mapmaker wiped a thick layer of dust from a metal plate fixed to the base of the mysterious sculpture.

Awkid joined him, intrigued by the finding.

"Zardraken Kaltas... First of his name, The Ruler of the First Kingdom, The Beholder of Peace, The Bloodline to the Beginning's End, The Timeless Wanderer. Here lies his knowledge, his lasting breath, and the bed of his soul."

"The Mystic Red King," Awkid whispered.

"The Necromancer?" Balamor asked, looking back at the statue for some kind of reassurance.

Awkid only nodded in response as his mind began to wander in all possible directions. He didn't know anything about the old king besides the same Anstian tale he told Balamor.

Cutting him from his line of thought was a realization – Balamor knew something between this place and the old Anstian tales didn't add up. "Wait... You said something about the 'sixth' Mystic Red King... What about the other five?"

"Maybe he was the first? Looks like some kind of crypt. If there really were six kings, they might all be buried here," Awkid suggested.

Balamor continued to wipe the remaining dust from the plaque to find some kind of inscribed date. "Born on the Last Breath, Died only in name..." Balamor read aloud. "The Timeless Wanderer... Or there was never more than one."

Awkid quickly contested the idea. "A human, living for over six centuries? I doubt it."

"Wouldn't be the first thing you've doubted on this journey," Balamor jested with a raised brow line. "Plus, you did say in that old tale this 'Mystic Red King' used his magic to extend his life. What were the exact words you used? Ah yes, 'blood rituals.' Perhaps he performed six of these 'blood rituals', becoming reborn — anew, as his own successor," he added, gazing out of focus in the afterthought.

"Or, like any other king, he had an heir to whom he bestowed his own name. Although, your version is much more creative," Awkid said with a smirk between his brown beard.

"You call it creative; I call it intuitive. Either way, one of us will be proven wrong, Mr. Anvorbeard," the young Wisebeard replied as he rose to his feet and started exploring the ancient chamber.

Awkid walked closely behind him, still uneasy about the possibility of some unexpected turn of events. He watched over Balamor closely, reminded of how much had changed since he first met the young mapmaker.

From saving his life on the Greatstone Pass, to him saving Awkid's life in the caves of Du'gahr's swamp. As the robeless halfling searched around the room with his journal in hand — taking notes and gathering information — Awkid realized that one thing hasn't changed. No matter the situation, Balamor's search for answers was undisturbed, and unrestricted, even by tragedy. It was admirable to the dwarf since he always let answers be bygones until now.

"Look at this," Balamor said, waving his hand toward the ground at his feet.

The dwarf approached him at the far end of the room, where Balamor was crouched next to a wall, holding something in his hand.

"It's some kind of green cloth, but this one end is cut," he said as he held the triangular piece up to Awkid.

The dwarf felt it in his hand, a familiar thin soft material only the high class could afford. "Silk... a piece of someone's clothing, perhaps a dress or—"

"Robes?" Balamor cut in, realizing he had seen such a color before.

Awkid stopped for a moment, thinking the same exact thing. "Perhaps," he said, handing the snippet of cloth back to Balamor.

38

THE FIRST DOOR

875, Summer's 58th Afternoon

Awkid looked around the cold stone room. Blue lit torches filled the place with an eerie dim light that wavered against the seemingly ancient interior. As he scanned the room, he noticed it wasn't exactly kept like one would expect in such a resting place.

On the left of him, were long wooden bookshelves nearly vacant of any texts. Across from them was a stone podium with a thick tome resting on top, standing near a carved stone wall.

Balamor lurked past Awkid, studying the large wall intensely.

Awkid went on his own to wander, carefully stepping between loose leaflets, trinkets, and various glass vials all scattered across the floor. Colorful powders coated parts of the stone surface, glittering in a rainbow shimmer. Past the clutter, he came closer to an odd circular wooden table at the center of the room.

For Awkid, the table seemed far from normal.

Eight bowl-shaped impressions around its edge meshed into a maze of deep grooves in its polished surface, suggesting more than simple decoration. All the finely carved channels convened at a larger circular indentation. Nothing laid upon its surface, no strange runewords could be found etched into the wood.

He rested both of his hands on the top, leaning over as he thought about its purpose. As with anything in the Mog Brush, magic must have been it.

"This table, it's strange... I don't like it. Why would a king request such a thing in his crypt, anyway?" Awkid asked aloud, turning his gaze to the young halfling across the room.

Balamor looked over his shoulder after finishing a sentence in his notebook. "Not sure, perhaps it's for his 'rituals' you mentioned before? Nonetheless, what's more interesting is this wall here, looks like some sort of index for the Runesong."

Awkid strolled over toward Balamor as he continued to scribble down his findings with a broken charcoal pencil.

Flipping to the next blank page in his notebook, he sketched the runewords found carved into the Blackstone wall.

With forty-five symbols available, only a handful of them were familiar, but he knew that soon the rest would become clear. The runewords were presented in three different sections that deeply intrigued the young Wisebeard.

Carved beneath each of the ancient symbols were what seemed to be some common tongue translations, like those on the cover of his six-page spellbook.

"These other words beneath, they're exactly like the ones in my book. In fact, all six are throughout this second region," he said as he pointed between the words of his spellbook and the middle portion of the wall.

"There's an obvious difference between each of the symbols here in the top two regions, and those found in the bottom region. They're smaller, more discrete carvings," he added while jotting down the remaining runewords; a series of curved, flat, and tilted dashes and dots.

As he finished the sketches, he contemplated the organization of the symbols on the wall, rubbing his chin as theories brewed.

Three regions of runewords engraved along a wall with their phonetic enunciations.

⼂∵‼⇧⸪✖⸀◉÷Ͼ⑴⚠☻☼⸔∧𝒩

In the topmost region, he noted sixteen different symbols presented in a single row. Of them all, he thought he had seen one on his travels. Now trying to vividly replay the days that had gone by, he thought back to his encounter with the Anstia guards on his way to the Forest of Nim.

In a snap, he rummaged through his worn leather backpack, shuffling through his runes, papers, and writing utensils with haste. Finally, he came across the metallic trinket he received two days ago.

"This key, the runeword on it matches..." he said as he held the key in hand, pointing to an inscription on the wall with the other. *"Lohn."*

The inscribed word upon the dark metal key glowed in a momentary pulse of a dim orange light.

He dropped the key from shock and watched the light fade with metallic dings against the cold stone floor. Shooting a puzzled look at Awkid, he quickly grabbed the key from the floor and stuffed it back into his bag. He made a note of the orange hue from its symbol before moving over to the strange polished wooden table and placing down his journal and spellbook.

In the middle region were eighteen different runewords laid out in two rows of nine. Six of those he found on his own spellbook, though not in the same order.

He had a feeling the two rows represented pairs but couldn't know for sure without some experimentation. He stared deep into the page at these eighteen runewords, recollecting times when he had seen others before.

Removing his metal flask from his belt, he held it up under the blue torchlight and scanned for some resemblance. He hadn't looked at the flask since the first day of his journey, and to his surprise each of the words imprinted on the metal surface matched those found on the cover of his spellbook; a detail he knew not to be taken as coincidence.

"I need to experiment. There has to be a system of some kind," he said while darting his eyes along the floor for something else to write on. "Here we are," he added before plucking loose pieces of parchment from the floor.

After gathering a dozen, he placed them on the table and tore the first one in half. On the first piece, he drew the symbol for a new word from the middle region, *Dran*; three waved horizontal lines each ending with a dot on its right.

Holding the ripped piece of parchment in his right hand and lifting his left forward he spoke the new word softly, *"Dran."* His voice carried along with a sky-blue shine that illuminated the symbol on the page.

A breeze seemed to emanate from his core up to his open palm, splashing against the loose pages across the table.

A moment passed before the parchment in his right hand dissipated into ash.

Unfazed by the outcome, he grabbed the second ripped portion and inscribed a symbol from the bottom region. A runeword he had only heard spoken until now; a simple pair of small backward slashes.

➜ ➜

Holding the paper once more, he spoke the familiar word, *"Ehn."*

An awkward pause ensued as he waited for something to happen, yet there was nothing, no colorful glow or disintegrating effects. At first, he thought he made some mistake, but multiple tries led to the same result. After thinking things through, he got a hunch, and quickly sketched the remaining symbols from the bottom section onto the same ripped piece of paper. He pronounced each of the eleven words carefully and in the order that they appeared, pausing after each word for a response.

━ ∼ ∥ ∥ ＼ ∣∙ ∙∣ ∪ ⋒ ○ ●

"Onos, Manas, Ahn, Dahn, Ehn, Mal, Sal, Moh, Khy, Asyr, Zahr."

As he expected, none of them produced a result. He snatched two more pieces of parchment from the table and transcribed different symbols from the top section onto them. He started his new experiment with one of the pages in hand, choosing the first of the three words he had drawn, *Deun.*

THE FIRST DOOR

"Deun Siras Lim," his voice spoke the Runesong with mystic tongue, hoping to conjure some kind of spell.

The runewords pulsed a dim flash of pale-yellow light before the page crumbled to ash.

Balamor looked around as the ash pile fell through his fingers, yet there was no obvious result besides the flash.

"Toying with magic is not a good idea. You don't know what will come of it," Awkid cut in sharply, opposing Balamor's brute-force methods.

"Not 'toying,' it's experimentation, a series of calculated guesses and a bit of trial and error," Balamor shot back, grabbing the next piece of parchment and preparing to finish his test of the strange words.

"Call it what you wish. We should be more concerned with getting out of this place rather than 'experimenting' with the same magic that got us in here in the first place," Awkid said, not convinced.

However, the hope of gaining Awkid's approval wouldn't change his mind anyway, he was onto something. He was almost certain that the Runesong was not only responsible for their imprisonment, but that it was also the key to their escape. Looking over his notes and adding a few more of his thoughts, he was sure the three sections were categories, all playing a separate role in the magic.

The middle section that had the most runewords was the only section to produce a noticeable result. Saying one of the words with the symbol in hand has consistently led to some sort of elementary action.

Raji caused healing, *Theas* changed the tree of Nim, *Hels* lit the torch, *Tyel* created a flash of light, and now *Dran* caused a gust of wind.

As far as he could tell, the remaining words in that section would cause similar effects using other elements. As for the top section, the only distinction between those words and the other eighteen below was the lack of some physical event.

Lohn, Lim, Deun, Siras – they all shined when called upon, yet there was the lack of familiar hair standing and numbness.

His only guess was that they required another elementary word to be utilized. His main questions might be answered if he could decipher the bottom region, since those had no effect whatsoever.

His last test would be using a combination of all three sections. With his right hand held out in front and the last piece of parchment in his left, he spoke the three simple words sketched on its surface.

"Lim ehn theas."

The page flashed a warm green light before Balamor felt a force rush to the center of his right hand. From the thin air around his open palm, a ball of earth formed and shot across the room, colliding with the pedestal in a burst of dirt.

Balamor felt slightly weakened by the act but more so, he was surprised at the outcome. He rested his hands upon his knees before rising and studying his right hand.

Awkid watched in silence, a slight sense of fear crossed him like the cold of a ghost. Even with the magic of his own arm, he knew Balamor possessed even greater potential if he could create earth from thin air.

"Look, over there," Balamor said, pointing toward a shining green light emanating from the pedestal.

They both approached the ancient tome atop its surface.

THE FIRST DOOR

Balamor leaned over the thick text and wiped the dirt from its cover. Beneath was the warm green glow, swirling within the bounds of a *Theas* runeword pressed into the leather cover. Below it in golden leaf, were two other words, *Awa Jar*.

The young Wisebeard placed his right hand on the book, the same mysterious force pulsed through it.

"Theas Awa Jar," Balamor said with a commanding voice.

The mysterious green glow shined brighter and the ancient book exploded open in a flutter of pages. The pages flipped on their own until the middle of the thick text was found. Across both pages were four lines of various runewords, like a list of some sort.

Each one contained the familiar word, *Theas*, and upon further investigation, each used runewords from each section on the wall.

Balamor's steel-blue eyes gazed deep into the lines of ancient symbols, now realizing a pattern throughout.

"Ah yes, I see. These symbols from the middle section, they are like the subjects and objects in common tongue, except they stand for some magical essence or element like fire or earth. So... Those in the top section are like adjectives or verbs, used to give the element some kind of form or direction, like the gust of wind or the magical dome covering this place... Which means those in the bottom section are like prepositions."

His finger scanned the glowing pages as he pieced his theory together.

"Prepositions?" Awkid sounded lost.

Balamor rubbed his chin as he tried to think of a good definition. "You know... like transition words, used to describe going from one thing to the next, or how things relate to one another?"

"Sure..." Awkid still sounded lost.

"That would explain why the top and bottom sections don't work without the middle section, just like a sentence requires a subject... Err... But it isn't a perfect match. Common tongue has more written complexity, whereas the Runesong is more implied... It's a good start. It should help me put a common definition to some of the symbols."

"Since you're one for solving riddles, how about you start with the one that has us stuck in this place," Awkid growled, looking around for some other means to escape.

"Understanding the Runesong is the only way we can get anywhere around here. Something brought us here for a reason, and I don't think it was to watch us die," Balamor replied as he began brainstorming a way to decipher the magical words.

"Optimism has you dreaming, halfling. Here we stand in the crypt of a supposed Necromancer, buried under a cursed land of war and death, and you don't believe this is some kind of trap?" Awkid asked menacingly, throwing his arms into the air.

"Supposed Necromancer, keyword 'supposed.' You said it yourself, 'don't let it fool you.' The Anstian Monarchy wrote those tales, Mr. Anvorbeard. The same people who would rather imprison those like you and me," Balamor shot back, not willing to succumb to the dwarf's arrogant nature.

"If this place wanted us dead, it would have let that giant finish us. It didn't, instead bringing us here. Now, give me some time to figure it out," he added calmly, only pushing Awkid closer to madness.

The chamber remained silent as Balamor studied his findings.

Time passed slower by the second for the dwarf who was now pacing across the room, looking for some switch or hidden door. He knew Balamor was right not to trust the old Anstian tale, but Awkid knew Balamor was too curious for his own good.

THE FIRST DOOR

A good journeyman would know that any place with one entrance and no way out was a trap. His hands searched behind the bookshelves and across the Blackstone walls, but he found no signs of an exit.

His leather boots scuffed against the floor lazily as time slipped by slower than he could imagine.

Balamor stayed focused on his research, using the remainder of blank pages to perform more of his experiments.

Various conjurations of elements flashed across the strange table, from small dirt mounds to balls of light appearing and disappearing at the mystical halfling's will.

From Awkid's perspective, the young mapmaker was quickly becoming the young mystic. Before, the strange halfling was merely strange, carrying strange items and wondering about strange places. But now, he was truly strange in the same way the Black-Robed Man was, performing miraculous feats of magic yet possessing the will to be an awesome terror. He knew his intentions were as pure as finding the truth, but the dwarf knew all good truths are buried by raging hands.

Balamor wrote in his journal more than any time before, filling entire pages with his thoughts on the subject matter. The point of his pencil soon became dull at the expense of noting his experiments with each of the outcomes. Occasionally he would flip to a list and cross certain hunches off and circle others in interest.

For anyone who read his notes, there was a need for incredible comprehension and attention to detail. Like any halfling, there was a method to his madness, a system as he would like to call it. That system was finally turning questions about the elusive Runesong into theories he could accept.

In his studies, he experimented with newer words from the middle portion of the wall and confirmed his original theory of pairs. He dubbed runewords from this section, 'elementary' words, such as light and dark, earth and water, fire and air, and so on. Seven pairs of dual elements, though a few were more ambiguous than others in their effects. He referred to the top section of words as 'manifestations.' With only a few of them remaining more elusive, he ascribed definitions he saw fit in his research. Some of the words resulted in different forms of the elementary words, such as a wall of water, a dome of light, and the bolt of earth from earlier. While others still had a list of possible definitions, some were reduced to one or two.

Finally, it was the bottom section of words which he knew the least – a section he labeled 'transition' words. Out of the eight he had in his notes, he noticed two, *Onos* and *Manas*. They were used in the same pattern throughout his own spellbook as well as the thick spellbook that rested upon the pedestal. The two runewords always appeared in the same order; *Onos* first, an element second, *Manas* third, and another element last.

He noted that these kinds of spells allowed him to turn one element such as earth into another such as water. As for the other runewords in this section, there was nothing concrete to go on. Using different transition words in a spell greatly changed the outcome, yet he had no clear description of each word's purpose or effect. He could only guess at their potential, which was far from leaving him comfortable. Using a word in a spell without knowing its effects was extremely dangerous.

He could spend days in this study, learning the words with further experimentation, however, enough time was spent in this chamber. Balamor was ready to find a way out, but not for the same reasons as Awkid. He wanted to know the reason he was here, and the reason the Mog Brush was nature's graveyard.

Awkid stopped his pacing at the center of the chamber and watched Balamor stroll to the pedestal and compare his notes to the shining page of the ancient tome.

A silence ensued that drew Awkid closer to the young mystic as he deciphered the Runesong upon the pages, writing down his phonetic translation on a new page.

"It seems like these lines are connected. Maybe this is one entire spell? Hm, I can only figure part of it, but all the words are here in my notes. It could lead to a way out," Balamor said in apprehension, glancing back at Awkid for some kind of assurance.

The cursed dwarf was nearly at his wits end, and replied simply, "If it does, I'll be the first through the door."

Balamor grinned and nodded. "Well then, I shall find the way out." With his journal nestled in his side and his square stone *Vis* rune in his hand, he began his translation,

$$-\therefore\; \widehat{\ominus}\;-\;\widehat{\Pi}\;''\;\Theta$$

"... *Onos vis deun, onos maur dahn theas...*" The first line on the left-hand page began to shine a ghostly pale shade of green, and Balamor's voice started to echo through the chamber with an unseen chorus.

A strange force emanated from the ancient text and waved against his white tunic and curly brown hair. As he read on, the powerful energy coursed through his blood and within the air around him.

$$\sim\; \vdots\vdots\; \mathbin{/\!\!/}\; \widehat{\Pi}\;''\;\Theta$$

"... *Manas lohn, ahn maur dahn theas...*" The young mystic's square stone rune was gleaming with the same bright light, like a star burning at the center of his palm. The room shook as the words were spoken aloud.

Awkid braced himself, grabbing the table to stop from falling over. The sound of stone cracking and grinding came from the bare end of the room.

Balamor was unfazed by the commotion and continued to cast the powerful magic from the book.

"... *Vis lohn manas mal payr...*" The young Wisebeard stared down at the pages, now with pale green glowing eyes. A passageway opened in the wall beside him.

Awkid stood in shock while Balamor unleashed a spell within the ancient crypt.

The roaring voice of Balamor Wisebeard finally came to an end as he delivered the final words of the mystical spell.

"... *Manas sal payr, mal raji dahn firos.*"

The shaking stopped, and Balamor fell to his knees, dropping his stone rune and notebook to the floor. As the magical aura surrounding the halfling quickly dissipated, the once bare wall of the chamber was now a seemingly normal doorway.

Awkid quickly grabbed the halfling from the foot of the pedestal and helped him to his feet. Whatever the spell was, it left Balamor feeling weaker than any time before. His hands were shaking as he gathered his belongings. After a few minutes, he finally caught his breath, and looked over at the cherry red wooden door, its ornate golden handle looked strange compared to the rest of the room.

Awkid looked at the door with wide eyes. *"That door... Its—"*

"The door from the old library!" Balamor cut in. "Well, Mr. Anvorbeard, I believe I've found our way out. Unless of course you wish to stay in this crypt," the young Wisebeard said with tired breaths.

THE FIRST DOOR

Awkid raised his eyebrow before Balamor reached for the doorknob and wrenched it open. White light shined from beyond, causing them both to cover their eyes.

"After you?" Balamor asked with an inviting gesture.

But Awkid was quick to change his mind, "Certainly not! This is not a good idea, halfling."

"Have you any other ideas, Mr. Anvorbeard?"

Awkid growled as he shielded his eyes from the light. "Your idea, you take point." His earthen arm gripped the door, holding it open for Balamor.

"Fair enough," Balamor replied as he advanced through the mysterious passage of Zardraken's Crypt.

39

THE LIBRARY OF MYSTICISM

62, Autumn's 40th Evening

A series of bells jostled in a peculiar tune as the thick wooden door opened and Balamor Wisebeard stepped through, crossing the dark threshold cautiously before the heavy door closed with a thud.

A moment passed as the ringing of the bells slowly dissipated into the ticking of a winsome clock. He stood still, scratching his head as he gazed upon endless aisles of towering bookshelves.

This new chamber was massive and furnished like a palace. Long stylish throw rugs covered the glossy hardwood floors, padding his footsteps as he crept forth. Large tables were occupied by books and robed strangers bent over them, deep in study. Some of the strangers were curious and looked in Balamor's direction. Colorful rays of light blanketed the chamber, coming from the massive windows of stained glass.

Balamor was mesmerized by the place, walking slowly as he tried to let its entirety sink in.

In every which way the aisles of books seemed to be, each was full of texts all neatly organized into groups.

Balamor recognized the musky scent of old paper and lingering dust, a library like his own, yet this place was far more exquisite, majestic even.

THE LIBRARY OF MYSTICISM

The tall wooden cases were lined with fine red felt and etched with masterful skill, all as finely crafted as the centerpiece of the large chamber. A tall grandfather clock stood at the center of a circular desk occupied by scattered papers, wildflowers, and the whistling of a whimsical tune.

The young mapmaker looked puzzled as he pushed further into the colossal library. Not only did it remind him of his own library, it started to dawn on him that he was here before – the stained glass, the polished floors and bookcases, the trove of knowledge, the clock.

The clock...

Strolling along suspiciously, the ticking sound grew louder. Balamor was drawn to the walls of books surrounding him. He brushed his fingers across their aged spines, observing each title as he proceeded toward the center of the library.

He glanced down the aisle where he saw the pristine body of the grandfather clock towering over the library. It was unmistakably the same clock he had seen the day before.

"This is the library from the Mog Brush..." Balamor whispered.

"Awkid, can you belie—"

His words were cut short as he turned around to find his companion was gone. He started to peek around the towering shelves to find the dwarf, but he was nowhere to be seen. His heart started to beat fast as his search came up empty.

The clock ticked on and on — each clicking tone more intense than the last. He tried to comprehend what was taking place. With every high tick and deep tock, Balamor ran through the days passed, from the vision he experienced that led him through the Bounds of Akinn to the humongous statues that saved him from the grips of a terrible giant.

Nothing was random. Nothing was unwarranted.

At this point the absence of Awkid Anvorbeard started to feel like yet another sign getting him closer to the truth. He looked around the magnificent library, strangers whose time was from another day, all preoccupied with learning something they did not yet understand.

Balamor was here for the same reason. He felt it in his gut. He just needed to figure out what he was here to learn. He proceeded down the center hallway gazing at the countless books lining the shelves.

All of a sudden, his footsteps came to a halt as his eyes fell upon a familiar text. Resting between other texts was a strange book. He pulled it from its place on the shelf and gazed upon its red cloth cover. The bold text, *Runes and Runewords*, spanned the red cover and the edge of its leather spine.

"I've read this book before. But, how is it here?" Balamor whispered to himself.

He continued walking as he flipped the pages and scanned its contents. Everything was the same, yet the pages lacked the same patina from before. The last time he had laid eyes on the same text was at home, in the Raehl. So far away from where he was now. It felt like ages had passed.

Now he could comprehend it, based on his own knowledge thus far, it was a text of more questions rather than answers. What struck him this time around was the date inscribed at its introduction: 12, Spring's 23rd Day. There was no name of the author, only a curious title, *The Learned Man's Voyage*. The search stopped at the next page as he found the portrait of a red-robed man.

"Already deep in study I see," a high-pitched voice said, seemingly amused.

Balamor looked up from the text as this voice continued.

"A good place to start, written by the bookmaster himself."

Now standing at the front of the central desk, Balamor saw a small man whose presence shocked him, leaving his mouth agape. Dressed in the same colorful attire, though in much better condition, this small man let out a final sentence that only compounded Balamor's confusion.

THE LIBRARY OF MYSTICISM

"Welcome to The Library of Mysticism, nice to meet you Mister...?"

Balamor was almost at a loss for words as the man inked his opalescent quill and held it out to Balamor to sign his name.

"Nim?" Balamor said, unconvinced by the man before him.

A jolly laugh accompanied the colorful gnome's retort, "You may be wise, stranger, but I would know the difference between Rootfolk and halfling." A wink from the fellow left the young Wisebeard bewildered.

"Uh... Sorry that's not my name. It's just that you look and sound exactly like a gnome I had met days ago. He called himself Nim."

The gnome rubbed his chin and squinted his eyes. "Perhaps his antics have you fooled. I am Giro Vidiro, a simple clerk. Though I am flattered, friend."

Balamor looked down at the scroll he was ready to sign and back at the gnomish clerk. He was lost as a moment of silence fell upon them.

"Is everything okay, sir?" the gnome said to him with a perplexed look on his face.

Flashing across his mind was a memory of Nim's words, a line that he thought aloud, *"Some papers to sign."*

Giro pointed toward the empty space and responded, "Um, yes, sir. You must sign your name here and you'll be—"

"On my way..." Balamor replied, finishing Giro's sentence as the memories of his time in the Forest of Nim started to replay in his mind.

"Yes..." Giro cleared his throat.

"And this list, I must sign it *because?*" Balamor inquired.

"Oh simple. Being the clerk of this fine establishment means I must know the names of all who cross the threshold."

"The threshold," Balamor said as he looked behind him toward the door he came through. Nim used the same wording in the forest when Balamor met him.

"Indeed, sir," Giro replied, perplexed by the young Wisebeard's behavior, as he reached for the odd quill in the gnome's hand.

Balamor proceeded to sign his name with elegance. The black ink soaked into the long scrolling list that the clerk had unraveled from the finely carved spindle built into his desk. The list was so long it furled around the wooden rod for what seemed like miles.

His signature was made in eloquent style amongst the others above, names he had never seen nor heard of before. The scroll was familiar to the young Wisebeard, as if he'd seen it before, but where he'd seen it was far beyond his recollection. Although he did know it had everything to do with the gnome sitting across from him. A gnome whose name didn't match the one he heard days ago.

After the young Wisebeard added his signature to the great list before him, he handed the prismatic quill back to the clerk.

The clock went tirelessly on as the gnomish man behind the desk studied the new name. He leaned over his large comfy chair and peered through a monocle that was resting in his vest pocket.

Balamor waited for Mr. Vidiro to respond, yet silence was all that accompanied a raised eyebrow. Gazing into Balamor's steel-blue eyes he seemed to search for something more from the mapmaker. The silence grew intense causing Balamor to look around the room suspiciously.

The gnome laughed aloud before he spoke. "Well, Mr. Balamor Wisebeard, I was not aware of your relation to our beloved bookmaster! Strange... He never did tell me he had another grandchild. If you're looking for him, he's currently searching the shelves for his own personal study." The gnome pointed rightward as he quickly cranked the spindle to return the list to his desk.

Balamor stayed quiet and nodded before walking toward the right side of the library. His thoughts of this place only became stranger after hearing what Giro Vidiro just mentioned.

Another grandchild? He wondered who this bookmaster was, and if this place was truly an illusion like Awkid would suggest.

As he walked, his concerns quickly diminished upon returning to the book he held in his hand. The portrait from before now became obvious. This was the same face as the statue who stood at the entrance to the crypt.

"Zardraken Kaltas," he whispered to himself.

The name and all of its titles were written below the masterfully painted depiction.

Balamor began to flip the pages, now remembering the first time he read the same text in his own home. His eyes were glued to the text while his bare feet pushed forward against the throw rugs in a pleasant saunter.

Passing by all kinds of strangers busy studying peculiar lines of text, Balamor could hear the whistling from earlier had returned, now closer than before. He shot a look in the direction of the tune to see a black-robed halfling man atop a ladder, removing books from the shelves and stacking them upon his left arm.

The melody this old halfling whistled was whimsical, almost mesmerizing, a song he felt lurking deep in the recesses of his own mind.

The old man waved his hand to the left ever slightly, and the ladder shifted in its direction. More books found their way onto the tall stack, each now being tossed to the top with ease by the mystifying stranger.

Swaying and tilting with every small motion he made, Balamor was sure they would fall to the floor below, yet the books never did. A few seconds turned to minutes as the young Wisebeard observed the old halfling in action.

His long pitch-black robes draped across his small frame and down the rungs of the rolling ladder at his belly, just as his gray beard did the same. Each new text he snagged from the shelves flipped open with a torrent of pages fluttering from beginning to end.

A simple nod or shake of his head made his decision. Those that he chose not to take would be flung back to their places on the shelves. How it was they made it beside their neighbors without trouble was beyond simple skill. It was something otherworldly that this old halfling possessed.

"This should do for now," he said, with a voice Balamor had certainly heard before. The voice of his grandfather, Farjadis.

It couldn't be! He waited to gaze upon the old halfling's face.

"How are they all going to fit in here, Bookmaster?" a young boy's curious voice said, frightening Balamor with utter surprise.

Glancing toward the youthful voice, he saw there were two children nearly as tall as Balamor himself.

They were standing on the other side of the aisle holding a rather small orange velvet bag.

Humans.

He could tell by their size. A boy and a girl no more than ten years of age. The boy wore simple, coarse clothes – a white buttoned tunic and tan knickers all sewn by hand – clean but not noble in any respect. His eyes were golden brown and his hair was curtained and black, cut like a commoner. The girl beside him had a face nearly identical to the boy, though her hair was long and brushed straight. She wore a long green dress tattered at the ends, handmade, and lacking any fineries that would show she was highborn.

Siblings perhaps? Balamor studied them as well, realizing their garb didn't fit the magnificence of the place they stood. *Orphans?* He thought, as he looked around for any sign of parents.

"Does my own size fool you? Am I so small as to not have this noggin of mine hold all of the kingdom's knowledge?"

Both children shook their heads, realizing the point to his retort.

"You and your sister have much to learn about the intricacies of the small things in life. Now, hold the bag open wide as you can," the old robed halfling replied to them through the darkness of his hood.

Balamor watched the boy and his sister follow the old halfling's command, glancing at one another as they stretched the velvet bag open. It was small even when compared to the size of a halfling.

Balamor was amazed at the spectacle this man was ready to perform but still skeptical of its final conclusion. His stroll gradually became a slow creep as he drew closer to the scene. The air became thick with every step Balamor took, his curiosity reaching its peak when the wise bookmaster — holding a tower of teetering books — twisted and waved a gesture around them.

Balamor held his breath.

A spiral of wind spun each book through the air, gliding it down effortlessly toward the bag below. In elegance, the texts descended in a helix into the orange velvet sack. One by one they twirled inside.

The children were stunned by how many there were, looking at each other in disbelief as the bag's size hadn't even changed.

The black-robed halfling climbed down the ladder as the twisting books continued their descent. Reaching the polished floor and strolling to the rippling carpet, his oversized robes trailed him. Pointing at the bag he snapped his fingers and hurried his walk, motioning the children to join him.

The spectacle was over and Balamor exhaled a gasp in awe at the magic he witnessed.

"Carry on now... As I've said, much more to learn," he said, shaking his wrinkled finger as he spoke.

The children closed the bag, lifting it in suspicion, its weight was the same as before. They slowly strolled further down the aisle, away from the awestruck mapmaker who remained motionless. He watched as the old halfling walked behind the two children, speaking wisdom and teaching them about history.

40

CENTURIES APART

62, Autumn's 40th Evening

he old bookmaster's voice was like a childhood scent baked into Balamor's mind.

"Wait!" the young Wisebeard shouted, his echo wavering through the entire library.

The trio at the other end of the aisle turned around. Books were everywhere one could look, small or large, marked, opened, some never before seen. Some were on tables and within crates, others like dominos populated long shelves forward and back.

The air felt stiff, the once familiar echo now a low drawn out muffle.

The old black-robed halfling held his hands behind him, staring down the robeless stranger facing his way.

"I think I know you... I've heard of you," Balamor said as he walked toward the old bookmaster.

The black-robed halfling gestured to the children to stay before he strolled toward the robeless stranger, still holding his hands behind his back. Intrigued by this halfling fellow and his presence, he followed with a soft reply.

"You have? Then who might I be?" The smirk beneath his darkened cowl fit the scene like a breeze upon the neck.

"You're The Black-Robed Man," Balamor claimed, feeling like it was all that made sense.

"I am? Or am I simply a man who *wears* black robes?" the old halfling replied.

CENTURIES APART

The two of them slowly walked to meet one another. The distance between them became shorter with each stride, and with it the semblance between this old bookmaster and Balamor's own grandfather became more apparent.

Balamor went on to describe his thoughts to the strange halfling. "The magic you perform, the students you have, it all matches the stories I've heard. Although, I wasn't aware The Black-Robed Man was a halfling..."

"You sound *almost* convinced, stranger. However, with no name for this man, how can you be sure I am him? Where did you hear these stories?" the black-robed halfling asked.

"A friend. He told me he traveled with a black-robed man once, to the Mog Brush. His students spoke fantasies about his ability to perform magic. He never found out his name," Balamor answered, now scratching his chin with uncertainty.

"That sure does sound like me," the man said while removing his long hood.

His face was eerily familiar – the steel-blue eyes and furrowed brow line. His long nose, the thin gray locks of hair, and the soothing smile showed more wisdom than the deep wrinkles of his face. The only difference between this man and Balamor's own grandfather was the long beard he had.

The young mapmaker knew this man was not Farjadis, yet he felt their blood was the same.

The old halfling continued, "However, I have never been to a Mog Brush and these students of mine are my first, only weeks into their study. Does this friend of yours live here in the First Kingdom?"

Balamor's confusion only deepened at those words. His eyes widened before he quickly rummaged through his bag with his open hand, plucking his journal from within. Standing only feet away from this strange black-robed halfling his hands were shaking.

"No, no, no... Wait... wait. *This* is the First Kingdom?" Balamor asked the man before him, flipping the pages of his journal for his list of names.

"Indeed... How is it you've gotten this far without knowing that?" the old man asked, amused by the idea.

"But that couldn't be true, we're in the Mog Brush. The First Kingdom existed centuries ago. How could it still exist now?" Balamor challenged the old halfling's knowledge.

The old halfling raised an eyebrow and studied the young man before him. His features were almost uncanny. His intuition told him this encounter was unlike any he would ever have. "Now? Tell me stranger, what year is it?"

"The year is 875," Balamor replied cautiously.

The old halfling's intuition was right, but his response was lost. He didn't show his perplexity like the stranger standing before him. Instead he turned to his pupils and spoke, "Gantis, what year is it we live?"

The young boy stepped forward, glancing between his master and the peculiar halfling he was speaking with. "The year is 62."

Balamor stepped back and looked around for something or someone to assist him. He stared at the boy who was yards away, now whispering to his sister and pointing in Balamor's direction.

Gantis? That name. Balamor remembered the name. It belonged to a man his grandfather Farjadis spoke of, a mystic. Yet this was merely a boy.

"62? That's over eight centuries... Wait, this student of yours, his name is Gantis, Gantis Jacs?" Balamor asked the old man.

"Indeed. You know him?" the old bookmaster asked, returning his steely gaze to Balamor.

Balamor nodded. "Not as a boy, but a man. An old man who helped my grandfather once, after the fall of Delsis."

CENTURIES APART

The black-robed halfling asked one last question, now staring into the eyes of the young mapmaker. "Who are you, traveler?"

Balamor was reluctant to answer, as everything around him seemed so unreal. But the man he spoke with gave him a look he could not mistake as an illusion. He felt a burning urgency in his eyes.

"My name... my name is Balamor Wisebeard," the young mapmaker replied, his voice overheard by the two children who tried their hardest to eavesdrop on the conversation. The old bookmaster looked back at them and then to Balamor.

"I see... Have you signed your name with our clerk?"

Balamor nodded, his nerves causing his hands to tremble and his eyes to dart. "He told me I was related to you. The sound of your voice, it's like the voice of my grandfather. But... But I know you're not him. He doesn't know magic."

"Magic is not known, it is realized, Balamor. Wherever you are from, it's by magic that we've met, centuries apart."

His wrinkled hand extended to meet Balamor's before he revealed his own name. "I am Jaric Wisebeard. I'm not your grandfather, but we do share the same blood."

Balamor hesitated to shake his hand, unsure about everything here. Yet, he knew he had to. As much as this old halfling was strange, he was the closest he had felt to family in so long. His open hand grasped the clutch of his ancestor and it was the furthest from an illusion as he could tell.

The simplicity of a handshake had never felt so visceral to the young Wisebeard.

Silence began to set in just as Balamor released his grip and held the red book in his hands, nearly forgetting it was there.

He looked at its cover — one he would never forget — and handed it to the old Wisebeard.

"This book... It's why I am so far from home," he said with a solemn tone.

Jaric accepted the book, glancing over its cover before he replied, "I'll be sure it stays in my personal library."

The young Wisebeard looked around the majestic library, a place he would never forget. The scent, the atmosphere, the records of knowledge lining the shelves. The thought of what it would become brought tears to his eyes.

"This place, it isn't here in my time, not like this. Something happens to this place. A powerful curse no soul should have to witness. Darkness lives here now... Amongst the death of countless men and broken ruins, tormenting all within! I wish I knew why. I wish I could do something!" he said, his voice raised with roaring emotion.

"You already have, friend," Jaric replied, his hand now resting upon Balamor's shoulder.

The words stuck in his head, like a relentless echo not waning once. He looked up at the old bookmaster and saw everything around him was paused.

The children were frozen in place, their eyes wide and staring in Balamor's direction. Jaric was frozen still, not a single blink in his eyes.

Suddenly the echo came to an abrupt halt and Balamor took a step back, his heart beginning to beat faster. In an instant, the black-robed Wisebeard's body crumbled to ash.

Balamor turned and saw the entire place was disintegrating before his eyes. The children and once passing strangers fading into lifeless mounds of ash and dust. The towering shelves of books began to keel over into enormous piles of gray.

Balamor started to run, dodging the crumbling remains of anything and everything that was the Library of Mysticism. With each stride, he felt his blood pumping faster than before. His entire lower body became coated in a thick layer of ash as he tore through the room.

The soothing aura of colorful light coming through the massive stained windows quickly dimmed as each dyed pane crumbled away. On all sides, the room was gray and lifeless. All the magnificence of the great library was left to a center aisle that led to the entrance.

Balamor, gripping his journal in hand, ran as fast as he could imagine. In seconds, he skidded to the door and pushed it open. All of his strength didn't seem like enough to move the large door. Nearly halfway open, Balamor slipped through.

41

FIRST BLOOD

212, Winter's 23rd Twilight

Balamor landed upon the dusty stone floor of a dim lit hallway.

The door behind him slammed shut, leaving him alone with the silence of his racing thoughts. Wavering blue torchlight flickered on the Blackstone walls, separated by gaps of pitch-black darkness. Sitting against the wall, holding his head in his hands, he closed his eyes as tight as he could.

Just as the torches upon the walls cracked and snapped so did his recollection of his trip to the ancient library. Every little detail flashed before his senses. The smell of the air, the sound of patient study, and the feeling of shaking hands with an unknown ancestor. It wasn't simply a vision; this time was different. It was like a dream. An experience, indistinguishable from reality.

Eight hundred years... he thought to himself, looking left and right down the semicircular Blackstone hallway.

Drops of water leaked from various spots above, forming small puddles along the floor. The torches all burned that same mystical blue fire as the runes. Balamor observed the long halls of carefully chiseled Blackstone. Their confines were both gloriously spacious and dismally abandoned. He felt terribly small, even smaller than his halfling size granted. It wasn't simply due to the immensity of his unusual surroundings, but rather his lack of usual company. Awkid Anvorbeard was gone, as if he never walked through that door.

Perhaps he never did. It was a possibility Balamor highly doubted. Awkid may be at odds with him most of the time, but Balamor was certain he wouldn't suddenly abandon him. After all that they had been through, and after getting this far?

Tears slowly rolled down to his chin and dripped to the floor between his ash-covered legs.

Not Awkid Anvorbeard.

They made a deal.

Any other dwarf wouldn't dare leave until the deal was finished, no matter what the deal was.

Yet, Awkid Anvorbeard wasn't any other dwarf, that much was a fact. From his lack of golden keepsakes to his otherworldly arm, Awkid was truly a misfit of his kin. Perhaps that's what drew the two of them together on this outlandish quest in the first place.

Nonetheless, they were far apart now, at least it felt that way. He wasn't sure what time he would find himself in now, or what instance he would appear in next. In one moment, he was exploring the depths of a buried crypt and in the next, he was strolling through a library eight centuries in the past. Any idea of where he was going fell by the wayside once he stepped foot in the Forest of Nim.

Each step forward pushed him further from his comprehensible mission to map the Mog Brush and closer to the alluring mysteries of magic. The Runesong was a siren's call he couldn't ignore, especially after saving Awkid's life with its power. The majestic glyphs and their enigmatic tongue needed to be further understood. After all, it might just be his only way to escape these strange halls and return home.

He thought about the spell he cast to open the doorway, wondering if he could use it to go back.

Opening his notes swiftly, he studied his translation of runewords for answers.

$$-\because \widehat{\underset{\bullet}{\circ}} - \widehat{\mathsf{i}\mathsf{i}}\text{''}\ominus$$

ZARDRAKEN'S CRYPT

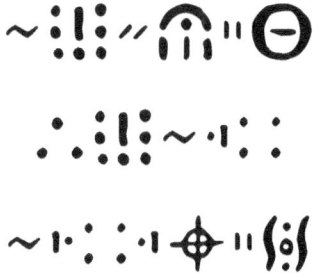

Onos vis deun, onos maur dahn theas.
Manas lohn, ahn maur dahn theas.
Vis lohn, manas mal payr.
Manas sal payr, mal raji dahn firos.

It was a lengthy spell indeed, which might explain why it weakened him as much as it did. Unfortunately, there was no obvious way to determine what each of the words actually meant. The runewords weren't giving away any clues on their own, though a few did help him make some far-fetched implications.

Theas was a word related to nature, having effects on the tree of Nim, the dirt of the Mog Brush, and perhaps the stone wall of Zardraken's Crypt.

Vis was a familiar word he associated with his strange visions, from the nightmare he had before he left the Raehl to the vision he had in the caves of Du'gahr's swamp.

Lohn was the word he found on his strange black metal key. He could only imagine why it would also be in the spell he performed to open the doorway. *Open, unlock, passage?* He thought of a few possibilities.

Then there was the word *Payr*, a word he first heard Nim speak when referring to his strange pocket watch. He'd also seen its symbol in a vision, the one he gestured across the Bounds of Akinn. Its meaning was shared by a clock and the Mog Brush, an element each shared.

Time?

He did travel eight centuries into the past, through a passage made of earth, only to witness a point in time that would have otherwise remained unseen. The deduction about the elements seemed reasonable. Yet there was one word he couldn't find even a remote meaning for — *Firos*.

He had only seen it once before, in the spellbook his grandfather had given him. He removed the book and searched its cover for the word. The last in a series of six, it was a word whose symbol was more complex than the others. Two dots and a circle sandwiched between a pair of waving vertical lines.

$$\{ \mathrel{\vcenter{\hbox{$\cdot$}}} \}$$

Perhaps this particular runeword was the reason Awkid wasn't here with him, and the reason he traveled to a place where his own ancestor happened to be.

The reason. There had to be a reason.

Everything that he witnessed, everyone he crossed paths with, every close call. Everything that led him here was undeniably improbable if not impossible. However, a reason for all of this would be something that eluded him. For now, he would be left with his gut feelings and a story few would even believe.

But it was real, and Balamor knew it to be true. What he had experienced on this journey wasn't some myth, though it was a tale that would certainly need to be told.

With a snap of his fingers, he scuffled through his bag and found his charcoal pencil. It was dirty, broken and waterlogged, yet still with its point intact.

Balamor breezed through the pages of his journal, dozens of them already filled with notes and sketches from the days passed. He came to a blank page and started making his latest entry. It was a sketch of his first steps in the Mog Brush, before it came to life. With haste, his lines were drawn, outlining knocked over buildings, men paused in battle, and most of all the leaning high tower at its center. A few notes were left on the page, some questions, others were clues, and few of them were answers.

Minutes went by as he hurried from page to page. From the beat down barracks to the thrashing lands of the Mog Brush he whizzed through his sketches, sloppy renditions at best, but enough to spark his memory. There was the raging giant that chased him and Awkid, the mysterious interiors of Zardraken's Crypt, and now the majestic Library of Mysticism.

His hands started to shake as he sketched portraits of Jaric Wisebeard and his two young disciples. Faces he knew were not of his own making but faces he had witnessed. The series of sketches were nearly complete when he heard a sound coming from his left, like metal shackles clanging in the distance. Muffled by the thick stone walls, the call of a horn started blaring.

Once, twice, and now a third time.

From his left he could make out the figures of men, suited in a dark armor. Balamor hurried and jumped to his feet, packing his notebook into his bag.

Shimmers of light outlined the dark steel figures accompanied by the sound of clanging armor plates. Balamor recognized them. They were the same armored suits he saw in the Mog Brush.

They advanced quickly, but Balamor was swift. His bare feet thudded against the stone floor as he escaped down the hallway to the right. Passing by the dim blue torchlight, the long hallway began to slowly curve left. He hadn't a clue where it led, or where he was for that matter. All that concerned him was finding a way out. Sprinting full steam down the hallway, he passed more doorways, closed and latched shut.

He didn't stop running through the winding path as the sounds of the soldiers closing in only quickened his pace.

There was an intersection ahead.

Right, right! His thoughts were racing almost as quickly as his feet.

Reaching the intersection, he darted right before he spotted more figures running his way. His small frame came to a skidding stop and turned around, retreating to his original path.

Now, the sound of metal crashing echoed through the hallways like a roaring crescendo of metallic teeth crunching down on the stone.

The horns sounded once again, only this time they were louder than before.

Balamor's chest was burning with every stride he made down the darkened hallway. He looked forward, and yet another stream of armored figures approached. There was nowhere else to go, only forward toward the next intersection.

A warm light came from ahead to his left and the final blast of the horn rolled through the halls.

He rushed toward the intersection as he took his *Vis* rune necklace in hand, hoping it would save him again. Breaking left toward the light, he ran. At the other end of the hallway was a soldier battling a sleek figure.

Their silhouettes striking against one another against the backdrop of a fiery war.

Balamor glanced over his shoulder. The looks of an army were still behind him, charging full force for the door. Gripping his rune tight, his mind focused on something else, something he didn't know but something he could realize.

∴

The young Wisebeard's body grew cold and numb as runewords flashed through his mind.

Ahead, the duel was over as the sleek fighter defeated the dark steel soldier, piercing him with a curved blade beneath his menacing helmet, arterial blood erupting from underneath and onto the figure's green tunic.

Balamor sprinted toward him, his eyes now glowing white as he spoke in a deep and foreboding tone, *"Ahn vis dahn maur, dahn tyel!"*

Light enveloped Balamor's body from head to toe as he charged forward.

Frightened by the sight of the young Wisebeard's gleaming figure, the sleek man stepped back through the doorway as a blue fiery light shined on him. Piercing through his back and breaking his silvery breastplate a black arrow struck true, a cool fire burning through his body.

In an instant, a hail of flaming arrows berated his entire body, bringing him to his knees. He watched as the young mystic Balamor disappeared before his eyes.

Balamor felt a slight jolt scatter across his skin and suddenly everything around him became silent. Balamor pushed past the fallen figure, shoving his dying body to the ground. Sharp features and pointed ears, his green tunic burning from scorching blue fire; it was an elf whose horrifying scream was eerily quiet.

Balamor stumbled by the flaming warrior and pushed through the doorway.

Outside the sky was a mix of swirling dark clouds and fiery arrows, racing toward the ground like fallen stars. He glanced to his right and was bewildered to see the same high tower as the one he had seen in the Mog Brush, yet here it was surrounded by the likes of a kingdom, one under siege by elven forces. The air was frigid, and the sun was faint as it set upon the war-torn landscape as Balamor looked for a place to escape to.

Sprinting through a city of Blackstone buildings, he looked for a way out of the deaf madness unfolding around him. Clashes of elves and armored warriors battled in the streets as blue fire whipped from rooftops. Arrows struck the ground along with the rain in a relentless wave, piercing Blackstone cobbles, and sending fire rippling through shattering cracks.

Blood covered the bodies of those fallen in battle. Countless elves and black-armored men lay wasted by the unfolding warfare.

Balamor's breaths became hoarse as his running seemed without an end. Dashing down a narrow alley, the young halfling rushed forward, splashing up puddles that washed the gray residue from his legs. Reaching the end of the alley, he felt a great tremor rumble the ground.

In an instant, the silence broke and the sound of devastation filled its place.

Balamor's body felt weak. He braced the wall of the building to his left as another quake almost knocked him to the ground.

The screams of men could be heard along with the cries of their retreat.

"Giant! Fall back to the keep!" The command was repeated by the armored warriors ahead.

Balamor emerged from the end of the alleyway where a regiment of iron-clad soldiers escaped down the street to his right. The young Wisebeard turned his head to the left where the colossal figure of a giant, wearing nothing but piecemeal furs was charging full force toward them.

With each step the giant took, the ground broke apart in an explosion of force.

Balamor was stuck, fear holding him in place as the monstrous figure sprinted.

The ground trembled as the foundations of buildings crumbled, throwing Balamor to the ground. The buildings cracked and buckled as powerful gusts of wind pushed against the giant. A deafening screech came from above and the wind shattered windows as it grew stronger.

Balamor regained his focus to see a torrent of blue fire crashing against the giant, burning all the furs on its body. The young halfling crawled from the alley and onto his feet where a beast shouted down at the massive figure in front of him.

Black scales covered its humongous winged body all the way to the tip of its long whip-like tail. Roaring once more, massive wings tossed debris through the air. A bright blue light emitted through the cracks of its scaly gullet before flames spewed from the beasts toothy snout.

A dragon.

There was no doubt about it. Balamor was awestruck by its ferocious nature. Razor-sharp claws gripped the giant's shoulders, digging deep into its thick skin. Blood gushed from within as the dragon's fire scorched the face of the giant warrior.

Flesh boiled in an instant and dripped down the giant's body, sizzling and popping as it splashed to the ground like oil from a frying pan.

The smell of burning flesh made Balamor nauseous and pushed him back into the crumbling alleyway. The giant was standing only by the grip of the black dragon roasting him alive. His grotesque face became a hodgepodge of charred bone and bubbling skin. He made no more noise as the stream of fire ended and the dragon discarded his body into a demolished building.

Balamor tripped over rubble and fell to his back, crawling away from the horrific screams of elves now being bathed in dragon fire. He cornered himself into a pile of Blackstone debris and closed his eyes.

The vicious sounds of war and death tortured his mind as he tried to wish them away. His heart raced with an unparalleled fear as he curled himself up in a ball, hopeless to escape the unfolding madness.

A low metallic horn rang from the distance, its jarring sound quickly drowning out everything else. Once, twice, and now a third time the horn sounded. The young Wisebeard kept his eyes clamped shut while the loud horn drifted into a silent breeze.

42

THE ROOTSTONE

310, Spring's 19th Afternoon

He could hear nothing else but the sound of the woods, rustling their foliage peacefully. Slowly Balamor took a breath, before he eased the clutch of his eyelids. Daylight softly pierced his vision as the smell of plant life filled his senses.

His blurry vision slowly cleared to reveal an old twisted tree standing before him. Its bark was gray and cracked while its drab foliage laid upon the gold-speckled soil. At the center of its bark was a hole, seemingly ripped and torn open from within.

Balamor rose to his feet from the foot of another dreary tree. The battle he was in was gone as quickly as the ancient library faded to ashes. He was somewhere else, and possibly in some other time. He couldn't tell when, but he thought he knew where.

He approached the old timber in front of him, recollecting his surroundings as a forest he had been in once before.

"... Nim?" he asked as his hand reached for the great wound the tree suffered.

His fingers brushed up against the bark.

A trace of gold residue still ran through the wood, glistening and sparkling ever so slightly. Splashing across his eyes like a wave was a vision.

A woman standing exactly where Balamor stood now. Her green robes waved as she spoke the Runesong. The same robed woman he had seen conjure a halfling from the earth.

THE ROOTSTONE

The same woman he envisioned before he reached into the Bounds of Akinn. A woman who he couldn't shake the feeling was Farah Lenook.

The branches of the old tree wrestled against a force radiating from her figure, helpless to resist her awesome power. A calm laugh could be heard as the tree began to twist and cripple. Its bark slowly petrifying as she spoke.

"Nim, that's what they call you? And I was told you were the strongest. Are you really the best the Rootfolk have to offer? Not bad, I suppose. A shame it is you chose the side of ignorance. I always thought the trees were above men and their short-sighted affairs."

The tree was now wilted and its lifeless struggle could be mistaken for the wind. At the center of its trunk was the familiar runeword Theas, twisted and rippled like water. Its shape began to change from a circled dash to a pair of vertical dots above a downward crescent. A symbol Balamor had seen before in Zardraken's Crypt.

Holding her open hand to the newly formed symbol, she spoke softly, "I'll always wonder why they didn't learn their lesson the first time."

The bark ripped open with a jolt of energy that shook the leaves from the ground. A gaping hole in the ancient tree revealed a large glowing emerald that floated to the woman's hand. Removing it from the tree, the gilded foliage fell from the branches at once, drifting to the ground like a dying breath.

Balamor stumbled back and fell as the vision ended.

Dead leaves covered his body as he realized what had just taken place here.

The tree remained motionless, yet Balamor felt a strange energy emanating from it.

He gathered himself and brushed the leaves from his body, looking around for a trace of the green-robed woman, but there was nothing she left behind.

The magical woodland was strangely quiet. No sounds of chirping birds or buzzing insects, only a long drawn out silence that bothered him.

He had been here before, but he was never alone like this.

His thoughts wandered and so did his legs, now slowly strolling him through the Forest of Nim. He glanced at the tree once or twice before it disappeared behind a lattice of other trunks. He didn't know where to go now, and he couldn't tell if right now was even the same year as when he had left.

The war he witnessed must have been later than his visit to the old library, based on the notes he had taken from Doryn Beldavale's own journal. Reaching into his backpack, he grabbed his notebook and searched its pages, trying to make sense of the mysterious shifts in time.

His assumptions were soon met with answers as he found his entry on Mr. Beldavale.

212, Winter's 3rd day.

He thought as he read over the stranger's words. It was a time when The First Kingdom was at war with the Fey. Perhaps it was written around the same time as the war he just witnessed. Nonetheless, it gave him confidence that the war took place after his trip to The Library of Mysticism in the year 62.

As he walked through the Forest of Nim, he wondered what time he was witnessing now. One thing he was certain of was that Nim was nowhere to be found. Not the Nim he recognized, anyway.

The vision that flashed before his eyes spoke of another Nim, a Rootfolk. The clerk at the desk of the library confirmed this other Nim to be one of these folk as well. If it was true, then what Balamor witnessed only compounded his confusion.

How could he remember Nim in his own time as the gnome Giro Vidiro from the year 62?

Something wasn't adding up, but his gut was telling him he was here in this forest to figure it out.

THE ROOTSTONE

There was now a puzzle of trees in all directions, and the way he chose to walk had no obvious destination. He returned his journal to his backpack when his stomach began rumbling. He realized he hadn't eaten in a day, maybe more so he stopped to search his backpack for something to eat.

The inside of his bag was a terrarium of the adventure he was on, filled with dust and soil, scattered papers and his three stone runes. He scattered the contents until he found what he was looking for. A baked potato and a stick of lamb jerky, the last of his stepfather's pantry and his only remaining meal. Thankfully he saved these for last, items he knew wouldn't spoil quickly.

Biting into the potato, its bland flavor made him yearn for home cooking. Days had gone by now. Days since he left the Raehl.

Knowing exactly how many days that was, went beyond his memory.

His walking continued as he ate his food alone. As much as he tried to not concentrate on his situation, he couldn't help but wonder why he was here again. The events he had been through were all too strange if not for a reason beyond coincidence.

The visions, the mysterious crypt appearing to save him from an early death, it seemed all too lucky, even for a halfling. Each new experience felt fated, as if something was guiding him to uncover this lost knowledge. Ever since he stepped through that strange door in the crypt, he wasn't sure he would ever return to his own time.

Perhaps he never left, and all of this was some spell, an illusion as Awkid would put it. *If it was, then why? What good would come from showing him these scattered points in time?* He wanted answers but there was nothing willing to make them clear.

310, Spring's 19th Night

Hours passed and his walk soon became a tiresome wander.

Fighting to stay awake, he whistled to himself. It was a tune he heard before from Jaric, but when he first heard it, it felt long before then – from his youth, a time when memories were filled with blanks. The song was simple and wonderfully peaceful, yet it was strange in its ups and downs and peculiar changes in pitch.

The trees shook from a slight breeze as dusk fell upon the land. His legs ached from seemingly endless walking, but his mind was taking notes.

One thing he realized was the biggest difference between now and his first time here – the rune-marked tree hadn't reappeared once. He looked for it everywhere, even frequently turning around in hopes to find it following him. Instead, he was met with more normal woods, a sight that nearly drove him mad. He felt like he was losing his mind here, and he knew this forest was relentless in keeping one within its confines.

For now, he would have to sleep, otherwise he may pass out somewhere in the open.

His tired frame slowly searched for a more discreet place.

Tree after tree, nothing seemed suitable. Scaling their towering trunks was out of the question. He was too weak and had nothing but a knife to help him. His eyes became heavy as lapses of time were quickly forgotten with each drowsy blink of an eye.

Suddenly, he tripped over something big. His weary body crashed to the ground, jolting him from half asleep to alert in a split second.

He looked behind him to see the long broken trunk of a tree, its gnarled roots exposed to the cold air. His concern soon became excitement as he crawled into its remaining foliage for shelter.

Moments went by as he nestled himself somewhere within the trees thick and broken branches.

The Forest of Nim remained silent as his eyes slowly closed shut, and he fell into a deep sleep.

43

PEACE OVER TRUTH

310, Spring's 20th Sunrise

ighttime passed quietly, yet for Balamor it passed in an instant as he stretched his frame in the brush of a fallen tree.

He opened his eyes as rays of light signaled the morning. Through the mix of branches of leaves he looked; a relieving breath followed as he didn't wake somewhere else. An unexpected hoot reverberated through the tree causing him to flinch and turn his head.

Staring down at him with big orange eyes was a large owl perched on a branch. Its body was unlike any he had seen before. Colorful shimmers of light came from within its milky white plume. It crooked its head and gave another holler.

Balamor didn't move, his eyes were fixed on the owl's strange stare.

"Tessa! Where did you fly off to?" a pitched voice yelled from the distance.

The owl swiftly jumped from the branch and fluttered its wings until it was out of Balamor's sight.

He gathered himself quickly, now realizing he wasn't alone. Staying silent as he could, Balamor crawled to get an eye on who it was that trekked the magical forest this morning.

Peering through the branches, he spotted a small man standing in a clearing of brush. The owl flapped its wings before perching on the man's shoulder.

Upon closer examination, Balamor could tell this was a gnomish man. Judging by his colorful attire and the joyful sound of his voice, Balamor was certain who this man was. Although he knew him by two different names, the man was the same.

The gnome spoke to his owl quietly before another man's voice came from behind him.

"Did it find anything yet?" The voice was deep and stubborn in its tone.

Approaching the gnome were four other figures. All but one wore a different color robes.

The one speaking was short and had a stocky frame. Flowing from his darkened cowl was a thick black beard. He wore deep blue robes lined with gold, covered by an ornately carved dark steel breastplate. His heavy pole-arm was fixed with a huge Blackstone ball nearly a third of his own size.

The gnome responded to him as he shook his head, "Not yet, Mr. Anvorbeard, but that only has me more worried."

Balamor could have jumped from his cover at the sound of that name but he remained still and continued to spy on the conversation.

"Indeed... The trees are too quiet this day. We should move with caution," the red-robed figure said as he began walking.

His face was hidden but Balamor had seen him more than once already. The crown upon his head was a telling sign this was the Mystic Red King, Zardraken Kaltas. Holding a long bone wand in his right hand and a flame-bladed short sword at his waist, his status was easily represented as the group's leader. Long crimson robes trailed his powerful figure and following behind him was a creature who stood feet taller than the rest of the strange company.

Made of grinding Blackstone carved with seemingly endless runewords, this golem-like creature walked with a brooding stature. His eyes were two deep holes set beneath the stony brow of his face — scanning the forest for any signs of danger.

The final figure strolled through the forest quietly. He wore plain black robes and grasped a wooden staff fixed with an amethyst stone. His tall lanky frame took long strides next to his party yet his focus seemed to roam elsewhere.

Balamor waited for more to unfold, unwilling to move until they were nearly out of his sight.

The mysterious strangers had an air about them that told of urgent business here. The Red King led the rest forward, his sense of direction showed his expertise in this place.

A moment passed before they disappeared behind a lattice of trunks and the young Wisebeard crept silently ahead. His bare feet treaded carefully behind the five strangers, between leaves, twigs and roots. His curiosity was at its peak with the like of another Anvorbeard around.

Who was this other Anvorbeard? Or any of these strangers for that matter?

Occasionally he would peek from behind his cover to keep them in his sight.

They quietly pushed through the Forest of Nim, leaving no trace behind besides the footprints of the rock creature, deep in the soil.

310, Spring's 20th Morning

Time slipped by as slow as Balamor took his breaths. Following behind the party of strangers, he was careful and his furry feet made not a single sound to give away his position.

The wind gradually picked up into frequent gusts. Drops of rain pattered the ground and left wet spots on his clothes.

Another storm was afoot and the strangers he trailed took notice quickly.

"A century later and this rain still leaves a bad taste in my mouth," the blue Dwarven figure said, holding his hand out to catch drops in his palm. His hand closed in a strong clench of a fist. "She knows we are close. Damn that witch! She will turn this place into a wasteland if we don't stop her!"

Finally, from his long bout of silence the black-robed man spoke to the dwarf. "We mustn't stray into that same darkness, Beylor. Don't forget, many years ago she was no different from us. She was our queen. It was grief that led her to fall from grace."

The dwarf grunted, nodding, and easing his grip to an open palm once again. He turned to the red-robed king who walked solemnly, looking toward the sky with his eyes closed as raindrops splashed against his pale face.

"This rain, why does it follow her? Why does it rage as we draw near?" the dwarf asked.

Zardraken opened his eyes as he answered, "Tears... Pent-up sorrow that will only worsen with my presence. This is the price I pay for choosing peace over truth."

Suddenly, the tall rock figure stopped and motioned his party to do the same. Kneeling to the ground, he felt the earth.

Silence ensued as the others waited for him to explain.

Balamor crept closer, his steps made in a gold shimmering mix of soil and leaves.

The rock figure's hand dug into the soil before he spoke. "Nim, his breaths are shallow. His essence is fading quickly." His graveling voice of stone was unlike any voice Balamor had heard before.

The brisk air was churning with rain and gilded leaves as the group finally met the remains of the dying tree of Nim.

Zardraken approached the torn open trunk, his pale hand coming from beneath his long sleeves to touch the gray bark.

A moment of raging quiet fell upon the forest as the others stood behind the Red King.

"She's taken the Rootstone," the king said, pressing his hand against the tree like a grave of an old friend.

"The Elves... Blindly following her hypocrisy," Beylor said, his words sewed with disgust.

"Peace over truth," the black-robed figure responded.

Giro Vidiro stood by them. Fear growing upon his face as he drew closer to the ancient tree. Tears dripped down his cheeks and sniffles stuttered his speech. "How could she? There must be something we can do to save him! Nim has done too much for us to watch him die! There must be something!" Both of his hands embraced the trunk of the old tree.

"A life cannot go on without a soul," the black-robed man said, kneeling and placing his hand on the gnome's shoulder.

The rain was coming down in heavy waves as the company of strange men stood by the tree.

Zardraken turned to the others. The darkness within his hood only deepened the urgency of his words. "If his essence fades, the forest will fade with it. All that conceals the kingdom will become rotten wood and soil. Without Nim and the shield of his forest, Farah will have free rein in the south. Mr. Vidiro is right. We must do something to prevent further destruction... One of us must stay behind."

"But without a soul," Giro contested.

"A new soul must take its place," the black-robed man said quietly, looking down as he pieced together the Red King's words. "One of us must give our soul? How can a man give life to a Rootfolk?" he added, looking up at Zardraken for answers.

Interrupting the question, Giro stood to his feet and quickly interjected, "I will do it. I am no mage, no man of power. I am a simple clerk who has nothing more to offer. Let it be me."

"No, I will not let you sacrifice your soul for our cause!" the black-robed man shouted over the sound of crashing rain.

"Gantis, listen to me! I knew this day would come ever since you were a boy! On the day that Wisebeard came to my desk, eight centuries before his time, he looked in my eyes and believed I was Nim. I thought he was out of his mind until I saw his name... Until he disappeared into a pile of ash before everyone's eyes!" Giro yelled; his eyes filled with tears as he glanced back at the dying tree.

Gantis looked inward for the memory of that day. Then it hit him, the entire scene flashing before his eyes. "Balamor. He said his name was Balamor. Even the bookmaster, Jaric, believed it was true."

"Whatever it takes, I will do it. Otherwise, she will destroy everything I know, and everyone I love," Giro said, looking at Zardraken with determination in his eyes.

Gantis gripped his staff and turned away from the party. A moment passed before he spoke. "What will happen to him?"

The rock figure towered over the party. His wisdom was obvious, simply by the strength of his being. "It's never been done, not like this. The two souls will choose their own path; however it is they see fit. They may trade vessels or both inhabit the same vessel."

"If they trade vessels?" Gantis asked, still looking outward from the forest.

Zardraken replied as he walked toward the towering rock creature. "Nim would die in Giro's vessel as a Bloodfolk, and Giro would enter Nim's vessel and become a Rootfolk."

"And if they both inhabit the same vessel? What then?" Beylor entered the discussion.

In a vicious crack, lightning struck close to the forest and the entire group turned at once.

Snooping from a bush, only yards away, Balamor jumped and fell onto his back when the sky flashed in blinding white light. Rising back to his feet and under his cover, he watched as a thunderstorm began to unfold upon the situation.

Zardraken looked at Gantis and Beylor and commanded them. "Both of you must prepare to break the spell before it is finished! I will do what I must to save Nim. Go, now!"

Gantis was reluctant to leave Giro behind, his hand reaching for him as Beylor tugged him away.

"We must follow the plan, Gantis. The world our king created will be lost if we do not succeed! There are no other options now. We must do what needs to be done!" Beylor shouted above the ferocious howl of the storm.

Lightning struck once more. Its violet arc shuttered down a tall tree and nearly split it in half. Shredded timber fell toward Balamor below.

He quickly dove from his cover and tumbled toward another tree. Muddy leaves splashed as he fell to the ground, soaking his clothes. Looking up from the forest floor, Balamor saw Gantis Jacs and Beylor Anvorbeard running through the forest; their robes rippling like a sea of cloth.

Gathering himself quickly, the young Wisebeard searched for the others.

Winds were raging, and the storm drenched everything around him. Sheets of rain obscured his vision making any signs of the remaining group lost to him. Above the sound of the intense rain, a writhing screech rippled through the forest with a deafening pitch.

It was an agonizing cry that slithered down his spine like a ghost. He knew what it was, but he didn't want it to be. His heart started racing as adrenaline pumped through his veins. In a flash, he started to run.

A faint memory of where Gantis and Beylor traveled was all that guided him. Balamor glanced back, a green flash shined through the misty rainfall behind him.

The silhouette of Zardraken and his rocky companion could be seen, but there was no clear sight of the fated Giro Vidiro. The green light intensified before another shriek rolled behind him. He faced forward and tried increasing his pace. The sounds of wings fluttering from behind him nearly drowned out the sound of crashing rain.

Parins.

44

A SIMPLE CLERK

310, Spring's 20th Afternoon

Zardraken Kaltas stood at the tree of Nim as the wicked storm raged around him and his rock companion. Giro Vidiro was in front of them, shaken from the sound of Parins shrieking through the Forest of Nim.

"What about the Parins?" the clerk shouted over the wailing screams and heavy rains.

The King threw down three stones and gestured toward them with a majestic display. They shattered in a sudden burst of pale green light before a dome arose to cover the three of them. The sounds of the storm and the raging Parins were muffled to near silence. The inky figures slammed into the magical shroud and turned to ashes. Giro flinched as one came after the next, their speckled remains collecting at his feet. "Worry not about demons, my friend. You will not be touched by their hands, not on this day," the king responded gracefully as he removed his hood, revealing his face to the old clerk for the first time.

His pale skin was sunken and aged, forming bags beneath intense scarlet eyes. Jet black hair flowed with streaks of gray down to his shoulders and a long goatee waved down to his chest. His face was strikingly ordinary considering his powerful role. Without the crown upon his head, he would look like a usual scholar.

"There is plenty of time for worry ahead, for now, we must focus on saving Nim." He removed a silver necklace from around his neck, its ruby pendant merely a shard of a once greater stone. "Hold this still, don't let it go no matter what happens. Understand?"

Giro nodded as he gripped the necklace firm, glancing down at it only once before returning his gaze to the Red King who continued his instruction, "Now, I need you to keep Nim in your mind as you close your eyes. Focus on something that reminds you of him, a memory, a tale—"

"A riddle, I remember his riddle!" Giro said as he squeezed his eyes to focus.

"A riddle? Tell me, Mr. Vidiro, how did this riddle go?" Zardraken asked while placing his hand upon his rocky companion's shoulder. The runewords engraved on its body began to glow crimson red.

The gnome hesitated as he heard the sound of the king's magic. "Yes, yes of course... let's see... My name is nimble in the beginning and always at the center of this inanimate forest."

The king spread his fingers wide. Streams of red light emitted from Giro's chest and twisted through the air, gathering at the king's fingertips.

The clerk went on, and so did the powerful spell. *"You can see my name within unimaginable places."*

The streams coming from the gnome's chest grew more intense, whipping toward Zardraken's hand and spiraling into a pulsing ball of red light. The light burst outward in a blinding flash — left in its place was the beating heart of Giro Vidiro.

"Like an eye in between the ending of dawn and the beginning of midnight." The ruby shard he held started to shine as the king removed his hand from the red glowing rock figure's shoulder. He approached the ripped open hole of the gilded tree, his red robes trailing his long strides.

"You can find my name through the trees and under the bushes, in the midst of the animals," the gnome said with a smirk, knowing his riddle was coming to an end.

ZARDRAKEN'S CRYPT

As Zardraken placed Giro's heart within the tree, pale fibers gripped it and slowly consumed it entirely. The king signed a symbol in the air, a circle with a dash that glowed a warm green. He pushed it toward the gaping hole and it sealed the tree back to its original state. In a wave, its golden colors returned and glowing foliage sprouted from its once dying limbs.

The glowing ruby pendant in the gnome's hand was streaming with crimson light that entered the now empty place of his heart. Only the silver chain was left in his hand when he finally opened his eyes, now the color of shining emeralds. "Now that you have heard my name, tell me Mr. Kaltas — *who am I?*"

"You are Nim," Zardraken answered.

"Correct! Although one may also say that I am merely a simple clerk, whichever he chooses!"

The king smiled before he put up his hood.

He and his rock companion watched as the gnome snapped his fingers. "Until next time!" The foliage of the gilded tree reached for Nim and carried him away.

45

A KINGDOM IN RUINS

310, Spring's 20th Afternoon

Balamor's feet ached as he ran through the stormy woodland with burning lungs. Passing by trunks and bushes, Balamor kept moving. His entire body was soaked by the thundering rain. Exposed roots nearly tripped him as he kicked up fallen leaves and left a muddy trail in his wake.

The forest seemed to be falling apart as lightning blasted open bark and ripped through entire trees. A large timber started to fall yards ahead of where Balamor was running.

As he drew near, branches from the surrounding trees started to move and twist. New leaves sprouted from them and the forest quickly became a green maze of vibrant life.

Balamor looked up as the falling tree coursed for his direction, its branches snapping and breaking through the thick foliage. His feet dug into the mud as he tried to stop and avoid being crushed.

An exposed root stumbled him and he crashed to the ground.

The surrounding brush suddenly bent and curled toward the falling timber. Branches wrapped around its thick trunk, gripping the bark like leafy tentacles.

Balamor jumped to his feet when the towering trunk was finally stopped from crashing toward the earth. Mud splashed as he resumed his sprint, the forest becoming thick with vegetation around him as he tried to catch up to Beylor and Gantis.

The storm only strengthened its powerful wind and rain as he moved further into the forest. Lightning flashed, and the thick mist barked with cracks of thunder.

Balamor glanced around him as he heard another screeching call erupt from his left and right.

The dark and foggy forest was roaring as he pushed forward, his eyes keen to the first sight of danger. Through heavy waves of rain to his right and left, he could see the dark silhouettes of Parins forming, their bodies a teeming school of winged imps.

Dripping in black ooze and ripping through the brush like fearsome predators, Balamor was surrounded by them, yet he was not their only prey this night. They were racing for something else, something much more alarming than him.

Balamor rushed forward, now amidst the pack of Parins racing toward an unknown finish. A single stone pillar could be seen ahead, a sign he recognized.

Last time he encountered the same pillars, he was close to the Mog Brush. Reaching into his bag in mid-sprint, he grabbed a metallic torch and held it in front of him.

"Hels!" he shouted.

A cool glow filled the runeword on its surface before a blue flame erupted from the wick and sent its cool light through the hazy fog.

Now feet away from the pillar, Balamor could see its shadow pointing off to his left. He quickly turned and quickened his pace.

Parins closed in on him from the left and the right, their barbaric figures tearing through the forest without regard.

Suddenly, the trees whipped their branches toward the wild creatures and ripped their hive bodies apart.

Balamor found the next pillar not far ahead and rushed toward it. Around him, a seemingly innumerable amount of Parins howled as the forest fought them from reaching their destination.

One of the pitch-black creatures quickly caught up to the young mapmaker and leaped from the ground toward him.

Balamor turned to face the creature and thrust the torch in its direction.

"Lim ehn hels!" His voice sounded otherworldly as he spoke the magical words.

From the burning torch in his hand, a blue fiery orb coalesced and shot through the air toward the bloodthirsty Parins. A bright explosion of blue fire engulfed the inky black creature. Tearing apart from their combined form, the winged imps burned and screamed as they flew wildly through the air.

Balamor kept running, the light of his torch finally revealing the pillar's shadow as he passed it. Turning and darting forward, he could hear more of the Parins closing in, their wings amplifying the sound of the crashing rain. He suddenly felt the cold of stone beneath his feet. He was close now, but the Parins were too fast.

Their agile humanoid figures ran on four legs like ravaging beasts.

His breaths became wheezy and cramps began stuttering his strides.

The forest around him thinned into a rocky cliffside. A dark chasm surrounded a walled fortress. The sound of rain roared and thundered as he slid to the cliffs edge.

He gazed into the abyss; its endless depth screamed at him to stop.

Dust fell down, but his short frame held strong and quickly turned around to face the Parins in a wave.

Their black humanoid forms dashed toward him, looking to tear him to shreds. It was a moment that slowed with anticipation. His thoughts were zapping by like lightning bolts but everything moved in such precise fashion, predicted by the focus of his mind.

Runewords flashed before him as he searched for a way to stop the demon-shaped figures from reaching their goal. *"Deun ehn hels!"*

A wave of flames pushed from his feet toward the onslaught of Parins. As it rippled forth, the waves grew in size, flames crashing into the Parins at a height of ten feet and searing their hive bodies. Breaking apart and screeching as they burned, the Parins fled, leaving Balamor cliffside and falling to his knees.

Weakness plagued his body as he struggled to regain his footing. Lightning struck the Blackstone ground near him, a static energy stood the hairs of his body.

He stumbled along the edge of the chasm. More Parins were charging through the forest and onto the stone cliffside toward him. The sound of a man's voice could be heard bellowing out the mystical runewords of a powerful spell.

Balamor could see the two robed figures of Gantis and Beylor, both of them churning forces of magic greater than anything he had yet witnessed.

They both stood across the Blackstone bridge that spanned the chasm.

The Dwarven mage held his spherical stone mace high in the air, wind swirling around it like a tornado sparking with tendrils of lightning. Gantis stood further behind him, his spellbook glowing and flashing in different colors as he held it in his right hand and read its contents aloud.

Spewing from the stormy spell and crashing around them, lightning zapped the charging Parins, throwing Balamor to his back.

Through the roaring storm, the figures of Zardraken Kaltas and his rock companion approached Gantis and Beylor.

An aura of light surrounded them as they walked without any sort of fear.

Parins crashed into the magical light and turned to ash in an instant.

The Mystic Red King paid no mind to them and reached into his robes to reveal a thick scroll. Unrolling it carefully, the two figures finally stood with the party – Gantis to the left and Beylor in front.

Zardraken released the open scroll from his hand and suspended it in the air with a mystical gesture. Placing his left hand on the Blackstone figure's shoulder, the engraved runewords on its body began to glow with a deep crimson light. The red-robed king removed a wand from his right sleeve. Waving it to-and-fro like a magical maestro, he began conducting the spell that was contained within the scroll.

"Moh theas, rhul mog ris manas nhir ehn firos. Onos moh theas manas khy theas."

His voice was deep and echoed with the power of a god. The spell was long and contained words he had never before heard. From the tip of his wand, a ghostly green force gathered and spread to the edge of the cliff and down into the darkness of the chasm.

Balamor looked over the edge where the once pitch-black depths glowed green. Metallic scrapes could be heard from within the chasm as he moved away. He crawled toward the trio of wizards and watched as the spell intensified.

"Ehn hyr mal payr, asyr raji dahn theas. Rhul aer, theas, hels, dran raji manas nhir ehn tyel."

The twister swirled around Beylor Anvorbeard's mace with fury, channeling the entire storm toward it. He slammed the Blackstone ball down into the ground with a mighty spike and the ground quaked. A monstrous stream of lightning funneled down the mace's handle and drowned the sound of the storm with a vicious warping crack.

Beylor stepped back and removed three stones he had stowed away in his robes and cast them toward his mace.

They scattered into a perfect triangle at the base of the twister and flashed in a violet light.

Gantis finished his own spell and fell to one knee, his book slamming shut as the entire storm was sucked into Beylor's glorious weapon.

A strange stillness fell upon them all as the sound of Zardraken's godly voice continued to roar.

"Vehs raji onos nhir manas maur awa vis mohr. Ehn siras wyl tyel lyras manas mohr."

Coalescing around the Blackstone mace, different energies coursed with magnificent speed.

Near the edge of the chasm, Balamor could see metallic figures crawling up and over the cliff. Suits of armor absent of any life gathered like an army around the Mystic Red King.

Thousands of them poured over the edge and onto the stone, clashing with charging Parins and fighting them off. Their black steel armor was old and covered in ash and dried blood – remnants of the men who once inhabited them.

The Red King's spell coursed through the living armor, its eerie green glow penetrating through holes and slits, seeping out of it like a ghastly soul. Parins broke apart into a flying barrage of hellish imps as they smashed into the magical soldiers without regard for themselves.

The floating scroll in front of Zardraken wisped away into ashes as his mighty voice finished the spell.

"Yev tyel lyras, manas asyr lohn. Onos vis mohr ahn hyr manas vis ehn hyr. Dros mohr manas zahr awa seht ehn tyel."

The final words echoed through the landscape and in a flash, the pent-up energy within Beylor's mace shot toward the kingdom across the bridge, a white tendril warping the air around it with blistering speed.

The blinding beam of white light exploded halfway across the chasm, splitting an unforeseen dome surrounding the kingdom. Like shattering glass, the dome exploded open and disintegrated to reveal a wasteland beyond.

Dark and dire, the relic of the once fine kingdom was now a twisted graveyard of death and earthly corruption. Like a graveyard for the corpse of nature itself, it was the *Mog Brush*.

46

TO ASHES

310, Spring's 20th Afternoon

he once strong and unscathed kingdom from moments ago was merely an illusion. Its true grim identity was now revealed by the epic spell the three mages performed.

Balamor's eyes grew wide as the illusory dome shattered before him.

The Mog Brush whipped wildly within its decrepit walls, tumbling debris and smashing them apart as they churned about a solitary standing high tower.

He gathered himself from the cliff edge and watched as the army of armored warriors gathered in formation around the Red King and his men.

Beylor picked up his mace and waited for his leader's command.

The red glow upon the king's rocky companion faded as the army marched into place.

Gantis turned to the three regiments of men who waited patiently. With a majestic swipe of his hand, their dark steel weapons quickly transformed into menacing longbows. The black-robed wizard gestured toward them once more. Fiery blue arrows whipped into shape, notched and ready to fly to their target. A raised hand from the black-robed man signaled the soldiers and they took aim at the sky in unison.

Across the narrow bridge, another army gathered, adorned in silvery armor over their green tunics. Judging by their slender forms and sharp pointed features they were certainly elves, the same elves Balamor had seen when he first entered the Mog Brush.

A series of banners waved in the heavy wind, emerald green with the familiar sigil of a gem braided in thorns.

Thousands of them stood at the entrance to the Mog Brush, untouched by the vicious soil within.

Their voices quickly turned into a rolling chorus that signaled their charge. Racing from the colossal archway of the old kingdom they moved across the bridge in swift fashion, blades and spears closing in on the Red King and his forces.

A simple nod from the king began their siege. Gantis was the first to give his own command. "Loose!" he shouted as his hand chopped through the air.

At once, the archers released their flaming arrows. A wave of blue fire filled the sky. The elves pushed forward as their numbers diminished. Dark steel arrows punctured through their gleaming plate mail, ripping their tunics and thudding into their bodies.

Just as those fallen were set ablaze, black smoke and horrid screams surrounded those that remained - those who charged swiftly toward the Mystic Red King.

Now, halfway across the narrow bridge, the elven onslaught was reduced to half its size. Heavy rains battered the stone and pinged against the black steel warriors.

With a roar from the bed of his soul, Beylor thrust his stone mace forward. "For Truth!"

Countless numbers of black steel soldiers charged across the Blackstone bridge toward the elves.

Following his men, the Red King walked onward, his strides strong and his fierce stature unbroken by the approaching elven forces.

Arrows dotted the bridge with whipping blue fire.

As the two armies collided, Beylor bludgeoned through with his mace.

Elven bodies flung off of the bridge and into the dark chasm, their screams meshing with the sound of the horrific war taking place.

With each blow, his Blackstone mace channeled more power. Orange streams of light collected around it, racing around its spherical stone top.

The battle was chaotic as the blue-robed mage forced the enemy back.

Huge bursts of energy tossed elves over the edge. Metal sparked against metal as blood soaked the stone bridge and the corpses of fallen elves were trampled on by their metal counterparts.

Balamor backed away further and further from the cliffside and into the forest, nestling himself at the foot of a tree.

Around him were the remains of charred Parin imps and puddles of muddy water.

He wanted to leave altogether but his eyes were fixed on the calamity taking place.

Zardraken marched across the bridge, his force pushing the fallen warriors out of his way as he removed a short sword from his side.

Runewords engraved on its blade started to glow in a blinding violet light.

Elves rushed toward him, attempting to strike him down at all costs. His glowing blade cut through them with ease as lightning left its edge and shattered their bodies into ash.

The Red King and his forces pushed across the bridge, leaving the elves with no choice but to retreat.

Gantis gestured once more toward the archers he commanded before a barrage of arrows soared through the sky in a wave of mystical fire.

The elves rushed back toward the archway as flaming arrows struck many of them down.

Beylor and the king pushed onward with their mission when the sound of a screeching beast echoed from within the Mog Brush.

Heavy gusts of wind toppled the fleeting elves as a monstrous figure lifted itself into the sky. Black scales covered its winged body as it spiraled upward above the high tower.

Balamor knew this beast was the same as before; the dragon that scorched a giant alive. Reaching far above the battlefield, the dragon settled in the sky, beating its massive wings and waiting to attack.

A bone-chilling roar rippled through the sky before it swooped down to destroy Zardraken and his forces. He thought it was the same dragon, but this time, something about it was different. Bound to its shoulders with thick chains was a leather saddle mounted by a lone rider; a rider whose satin green robes waved in the wind as the dragon plunged through the air.

Zardraken held his shining sword to the sky. A violet tendril of lightning sparked from its pinnacle as his red robes slowly floated and waved. In an instant, the Red King disappeared in a blinding flash of light.

Blue light shined through the dark scaly gullet of the dragon, its humongous body came low to the ground and smashed into the top of the Blackstone archway.

Tumbling rocks crushed the front lines of the Red King's siege, but his forces pushed on, climbing the rocks in droves and advancing beyond the kingdom walls.

Blue dragon fire engulfed the end of the narrow bridge, melting the dark steel warriors in liquid metal. The torrent of fire streamed down the bridge, decimating those desperately crossing.

From atop the dragon's back, the green-robed rider leaped off and vanished in a flash of white light.

Balamor's hairs were standing on end as a strange energy drew from his body. The air around him was crackling as small wisps of electricity popped in and out of existence.

The dragon glided over the chasm when the sky suddenly ripped open in a violet flash.

A gleaming arc of lightning struck the dragon's back, ripping through its body to meet the Red King's blade as it pierced the base of the dragon's neck.

The blade sliced through the scaly beast with ease. Red blood poured out from within, drenching the Red King from head to toe. The dragon cried out as it tunneled toward Gantis and his black steel archers.

A gory wound extended from its neck to the base of its gut, gushing with blood and billowing blue fire.

Gantis moved his men as fast as he could before the dragon smashed into the ground, scraping its black scales across the stone and sending sparks into the air.

A dusty cloud settled, and the beast laid still.

The war kept raging on as its limp body formed a crimson pool.

The king walked toward it, blood still dripping from his robed body. The Blackstone figure joined him as he stood by the dragon's monstrous head. The scales were like polished stones layered upon one another. Zardraken placed his hand between a pair of twisted bone-white horns.

A ghastly whisper reverberated like a raucous wave through the air, absorbed by the trees where Balamor was hidden.

The young mystic could hear the words as though he spoke them in his own mind.

"Yus mal, mog ehn hels, dahn firos."

A force left the king's palm and shuttered through the dragon's corpse, rumbling the landscape around it.

The Red King and his companion slowly backed away from the beast as seizures riddled its bones and shook it back to life.

A reanimated version of the dragon arose, a lame and lifeless vessel whose scream was a gurgling cry of pain. Its piercing roar deafened the battlefield as gore and guts hung from its body.

The king walked toward the beast as it looked around with ghostly white eyes. It lowered its head in a bow as the king climbed up and into the leather saddle.

With a ground-shaking lunge, the dragon lifted into the air. Innards and gore hung from the wound across its gut, yet it was flying in painless fashion.

With heavy beats of its wings, the king and the dragon soared toward the Mog Brush. Passing crumbling walls and swirling ruins, a grotesque cry tore through the sound of battle. Strafing left and right, the black-scaled beast zeroed in on the high tower at the center of the wasteland.

A resounding rumble and cloud of dust erupted as the dragon crashed into the tower.

As the dust cleared, flashes of light boomed from the tower, thunderous echoes roaring with authority.

Gantis gestured his hands and a magical power waved the long sleeves of his robes. In a snap toward his remaining soldiers, their bows morphed into long ornate spears made of shiny black steel. Thrusting his hand forward, he gave his command, "For truth! Charge!"

In unison the three regiments of warriors charged across the bridge.

Passing by the black-robed man like a metallic wave, the armored pike men raced.

The soldiers ahead battled fiercely with the remaining elves as Gantis moved in on the scene. The large rocky figure led the new charge, his footsteps rocking the bridge with heavy thuds.

The Mog Brush whipped and twirled the ruinous landscape, tumbling entire buildings and carelessly destroying the reinforcements of elven soldiers along with their black-steel counterparts.

The high tower continued to boom and flash when the air became strangely still and absent of even the faintest breath.

Balamor grasped the bark of a tree and widened his eyes in anticipation. Breaking the stillness was a blinding flash that lit up the sky.

A shock wave rippled from the high tower in all directions as a milky dome spread from above the tower's peak. The sound of gruesome war and death turned to utter silence as the dome's edges covered half of the bridge and reached far into the chasm.

Gantis retreated from the magical force field with a jump backward and a swipe of his hand below him. A gust of wind carried him back away from the milky shroud as everything within was consumed by it and made eerily still.

Standing at the edge of the dome, Gantis looked onward, his mind was racing so much a breeze could be felt shifting the still air. Balamor was left equally awestruck by the magical spell. Curiously, the young halfling was drawn closer by the sight of the powerful magical dome.

Its size was immense, but he had seen it once before.

He had been here before... or was it after?

Slowly and cautiously, he moved toward the bridge as the black-robed man stood halfway across, gazing inside.

The young Wisebeard came to a halt at the edge of the chasm. He felt the air was still absent of breath. He exhaled as the robed man peeked over his shoulder.

"Gantis?" he asked with a voice filled with confusion and sudden fear.

The black-robed man turned around as the young Wisebeard called out his name.

Now facing him, Balamor couldn't find any other words to say.

Gantis walked forward as his memory of the young halfling became clearer. He had seen him before, many, many years ago. His appearance now left the black-robed man bewildered, as if no time had gone by since he had last seen the young man. The clothes and the uncanny resemblance to Jaric and descendants of the old Wisebeard.

Silence clung to every second. An eerie feeling grew deeper and deeper in the pits of their stomachs.

"You. What is your name?" Gantis asked in a commanding tone, his voice echoing in the stillness.

Balamor didn't answer. His hands began to shake and his only instinct was to back away from the tall and powerful man who started approaching him. The further he retreated; the faster the black-robed man's long strides became.

"No, wait! Don't leave!" Gantis yelled, but it was too late.

In an instant, the young Wisebeard faded and wisped away into ashes amidst a gentle yet breathtaking breeze.

There, the black-robed man stood, now a second time having witnessed the same young halfling turning to ashes.

47

ECHOES

875, Summer's 62nd Dawn

he sound of dust could be heard as it lingered within the dark crypt of Zardraken Kaltas. Through the still air of the chamber and past the ornately carved sarcophagus of the last mystic red king rested the soul of the timeless wanderer. His physical body was far away from his remaining spirit; charred and withered was his corpse, whose place lies in the moment of his death.

Now, free of flesh and blood, he waited patiently for a particular halfling to arrive in his chamber. His thoughts echoed from wall to wall, only scratching the surface — like they had been for centuries.

A series of thoughts, profound and beyond what the hands of time have revealed thus far. It was these thoughts that the wanderer found few men were capable of comprehending. To the common folk of the world, eventualities always cease to have means in fragile actions. Moments of great importance big and small can all be seized upon with precise action. This the wanderer knew to be certain. From the slightest pluck to the mightiest strum, each note reverberated through generations to come.

There was one moment that raced through his being this day, a moment the young Balamor Wisebeard would also bear witness.

Ever since that moment, when the wanderer's mortal body was vanquished and his soul set free, his thoughts were aligned on finishing the plan he had started a thousand years ago. Lost to him for centuries was this grand mission, repeatedly caught in the obscurity of his mortal lives and the emotions of flesh and blood. With each physical end of course, came another physical beginning.

Timeless is his being, yet his vessel is reborn anew, a necessity after existing for so long as a purely magical force. Time was running out before his essence was completely drained by those who spoke the Runesong, though he was unconcerned with that fact. Everything had gone accordingly thus far, and soon enough the bloodlines would be on their course.

His efforts to bring them together, as he has done so many times in the past, would start with the young Wisebeard. He knew his presence, the moment he crossed the Bounds of Akinn and entered the Mog Brush. With all the power remaining in his soul he had fought to see the young mapmaker.

Now, he knew the waiting would finally end, and with it, his time as King Zardraken would also end; merely a steppingstone in the grand scheme of things. The Red King would again return as a new man. The day he would need Balamor's hand would be the day he remembered the truth that he knew now.

48

FIVE PAGES

875, Summer's 62nd Morning

warping crack thundered through the halls, breaking the stillness of the air and echoing off the walls of Zardraken's Crypt. Standing in a dusty room surrounded by darkness, Balamor Wisebeard exhaled and felt coldness consume his breath. Still holding the black metal torch in his hand, he held it out in front of him.

"Hels," he whispered.

In a flash of fiery blue light, the floor below him shined.

Balamor cowered down and kneeled to the floor when he realized his surroundings. Standing on a narrow Blackstone catwalk, he was faced on either side with a wide chasm, whose bounds were obscured by darkness. He was frozen in fear as his torch burned its blue light.

Glancing behind him, he found no door, only a few visible yards of a jarring footpath. He stood up carefully and began to breathe as he slowly walked forward.

Each step pushed him further down the dark and unknown path.

His body was weary from the journey, but his mind remained undeterred. There was something he needed to know, and it was as simple as that. That's what it has always been about since the day he discovered the uncharted land from his own transcriptions. He needed to know what was here.

After each day though, it became more than the simple label and geography that he wished to obtain. It became a mission to seek the truth behind magic itself. He didn't know why but moving forward had always kept him alive. Now, he felt closer than ever to completing that very mission he delved into.

Bellowing deep from the depths of the chasm, something roared.

From within the darkness, a neon green glow began to intensify, filling the bottom of each chasm.

Balamor focused his eyes forward and quickened his pace.

A bright green glow slowly lurked up the walls of the once dark and seemingly bottomless pits. The sizzling and popping of something below him made his curiosity grow.

His feet thudded against the stone as he looked down to his left.

Deep below, a neon green pool of bubbling liquid was rising fast. He wanted to run but he couldn't risk one slip on the narrow catwalk. His only choice was to proceed with caution.

Facing himself forward, he held his arms out at his sides to keep balanced.

His furry feet began to catch stride, yet he didn't know for how long it would last. There was no obvious end in sight and the chamber grew hotter by the second.

The sizzling acidic fluid filled the chasms fast, and the room was beginning to glow with a waving chartreuse light. An intense heat warped and waved the air.

Sweat was dripping down into his eyes and soaking his white tunic.

The great chamber was glowing bright when he rubbed the sweat from his eyes.

A sound started to ripple through the burning acid. A sound of a beast, a growl of mighty proportions.

He squinted his steel-blue eyes to peer through the warping air.

In the distance, a wavering threshold fitted with a thick wooden slab.

ZARDRAKEN'S CRYPT

A door, a way out! The young Wisebeard thought to himself as he proceeded to jog down the narrow catwalk.

A huge splash of acid flung from below and crashed against the wall of the Blackstone footway. The pools were nearing the height of the footway when Balamor saw something massive whipping through the air to his right.

Crashing against the Blackstone and knocking the young halfling from his feet was a gangling tentacle covered in slimy teeth-riddled suckers. Inky purple in color and immensely strong. More of them sprung from the acid pools on either side of him.

Balamor laid upon the quaking footpath when he heard the beast roaring from below.

The chamber was hot, and the walls shook from the powerful screech.

Gripping the metal torch tight and gathering his bag, he got to his feet and ran down the catwalk.

Behind him, the monster's vicious tentacles smashed against the Blackstone one by one. The path started to break apart and his small strides were barely enough to outpace the beast. Anticipating the young halfling's speed, the acidic monster grappled the stone from in front of him and ripped the path to smithereens.

Stranded on a lonesome pillar of Blackstone, Balamor could see the doorway ahead, but the gap was too far for him to jump. He needed to think, but his time to do so was cut short with a whipping crack of stone as the monster constricted the pillar with its slimy limbs.

He nearly lost his balance as the pillar swayed back and forth. Quickly securing his belongings, he closed his eyes and went over the runewords of his next spell. His fingers snapped as an idea burst from his mind. Looking around for a piece of stone, he needed to craft a new rune.

Snatching a large flake of Blackstone, Balamor removed his silver dagger. The sound of crunching stone and slithering below shook his nerves, but he was determined to escape.

A makeshift series of three dots and waving lines were as close to the word *Dran* as he could get.

Returning his dagger to his waist and tossing his torch into the acid, he gripped the rune and waited for the moment to jump across.

The pillar dropped downward as the stone beneath it crumbled.

Only a few yards away from the acid, the tentacles spiraled toward him and the beast growled in hunger. To-and-fro, the shaky pillar rocked as it was consumed by the dark monster.

Balamor said the words over and over in his head as the moment to jump approached him. He took a breath and made two steps before the stone pillar was completely crushed. Leaping through the air with his open hand aimed behind him, he yelled out his spell, *"Deun ehn dran!"*

Gusting from his palm, a blast of heavy wind thrust him forward just before a rogue tentacle could snatch him in midair. His small frame slammed into the broken edge of the remaining catwalk.

He fought to stay grappled onto the cliff edge as the rest of the pillar toppled into the pool beneath his feet.

Popping and boiling, the acid dissolved the stone debris, and it was rising quickly.

He felt his muscles cramp and the bones of his hands ached as he climbed up the edge. His lungs were on fire by the time he made it to his feet, but the beast wasn't finished and it lunged its gnarled limbs toward him once more. He started to sprint, desperately trying to get away, but this time he wasn't fast enough. In what felt like the blink of an eye, the monster's tentacle whipped through the air and snatched him up by his ankles.

The slimy appendage gripped him so tight it started to singe his flesh. He writhed in pain as he struggled to break free.

His hand finally gripped his silver dagger and pulled it from its sheath as he was lifted into the air. The monster's grip was squeezing his bones and its viscous suckers tore through his clothes and into his skin.

Just as his bag started to slip from his shoulder, he sliced into the massive tentacle with all of his might and the beast let out an earth-shaking roar. Its slimy limbs suddenly released their grip, sending him falling toward the stone catwalk below.

Plunging toward the ground, the young mystic and his leather backpack bounced and thudded. Spilling from within the backpack were several of the precious items he had from his journey.

His map, his runes, his journal and the fragile spellbook his grandfather gave him. He couldn't afford to lose it all, not after coming this far.

The air was knocked from his lungs as he squirmed toward his belongings.

The ground rumbled and the contents of the bag shifted. Balamor crawled toward the edge as the stone footway began to crumble. The young mystic regained his footing and gathered his map and journal before scrambling to retrieve the remaining runes and book. The sound of the monster grew loud once more, standing the hair on the halfling's skin. In a snap, its tentacle gripped the Blackstone cliff, sheering it from the edge.

Balamor stretched his small arms out toward the last item, his six-page spellbook. The pages fluttered open before the young Wisebeard snagged the last of them. A breathtaking tear through the parchment left his jaw agape. In his grasp was the last page — torn on its inner edge — while the remaining five pages were devoured by the acid.

The monster screeched from below and in a shock, Balamor jumped to his feet and started running toward the door.

Grabbing his bag along the way, he quickly reached the wooden door and yanked on the iron rung fastened to it. He struggled to pull the heavy door open as he heard the monster lunging and whipping its tentacles toward him. Now the entire edge was consumed by its slimy body, bits of Blackstone crumbling in its ferocious beak as it cornered the young mystic. He pulled the rung over and over before he finally saw it, a symbol he had seen on that strange black key. He gripped the iron rung tight and spoke, *"Lohn."*

He saw the dotted symbol flash bright orange and the massive door released from its lock. Dust fell to the floor in a plume as Balamor drug the door open. The monster gave everything it had to devour the young mystic. Its tentacles and beak charged with all of its might, destroying whatever remained of the cliff. Balamor rushed around the door with barely enough space for him to squeeze by and pushed himself through the small passage.

49

THE MYSTIC

875, Summer's 62nd Noon

mashing into the door and slamming it shut, the horrific monster could be heard raging from behind. The young mystic barely escaped the creature's grasp. His lungs burned and his muscles ached as he collected himself.

Balamor stood within a new chamber, a much smaller room whose confines were illuminated by a dim blue torch above the doorway at the other end of the room. The flickering torches crackled in the otherwise silent chamber. Dust lingered in the air, forming cobwebs and coating the Blackstone surfaces in a dirty film.

The chamber was much smaller than the last. Within, Balamor could see a series of stone caskets on either side of him. Three on his right and three on his left; their chiseled features were carved with impressive detail.

He studied them as he strolled through the corridor, wiping the dust off each of them and inspecting them one by one. Upon them were dark steel plates, each engraved with a different name.

From his left side to his right he read the nameplates upon the caskets — *Jacs... Valorhorn... Anvorbeard... Riftenhale... Beshmere... Wisebeard.*

He heard of them all before, with the exception of one – *Riftenhale.*

He removed his journal and flipped to his newest section, *Names of Legend.*

With his pencil, he scribbled the name down, certain he would learn more of it in the future. He closed his book and gazed upon the sarcophagi before him. *Beshmere.*

A name he had come across on more than one occasion, although finding it here was strange considering what he knew about the name. Based on Doryn Beldavale's accounts of Beshmere, they were against the first kingdom.

Why would their name be inscribed on a casket where the first kingdom once stood? And who was inside?

With these new questions running through his head, he started to wonder about the contents of the other Blackstone casements. Bearing the short but powerful last name *Jacs,* this first stone bed was the only one left open. Lying upon the floor behind it was its stone lid.

The young Wisebeard looked inside.

There was no corpse within. In fact, it seemed completely empty. He felt around for anything hidden but there was nothing.

Did this sarcophagus belong to the famed Gantis Jacs? How?

Questions and curiosity filled his mind. Slowly he moved across the room, approaching the Blackstone casket inscribed with his own surname. His nerves started to race.

His shaking hand reached for the stone surface when the shuttering of its stone lid caused him to jump. Slowly, the heavy stone top slid open and fell to the ground.

The young Wisebeard stood back and waited for something to happen.

The resounding stone crash slowly faded into silence before he moved closer to the open sarcophagus. Cautiously, he leaned over the edge and looked inside. Expecting a preserved corpse to be resting, he was surprised to see no such thing. Instead, there were two items contained within.

He reached inside and removed the first.

A small and narrow wand made of a twisted amber wood. It was finely polished and extended twice the size of his hand in length. Engraved with three familiar runewords, Balamor studied them.

Theas, Dran, and Raji.

He looked around suspiciously before moving on to the next item inside the open sarcophagus.

It was dark within the stone box as he tipped over the edge and reached his hand into the shade. Feeling around the confines, he finally held something – cloth that had almost slithered in his hand.

As the suspicious Wisebeard pulled it from the ancient burial site, it started to move. He jumped back and the mysterious cloth rose into the air and held itself in place.

The young Wisebeard was sure of it. They were pitch-black robes, the same as those his ancestor Jaric wore. Long and draping over an invisible force, it was an energy that embodied a small man.

Balamor aimed his newfound wand at the strange robed spectacle. *"Lim ehn dran!"* he shouted.

The second word on his wand glowed with a bright sky-blue light. Balamor could feel a force pulsating from his body and rushing through the ancient wand.

In a blast, a bolt of swirling air left the wand and spiraled toward the strange robes. Twisting from its path, the majestic black robes dodged the spell and zoomed toward the young Wisebeard.

Splashing over him like a wave of cloth, the robes adorned his small body before he could muster another spell. He fought to escape but to his surprise the fine black robes rested upon him normally, no longer wrestling with some kind of force behind them.

He studied the long cloth for a moment while holding the short wand in his hand.

Although they seemed to have a mind of their own, Balamor couldn't resist such fine robes, especially considering who they once belonged to.

As he stood inside the small chamber facing the next doorway to Zardraken's Crypt — now cloaked in mystical black robes and holding a very ancient wand in hand — Balamor took a deep breath and reached for the ornately gilded handle.

He pulled the door to the king's chamber open with a jarring creak and the next room was upon him. As he stepped through the threshold, he felt a cold air shock his bones unlike any he had felt before.

It was more than a mere frigid chill. There was something lingering within the confines of this place. Slowly the door behind him closed, and an echoing thud turned his head.

In a flash, the torches upon the walls lit in unison and filled the room with an appropriate cool blue light.

On a stepped plateau rested a large and intricately carved Blackstone sarcophagus. Unlike the others in the previous chamber, this new funerary box was a masterful work of stone. Etched into it were twisting and weaving designs accompanied by a plethora of runewords. Ridges and folds of stone flowed from the top of the ancient bed where a metallic plate rested upon its intricate stand.

As the young mystic Wisebeard approached the steps, a blue flame awoke at the center of the plate. It wavered calmly and flickered its cool light with a strange force. Balamor arrived at the foot of the ancient sarcophagus where he studied the strange fire closely. The small blue flame seemed to be breathing with each flaring pulse. A deep indigo light emanated from the center with every beat, turning into a bright fiery blue ember at its tail.

Balamor was awestruck at the sight of this majestic fire, as if it was staring into him with unseen eyes, as if it knew more about him than he knew of himself.

The heat of the flame grew with intensity as the fire upon the sconce-like plate exploded into a massive flaming figure. Whipping flames raced upward, conjuring the looks of a tall robed man with a crown upon his head.

Balamor fell backward down the three stone steps as the mystical being presented itself. He recovered quickly and looked up to the figure in awe as the coldness of the room was quickly overwhelmed by the fiery energy of this powerful figure.

He held his wand to the strange being, his mind racing through runewords to react to whatever came next. He waited as the being fully coalesced in the blue flames and settled upon the silvery plate.

A disembodied voice spoke, *"More than words are the likes of magic, my dear friend. Let us not waste time in confrontation. The truth knows where all men fall in place of reason. You, a young man whose principle is beyond the grips of mortal bias. It will be you, I choose to give my parting wisdom."*

The message echoed through the chamber, dimming the torchlight with each emphatic note.

Balamor lowered his wand and spoke firmly, "Truth is what rises above the nature of time. Finding that truth is my mission, no matter the stakes." Rummaging through his bag, he removed his journal and began recording his encounter with the awesome being.

"Know this, young Wisebeard, it is time that gives truth fortitude, and yet it is time that consumes the evidence of it. As we stand here now, time caresses every fiber of reality, without hindrance. Twisting, turning, warping the nature of all that was into all that ever will be. Waves spawned within the deepest fathoms of the ocean are crashing into shores of virgin sands. As we stand here now, the entire past stands with us, as

does the future. The young Balamor Wisebeard stands side by side with every one of his reflections. The truth is the one thread that entangles the rest, at every turn and every single instance, the truth reveals itself."

Balamor was scribbling down the flaming figures words as carefully as he could while trying to absorb the wisdom himself before he shot out a question. "Are you Zardraken Kaltas? The sixth Mystic Red King?"

The mystical figure answered swiftly, *"Zardraken was my final name. Kaltas is my everlasting title. Of the twenty-six Mystic Red Kings to have ever walked the earth, Zardraken was the last. I, too, stand side by side with all of my reflections — Zardraken Kaltas, twenty-sixth Mystic Red King — is one of them."*

"If Zardraken was the last of twenty-six, will there be a twenty-seventh?" Balamor asked, perplexed by the new information the mystical king revealed to him.

"There is another, though his time is the first time, and his name is the first name. Born on the First Breath, and to die only in name. A king whose early reflections will be mired in corruption. A king who you will bear witness," the Red King responded, his voice echoing off the walls of the main chamber.

"You're the last of twenty-six names... Zardraken... The clock from the library! I see... That would mean the name of the next king begins with an 'A.' What will his name be?" Balamor inquired.

"You will come to learn his name soon enough, young Wisebeard," Zardraken replied.

"How do I know this is not just another illusion? Ever since I walked through that door, I can't trust what I see is true."

"Young Wisebeard, all you have witnessed is no illusion. I am no illusion. Those who cross through my portal see only what is real."

"Your portal? The door that led me to the library...?" Balamor asked as he looked into the beings piercing eyes.

"Indeed. The spell you performed, opens my portal, a passage through time for those with mana coursing through their blood. Through that passage, a series of truths once unknown is revealed. What you have witnessed beyond this portal is a matter of lineage."

"Lineage... My grandfather told me my lineage was special, that only I could prove it... What did he mean?"

"You, Balamor Wisebeard, possess the blood of the Scrivenkin. The Wisebeard name is the last living name of that bloodline."

Balamor wrote down the strange title before he spoke, "Scrivenkin?"

"The curators of knowledge, past, present, and future. The Scrivenkin were the beholders of the truth. Once consisting of four families, only the Wisebeards remain, a family of bookmasters, the great Scribes of the Runesong."

"What about the other three?" Balamor inquired.

"The Tipsyhill Alchemists, the Humfellow Bards and the Farfoot Wayfinders. All names which cease to exist," Zardraken replied.

Balamor promptly flipped to his *Names of Legend* and added the new families to the list along with the name of the bloodline.

His notes were finished before he asked, "You said something about 'those' who cross your portal... Well, I wasn't alone, what happened to—"

"Anvorbeard, the cursed one?" The fiery apparition finished the question.

Balamor nodded.

The mystic king continued, *"His past and the past of his ancestors are not the same as yours. His time in my crypt will end soon, but it will not be me who answers his questions as I am answering yours. That duty will be yours to perform, as Scrivenkin, you will bear the knowledge I hold and the knowledge of all unknown."*

"How? I barely know what this place is, or who I am for that matter. How can I learn everything you know before it's too late to do anything about it?" Balamor asked, feeling overwhelmed by the Red King's words.

"Knowledge is not to be acted upon but acted with. You have more than you know. The door has once been opened by your words, young Wisebeard. The choice is yours to open it once again."

"The portal..." Balamor whispered. He remembered copying the spell into his notes.

The mystical king's words disturbed him. Everything seemed to rest on his shoulders. He realized how serious this journey had become, yet he never knew it would bring him here, face-to-face with the spirit of a mystical king. He had so many questions, yet he didn't know which of them to ask.

Suddenly, a memory gripped him – one task on his mission to the Mog Brush, a name he promised to find for Awkid.

"The Avennoth, what is it? And who cursed Awkid Anvorbeard with it?"

"A great calamity awaits the Anvorbeard. Bewitched by a spell forged in a chaotic war long before the time of men and their kingdoms. Soon to face the finality of it, it will be his deeds prior that will balance the devastation the Avennoth will bring... Though it depends on the scale of time in which one lives. The spell within your friend has yet to be finished. Be cautious, young Wisebeard, for the day will come when the spell is complete and the dwarf will cease to be Awkid Anvorbeard. The man you once knew will succumb to the monster that was birthed into his bones by the one called Lenook."

"Farah Lenook," Balamor whispered as he clenched his notebook.

"A woman whose mind has been twisted by paranoia and ill-sought justice. Her actions have tilted the scales of

balance further than I anticipated. My own mistakes are to blame for her madness."

"Peace over truth... I heard you say it once, in the Forest of Nim. What does it mean?" Balamor said, speaking the untold thoughts of the ancient king.

"Truth is not justice, as justice is not what is real. It is what fills the gaps of a damned reality torn with pain. Tell me, young Wisebeard, as loved ones die at the hands of those alive, is it true that the death of the executioner will replace the life of love lost?"

"No..." Balamor answered.

"Is it true that the wrongs of one should be corrected by the reasoning of those done wrong?"

"Well... I—I don't think so..."

"Know this young Wisebeard, those truly wronged feel a depth of pain only fallacy can fill. No form of reality, no remedy, no spell, nothing that is real can annul that pain. Not the death of others responsible, not the manipulation of innocents, not reciprocity!" The Red King's flaming figure flared with intensity as his otherworldly voice shouted.

A moment went by before the flames settled back into a calm blue and indigo shade.

"Justice is what gives peace to those wronged, peace only obtained in foresight... This I did not know at the time it mattered most. When those I loved were done wrong, I believed it was just to keep them from the inevitable danger of truth. I chose their peace for them, rather than the true peace they might one day achieve. Peace does not follow the truth, and when the truth alone arrives, it will be those who the truth has caused pain that demand justice instead."

The flames of Zardraken's shade crackled as Balamor recorded his words. The sound of his voice became garbled as his figure lost heat. *"You will be faced with the same choice, young Wisebeard, and the decision will come to change the world more than any other."*

THE MYSTIC

Balamor was scratching more of the ancient king's quotes into his journal as silence fell upon them and the coldness began to fill the room. He looked through the shoddy pages of his notes, scanning the numerous questions he asked.

Now, with so many of them having answers, so few of them seemed left. There was one thing that eluded him thus far, and it was the answer to the first question he asked on his journey.

He glanced up at the shade of Zardraken Kaltas as he was about to ask when he saw the last of its dwindling flames swell. *"My time has come, young Wisebeard. I must leave this world to you now, be vigilant, protect the sacred and remember, evil has no face."*

"Wait! I had one more question!" Balamor yelled as the flames of the mystic red king suddenly dissipated into a puff of ash and smoke.

Of course that one question would remain unanswered, lingering in his mind almost as long as the ashes lingered in the air.

What is the Mog Brush?

He coughed as a dusty cloud fell before him.

With the plume settled, all that remained in the metallic sconce was a pile of gray ash smothering three papyrus scrolls.

Balamor looked around the cold room before he walked up the steps to the sealed Blackstone sarcophagus. Silence surrounded him as he gazed at the three scrolls covered in ashes. They were the same three scrolls he had from the visions — *the same ones demanded from him.* His shaking hands reached into the pile atop the metallic plate and removed the first scroll.

A timeworn papyrus rolled and tied with a red satin ribbon.

At a first glance, the scroll could be mistaken for a simple document. But it was the context that proved otherwise.

ZARDRAKEN'S CRYPT

In the ashes of Zardraken Kaltas, these documents were far from simple. They were unmistakably magical and obviously more powerful than the papyrus they were made of.

Balamor claimed the remaining two scrolls as he looked around suspiciously.

Each tied with blue and purple ribbons, respectively; the three scrolls seemed identical in size. As he carefully put them into his bag, he glanced back at the ashy pile and saw something green poking through the gray mound. He finished with his bag and leaned over to investigate the remains further.

As he moved closer, it became clear what he saw was another ribbon. Yet, there was no scroll with it. He pinched the green satin band and slowly pulled it from the ashes.

Unlike the others, this ribbon was left untied and stained in deep red. As he removed the green ribbon, a breeze started to flow through the chamber from further ahead of him.

The ashy remains began to wisp away as the breeze became more intense, churning the stale air and flickering the torches upon the walls.

The sound of grinding stone jolted the young Wisebeard as the dim lit room started to fill with light.

From the opposite side of the chamber, a stone door slowly lifted and with it, the chirps of birds and skittering of insects spilled into the silent chamber of Zardraken Kaltas.

Balamor ducked behind the sarcophagus and hid as the door continued to open.

After a moment, the heavy aroma of the forest permeated through the crypt.

Balamor waited behind the Blackstone casket, gripping his bag and newfound wand firmly. His ears were all he could depend on, and what he heard over the noise of forestry was a familiar whistle.

A tune that drifted through the air and into the young Wisebeard's memories, growing louder as the door finished opening.

THE MYSTIC

The whistling stopped and an awkward pause made Balamor's curiosity grow.

"To know to go where no one goes, the one who goes knows not where to go. For where to go is not a where to be known, as nowhere is known as a where to be shown," a jovial voice uttered, the tongue twisting verse before a metallic flick snapped the air. "So now, Mr. Wisebeard, now that you know the difference between nowhere and a where that is known, riddle me this... If two trek south to somewhere who is someone going to know where?"

Balamor slowly peeked over the sarcophagus, his blue eyes were squinted as the day-lit forest changed his focus.

Leaves and vines hugged a narrow hallway that seemed to be an exit from the crypt. Standing in the exit way was a small colorful gnome, unmistakable now as both Nim and the old clerk, Giro Vidiro.

Two trekked south to somewhere, yet only someone knows where.

"Nim? It was you! You knew I was going to be here," Balamor said with wide eyes.

Looking at his timepiece and leaning against the Blackstone archway the gnome chuckled and nodded.

"Indeed, but it is you, Mr. Wisebeard, who won the race." He clicked his watch shut.

Balamor slowly walked from behind the sarcophagus and threw his backpack over his shoulders.

"What year is it?" Balamor asked the gnomish fellow.

"The year is 875," Nim answered swiftly with a wink.

"Good, good," Balamor replied as he dusted off his black robes and walked down the stairs toward the doorway. He walked through the doorway quietly. Exhausted and weary from his journey, his steps were drained of energy. As he reached the colorful gnome, he let out a sigh and stretched his body.

"Now, I think it's time I went back home, Mr. Vidiro."

"I couldn't agree more, friend," Nim replied with a wink as he motioned Balamor into his forest.

The stone door ground shut as the young mapmaker left Zardraken's Crypt and walked onward.

His journey to the Mog Brush was finally complete, yet his adventure back was only beginning.

Removing his flask and taking a long swig, he finished the rest of his water and started to whistle a tune he would never forget.

Nim joined the young Wisebeard and their whimsical song drifted softly through the forest along with their figures, slowly fading beyond a lattice of trees.

50

THE BLACK-ROBED MAN

875, Summer's 62nd Night

he Raehl was steeped in silence as the sun had finally begun its descent over the forested hills of Gwendilae. Orange rays of light blanketed the halfling village as the clouds of a recent storm rolled off in the distance. The occasional owl's hoot was the closest thing to a crack of thunder, and even that had some of the halfling workers on edge. After days of storms, the constant state of repair to the town was finally over, yet the townsfolk seemed to be dealing with a different form of hardship. Losing loved ones to the ebb of time is never an easy thing to accept. Any sense of normalcy would long await the Raehl, and with the arrival of a familiar young fellow that was more than apparent.

Hurrying across the fresh oak planks of the rope bridge was his calloused and aching set of feet, eager to reach their destination. They moved confidently over the ravaging waters of the River Faric. The farmers recognized the short figure as the same young man who had embarked on a quest over a week ago.

As the figure walked by the freshly turned soil of the fields, one of the farmers stopped him with a call of his name, *"Balamor?"*

The young halfling stopped, seemingly bewildered at the sound of the name. He looked back at the farmer who was adorned in a long black cloak and holding a flower in his hand.

"I— Farjadis... He—" The farmer looked down at his feet as he searched for better words.

THE BLACK-ROBED MAN

"What happened? Where is he?" Balamor asked. A pit formed in his gut as he took a good look over the small town.

At a first glance, the town seemed to be the same as any other halfling village; a series of well-lit holes all neatly decorated, the scent of a feast billowing through the streets, and of course the company of its humble occupants.

Suddenly it dawned on the young mapmaker; hanging dreadfully over each halfling home was a black banner that could mean only one thing — there was a funeral to be had.

A breeze sent a shiver down the Wisebeard's spine. He clasped his bare arms for warmth. His lack of any robes was to blame, but in his mind, it was the farmer's words that gave him real goosebumps.

Balamor looked into the farmer's eyes. He could see sorrow and even a sense of fear, but it was the farmer who saw something else completely when looking back. It was a look the farmer thought a halfling couldn't make, let alone witness. It was ugly and full of hate. Somehow it was both blank and twisted, but most of all it was devoid.

Devoid of... Something.

The farmer looked away.

"What happened?" the mapmaker asked with a strict tone.

"We found him in the early morn... Was as pale as a ghost down in that old library. I'm sorry, we tried but—"

"The library, show me," the steely eyed mapmaker said. His mind seemed somewhere else completely, and the farmer was without a breath to give.

What would happen next?

The thought gripped the farmer as he strolled with the young halfling by masses of other black-garbed halflings, the candles in their hands were yet to be lit.

Balamor looked over his shoulder left and right. His eyes were darting around the crowd.

Dressed in all black-flowing garb they seemed like they were all that same, eerily familiar person. Soon every door he saw became a new concern, and every halfling that was traveling to the center of town was another possible danger. He stayed on his toes but kept his head down as he trailed the farmer.

Perhaps the farmer merely had a different perspective, but after seeing the young mapmaker leave over a week ago, he could sense something changed, something happened to him out there beyond the Faric. He wasn't like the rest of them, that much was always true, but now, he seemed like someone else completely.

Everyone silently watched as the young Wisebeard passed through the Raehl, all the way down the main path and toward the original home of his grandfather Farjadis Wisebeard. Now it belonged to another halfling family.

They passed a wooden sign inscribed with the fancy title of its occupants.

Oakfoot.

Balamor felt the sign for a moment. It was handcrafted by a strong yet skilled carpenter, the kind of halfling who had a look that was far from a scholar.

The farmer pulled the heavy door open. A long creak echoed through the hollow hole. Stale air escaped in a plume of dust. The place hadn't been cleaned in days, and there was a strange stench only a few with a trained nose could smell.

The young halfling could smell it.

It was the smell of a familiar magic, nefarious and known for taking its toll over time. It was the smell of Whispering Wine.

He didn't bother sharing the knowledge with the farmer, more pressing concerns were at hand. He needed to find them. That's what he came all this way for.

The farmer strolled through the kitchen and toward another wooden door. With a pull, he let another dust plume escape, the scent of paper was unmistakable.

THE BLACK-ROBED MAN

"This way..." the halfling said as he descended a spiral staircase. Balamor trailed down the steps behind him and through the basement archway before brushing the dust from his dingy white tunic.

There they stood, in a narrow room full of bookcases and shelves, yet all the books were gone. Dust remained in their places, in patterns suggesting that someone had taken them — and in a hurry.

He approached a table with shaking hands. His palms should have been sweaty but instead they were dry as ash and so, so cold.

"The books..." he said, unsure where to even begin. A fist formed in the meantime.

The farmer felt the tension in the air and stepped in to explain, "Your stepfather... It was days ago, he took the old caravan and left. Perhaps he—"

Balamor slammed his open hand down on the table. A teacup fell over and spilled its contents upon the wooden surface. Dust billowed into a cloud as Balamor huffed a single name through his teeth, *"Oakfoot."*

He let the tension settle before he shot a look over his shoulder. "And Farjadis? Where did you take his body?"

The farmer looked down and paused. "To the pyre... Built him one yesterday, the whole town did. With no family mound to be buried in, it was agreed he would find rest with the winds."

"Soil, Ash... It makes no difference, just remains anyhow," Balamor replied.

Silence resumed as the young halfling leaned over the table and stared down at its surface. He pressed his finger into the thin layer of dust and slowly began to draw a symbol of *Hels*.

$$\cdot \overset{?}{\underset{\circ}{}} \cdot$$

Balamor felt the power of the magical word and the fire it could bring. "All of us will fade away, but only some of us shall burn bright when we do. Wouldn't you agree?" Balamor said as he turned away from the table.

"Yes, indeed," the farmer answered. His eyes drifted toward the empty shelves and then back toward the young halfling who stood before him. "Is it true? Everything they say about you Wisebeards and your magic?" he added.

"Honestly, I can only wish it all wasn't true, but it is. Figuring out what to do next is the real question." Balamor paused, lost in the unraveling of the plan he had worked so hard toward executing. "Well, let's get on with it then," he said as he motioned the farmer toward the doorway.

They ascended the stairs quietly. Balamor trailed the farmer who entered the kitchen and held the door open for him. Balamor passed by the kitchen and reached the dining room when a jarring creak came from the hinges of the basement door.

He snapped his head back to see the farmer pushing it closed. "No. Keep it open... *Keep all the doors open.*"

"Of course..." the farmer said as he left the heavy door ajar. He walked to the front door and opened it promptly.

Balamor proceeded down the hallway and opened every closed door he could find. Finally, he reached his own room, yet it felt like the room of a complete stranger.

He walked in and approached the desk quietly. As he reached for the handwritten note upon its surface, the sound of a distant violin broke the still air. It was a song played only in times of loss. The only kind song the halfling people took no joy in performing.

As he read on, the melody continued. Soon it was accompanied by the deep tones of the cello and a hymn that epitomized the somber atmosphere of the ceremony.

He reached the note's end when he looked up at himself in the mirror. Steely blue eyes stared back.

THE BLACK-ROBED MAN

He crumpled the note into the palm of his fist, squeezing so hard his knuckles turned white.

"Mr. Wisebeard?" the farmer asked, now standing in the doorway of the same room.

Balamor looked up at him. Rage seemed to fill his eyes and perhaps rightfully so. Either way, the funeral was to be had; tradition to be followed — that much the farmer could be sure of. "The sun sets upon us, I'm afraid. I know it's the worst burden to bear, but... As tradition dictates, the next of kin must light the pyre."

"Of course," Balamor replied as he dropped the crumpled note on the desk.

After a moment the two halflings strolled out of the house and were on their way through the town. The farmer now trailed the young Wisebeard, along with the rest of the attending halflings, of which there were many. Those who didn't attend had their reasons. Some of the halfling folk weren't the type for funerals, others had one too many in the past week. Both could be found in The Watering Hole, washing away their aches with a pint of Jollymead. Balamor passed by the place on his way to the town center, the scent of alcohol particularly strong this time around.

As he walked with the crowd, he remained as paranoid as ever. Every which way, there was a man in black robes grasping a lit candle. Even the children had the young Wisebeard on edge. As he drew closer to the pyre, the sound of the music had taken over.

The crowd moved around the pyre like a carousel, each robed halfling lining its base with all sorts of flowers. The young Wisebeard watched the crowd grow as he stood by the pyre waiting for his moment to speak.

The town really admired the old Wisebeard and what he stood for. For years they kept his secret hidden and let him grow old in the comfort of their village.

ZARDRAKEN'S CRYPT

They gathered for Farjadis in droves. Almost the entire town was present. Balamor turned to the pyre as the song started to come to an end. There his grandfather lay in an eternal rest, waiting to pass on. The last Wisebeard — *or so he thought.*

It was at that moment that Balamor realized Farjadis was really gone. After all these years and almost as soon as Balamor had found out about it all.

Ultimately though, he felt defeated. Even with his original task completed, Balamor had failed in his mission to secure the library and the Bloodstone. All the books and stone were gone, along with his stepfather. Balamor was certain that he'd taken them with the caravan.

All along it was true. As true as the death of Farjadis was now; Balamor had become the last Wisebeard, the only one to carry on the bloodline. The young halfling grew angrier just thinking about it all. Just as he was about to burst, the music stopped and a windy silence filled its place. Surrounding the young Wisebeard at the funeral pyre were dozens upon dozens of halflings, each holding a fiery candle in their hands.

He closed his eyes and took a deep breath. The crowd waited for him to speak.

Balamor reached for the torch that one of the robed elders was holding and began, "As the sun sets upon the hills, we are tasked with setting a flame to the past and to those who've passed away. Farjadis was very important to you all. That much is obvious by the gathering his death has brought. He was a man of many secrets, and for many years his secrets have been guarded by you all. Some of you may know the stories, some of you may not. Some may believe what they know, others may be skeptical. I am here to tell you all the truth; about the Wisebeards, about the books, and most of all, about the magic they wield." He strolled by the crowd and lit his torch from the wicks of their candles. The halfling villagers waited patiently as the flame slowly engulfed the torch's end.

The young halfling continued, "*Magic...* it is indeed real. It's no figment of the imagination, no trickery or illusion. In fact, magic is why we are all gathered here in the Raehl — of all places. Farjadis chose to hide in this place for a reason. Because magic would be the only way to find him. Centuries ago, the Wisebeards were the proctors and protectors of this magic. They helped bring all of mankind together for the first and only time in history, during the days of the First Kingdom. They brought peace and security to the world with their magic. It seemed the future was looking bright for everyone, but peace on a scale like that had to come at a cost."

He approached the pyre with the torch fully burning in his grasp. "The Wisebeards had a clear choice, as did the Red King who they gave counsel... What do people deserve?" Balamor studied the crowd, watching as his question made them uneasy. He finally held the torch to the pyre, the scarlet flames leaped from its end and onto the lattice of branches, logs and kindling. The fire spread around the base of the pyre with unrelenting speed. Balamor held out his hands as if they were scales weighing two options. *"Peace or truth?"*

The crowd began to look at one another as the question sunk in. It seemed unfair to even compare the two things, to choose one over the other.

"Their choice would lead to centuries of war," Balamor said as he held out an open hand. "To a divided world and ultimately, it would lead to this very moment."

With a mesmerizing twist of his fingers, a strange vial coalesced. Its glass was that of a teardrop shape and pressed into its surface was a square of four dots. Within the vial was a ghostly green substance that twisted and moved with a mind of its own. It seemed trapped by the glass container, like a prisoner yearning to break free.

"Ignorance is what they chose. Ignorance imposed upon people so that peace could exist!" Balamor shouted. The fire was blazing behind him, nearly engulfing the entire wooden structure.

Balamor studied the vial as he went on, "Back then the Wisebeards knew peace was merely an illusion. To them, the illusion of peace was far better than the reality of the truth. They knew what the truth would bring. Pain, suffering, chaos. They chose the illusion instead."

The flames cracked and popped as they consumed the remains of Farjadis Wisebeard. As the crowd watched the old halfling wisp away, his grandson waved his open hand at them with a mesmerizing twirl.

Slowly, the features that made him so similar to the old man melded into the striking features of someone else completely.

Steel-blue eyes changed to a deep aquamarine hue. Rounded ears now came to a sharp point and a once shaggy square jaw turned soft and feminine. Their short body grew tall and narrow and their voice higher in pitch. Soon even their white tunic morphed into a long satin green robe that flowed to the ground. Hanging from their neck was an emerald pendant that shined in the warm fire.

Finally, the Elf Queen — the mysterious green-robed woman — emerged from under a halfling guise she regretted taking in the first place. After all, being in Balamor's skin only proved she had failed in preventing his existence all along.

Farah Lenook studied the awestruck crowd before opening the cap of the strange vial. "The truth is, as convincing as they may be, illusions only cover up our chaotic nature, masking who we truly are."

Whipping and screaming like a monster, the flames grew hot and unwieldy; intensified by the power she possessed and the pain she harbored. From beneath her robes she removed a long bone wand and waved it over the vial.

"Now the Wisebeards run and hide, desperately avoiding the repercussions of their choice, of their illusion, of their magic.

THE BLACK-ROBED MAN

They fooled you all into thinking those old books would keep you safe, but no one is safe, even after their death," she said as the cold ghostly vapor arose from within the vial.

Her eyes began to glow the same eerie green hue as she spoke the ancient words of a mysterious incantation. The vapor swirled out of the vial with a screeching yell as a face appeared in its cloudy form — *the face of Farjadis Wisebeard.*

The crowd panicked and tried to flee, but the Elf Queen's magic was too powerful for them to escape. The Rootstone upon her neck shined as her wand gestured rhythmically toward them. Pale roots rushed through the soil and latched onto them, wrapping around their bodies and pinning them to the earth.

The wailing spirit of Farjadis Wisebeard surged into the fire upon a flick of the Elf Queen's wand. His ghostly form merged with the flames and twisted into a fiery wraith that towered over the Raehl. Orange and red flames turned to a bright and hot blue that filled the town with flickering light.

The funeral pyre was merely a charred husk of halfling tradition by the time Farah Lenook had finished her spell. She stood defiant with her long bone wand in one hand and the empty vial in the other. A force emanating from her body left her unscathed by the flames rushing around her.

Blue fire spread across the roots and up the bodies of the halfling villagers. Their black funerary robes burned hot and wild in the night and their screams tore through the Raehl almost faster than the fire itself.

The flames flooded the streets, swallowing whole mills, porch fronts and gardens. The giant figure roared as it smashed its fiery hands down on halflings and their hillside holes, pulverizing them into mounds of charred rubble and ash.

Farah Lenook watched as the halfling village was brought to ruin by the raging spirit of Farjadis Wisebeard. As satisfying as it was to watch the Raehl being reduced to ashes, Farah was far from pleased. The library and the Bloodstone shard were in the hands of that slimy halfling in Mesmir. She should have disposed of him when she had the chance. Nonetheless, Idhissat would find him, along with every other Bloodstone shard there was. Soon her newfound pet dragon would wake from its much-needed slumber and with it she would hunt down every last remnant of the Old Kingdom.

An hour had passed before the final screams of the Raehl were taken by the fire. Farah twirled her wand, and the wraith lurched toward the burning hole of Barris Oakfoot.

The monstrous figure funneled through the open doors of the house. The flames that devoured the Raehl trailed behind it like a fiery cape, filling every room with its destructive jet blue embers. The wooden walls were engulfed in flames as the wraith forced itself through the halls and down the spiral stairs that led to the cold and dark library.

The dusty symbol of *Hels* that Farah had left on the table glowed a fiery blue light as the wraith approached.

·?·
○

The entire halfling hole started to buckle and collapse as the fire burned away the supports.

The wraith of Farjadis crawled through the library, setting ablaze the empty wooden shelves and scraps of paper that littered the floor. The blue flames had finally reached the runeword upon the table when the Elf Queen snapped her fingers.

In one swift fashion, the flames were pulled into the contours of the shining symbol. A final roar erupted from the wraith; a burning screech that twisted and faded away to nothing. The symbol slowly faded away leaving an engraving in its place. Moments passed before the ceiling caved and the rune on the table was buried by a mass of rubble.

A cloud of ash and smoke joined that of the surrounding village as the green-robed woman approached the demolished halfling hole. As she drew closer, she could finally make out the ruins.

All but the front doorway had fallen in. The charred circular door was still left on its hinges. She hurried toward the open door, when a gust of wind rushed from behind her. She pointed her bone wand toward the door and yelled, "No!" A force spawned from its singed end and gripped the door — but she was too slow.

The gust of wind slammed it closed and something else wasn't letting it budge. The hairs on her neck stood up straight. She knew he was here; she could smell that strange magic only he possessed.

The door pushed open and out stepped a man adorned in long black robes. His face was hidden beneath his dark hood but his hunched stature showed he was a very old, old man.

He whistled a strange tune only few people ever heard as he strolled toward the green-robed woman. She remembered it. It was a song she hadn't heard in centuries — a lullaby from her childhood. The man finished with the tune as he waved his pale hand toward her.

She was frozen in place, not even a word could break through. Her eyes studied him but even up close his face was only darkness. The Black-robed Man stopped just feet away from her and spoke, his voice sounding deep and otherworldly. *"Farah, please forgive me. I have failed you, so many times now. No matter how many doors I open. No matter how many times I've tried, I cannot save you from yourself."*

A tear rolled down her cheek and her heart started to beat faster and faster. She wanted to break free but his magic was far stronger than anything she could imagine. He held his hand out to her and revealed a symbol pressed into his palm.

His figure crumbled into a mound of ash right before her eyes. The wind gusted once more and the remains of the black-robed man wisped away, leaving Farah Lenook lost in yet another set of ruins.

EPILOGUE

875, Summer's 85th Night

S*tars* filled the sky, stretching far and wide as the world clock ticked on, unrelenting in each and every successive tock. Weeks had passed since the Raehl had been lost, but the story of its fall wouldn't go unheard for long.

Far into the High East — in the gnomish city of Halden's Burrow, a shoddy old town to say the least — there was a human stranger who contemplated his own mission over a pint of Doryglor mead, a local favorite with a lingering aftertaste.

He was a drifter who found himself hunkered down on a rainy night in the glorified shack that was appropriately titled, The Hogworm. Within the dreary confines of the crumbling establishment were the usual suspects: Gamblers, drunks, thieves, ear moles, and of course, the obvious passerby.

Sticking out like a sore thumb, this new stranger sipped down his mead and did best to avoid contact. Hours had passed by since he arrived and only once did he need to show the steel of his blade.

That all changed when a halfling fellow walked through the door. Dressed in a brown hood and tan garb, he was equipped with a heavy hammer that proved his laboring occupation as a bridge builder. The sturdy halfling man sat at the bar atop a shabby cushioned stool. Upon his back was an oversized bag filled and fitted with a small bedroll. A traveling halfling, who was far north east from his native territory.

It was a long journey for a halfling to be on, and so his presence intrigued the human stranger who he kept an eye on him.

EPILOGUE

Drinking and merrymaking carried on at The Hogworm for the next hour before a boisterous dwarf began to tell a story that captivated nearly the entire bar.

A tale of a Dwarven warrior whose weapon swallowed storms. The common folk jested about the legend the dwarf spoke of before following with myths and stories of their own. Not before long, stories were being shared by each man and the next.

The human stranger listened closely to each story, many of which had their roots in truth. One by one, each of them spoke, some with jovial jibes and others whose words put the crowd in awe.

Finally, the halfling traveler was called out to tell his own story, and he promptly ordered himself a new drink. "So, there I was in my hometown the Raehl, drinking a fresh round of cold Jollymead at The Watering Hole. After a long day finishing repairs on the bridge and still grieving from a string of recent losses, I managed to loosen up a bit. Even as the town was busy with another funeral, some of us tried to catch a few laughs with friends..."

The gnomish bartender leaned on one elbow and poured a fresh drink into the halfling's wooden stein.

Silence lingered as the halfling took a swig and gulped it down.

"It didn't last long... First, we heard the screams, so loud it drowned out the sounds of the tavern. We hushed down and everyone raised brows before I ripped that door open. Like the heat of a furnace, the air outside took my breath away. One look to my left and there it was..." The halfling looked around at the quiet crowd of The Hogworm. His look sold the story before it was even finished. "A demon made of twisting flames, taller than anything in sight. Like a monster, it ripped through the town setting everything and everyone in its path ablaze. That smell... That gut-wrenching stench of burning flesh carried by clouds of black smoke, choking your lungs and stinging your

430

eyes. Men, women, young and old, their screams were all the same that night."

Shouting out in drunken fashion, the obvious question was thrown at the halfling traveler. "Well wh-what did you do?"

The halfling man hunched over his mead, waiting a moment before he responded with two simple words. "I lived."

His words fell into an awkward silence as he chugged the rest of his drink.

"Lenook," a voice cut through the silence.

Glancing in its direction, the crowd focused on the human stranger who sat alone at the bar, swirling his mead in his stein. He wore a suit of dark steel armor draped with a long dingy white tunic. His skin was dark, riddled with scars and wrinkled with age. His messy black hair and thick goatee were matted with days of dirt and sweat. He was a vagabond; whose rugged plate mail showed his battle worn past. Beside him, a traveler's backpack, at his hip, a veteran's blade and upon his tunic, the black sigil of a cane and sword crossed below a curved horn — *the sigil of the Valorhorn.*

ACKNOWLEDGEMENTS

I can't stress how much it means to have the support of those around you when you are pursuing your wildest passions. Everyone can get lost in the wild and it's those who picked you up when you went down and kept you from falling by the wayside that really deserve a special shout out, without them I would not have made it here to tell you all the next tale.

First and foremost is the love of my life and my best friend, Joslyn. Without you reading the rough drafts along the way, listening to me babble on about the plot and continually pushing me to finish this first book I truly doubt I would have discovered how much I really love doing this. Thank you for being there every step of the way even when it seemed like I would give up and throw it all away. You are the rock that keeps me grounded and gives me a place to fall when I reach for the sky. I love you.

Of course, if you get to know me you'll realize I tend to be a lot to handle and no one knows that more than my family. Growing up everyone knew I was very loud and even more ambitious. Two traits that haven't changed a bit. Ever since I could pick up a pencil you've all helped me grow as an artist and as a person. As much as we've had our disputes and disagreements, the best of times were had with you all. Mom, Dad, Aunt Kim, Uncle Den, Ian, Cady, Justin, Brian, Timmy, AJ, and many more who I haven't mentioned by name, thank you and I love you all for your unbridled criticism and your loving support. You all may be a wild bunch but I couldn't ask for a better family to reference and share stories about!

As one doesn't have a say in family, they surely do with their friends and I couldn't have picked a better group of friends to surround myself with. Together we have always been involved

ACKNOWLEDGEMENTS

in some creative endeavor that has shaped my own passions to this day. We have been forging our own worlds for as long as I can remember and it was those early makeshift comics and games that made me the artist I am today. Without the collaboration and support of you all I would never have written this book nor would I have discovered my passion to tell stores. Emmanuel, Kirby, Bret, Andrew, Allen, Tyler, and many others who have made their friendly acquaintance, thank you all for being a part of this story and driving me to reach further and further into the universe with my imagination.

Lastly, but certainly not least, are those who have really helped me with my writing and getting this thing off the ground. Stepping foot into this big and wild writer's world and finding my place in it has always been a challenge. Angelina, Nathaniel, Mary, as well as Sarah, Mia, Lila, Matt and the rest of the TL;DR Writing Community, thank you! Those who have extended your hands, who have given me your ears, your services, your resources and brilliant minds to pick, I am grateful for you all pushing me to be a better writer and for helping me bring my works to life!

GLOSSARY

Anstia: *The region in which the high kingdom of Anstia resides and directly governs.*

Anstian Kingdom: *The ruling kingdom of the south, one of the five human kingdoms, also known as the High Kingdom of Anstia.*

Anstian Monarchy: *The royal family of Anstia which directly rules over the people of Anstia and is recognized as the ruler of the human domain. The royal house which occupies the throne is selected by way of victory in the Anstian House Games every quarter century.*

Avennoth: *A mythical creature created by reading its four parent scrolls, the Scrolls of The Avennoth. When the spell is complete, the Avennoth is prophesized to bring the world to destruction using the combined powers of all folk (Bloodfolk, Rahkfolk, Wyndfolk, Merfolk and Rootfolk)*

Beshmere Arm: *A group of nomadic hunters who follow the ancient teachings of a gnomish man named Beshmere. Originally on a mission to defeat all evil ways of magic, their interpretation of Beshmere's word has radically shifted over the centuries to defeating the ways of magic itself.*

Blackstone: *A type of stone as black as coal but stronger than granite. It was first forged in the calamity of the End War.*

Blood Wars: *A series of conflicts between the forces of Mankind. The battles fought between the First Kingdom (the old kingdom), the Human Kingdoms, The Steel Isle, and the Free Dwarven Clans.*

Bloodstone: *An ancient crimson colored gemstone that was created by the Merfolk as a means of pacifying the chaotic nature of the Bloodfolk. Once a larger gemstone, it was split into shards, each of which has only a fraction of the true stone's power to pacify any Bloodfolk.*

Dwarves: *One of the four races of Mankind and natural inhabitants of the Dahris Mountains beyond the Great Divide. Their short and sturdy mountain-dwelling bodies are adept at working all kinds of earth and stone, resulting in a level quality far beyond anything the other races could produce.*

Elves/Fey: *A race created by the Elf Queen using the fourth scroll of the Avennoth, mixing the souls of men and binding them to the remaining life of the Whispering Tree. Elves are pale slender human-like people who possess a natural magical connection to the Windsong.*

ZARDRAKEN'S CRYPT

End War: *A mythical war between the First Folk over the birth of Bloodfolk and rise of Mankind which resulted in the creation of a demon known as the Torchfolk. This demon ravaged the earth for centuries, burning forests to a crisp and choking the atmosphere with its smog breath. It is said that the End War was put to rest when last men of Delsis, the orphan children, used the tip of the demon's metallic horn as a call which cast down the demon.*

Familiar: *A being, usually in the form of an animal, which is created or possessed by a magical spell to be used as an extension of the caster.*

First Folk: *The first beings of the natural world. The Rahkfolk being the eldest, followed by the Merfolk, the Rootfolk and the Wyndfolk. These four races shaped the world and gave birth to a new type of folk, the Bloodfolk, which led to the rise of Mankind.*

Gnomes: *One of the four races of Mankind and natural inhabitants of the forests and meadows of the High East. Their tiny meticulous nature has gifted them with the ability to craft clockworks and other complex machinery unfathomable to the minds of other men.*

Golems: *A type of Familiar whose manlike-body is of crude materials held together temporarily by a singular source of power usually found in the place of man's heart.*

Halflings: *One of the four races of Mankind and natural inhabitants of the plains and forests of Gwendilae. There small and stocky builds gift them with marvelous woodworking abilities which have led to some of the finest mills and bridges ever seen.*

Higher Hand of Anstia: *The spiritual group of monks whose council guides the policies of Anstian Monarchy by way of the wisdom of their enlightened oracle. The power of the Higher Hand is supreme and is the only power capable of passing judgment upon any man.*

Humans: *One of the four races of Mankind and natural inhabitants of the Lowlands of Leylancarr, though they have spread to all corners of the south. Their taller athletic bodies have granted them the ability to hunt game and fight in battle, leading many of the greatest wars ever waged.*

Knights of Valorhorn: *A group of orphaned knights whose sworn duty was to protect the famous horn used to defeat the demon of the End War and guard the magical knowledge of the First Kingdom and its leader, the Mystic Red King.*

Merfolk: *Second-born of the First Folk, the Merfolk are said to inhabit all bodies of water found across the lands. Their beautiful forms are made of the water itself and can disguise themselves as almost any other form. Their* water-coursing magic allowed them to create powerful potions, the most influential being the creation of blood and thus the Bloodfolk.

Mystic/Mage: *Someone who has the ability to channel the ancient powers of magic.*

Mankind/Races of Man: *Four distinct groups of Bloodfolk who possess a level of intelligence comparable to that of the First Folk. Mankind consists of the Humans, the Dwarves, the Gnomes and the Halflings.*

Necromancer: *One who practices blood magic and the dark arts.*

Paak Swarms: *Carnivorous insects native to the Paak Lands west of the Dundur Mountains. These insects gather in swarms which can grow to the size of a large pond or even a small lake. Feeding off of flesh and blood, these swarms are known to decimate livestock and men alike.*

Parins: *Strange imp like beings which travel in hives and form themselves into the shape of men. Their black inky figures dwell in the rock crevasses of the Forest of Nim in the day and usually feed off of various prey at night. It is said their human forms are that of fallen souls of the Blood Wars.*

Rahkfolk: *First-born of the First Folk and natural inhabitants of the northern mountains beyond the Great Divide. Their large hulking figures are made of the stone itself and their rocky skin is imbued with the words of the Runesong. Their earth magic allows them to manipulate the stone in magnificent ways, but the Runesong upon their bodies is capable of unlocking magics beyond their own.*

Rootfolk: *Third-born of the First Folk, the Rootfolk are the creators of the world's flora. Their bodies are that of towering ancient trees whose bark and foliage are majestically tinted with a precious color unique to the area. Their gesture magic grants them the ability to manipulate other flora through the dense network of roots connected to them.*

Rootstone: *An emerald stone which is found at the heart of each of the Rootfolk. These magical stones grant its controller the ability to manipulate and pacify to the flora of the Rootfolk's forest.*

Runesong: *A magical force used by the First Folk. Although there are many forms in which it is expressed, the most widely known is its written form, known as Spells.*

Runewords: *A magical language used to create spells which tap into the Runesong. There are three known types of runewords: element words, transition words, and manifest words.*

Scrivenkin: *An ancient group of halfling scholars who were tasked with studying all knowledge pertaining to the Runesong and forging spells which* *were then compiled into spellbooks. Until the first of the Blood Wars, there were four main families who carried out this patient work for centuries, the Tipsyhill Alchemists, the Humfellow Bards, The Farfoot Wayfinders, and the Wisebeard Scribes.*

Searing Yemmings: *Packs of small squirrel-like creatures of the High East lands whose bodies are said to spontaneously catch fire, causing wild brushfires, killing and displacing the other fauna.*

Spell: *A sequence of Runewords which are arranged in a particular order to produce magical effects.*

Spellbook: *A compilation of smaller spells arranged across volumes to produce very powerful and complex magical effects.*

Swords of the Steel Isle: *A band of the most talented swordsman the Steel Isle had to offer. After the Swords of the Steel Isle were united by Du'gahr, the crown prince of the Mezar Vas, they went on to conquer all of Wynspur and even parts of the Southland.*

Tarwolves: *Massive wolves with bright yellow eyes and whose fur is coated in hot black tar. Like their natural wolfish counterparts, Tarwolves are native to the forests of Leylancarr. They're know to travel in large packs of six or more, hunting the lesser beasts of the lowlands.*

Vespine Oak: *An ancient type of oak lumber that is specially treated to make it resistant to burning as well as other harsh weathering.*

Wraith: *A spirit whose unbound soul is trapped by a spell in some kind of rudimentary elemental form. Unlike familiars, wraiths are not an extension of the caster.*

Wyndfolk: *Fourth-born of the First Folk and creators of air and the wind. Their bodies coalesce in the clouds towering far above Mankind. Their magic has gifted the flora and the fauna with the air they breathe, and with its mighty breath the Wyndfolk speak their magic. It is said that during the times of the End War the Wyndfolk turned themselves to Dragons in an effort to relinquish the Torchfol.*

WORLD ATLAS

NORTHWEST

NORTHEAST

SOUTHWEST

SOUTHEAST

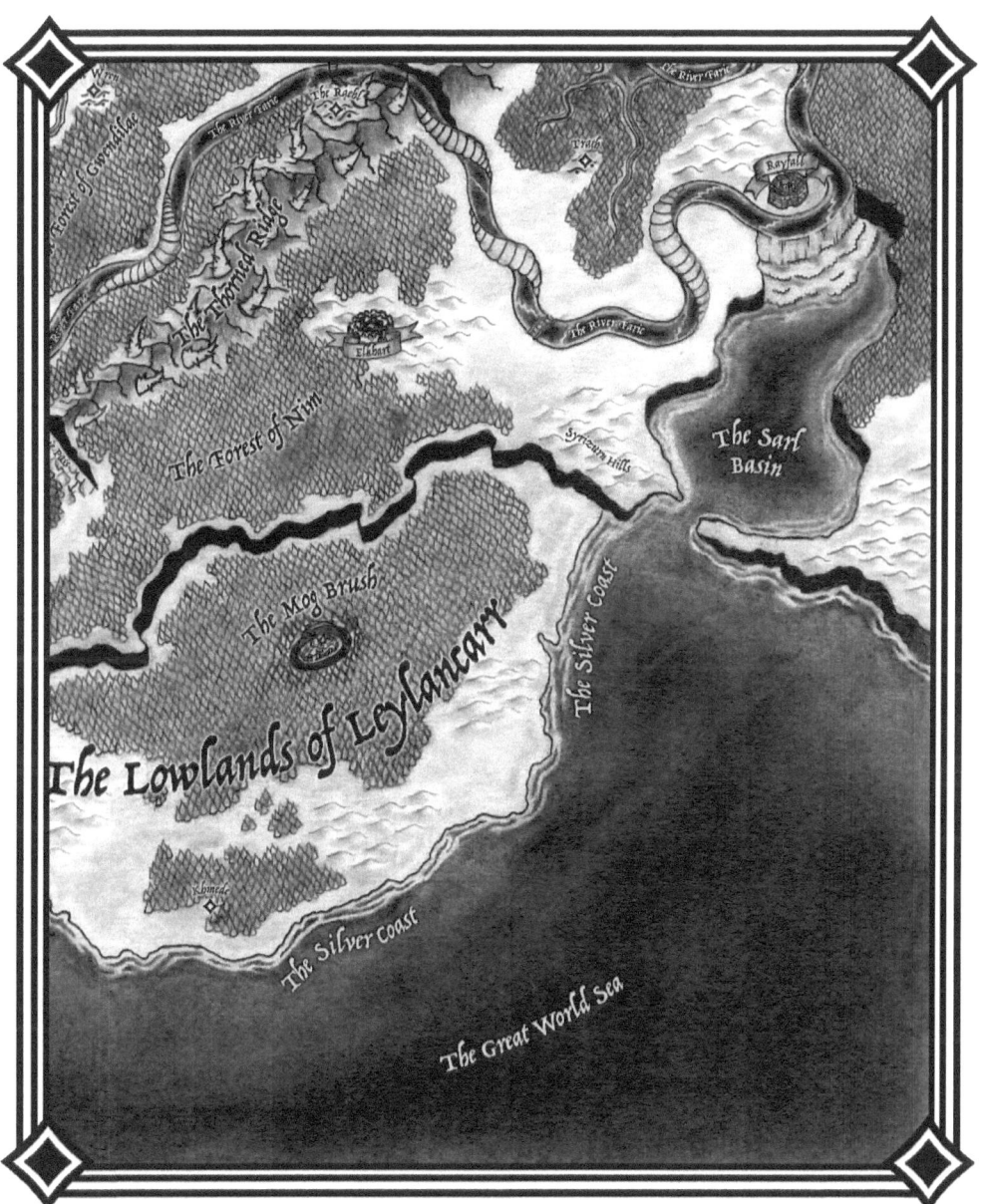

www.ingramcontent.com/pod-product-compliance
Lightning Source LLC
Chambersburg PA
CBHW020230110726

47898CB00004B/1211